I0676176

Snow Blind

Book 2 in the *Silver Blades* series

Lisa Mortara

Foil Books

Also by Lisa Mortara

Silver Blades

In the Shadow of the Eiffel Tower

Registered with the U.S. Library of Congress

Foil Books

Cover design by Lynne Pierce
Front-cover weapons and back-cover photos by Lisa Mortara
Bottom back-cover photo: a corner of Castel Grande (Great Castle) of Bellinzona, Switzerland

Chapter 1

Erika Rivoli looked away from the Swiss psychologist, out the window into the late-afternoon gloom. This was her third session with him and she could no longer put off confessing her dream, not if she hoped to get help from this psychologist for her insomnia and intense headaches. Finally she met Dr. Betz's steady stare, her emotions repressed like packed-down snow, her voice even: "In my dream I sleep with my brother and I kill him," she uttered almost matter-of-factly.

The psychologist didn't flinch. And yet, thought Erika, *why should he*? Instead, as she had made him wait, he did the same with her. Then his head tilted a fraction and a faint smile crossed his eyes. The smile lingered before at last he gave a long professional nod and pronounced a bland: "Interesting."

How else should a shrink respond to a bomb like that—*fascinating...extraordinary?* Neither seemed suitable for 1980 when nothing seemed shocking anymore. His curiosity was piqued though, and whichever school of psychology Dr. Betz followed, she liked him. Then again, he was only the second therapist she had seen in all her twenty-six years of life and very *unlike* the pushy, presumptuous woman she had once seen two years ago in San Diego, where she was born and raised. *San Diego, USA, Turin, Italy, and now Bellinzona, Switzerland.* And always, it seemed, on the run.

That, she hadn't told Dr. Betz—that she was on the run. No one must know. Erika had found Dr. Stefan Betz, chosen him at random on one of her walks through the city. A polished brass plate inscribed with his name gleamed next to the door of the five-story, terracotta-roofed building which his office occupied. Her insomnia and headaches had been surging like

1

the surfers' waves at Mission beach. On top of that, now that winter had arrived in the Alps, with its three-pronged attack of wind, cold, and snow, she also felt lonely, and isolated. Still, what should she expect? She had chosen this bizarre path she was on.

Erika waited, studying Dr. Betz and his dark, sturdy looks, his sharp chiseled cheeks and nose that reminded her of a Medici bust she'd seen in a Florence museum. Maybe, as he gazed back at her own blond, blued-eyed looks, he wondered if she was lying about incest and fratricide.

"So that is the gist of your dream?" he finally asked, dark brows inching higher.

"*Già*," Erika answered. *Right*. They were speaking Italian, the language of Switzerland's Canton Ticino. "Not your average recurring dream, I imagine." Her flippancy sounded phony to her, but it was the only way she felt comfortable expressing herself about the dream.

"Who can say what *average* is? And your headaches start when you wake up from these dreams?"

Erika nodded. "The dreams come right before I wake up in the morning, and sometimes in the middle of the night. Combined with the headaches they make me feel like I'm trying to pull myself out of a vat of cement in the morning."

Dr. Betz made a swift note on his pad and looked back up. "You're from California. How are you dealing with this severe winter month of January?"

Ah, he thinks the jolt from palm trees to pines sagging with snow might have something to do with my condition. So far he hadn't asked what *brought* her to Switzerland, which was just as well, though she had a cover story for that.

"I'm used to the cold. I lived in Turin, Italy before I came here."

"Your Italian is very good."

She acknowledged the compliment with a slight nod which she hoped came across as modest. Her Italian was at least fluent. "My grandparents spoke the language." His Italian was good too. They both had accents, his German, from German-speaking Switzerland, no doubt.

"So how long have you been having these dreams and headaches?"

She made as if she were considering it, though the calculation was easy. "About two months." Since right before she'd fled Italy in November. She didn't reveal that connection. She just wanted help, relief, without telling her whole life's story.

"Can you describe the dream?"

Erika shifted on the corner of the brown leather sofa. She was comfortable, the room felt cozy, lit by a low lamp, tomes crowding cherrywood bookshelves, a heavy wooden desk covered with papers behind the doctor's swivel chair. Out the window, the light was fading, the gloam of an overcast sky. She felt even warmer looking out at the cold, the lonely cold, and didn't want to leave.

"Do you feel you can tell me?" he asked.

Of course he would want to know the dream in detail. His sharp, stony features seemed to demand it. Yet his voice was so mellow, a mild baritone, that the man channeled calmness. And unlike the pushy old shrink in San Diego, he was on the young side, maybe late thirties.

She drew a silent breath and began to narrate, once more as if there were kilometers between them, as if someone else was speaking. After finishing, she blurted with a half-mocking chuckle, "Is that Freudian?"

Dr. Betz returned a non-committal smile. "Oh, I think there's more to it." Outside, crooked tree limbs glowed black against a sky turning from white to grey. "Maybe you'll choose to share more about that at our next session."

Erika nodded a slow assent.

The train brought her to the base of an icy mountain, to the station of Cobbio, the village where she lived, in a house she didn't own—not a home, but a hideout. At least there was a twenty-minute train service back and forth from Bellinzona. If not she would feel trapped in this village of a few hundred people, caged in by hoary mountains. She hiked up the terraced hill that held the village, the cobbled roads and paths cleared of snow. No worries about slipping, for this was Switzerland: snow was plowed and shoveled practically before it hit the ground.

She let herself into the three-story, one hundred-year-old house. The owner, Romano Rosselli, lived in San Diego and had been a friend of Erika's grandparents. It was he whom she had contacted from Turin to ask if she could stay in the house. She wouldn't pay rent, they'd agreed, only utilities. His niece in Cobbio had given Erika the keys. What made the house a good hideaway, apart from its remote location, was that no one could trace her now that her grandparents were deceased, and Romano Rosselli was not a friend of Erika's parents or any other of her relatives.

She lit the kerosene stove in the kitchen, the only source of heat in the entire relic. Spacious as the house was, she lived in the kitchen next to the stove's radiant heat. It warmed her quickly, and she shed her coat and settled at the kitchen table to write a letter in Italian:

The translation into English of the exposé continues to go well and I can't wait until the story hits the press. I still haven't noted anyone I consider suspicious here in Cobbio. Of course, Bellinzona is different, with about 17,000 inhabitants, I was told, and all of them strangers to me. But I haven't spotted any tails, and you know how vigilant I am.

This was the gist of each of her letters to Giorgio Testa, the newspaper owner turned investigative journalist. She was lying as low as possible, as was Giorgio, both of them having fled Turin, Italy, and DIGOS, the Italian security services. Giorgio, now in Cluses France, had taken to hiding in a larger community, while Erika in Cobbio needed to trek back and forth by train to Bellinzona for provisions greater than groceries. She didn't mind the commute at all; since the arrival of January she could feel cabin fever creeping up on her.

She finished the letter, then remembered she had to prepare the garbage for pick-up the next morning. This time she tied it up with the attention a professional would give to a Christmas present. Last time she'd been careless and the garbage collectors had left it.

She turned on her transistor radio and settled back to read her novel, legs propped on a second chair facing the kerosene stove. Heat enveloping her legs, kitchen light shining down, she felt almost cozy. Thank God the house was equipped with electricity. And plumbing, though the bathroom had been configured in later years at the end of a long outdoor balcony on the second story. When taking a shower she'd cringe in the cold room, then jog back in her bathrobe across the frigid balcony into the house and onto its equally cold stone floors. And of course there was no washing machine. *Christ, she was either a wimp or else just crazy to stay here.*

At least the house was piped with hot water and furnished with a modern stove to cook on. After dinner she took the garbage bundle out and looked skyward. No, she wasn't crazy to have chosen this place. The lights from dwellings on the distant mountains gleamed like stars suspended in the valley. These *hanging lights* of Cobbio never ceased to amaze her. As much as she complained, the beauty of this landscape fed her like bounty from heaven.

She shivered and hurried back inside, blowing warm air on her hands. Maybe later this evening (it was always hit and miss) she might receive the BBC on her radio—news from London, where Ian Westcott lived, Giorgio's and her contact and potential publisher of the exposé Giorgio had written and she was translating. Do you listen to the radio as well, Ian?

At eleven she shut off the radio and the kerosene stove. She filled two thirty-three centiliter glass bottles with hot water and brought them upstairs to tuck under the bedclothes at the foot of her bed. This was how she fended off the sub-freezing cold. Bundled in pajamas, she climbed in under the eiderdown and sighed as her feet hit the hot zone.

It was still dark when a dream descended on her like an avalanche. This time, however, her antagonist was not her brother but Claudio Voghera, the DIGOS agent hunting her. They'd had an affair some months ago, he'd even taught her some tricks of spycraft. Now Erika and her journalist partner Giorgio Testa felt certain Voghera and DIGOS were tracking them to stop any publication of a scoop that could rock Italy's democratic standing throughout the Western World. Hunting them down: not only to intercept their manuscript, but maybe to make Giorgio and her disappear as well. After all, look what they'd done to Matilde Fassino.

In Erika's dream Claudio Voghera burst onto the scene as a wolf with a handsome face and a mocking smile. His grey-blue eyes and silvery fur glinted as he galloped under moonlight following her scent. He knew her odor, knew about her past, knew why she might seek psychological help. Tongue lapping icy air, he crossed the mountains from Italy into Switzerland. In a sliver of a second he was approaching Bellinzona's three castles. With a supernatural leap he reached the ramparts of the highest castle on its hill. And then he was standing erect and tall, fully shape-shifted to the human Claudio. Armed with a broadsword he now surveyed the frozen land with an equally frozen scowl. His blue-grey eyes glowed impossibly large, saw far and wide. The belltower of Cobbio's high church caught his telescopic gaze, then the hundred-year-old house with the frescoed name *Casa Rosselli* on its outer wall. Claudio's cold silver gaze, like sinister moonlight, slithered through Erika's window.

She woke with a gasp, flung off her covers and stalked to the window where the moon was indeed plump and shining. She closed the drapes and returned to bed, turning on her nightlamp and reaching into the drawer of her nightstand. She pulled out her switchblade, the one she had taken from Claudio in a fight a year ago. With the press of a button on its handle, the blade flicked open with a ringing click. Satisfied, she gave its handle a confident squeeze and returned it to its abode. She was good with blades.

Chapter 2

The next morning Erika performed her workout: thirty pushups, a thirty-minute jog round and round the kitchen and tiny cold sitting room, to the music of her radio. She stayed indoors so as not to draw attention since no one seemed to jog in Cobbio. She did her fencing exercises— duck-walks, lunges, balancing exercises on each foot. She practiced her lunges with a used epée she had bought in Bellinzona. Someday she would get back into the sport that had netted her prizes in San Diego. Maybe Dr. Betz could be of help there as well, after they'd sorted out her debilitating dreams. She looked forward to seeing him again, to his soothing voice, to his kind demeanor. And since she was unemployed, receiving only the money Giorgio sent her from France, Betz had offered to waive his fee during this initial phase of treatment. Maybe it was her unorthodox dream that now kept him tethered to her case, though "unorthodox" would probably not be Dr. Betz's choice of word. As for the dream itself, she wondered how long she could keep from conveying its true magnitude to the unsuspecting doctor. At least last night's nightmare had changed nemesis, from her brother to Claudio, the hunter from DIGOS, which was almost like getting rid of a headache by banging her thumbnail with a hammer. Naturally, she would not relate this second dream to Dr. Betz. All things considered, she felt she had a sort of ally in the man (unwitting as he was) at a time when her collaborators were few and literally far between.

The work-out made it easier to face the cold outside on her way to the shower in the bathroom at the end of the balcony. Still, after finishing she returned at a jog back into the house, pulled her clothes on in the frigid bedroom, and hurried down to the stove-warmed kitchen. It was time to get to work.

To the end of the table next to the stove she moved her portable typewriter and the papers Giorgio Testa had sent from Cluse, France. The manuscript's first stop had been Bern, where Giorgio's Swiss-French collaborator Régine Farigoule lived. It had been Régine, a fellow journalist and friend to Giorgio, who had hooked them up with the Brit Ian Westcott of *The Guardian*. Commuting to Bern, Erika had fetched various segments of the Italian scoop one by one, with one last installment left to pick up. Once translated into English, the story's dissemination was all but guaranteed world-wide attention.

Erika settled onto a chair and shuffled through papers she had already typed in English. As translator she had leeway on how the story was expressed, but she'd remained faithful almost word for word to the original Italian, to her friend Giorgio's eloquent-while-explosive style. She pulled out the first page of her work, entitled—FASCIST COLLABORATOR MURDERED BY ITALIAN SECURITY SERVICES—

Yes, she finally decided, liberties should be taken here to deliver a maximum punch to anglophone readers. With a pencil she scratched out FASCIST and replaced it with AUSCHWITZ. Fascist spoke volumes to Italian audiences. AUSCHWITZ COLLABORATOR would have a bigger impact abroad, she thought. NAZI COLLABORATOR would even be punchier, however Matilde Fassino, the now-deceased octogenarian in question, had not belonged to the Nazi party. She and her banker husband had been fervent followers of Mussolini. In Turin the couple had blackmailed Jewish account holders, denouncing those who wouldn't pay to the fascist government, all but guaranteeing their transport to Auschwitz. The modern Italian government had turned a blind eye to Matilde Fassino's past. After all, her husband had died after the war, and how much harm could the little old woman have done even back in the day?

Plenty, Erika knew. And rumors still swirled about the woman's "diamond stash," diamonds also stolen from Jews. Then, out of the blue it seemed, DIGOS had taken Fassino out, the operation orchestrated to look like the old woman had died of stroke-related complications. But Erika knew otherwise. Matilde Fassino had become too inconvenient. In an aggressive, drunken state, Claudio Voghera had told her so. That had been the moment of reckoning. The knowledge had compromised her. She could not keep such a secret. She had to get away from Voghera—literally decamp. And so she'd told Giorgio the journalist, and a collaboration based on camaraderie had been born: she, Giorgio and Régine. They had a scoop and Erika had a role to play in her translating job.

"Yeah," Erika said aloud in English, reviewing the change in the title. "Definitely better." It was the only thing she had gone back and altered in her translation so far. Time was ticking down, Claudio and the DIGOS hounds were surely on her heels, and she had to go to Bern tomorrow to retrieve the last tranche of Giorgio's story. She would have liked to have already sent the first part of the translated scoop to London but Ian Westcott wanted the story in full. Well, soon he would have it.

Erika's roundtrip train ticket from Bellinzona to Bern lay in a drawer of the credenza in the chilly living room. Out of compulsion she went to check it again. Naturally nothing had changed: departure from Bellinzona at 8:06; change of train in Lucerne; arrival in Bern at 11:35, just in time to meet Régine Farigoule at noon at the city-center's the Bear Pit. She had made the same trip before, getting up at six o'clock to first catch the train from Cobbio to Bellinzona. Nothing to worry about...if she didn't *think* about it too much...

Another night passed with no dream about her brother nor, thank goodness, about Claudio. Maybe the sessions with the shrink were helping. Darkness still tarred the sky when she left the house, a few *hanging stars* accompanying her on her walk down the hill to the train station. Mountain folk high up were rising and their lights signaled life in the gelid night.

Foot traffic in the station conveyed the same. Among milling commuters speaking in hushed pre-dawn tones, she bought her ticket to Bellinzona. Then she waited for her train and listened—listened carefully, as she always did when leaving the house. Accented speech revealed much. In the village, everyone, though they knew Italian perfectly well, spoke to one another in the dialect of Canton Ticino, a form of Italian similar to dialects of northern Italy, including the region of Erika's relatives. Erika understood much of it, but what mattered was anyone she heard *not* speaking "*dialet*," either in Cobbio or Bellinzona, because they had to be an outsider like herself; such as Dr. Betz, presumably from German-speaking Switzerland. When the locals spoke standard Italian, as they did with her, their accent rang with a charming sing-song. If she happened to hear someone speaking Italian without this accent, in Cobbio's stores or its café, she tactfully asked about the person.

In the Bellinzona station she naturally heard more standard Italian, and in Lucerne, mostly German, and finally in Bern it would be German and French. Beyond Cobbio, who knew where her enemies might lie?

On the train out of Bellinzona she might have let her visual attention relax a little. She wasn't sure, but at Bern's famous Bear Pit, apart from the bears lumbering around the snow mounds in their zoo-like enclosure, she noticed a man who could have also been in the Lucerne station. Was he at the news kiosk buying a magazine while Erika scanned the newspaper headlines? Same camel hair overcoat and matching flat cap...same mustache? Maybe not, but in any case she would keep an eye on him.

Few people were bear-watching today, the bears keener on the cold, and finally the man moved on. She watched him stroll back towards the street that sported a statue of a standing bear dressed in medieval armor—the bear, Bern's emblem. She continued to peer in that direction, sufficiently absorbed not to notice the arrival of her contact.

She heard something metallic hit the sidewalk. When she turned, Régine Farigoule was bent over picking up her keys about two meters away. The two women made eye contact and Erika turned back to the bears. After a couple of seconds Erika moved towards the other side of the pit, then left the area all together. It was the first time she had launched the signal: she would head for a café and Régine would go back home and wait for Erika's call, after which Erika would join her in her apartment. Again, Erika considered a possible coincidence involving the man in the camel hair coat, or the possibility of mistaken identity, but was satisfied with having given Régine the signal. In fact the maneuver kind of thrilled her. And she was sure Régine would agree that it was better to be cautious than caught.

Buzzed into Régine's building, Erika adjusted her belongings before calling for the elevator. She slung the messenger bag, worn crossways across her chest, back over to one shoulder, then moved the switchblade she carried in her right coat pocket to the back pocket of her corduroys, pulling her sweater down over it. She carried no purse—too awkward if she was accosted—her money, ID, train tickets, and essential items populating various pockets. Yes, the hypervigilance could be tedious, but she was used to it—had gotten acclimated even before this entanglement, for this wasn't her first perilous conflict with Claudio Voghera.

Régine, hand on Erika's shoulder, ushered Erika into her flat, relieving her of her grey wool overcoat and, for the first time, commenting on the spartan nature of Erika's winter attire. "No scarf, no gloves?" she said with a little laugh.

"Too cumbersome," Erika half lied. Last year, her scarf had almost got her killed and gloves made it impossible to manage her knife in a pinch.

"Well, you're awfully hardy." Another modest laugh from Régine, who seemed to treat Erika with a slight deference. And yet Régine was one of the friendliest, most accommodating people Erika had met in Switzerland. Partly, Erika surmised, because they were both friends and allies of Giorgio's.

The two spoke Italian for the most part, throwing in English every so often. Then Régine handed over the last installment of Giorgio Testa's scoop, Erika tucking it carefully into her messenger bag. Over coffee they spoke about the security precautions they'd taken at the Bear Pit. They shared their worries about Giorgio, whom Régine had met at a journalism conference in Geneva five years prior. Régine, who now worked at a French-language television station in Bern, spoke so fondly of the big husky man that Erika wondered if the two mid-thirty-year-olds had been lovers. Naturally she didn't ask, though by this third meeting she did feel she could inquire about her contact's given name. "I've never known anyone else named *Régine*."

"Well, it's old fashioned," Régine admitted with another polite little laugh. "But you've probably come across other names in Switzerland that are a touch démodé."

Erika let her gaze sweep subtly around Régine's sitting room and decided that her name and her surroundings suited each other. Classical décor, French provincial furniture, a bit like Erika's own grandmother's stuff. "True," she said. In Cobbio the postman was named Tarcisio and the café owner Plinio. "Makes me almost think I can trust anyone as long as they have an old-fashioned name!"

Régine shook her head. "I'm so sorry the Italians present trouble."

Trouble was putting it mildly, though Erika kept the particulars of her fears to herself, which was why she'd moved her knife out of her coat pocket, so it wouldn't accidentally fall out when Régine took her coat.

Régine offered Erika lunch but Erika declined, having eaten in the café during the half hour she'd killed after leaving the Bear Pit. She probably shouldn't stay long anyway and put Régine at risk.

"So, this is the last of the scoop," Erika said, as she gathered up her messenger bag.

"Unless Giorgio sends additional material. But you and I will keep in touch."

Before Erika left the flat, Régine checked the street below from her window, as she had off and on during the visit. "No one loitering," she confirmed.

As Erika walked to the train station under the medieval stone porticoes of historical Bern, a strange sense of anti-climax filled her. She now had the final part of the exposé to translate. And then what? She'd also felt strange when Régine pointed out what a "hardy" constitution Erika must have, with Erika braving barely-above freezing temperatures and snowy landscapes with no gloves or scarf. Did the petite French-Swiss woman, with her bright smile and peaches-and-cream complexion, see Erika as some kind of American Amazon—five foot ten inches and not even carrying a purse?

A sense of alienness joined the anti-climax during her train rides back to Cobbio. She thought of her old empty house—she was the only person she knew in ultra-modern Switzerland who lived in such primitive, hermit-like conditions.

When she finally arrived in Bellinzona, instead of taking the next train to Cobbio (trains ran back and forth all day and evening) she left the station, vaguely justifying the stopover with picking up more bar soap at the mega-grocery store Migros.

But instead she turned the other way. Bellinzona's lowest castle towered over the store and town, and with the winter light dissolving quickly, she decided to make a last-minute visit there. The castle was one of the best-preserved medieval specimens she'd ever seen and she never tired of strolling through its ramparted precincts.

As she climbed the path next to the castle walls, she suddenly smelled a musky-sweet odor. She stopped and inhaled. Someone was smoking weed nearby—no mistaking it. She entered the castle grounds, the odor growing stronger. A uniformed man walking across the frosted grass, lifted a cigarette to his mouth. When he spotted her, he cupped the cigarette.

"Sorry," Erika said, "is it okay to be here at this time?"

The man was young, even in the twilight she could tell he was about her age. He stood staring at her—no one else was around. The hand cupping the cigarette moved behind him.

"Don't worry," said Erika, smiling, "I don't mind that kind of smoking." In fact the scent nostalgically reminded her of America.

The young guard brought the cigarette back in front of him. "I shouldn't be smoking anything here," he said, "it's just that it's cold and I'm about to lock up."

Erika took a few steps towards him. "This place is great. I get such a fantastic feel for history when I'm here."

The young man instantly joined her wavelength. "The castle was constructed in the 1300s, when Bellinzona was under the dukes of Milan."

"So that's why the locals speak a similar dialect."

"Do *you* speak our dialect?"

"No, but I understand a lot of it."

They were speaking standard Italian. The young man, who introduced himself as Marzio, suddenly lifted his cigarette, maybe thinking it might burn him but finding it had gone out.

"Go ahead and relight it," said Erika. "I don't mind."

It was mostly dark now, but as Marzio struck a match and drew on the joint, the glow illuminated his face, and his eyes turned large and blue. He offered her a drag.

In the familiarity of his local accent she felt herself relax. And she had to admit that this bit of masculine attention felt good today. She hadn't smoked weed since back in San Diego and just one drag wouldn't get her stoned, so *hell*, why not? She inhaled, let out an unexpected cough and returned the joint. Her throat didn't burn too much since she'd only recently quit smoking cigarettes.

"Do you live in Bellinzona?" he asked her.

"No, in Cobbio. In fact I've got to get back."

"Oh!" He took one last drag, ground out the joint on the sole of his shoe, then dropped the butt in his jacket pocket. "I live in Cobbio too. I'm on my way home after I close up the castle."

In that moment the image of her messenger bag jumped to the forefront of her mind. She shouldn't have said where she lived.

"My car's in the shop," he said, "so I'm taking the train home. What about you?"

What could Erika say? By this point, several people in Cobbio already knew her. What was one more?

As predicted, the drag of weed hadn't gone to her head, but it did bestow a sense of warm well-being. She smiled. "It's the train for me too."

Marzio locked up, collected his things, and he and Erika walked out of the castle grounds together.

Marzio—she'd heard the name in Italy, but at least this Marzio spoke Italian with the sing-song accent of the Swiss Alps.

Chapter 3

Claudio Voghera considered the espresso machine on a café counter in downtown Turin. It was ten o'clock in the morning, therefore he should drink coffee. Paradoxically, he had a lot on his plate now that he'd been suspended from DIGOS.

"*Cazzo di* Erika," he swore to himself. *Fucking* Erika, he added in Erika's own English language. He had learned the word from her and now liked how it sounded next to her name. She and that fat fuck journalist Giorgio Testa and their writings could ruin him for good with the intelligence services. Put him permanently out in the cold over his indiscreet leak about the assassination of Matilde Fassino. Slips of the tongue had got other operatives banished, but Voghera had never made a mistake like this until his involvement with Erika. And damn her if she thought he would sit idly by during his unpaid suspension from DIGOS, while she used his indiscretion against him! As if they'd meant nothing to each other!

He looked out the café window at the skiff of snow on the street and the bustling, bundled passersby. *Literally,* out in the cold, he muttered to himself.

"*Signore,*" the barman said, briskly turning towards him to take his order.

Voghera stared at him, or rather looked through him as he further weighed his choices. "*Un caffè,*" he finally ordered.

The barman pivoted towards the espresso maker, only to stop at another request from Voghera: "With a glass of white wine on the side."

White wine was nothing, thought Voghera; it got him through the morning and, with the offset of coffee, amounted to net zero intoxication.

The espresso, *ristretto* style, took all of two sips to finish, the wine, not many more, and when he spied the postman outside he left the café and followed him up the street to the *Cardinale* newspaper office. Voghera waited for him to make his delivery, then entered the *Cardinale*.

The caretaker behind the counter greeted Voghera with a set jaw and worried eyes. To Voghera's raised eyebrows he firmly responded, "No news."

"Nothing from France?" Voghera insisted, strolling to the counter and picking up the mail. True, no envelope bore a stamp labelled République Française. And yet, Voghera knew (from a DIGOS agent who still talked to him) that Giorgio Testa was somewhere in that country. He tossed the envelopes back on the counter, one falling behind it.

"Listen," said the lean, elderly caretaker, bending down to pick it up, "I've told you they're not publishing anything right now. You know it's not a large press." The man threw his hands up, indicating the miniscule office of the socialist newspaper, which occupied only the ground floor of the building that housed it.

"Still," said Voghera, his grey eyes impassive, "you wouldn't want anything to happen to this place. Like that fire a year ago..."

The caretaker's brows inched anxiously together. The fire, set last year by neo-fascist punks, had destroyed the front office and killed Giorgio Testa's friend and partner in the business; it hadn't been all that long since repairs were completed.. "I've told you I don't know where Giorgio is, and I don't want trouble. I only—"

"You only *work* here, which means you're getting paid— don't deny it."

The old man squared his scrawny shoulders and tensed his jaw once more. "I do get paid, but by a group of businesses in the neighborhood to do maintenance and keep an eye on things. Nothing more."

Voghera didn't argue, he already knew this. And he knew he would get nothing out of the man unless he threatened to rough him up; then he might still get nothing, and gratuitous beatings were not his style.

"I'll be back," he said, throwing the man a cold grin. "Save the mail for me."

Cazzo di Giorgio Testa and his two-bit paper. Naturally, nothing was being published right now since Testa was almost certainly working on a scoop that could net him more than he'd earned off the *Cardinale* during the paper's entire existence. As he left the shop, he glanced up at the metal sign of a cheerful little American redbird, protruding from the building's façade above the door. Voghera was apolitical but still found the mascot irritating. It reminded him of how a fat rinky-dink publisher, who probably had a bird-sized dick, had flown away and avoided capture.

The publisher and *Erika Rivoli*. Voghera had tried to put out feelers, DIGOS was looking for the two as well, but other than getting that whiff that Testa was in France, he'd learned nothing. Granted, he'd got a late start, hadn't figured out what the two were probably up to until a month after they'd disappeared from Turin. He longed to jump in his car and take to the trail himself. For the time being, however, he needed to monitor the situation here in Turin. Which meant he must pay a visit to Signora Eugenia Sillano, whose attic flat Erika had lived in before she'd disappeared.

A few doors down from the Cardinale, Voghera reached his car, then rethought unlocking the door. Here on Corso Reggio Parco, it cost nothing to park. On Via Garibaldi, where Erika used to live, it would be almost impossible to find a slice of space to slip his car into. He zipped his black parka full up and waited at the tram stop.

On the ride to Erika's neighborhood, he couldn't stop his resentful musings. Overall, he and the American expat, who taught English at the Manhattan Institute in Turin, had enjoyed a passionate, fun-filled few months together. *Cazzo*, he'd even taught her some tricks of his trade—how to tail a target, how to spot a tail on oneself, how to pick a lock and cut telephone wires...

The thought made him cringe with embarrassment. He wanted to grab her by the hair, just like the time he'd first encountered her, only this time shove her to the ground, groveling. How dare she betray him like this!

And his outrage only increased when he remembered their last lovemaking. How she would push his short, dark bangs back before she kissed him. How he'd shaved off his mustache for her because its bristles irritated her skin when they kissed—those luxurious kisses he'd bestowed on her mouth, on her breasts, and everywhere. Their bodies meshed in a way that sizzled to the touch. She'd said so herself—that just touching his arm could send a frisson of electricity through her, that the patch of dark hair on his fair-skinned chest made her mad to caress him.

Christ, almighty!

Inhaling deeply, he reined in his self-flagellation. The tram stopped two buildings down from his target. Erika's landlady, Signora Sillano, had never met him. And though he'd visited Erika's flat, he and Erika had always used his place for their intimate rendezvous. He extracted a business card from his wallet, ready to present himself as David Rosasco, Private Detective. "Didn't Signora Sillano know that Erika's American family was trying desperately to find her?"

Who could ignore a line like that?

He pressed the buzzer next to her name on the plaque listing residents.

"Sì," responded a mature-sounding woman's voice.

He executed his cover explanation, then waited.

Finally came, "Are you listed in the Turin phone book?"

"Not yet," said Voghera, and presented his second line: "I've just moved my business from Milan to Turin."

Certainly the signora must be asking herself how Erika's family had found him so quickly if he'd only recently moved his business from Milan. Voghera waited for the question, but it didn't come; instead she buzzed him in. With no elevator in the building, he climbed the four flights of stairs, wondering all the while if Erika had told the signora about a certain Claudio Voghera breaking into Erika's attic flat last year and giving her a black eye. Erika, on the other hand—and he now found this hotly embarrassing—had wrested his switchblade away from him. She'd brandished her own knife, a stiletto; she was handy with blades, he had to admit.

If Erika had described Voghera to Signora Sillano, the signora didn't let on. His hair was short now, an old-fashioned cut shaved in the back and on the sides. His mustache had grown back and he now had a good start on cultivating a beard. The signora merely glanced at his card and ushered him into her kitchen. Like many old people (Sillano had to be at least seventy) she preferred to talk in the kitchen. She wore thick winter stockings with her wool skirt and her grey hair was pulled back in a bun. Probably came from peasant stock, a country bumpkin.

"As I said downstairs," he began, once the signora had served coffee and settled at the table across from him, "Erika's parents, Alan and Cheryl Rivoli, are anxious to know what's happened to her."

Signora Sillano examined him with hooded eyes that blended with her heavily-lined face, so that Voghera found it difficult to distinguish any particular expression—whether she'd fallen for his cover, whether she feared him, whether she suspected his true identity, all remained cryptic.

"Was it Erika's father who contacted you?" she asked.

"No." Voghera was ready for this question. "Mister Rivoli had an interpreter call who speaks Italian, a go-between, so to speak."

"Of course," said Erika's landlady. She let leak a faint smile. "I'd forgotten Erika is the only one of her American family who speaks fluent Italian." Though the smile was barely discernable, Voghera sensed he was being challenged.

"Yes, it's unfortunate the American relatives can't communicate in Italian," he said, though naturally he felt the opposite.

"But isn't one of her grandparents still living?" the signora asked.

Such a mild, unassuming tone the old woman's voice carried. And yet this last question was blatantly challenging. Both of Erika's grandparents were deceased, and doubtless Sillano knew it. Her wrinkled hands so modestly resting on the flower-patterned oil cloth, her placid nunlike gaze, made him want to laugh.

"Unfortunately both grandparents have passed away," Voghera replied, shaking his head in mock commiseration. "And her mother is Anglo-American—at least that's what I learned through the interpreter."

"True."

"Do you know any of her relatives here?"

"No, so far I haven't had the pleasure."

The old woman, still serene as a Roman statue, was beginning to get on Voghera's nerves. And he found the cuckoo clock mounted on the wall above her head irritating as well. It had just gone off, its mechanism shrieking and clanging throughout the room as if to give notice that he was in enemy territory. Signora Sillano would somehow communicate his visit to Erika—he could feel it in his sinews—but how?

"Do you have *any* idea where she may have gone?" he asked, suppressing his annoyance, all the while knowing Sillano's answer would be *no*. "After all it's been almost two months..."

"Signor...*Rosasco*, is it? I've been thinking about it myself. Most of her belongings are still in her flat, so I've expected her to return. But now," she shook her head stoically, "I don't know what to think."

"Have you notified the police?"

A second's pause ensued, and though the signora remained inscrutable, the hesitation spoke volumes. He craved to know the content of those volumes.

"No," the signora said. "Erika did say she had to go away, so I've respected that."

"And she wouldn't say where, or when she's coming back?"

The signora shook her head again.

"You have *no* idea? Never had a phone call from her?"

"I wish I had."

"But you're keeping her things in the flat you own without earning any rent?"

"I'm not dependent upon the income. I'll give her time to come back."

The woman was made of stone. But there had been that slight fissure "Well," Voghera said, "Erika's parents don't see it that way, understandably. They really need to locate their daughter and they've engaged me to do whatever it takes. So I'd like to ask a favor...Could I take a look at her flat?"

This was the real reason for his visit. He'd never counted on getting much information from the signora. And when she answered, "No, I'm sorry but that would be an invasion of Erika's privacy," he just nodded in acceptance.

He thanked Signora Sillano and got up to leave, dropping his card on the table and asking her to please call him at his new Turin number if she happened to remember anything or learn something new regarding the case. *Typical detective leave-taking words*. The number was that of his own flat, but he didn't expect her to call. What he didn't mention was that he would be back to have a look at Erika's flat on his own terms.

Chapter 4

When Erika had first told Dr. Betz that her dream of fratricide was ongoing, he'd looked at her with what she could only describe as detached concern. Probably a professional expression. At any rate, she knew he would follow up on the subject in this latest visit.

"But the dream *did* stop for two nights in a row," she said.

"Which nights?"

"For two nights after I saw you last week." Maybe that was hopeful.

Dr. Betz gave a confident nod and told Erika the pattern was to be expected. "And the other dream?" he asked in a quiet voice.

Erika hesitated. Not because she felt more embarrassed about dreaming of sleeping with her brother versus killing him, but because she thought she *ought* to feel more embarrassment.

"Yes," she said, "but the two don't always come together, and not always on the same night."

"Does the narrative of each dream vary?"

For a moment Erika reflected. "The one about killing always has us fighting and me stabbing him with a knife, the same thing I described last week." Again she paused, and this time she did feel rather awkward about recounting variations on the incest dream. The light in the room oozed its usual calming, yellowish-warmth, while outside the window a steely grey sky persisted.

Erika diverted her gaze to it, spoke as if from that distance. "The dream varies some...different acts, you know...um..."

"Is there any hostility involved?" the doctor mercifully cut in. "Any *crossover* in feeling with the other dream?"

"No." Erika's answer might have puzzled him, but then she still hadn't told the doctor the entire story behind the two dreams, and doubted she ever would.

"You know," he went on, "every part of our dreams represents us; they are part of us. They are a creation of our *selves*."

Erika thought that sounded reasonable.

"And we all harbor masculine and feminine energy, which can vary in intensity, given our state of mind at a given time. Your two dreams would indicate in one case a balance and in another an imbalance in your masculine energy." The doctor paused and waited, still with that same detached look of concern. "Do you see where I'm going?"

Erika thought she did. His head was slightly atilt and she figured he might be a psychologist who liked to use the Socratic method, if shrinks did that.

"I guess," she ventured, "the dream about killing my brother shows I've got too much masculine energy going on?"

"Quite possibly." Finally, a soft smile from the doctor.

"But the other dream..."

"Indicates a levelness, a harmony, rather than a surge in masculine energy, since you've told me there is no hostility." Dr. Betz sat back in his wheeled office chair and remained silent for a time, though his eyes never left Erika. "But," he said at last, "we're only chipping the tip of the iceberg, I'm afraid, considering the dreams persist. And," he added sympathetically, "you don't seem to be benefitting from them."

That was the truth. Just before she'd woken this morning, she'd dreamt she and her brother were dueling with fencing blades—she with the used épée she'd bought in Bellinzona, her brother with a foil, a weaker weapon, so to speak. So a variant had indeed occurred in her dream of fratricide. At times she would stab her brother with a stiletto, at others with a sword. She hadn't revealed the latter because she wanted to keep her former fencing sport private.

"Where is your brother now, by the way?" asked the doctor, after jotting down a note.

Again, Erika was slow to respond. "He's in prison."

"I see. Might this have something to do with dreaming of stabbing him?"

Jesus, this was getting complicated. All Erika wanted was relief from the dreams and the headaches they provoked. Still she knew dialogue was necessary to therapy, otherwise she wouldn't have chosen this course.

No, there was no connection between her brother being in prison and the stabbing dream, and she said so to the doctor. "He ended up in prison because of his stupid involvement in a criminal scam."

"No resentment on your part?"

She was glad this therapist didn't press for details that weren't relevant. She would have to invent a story if Dr. Betz asked for more on why her brother was in prison, or where, for that matter. She shook her head. "No, I just think he acted like an ass. He shouldn't be in prison too long."

"So how do you *feel* in the dream when you're fighting and stabbing your brother. Try to put yourself there."

Erika didn't have trouble with that. It was the fencing version that filled her mind as if she were dreaming right now. She folded her arms and bent slightly at the waist. "I feel horrible. I don't mean to kill him. I only want to show him he's not superior just because he's our father's only son, and our father prefers him..."

"Go on..."

"I was born first, then my brother came along four years later, and as soon as he got old enough to play catch and go hunting with my dad, I was left behind. I don't *hate* my brother, I just want him to see that I count too. I certainly don't want him to die!" Erika straightened and tried to draw a stabilizing breath that instead came in stutters.

"Breathe deeply now," said the doctor, demonstrating the

technique. "Inhale through the nose and exhale very slowly through the mouth." He nodded. "That's better. Three times, now."

Once Erika opened her eyes and steadied her gaze, Dr. Betz made sure she was all right, then said, "So there might be some feelings of guilt towards him."

Erika sighed—yes, there was. Both dreams provoked headaches, and just talking about the stabbing one had caused her chest to constrict and her ears to burn hot with blood. The deep breathing did help. The doctor told her to practice it whenever such tension befell her.

"So let's put guilt aside for now," he said. "We're nearing the end of the hour and I think we should end the session with your describing how you fill your days. Is that all right?"

Erika nodded, though here she had a cover story as well.

"What brings you to Canton Ticino?" Dr. Betz asked. Strange that he hadn't asked this question two sessions back.

"Well, I'm writing a novel that takes place both here and in Italy. Now I'm *here* to do research." Lying so blatantly didn't come easy to her, but since she'd entered into this dangerous endeavor with Giorgio Testa she'd known lying would be necessary to protect herself. Doing so in Italian had come easier, a language at a distance from her native English, like a cousin once-removed.

"So you're learning about the culture and people here." The doctor gave an approving smile.

"Oh yes."

"And you've gotten to know people? Because working alone, especially in this isolating weather, doesn't always bode well for mental health."

"I have met some people in Cobbio, mostly shopkeepers and so forth that I deal with." There were the relatives of the owner of the house she lived in, but she didn't see them on a regular basis. The owner lived in San Diego and had been a friend of Erika's grandparents. It was Romano Rosselli whom she contacted from Turin to ask if she could stay in the house.

His niece in Cobbio had given Erika the keys. What made the house a good hideaway, apart from its remote location, was that no one could trace her now that her grandparents were deceased, and Romano Rosselli was not a friend of Erika's parents or any other of her relatives.

"No friends yet?" the doctor asked.

"Not really." Because of her dodgy situation she hadn't tried to befriend anyone, including Romano Rosselli's relatives, though a few had offered their hospitality. There was her contact Régine whom she was growing fond of, but they had met only three times, and Régine lived in Bern. Then there was the Irish couple who had bought an old stone farm building in Cobbio to renovate with an ultra-modern interior. They spoke enough Italian to get by, she'd discovered when meeting them one afternoon in the village café, but thought it grand that there was another English speaker in the village and said they'd like to invite her to dinner some time.

Then, with a slight uptick in her pulse, she recalled her latest acquaintance, the guardian of Bellinzona's downtown castle. *Marzio*. How strange to meet a reefer-smoker here in the backwaters of conservative Switzerland, when she'd had no such encounters in a metropolis like Turin, nicknamed the Little Paris.

She told Dr. Betz about the Irish couple. "They're a bit older than I am but they're awfully nice."

"Good. Get out as much as you can. Meet people your age too," he said, closing his notebook to signal the end of their session. "Will I see you next week?"

Erika agreed and they stood and shook hands. No doubt the doctor would be pleased to know she had actually met someone her age. Still, she wasn't sure she would tell him about Marzio.

Dusk was drawing in as she left the building, her thoughts still on the guardian of the castle. He'd suggested they meet again since they both lived in Cobbio, but she hadn't committed to

28

anything, and merely offered casual acknowledgements of the *when-I-get-time* kind. He'd answered, "Well, you know where to find me."

Indeed she did. She couldn't help thinking of him every time she glimpsed the castle. Frequent masculine company was tempting, yet the fewer people who got to know her the better.

Once home, Erika lit the stove and settled next to it, thinking. Before long a warm lethargy took hold of her that pushed away her normal desire to turn on the radio and make dinner. She wasn't hungry, only weary and almost hypnotized by the penetrating heat. She had told Dr. Betz of her rivalry with her brother for their father's affections. On the surface, some might agree that a history like that could lead to fratricidal dreams. Yet the doctor had not affirmed the connection. He hadn't even used the term *fratricidal* in either of their two discussions of her brother. Instead he'd gone off on "masculine and feminine energy," and a balance needed between them, which did sound reasonable yet didn't make her feel much better about her dreams and about her brother, in general.

But you haven't told him everything, she reminded herself, as if she truly *needed* reminding. She sighed heavily, didn't want to leave the heat of the stove, but finally gave into a growl and contraction in her stomach. She got up and poured herself a glass of local red wine. Then she pulled a hardboiled egg out of the little fridge and started peeling it to slice into a salad. There was bread left over from this morning, a bit hard but it would do. A cold supper to complement the chill that crept back just by her stepping away from the stove. The cold that reminded her she was alone and that Dr. Betz was the only person she could have a heart-to-heart talk to in over two hundred kilometers.

Chapter 5

Claudio Voghera parked under the plane trees next to the sidewalk of his apartment building in Corso Brescia. As he locked his car door he glanced across the street, shaking his head in disapproval. More graffiti on the concrete wall. Today's addition, a big circle with a cross through it. *Goddamn Fascists*. The hammer and sickle, for now absent, also made frequent guest appearances on the wall. *Goddamn Communists*. It took the city forever to clean up graffiti in this neighborhood, despite its being decently middle class. Unlike in the historical and upscale areas where the mayor and his clique ordered swift action to rid palaces and castles of hooligan and dissident daubings.

Neofascist symbols, Communist symbols, Anarchist taggings—there'd been a street war going on in Italy for years and it wasn't limited to mere graffiti. Terrorist battles between Communist and Fascist gangs had kept DIGOS scrambling for practically his entire career, and he was only thirty-two years old. Last May, the Communist Red Brigades had kidnapped ex-premier and Christian Democrat Aldo Moro and assassinated him. Even Erika had got swept into the fray last year, nosing around some associates of the Red Brigades. Now she was capitalizing on her experience and almost certainly in league with journalist Giorgio Testa. They knew too much and had to be stopped.

Voghera unlocked the black wrought-iron- and glass door to his building, checked his mailbox, and took the cage elevator to the fourth floor. Inside his flat, he stripped off his tie, mixed himself a Negroni, then sat on his sofa to reflect on the day's unspooling. After leaving that mule Eugenia Sillano he'd proceeded to canvas the neighborhood. Flashing Erika's picture, he'd questioned every merchant in the zone. All claimed to know nothing and several voiced concern. "Such a pleasant and cheerful young woman," the pharmacist had said. "I hope nothing's happened to her!" Then, there was Erika's local café, the Déjà Vu, whose owner knew Erika well enough to express more than hope-filled clichés.

"Erika's been coming to my establishment for a year now," Fausta Fabri had said. "If she'd gone away for good I'm sure she would've let me know."

"But she did tell you she was going away *for a while*?" Voghera asked, sipping an espresso at the Déjà Vu's counter.

"No. And it's been over a month since I've seen her, so I'm glad her parents have got someone looking into to it."

The woman seemed sincere, though her hazel eyes held a strange far-off look. Maybe she was just an aloof type, reservedness a common cultural trait in Piedmont. And plenty of people in Turin believed in the paranormal, considering the city's historical—and current—reputation as a point of occult energy. With her café called Déjà Vu, the fortyish Fausta Fabri could well be one of them.

"Has she mentioned any places she might like to visit?" he asked.

The woman cocked her head as if considering Voghera for the first time. In his suit and wool overcoat, a homburg set at a jaunty angle, he fashioned himself a classic gentleman detective.

Thoughtfully, she said, "Everybody talks about places they'd like to visit, don't they? Paris, London, New York...but Erika would've mentioned if she were going to one of those cities."

"Maybe somewhere closer to Turin?" Voghera suggested.

Fausta Fabri shrugged. "The Matterhorn?"

Voghera thought she was joking.

"I only say that," she explained, "because when I first got to know Erika, I recommended she go up to Superga to see the view. You're from Milan, Signor Rosasco, but Superga's one of the highest hills in Turin. If you're lucky to be up there on a clear day you can see the Alpine Arc. Erika did that and said she'd spotted the Matterhorn. Said she'd like to go to Zermatt sometime..."

That was all Voghera had got out of the Déjà Vu's owner. Now, he drained the last of his Negroni and went back to his drinks trolley to make another. *Shit.* He thought he had another bottle of gin. What was left could barely make one more drink. Well, it would have to do. He poured the rest of the gin into his ice-filled tumbler, found it to be on the stingy side, and accordingly reduced the requisite portions of Campari and vermouth—three parts of each being standard, though Voghera preferred to go heavier on the gin.

Well, he could say he'd reduced his alcohol consumption for this evening. He sank back down on the sofa and held the tumbler to his newly-aching forehead. Drink had gotten him into this mess, no denying it. During an evening of cocktails and wine and brandy he'd let slip the truth about the death of the old Fascist Matilde Fassino. Erika had been so eager to learn about his craft. Before coming to Italy the CIA had recruited her, then ultimately rejected her. The elephant chip on her shoulder had ridden with her all the way to Turin and he, Claudio, had indulged her spy fantasies, and then let down his guard.

And got blindsided by the consequences. Heat rose to his face and he took a final pull from his drink, savoring the bitter-tartness of what would be his last Negroni of the evening.

He slammed the empty glass on the coffee table. The problem was he'd genuinely liked Erika, had even allowed himself to feel sorry when it came to her parents and brother. He pictured her, and this time his urge wasn't to grasp her blond hair and force her to her knees, but to bury his face in her hair, then kiss her, imagining her here with him where they'd always made love—

"*Cazzo*." He got up and went for the whiskey on the bottom shelf of the trolley, poured himself a shot and downed it. Straight Bourbon wasn't his habit and drinking shots made him feel more an alcoholic, yet he needed to iron out his nerves and quit thinking about the Erika he once knew.

He returned to the sofa and to his gleanings of the day. He needed to search Erika's flat but would wait until tomorrow night. Once more he reviewed what the owner of the Déjà Vu had said. Voghera believed her, overall. In the past Erika had referred to Fausta Fabri as a *casual* friend. So no, Erika probably wouldn't have told this woman where she was going. And yet, that statement about the Matterhorn...Voghera himself had never heard Erika mention the mountain, but now it intrigued him. He would let it percolate. In the meantime he went over his plans for tomorrow.

He plucked his notepad off the coffee table and checked off "Visits to Sillano and the Déjà Vu," jotting an asterisk next to Déjà Vu. He still needed to visit the Manhattan Institute, where Erika taught English as a second language. Not a lot of hope there either, he surmised, but if you left a stone unturned it could end up coming back to strike you in the head.

The next day, after leaving the Manhattan school, he felt safe figuring no stone would return to pelt him from that institution. The secretary, whom he'd first questioned, didn't even like Erika. "She ran off like this last year," the woman had scoffed. "You'll see, she'll turn back up again with some excuse or another."

Voghera had looked askance at the bleached blonde with the dark eyes and black-penciled eyebrows. No use bothering with her any further. Erika had already labeled the woman a *classic bitter bitch*, citing a particular time when Erika had called in sick and the secretary had threatened her job. She didn't like Erika, and Erika would not have told her where she was going.

The director of the Manhattan school, on the other hand,

with his limited time to talk to Voghera, had voiced no complaints about Erika, saying she'd called him directly about her sudden emergency leave of absence. The middle-aged, bespectacled fellow had alerted the staff for coverage but hadn't a clue where Erika had gone. "I do have to admit," he'd said, removing his glasses and polishing them with a crisply-ironed handkerchief, "I *had* been a touch irritated about her absence, but now that her family have called in a private investigator," he nodded at Voghera, "I only hope she's all right—I mean I've always hoped she's all right, don't get me wrong—"

Voghera said he understood.

He questioned some of the staff who weren't busy in classrooms—once more, no ideas of where Erika could have gone. Then he left, acknowledging it would make no sense for Erika to inform *anyone* in Turin of her whereabouts, even Eugenia Sillano, though Voghera would still stake the inheritance his deadbeat, deserter father would never leave him that they were in communication. Remaining on his list were Erika's relatives in nearby Asti. She visited them from time to time, but once more it made no sense for her to reveal her plans to them. Should he kick up those stones in Asti? *Probably*, he sighed. But first he had a flat to search.

That night Voghera appeared in front of Erika's building in Via Garibaldi dressed in black jeans, black turtleneck, black shoes, and his black parka. He'd left his car parked a few blocks away in Piazza San Carlo and now checked his watch: eleven-thirty—early enough for someone in the building to still be up, but late enough for many residents to have battened down the hatches. He counted lights still burning in the flats he'd matched up with names listed on the building's plaque. One flat of two on the first floor had a room lit, and one flat on the third showed both its windows illuminated through sheer curtains. The entire fourth floor, the Signora's floor, was a reassuring black stripe across the front of the building.

To avoid being spotted picking a lock at the building's entrance he rang the buzzer of the night-owl on the third floor.

From the speaker, a male voice croaked an unsure, "Sì...?"

"Signor Zucco?" Voghera voiced apologetically.

"*Sì*...who is this?"

"I'm sorry to bother you so late, but I'm Eugenia Sillano's cousin Elio, staying with her, and I got locked out. My cousin's asleep, but I saw your light on and—"

"Signora Sillano's *cousin*...?" the croaky voice came back.

"On my mother's side—her mother and my grandmother were first cousins," Voghera said, imagining Signor Zucco's both puzzled and skeptical look. "Anyway, I've come home late and realized I took the wrong key to the street-door with me. Can't get back in, and I don't want to wake my cousin. As I said, I saw your light on—"

Voghera heard a tinny mutter, then *buzz buzz,* the door clicked open.

Inside the foyer Voghera reminded himself that Signor Zucco might mention Cousin Elio to the signora when they next crossed paths. The thought was a mere minor note. If the signora suspected "Detective Rosasco" as the intruder, what did it matter? If she or Zucco wanted to call the police, who cared? They would obtain *zilch*. He'd written off Sillano anyway, a silent old tomb fit for Turin's famous Monumental Cemetery.

The old building, part of the city's historical center, didn't have an elevator. The pro: no clanking sounds to give him away. The con: he would have to walk up the four flights of stairs, passing Signor Zucco's landing, then take the stairs to Erika's attic flat.

With no choice in the matter, Voghera commenced gum-shoeing his way up the marble steps.

As he approached the third-floor landing he slowed to listen for sounds wafting from the Zucco flat. Standing still in the dark (he didn't want to turn on the stairway light) on the top stair before the landing, he heard nothing. Then, as he crossed the landing, he heard the cranking of a key in a lock—Signor Zucco, it seemed, had calculated the time it would take Cousin Elio to reach the third floor. Gripping the banister, Voghera lunged up two stairs, then stood silent, listening to Zucco's door creaking open. The stairway light blinked on. Voghera tiptoed up another two stairs and waited out of sight. He heard a man clear his throat—Zucco, no doubt, rubbernecking from his doorway. After a couple of seconds, Voghera heard the door close and the clatter of its lock.

He hurried up to the fourth floor, passed Eugenia Sillano's door, and continued the few stairs up to the landing of Erika's attic flat. There, he turned on his flashlight and examined the door's lock. He hadn't encountered it since last year (the one and only time) when he'd simply used a skeleton key in the old warded lock and strolled into the flat to wait for Erika. How he had underestimated her then! Arriving home, she'd noticed the door open a crack and entered with her stiletto blade flashing. He'd pulled his switchblade and from there a duel began, ending with his losing his knife, though he did land a punch to Erika's cheekbone. Afterwards he'd felt awkward about that, though he'd only been doing his job, trying to get Erika to quit snooping around his operation. It hadn't worked, and to this day she was still in possession of his switchblade.

Now he examined the new second lock installed in the door. He took out his long skeleton key and opened the old lock, then pocketed the key, placed the mini flashlight between his teeth, and pulled from his inside parka pocket a lockpick set. After what seemed a sweaty eternity in the overheated building, his flashlight slippery with saliva, the lock yielded and he walked in.

Aiming his light downward, he moved to the floor-to-ceiling double windows that opened out onto the building's roof. Finding both sheers and drapes tightly closed, he felt comfortable sending his spray of light roaming round the room. Illuminating the fold-out sofa bed, armoire, and entry table, he then proceeded to the kitchenette, and finally to the bathroom. No messes, no loose papers; unless Signora Sillano had picked up after her, it seemed Erika had left in a deliberate and orderly fashion.

So now for some deep scouring. Voghera started with the kitchen, examining the contents of all drawers and cupboards. He did the same in the bathroom. Just the bare basics seemed to be gone. A bottle of shampoo, a couple of blond hairs stuck to it, still sat on the shower floor. He checked the drawers in the entryway table. Erika probably used it for a desk, for he found writing implements, stationery, a spiral notebook, its top pages torn off, the remaining pages blank. In a drawer's corner, his light unearthed a few business cards which he examined then pocketed. Finally he went to the armoire, wincing instinctively as the doors squeaked open. Many items of clothing remained. One drawer contained a tarnished watch next to a pair of sunglasses and a two-piece bathing suit. For a moment he stared at the suit. Then he picked up the bikini bottoms and brought them to his face, crushing them as he inhaled deeply. He remembered a warm day the previous October when he and Erika drove south to a beach on the Riviera and swam. He'd licked salt from her chest, her neck, her ear, making her breath deepen, her skin quiver with desire. Did he love her? No—his work had always prohibited romantic emotion from taking root in him. Had he enjoyed her? Yes, immensely, and immoderately (considering her betrayal). Abruptly he opened his eyes and dropped the bathing suit back into the drawer. One fist was still clenched, though his anger was now receding. Nostalgia verging on sorrow lingered—and was *absolutely impermissible*. Exhaling steadily he picked up the sunglasses she'd worn that day at the beach and played his light across them. Already he was thinking of where one wouldn't need shades at this time of the year. Not in overcast Turin and most of northern Italy. And unless you planned for the possibility of snow blindness, you wouldn't take them to the *Matterhorn*. But who on the run considered that kind of contingency?

Voghera returned the sunglasses to the drawer and slowly closed the armoire doors. With a shade of a smile, he locked up the flat and made his way gingerly down the stairs and back out onto the street.

Chapter 6

Journalist Giorgio Testa's sunglasses sat on his restaurant table as he finished his lunch of steak-frites. The French did beef well, but still he missed his own cooking, particularly his pastas, boiled perfectly al dente. Although the French managed good sauces, if the pasta wasn't cooked just right you might as well ignore it and sop up the sauce with a chunk of delicious French bread.

He asked for the check, so he could head back to his room in the inn in Menton, France. It didn't do to linger in restaurants or frequent an establishment more than once, especially when you were a man of his size and bulk. His wasn't exactly saggy or flabby fat, and he liked to view much of his bulk as muscle; yet if some undercover dick from DIGOS were to ask here on the Côte d'Azur, "Have you seen a tall fat man with an Italian accent dining here?" a waiter's reply would be a swift and incisive *yes*. With that, he thought of that prick Claudio Voghera. How in hell had Erika fallen for him? Any man who would give a woman a black eye...yes, Erika had insisted the fight was *mutually defensive*; and yet, if Voghera ever came sniffing around here, Giorgio would fling his skinny, *swimmer's-build* (Erika's irritating description of his physique) off the ramparts of Roquebrune's castle, towards the bay below.

Well...*he would if he had to*. In principle, he shied away from violence. People almost always viewed him through the lens of his size. When he was a child, kids tended to either mock his bulk or fear it. Other boys had trod carefully around him, and if they picked a fight they usually lost, which quickly transformed their jeers into fear. Adults he didn't know usually approached him with either humble or unsure smiles. Since young adulthood he'd done what he could to avoid physical conflict. But when it came to the menacing of Erika, or of any woman for that matter, his fists would be ready.

Again, he shook his head at Erika's former crush on Voghera, as he drove his used Peugeot along the narrow, snaking Upper Corniche above Monte Carlo. That Voghera was a pretty boy with a winning smile had to have played its part, though Erika would probably never admit it and Giorgio didn't plan to ask. And of course Erika had longed to be a spy. The girl was complicated, especially when it came to that business with her brother. And yet she and Giorgio had survived a test of fire together last year that had soldered their friendship beyond a fissure of a doubt.

Negotiating another curve on the Corniche, he thought of Erika in her ice-encased hideaway in Switzerland. She ought to move soon, even though if DIGOS had been activated, Giorgio would probably be their primary target. He'd already moved once while writing his exposé on the assassination of fascist Matilde Fassino by the Italian intelligence services. He'd first hidden out in the low-profile, French Alps town of Cluse. Then he'd left Cluse and come down to the French coast. Moving around also made Erika and his postal correspondence seem more secure. His current refuge was a small country inn situated in the hinterland of Menton. But he knew he would have to move again soon. Not that he wanted to leave the sunny paradise of Alfred Hitchcock's *To Catch a Thief*. He could hardly boast of living it up here, unless looking over his shoulder most of the time was equivalent to strolling along the pebble beach under the palm trees. He thought of transferring to Bern, near his collaborator Régine and where he would also be closer to Erika.

Granted, Erika's hermitage in Cobbio would be hard to beat in terms of seclusion, and her expenses amounted to a pittance compared to his own on the French Riviera, even during low tourist season. And naturally he would have to continue paying most of her expenses if she moved. She always said she had money saved, but how much could that be from teaching English as a second language? He, on the other hand, had received a nice payout over the arson attack on his newspaper, *Il Cardinale*. The office in Turin, though repaired, remained closed for the time being, so no expenses piled up apart from rent and utilities and what he paid the custodian through a secret go-between. His life, his livelihood, and his life's work had almost gone entirely up in flames last year. His business partner and friend of fifteen years had perished in the fire and Giorgio had ended up in a hospital burn unit.

His pulse quickened just thinking of the neofascist pigs who had chucked those Molotov cocktails into the *Cardinale's* office. This almost decade-long street war between Neofascists and Communists had made him an unwitting target of both sides. He leaned to neither extreme—he was a Socialist, and that was reflected in the content of the *Cardinale*. Still, both sides had attacked him, and now he faced a third assault from the intelligence services of Italy's center-based Christian-Democratic government. And yet, he was forced to admit he had brought this present situation on himself through yearning to make a big scoop—but that type of dream was native to journalists like him: it was in their DNA.

He inhaled this sense of pride, squaring his shoulders and clenching the steering wheel. *If those DIGOS bastards were after him, they would not defeat him.*

On the wake of this intonation a car came racing up behind him, a little sports job from the looks of it in the rearview mirror. "*Cazzo,*" he swore and sped up a fraction. The switchbacks up here on the green-grey terrain above Monte Carlo were treacherous—only two lanes, one for each direction, with no divider, and on his right a drop of hundreds of meters. He slowed to take a curve, swung around it, only for the bastard behind him to run up on his ass again and this time honk his horn. *Shit*, there wasn't enough road between curves here to pass. Who did the idiot think he was, Cary Grant?

The guy edged closer and for a heartbeat Giorgio thought of tapping his brakes to warn the jerk back, but their cars were dangerously close. Close enough that Giorgio could identify the car's make and model—a FIAT Spider, its engine changing notes as its driver shifted gears. With this kind of bravado the guy should be driving an Alfa Romeo. Then a thought turned his sweat cold: *an agent from DIGOS trying to run him off the road would not drive an expensive car.*

He accelerated, then decelerated and braked to engage another curve, his tires squealing with the effort. Again the bastard ran up on him and honked his horn. Was he crazy? If Giorgio went over the cliff, the imbecile might very well follow.

Sweat trickled from his hairline but he dared not raise a hand or arm to keep it out of his eyes. He accelerated hard again but the bastard matched his move, this time jetting out to pass. Around the corner appeared a van in the oncoming lane. Its driver honked nonstop and swerved to the right, almost scraping the mountain's side, while Giorgio's heart raced like runaway kettle drums at the climax of a symphony. His hands, in virtual rigor mortis on the wheel, steered the Peugeot a sliver to the right, though when he looked down it felt like there was only a millimeter between him and the dizzying drop. The Spider slipped between the two vehicles, shooting ahead and fishtailing around the curve out of sight.

Slowing to a crawl, Giorgio gave a glance in his mirror in the direction of the vanishing van, figuring the driver's heart was hammering as hard as his own. Then he picked up speed once more, his hands finally looser on the wheel. Still, by the time the road descended to Menton his shoulders were aching. He stopped at a red light and felt an attack of heartburn. Unwilling to blame it on his close call on the corniche, he assigned it to the consumption of multiple steak-frites and too many Napoleons for dessert. By the time he rolled into his parking place at the inn, nausea had crept up to join the assault on his digestive system. *Not enough exercise*—correction: *no exercise*—he added to his list of bad habits.

Inside his room, he filled the bathroom sink with cool water and plunged his head into it. He dried off and sprawled out on the bed. The heartburn and nausea had retreated, but he could still feel his heart beating, a strange sensation when at rest. He eased off the bed to fetch the bottle of cognac he kept in the armoire—a tried-and-true digestif, he assured himself, as he poured a shot. A minute or two after downing it, he could no longer register his heart beating. *Better than a tranquilizer*, he sighed, glancing at the bottle of Remy Martin. Gradually he drifted off to sleep.

Chapter 7

Erika tugged on a hank of her hair, sighing in frustration. This final part of the translation was not going smoothly. She was glad she hadn't sent the first parts to agent Ian Wescott in London, as one of those portions needed further work too. Maybe she was letting perfectionism undermine her, but if this exposé was going to land in a high-profile British publication, perhaps finding readers throughout Europe and the U.S., she needed to fine-tune it as much as possible. *Keeping true to the author's style while rendering the translation comprehensible to the target reader.*

Easier said than done.

What caused Erika most difficulty was the issue of moral ambiguity about how to view Matilde Fassino. Should the Italian intelligence services have allowed the old fascist woman to be kidnapped in the first place in 1977, when her war crime dated back to 1943? Should DIGOS have used the frail petite octogenarian as bait to capture communist terrorists?

Certainly Matilde Fassino's war crime had been monumental on a personal level, while perhaps a mere sinister thread in the larger harrowing tapestry of the Holocaust. The thread was long and thorny. She and her banker husband had blackmailed the husband's personal secretary out of her savings in the bank. "We'll protect you, young Jewess, as long as you pay." What Matilde hadn't known was that her husband had been double-dipping, extracting payment of a more intimate kind from the innocent, single secretary. Extortion on two fronts. When Signora Fassino found out, she sounded the alarm to the authorities in jealous outrage, and Sara Lattes, already a natural prey, became instantly hunted by the police—Auschwitz bound if she was captured. The old banker Ercole Fassino, in a monster's moment of tenderness, tipped off Sara who fled from one bolthole to another in Turin's metropolis, finally escaping to the countryside. There, she was taken in by none other than Erika's Turin landlady Eugenia Sillano, who at the time still lived in her native village. For almost two years, until the end of the war, Sara lived literally underground, hiding in a dirt-walled enclosure below the farmhouse's wine cellar.

Erika read over this part of the story, never ceasing to marvel at its capacity to make her shiver—the courage of Signora Sillano, the suffering of Sara Lattes, the bone-shaking fear they must have both endured during those years of war. Sara Lattes emerged alive but certainly not unscathed either emotionally or physically. Those years of living between cold, damp dirt walls, only emerging late at night, had irreversibly weakened her. She developed tuberculosis and died in 1963, leaving a husband and a thirteen-year-old son. That Erika had first learned of the appalling story from Sara Lattes' son Paolo made it all the more gut-wrenching. For a moment she closed her eyes and rubbed her forehead with the heel of her hand.

She flicked her fingers and focused back on her work. Considering Fassino's crime, Giorgio Testa had dutifully asked in his journalistic piece whether DIGOS had or had not broken ethical or moral laws by helping to set up the old woman's kidnapping. He was leaving it to readers to make up their own minds. Erika couldn't guess how they would respond, for she herself still couldn't decide. Fassino had evaded international justice, all eyes focused instead on her husband who died of natural causes soon after the war. That Signora Fassino had suffered a major stroke following her kidnapping over a year ago made an assessment even harder for Erika. But Fassino's assassination to protect the intelligence services from possible revelation and scandal had ended the debate. Erika had told Giorgio, who then unleashed his scoop, enlisting Erika to translate the story into English. It was an exposé for which Giorgio and she were promised handsome remuneration by *The Guardian*.

And all tied back to Claudio Voghera's indiscretion. He'd been spiraling downward with drink in the two months he and Erika were together. Towards the end he'd slung sarcastic slurs her way, then finally hit the concrete bottom of drunken irresponsibility by letting slip DIGOS' role in Fassino's death.

They were in his flat, having finished dinner, with Claudio on his second brandy. Noting her shocked face at his admission, he'd flushed briefly, then aimed an accusing finger at her.

"Why so shocked—uncomfortable with the *real* world of spies?" He grunted, pushing away his dinner plate.

Erika said nothing. Up until now, domestic state-sponsored assassinations had been stuff of another world to her, mostly executed in autocratic realms that seemed distant from Italy.

When she shook her head in disbelief, Voghera snapped back: "*What*—don't you believe she deserved *some* kind of punishment?" Suddenly he seemed perfectly sober, and Erika pounced on the opportunity to punch back with the ethical question.

"*You* do, then?" she asked him. "You believe she deserved to die...?" She would make him take a stance one way or another.

"This isn't about *me*." He slapped his hands on his thighs and leaned in. "You're the one who can't let it go. I know the whole thing still bothers you."

"You mean how the kidnapping of an eighty-year-old woman caused her to have a stroke?"

Claudio shook his head, smiling sourly—

"*Drugging* her while you kept her locked up," Erika continued before he could answer. "And then when you couldn't trust her to keep quiet about it you actually— "

"It wasn't *me* who did it!"

Who *killed* her, he meant. He had no qualms about the kidnapping, no haunting intellectual or humanitarian dilemma about the trauma as a cause Fassino's stroke.

"*Could* you have killed her, if they'd wanted you to?" Erika pushed away from the table and rose. Voghera did the same and they stood facing each other across the table, poised for the inevitable upswing in their duel.

For a good while Voghera stared at her, his expression giving nothing away. Then, quietly, he said, "Do you remember that talk we had last year when you came to visit me in the hospital?"

Erika narrowed her eyes uncomfortably at this change of tack.

"You had all sorts of guilt back then about the major shit you'd done in your life." His brows arched, a taunting prompt for her to remember—*as if she could forget.* "I told you then that some things in life you just can't *predict or control*," he continued in a lecturing tone, hands on his hips.

If anyone didn't need this lecture, it was her. Erika drew a defensive breath but wasn't sure how to reply.

"Back then," he said, falling back into a posture of easy confidence, "you even brought up me giving you the black eye. I said I didn't always like how things turned out, but I had a job to do." He waved a dismissing hand. "I don't let who's a Fascist terrorist or a Communist or an Anarchist enter into my work. I care only about keeping order. That's why I do the job."

He hadn't answered her question, he was digressing, except for the *black-eye* statement. There had to be only one reason to bring that up—another *reminder*. Now he was walking around to her side of the table. She stiffened, her pulse ticking up, but she tried not to let her tenseness show.

"Listen," he said, looking stern, his face just inches from hers. "Call the fate of Matilde Fassino some kind of cosmic justice. Call it whatever you'd like, but what's done is done. Don't keep vomiting it all up because you'll go nowhere with it. You'll end up like you were last year. And," he added with a note of cutting condescension, "you'll never be *spy* material."

She didn't let her impulsive tongue strike back. She knew what a blow from Claudio felt like. But she did have another question to ask.

"And one last thing," he said before she could speak: "Don't tell *anyone* what you know. You'll bring down on yourself the wrath of the entire intelligence and security apparatus."

And your wrath too, she suddenly recognized with crystal clarity.

A gauntlet had been dropped in the miniscule space between them, but she would not step back, either literally or figuratively. Instead she went on to pose the question whose answer she knew would not be forthcoming. "So how did they do it?" she asked, in the voice of a curious spy student. "How did they force Matilde Fassino into 'another stroke'—the one that she *supposedly* died from?"

He grunted, took a step back, then offered out of the blue: "How about a nightcap?"

The only "cap to the night" Erika could envision was catching a tram home. She told him so, in so many words. As she gathered her things she felt his grip on her bicep. The memory of their explosive first encounter returned to her in a shuddering rush. *Back off, Erika, if you know what's good for you,* had been his warning a year ago, after he'd grasped her hair and pulled her ear to his lips. Personal outrage had pushed her further down the path to unraveling the secret of Matilde Fassino.

She hadn't been deterred then, and now as she sat at her kitchen table in Cobbio, she lifted her arm and slapped her bicep in a *fuck-you* gesture. Soon afterwards, her typewriter keys resumed their resolute clicking.

When Erika looked at her watch she immediately stopped typing. She had an appointment with Dr. Betz in Bellinzona in an hour and a half, and she also needed to make a phone call.

There was no phone in the hundred-year-old house in Cobbio, and even if there had been one, she would not make any calls from her refuge.

Commuting so regularly back and forth from Cobbio to Bellinzona, she let herself be lulled by the train's rocking rhythms, the cocooning heat of the carriages and the sharp metallic smell of Switzerland's clean mechanical efficiency—rarely a scent of industrial grease or a sight of dark grime in crevices. With the winter-white landscape coasting past clean windows, she could have easily luxuriated into a trance this afternoon, only Claudio Voghera kept intruding on this peaceful scene. She really would like to know how the agents of DIGOS precipitated Matilde Fassino's final and fatal stroke while she was convalescing at home. And so would her partner, Giorgio.

One final time she'd tried worming it out of Claudio, and that was the last time they'd seen each other. Her insistence had made him come to a halt on a foggy Turin sidewalk and accuse her of conniving to bring him down. "And you can't do it by yourself, so who are you working with?"

At that she clammed up, for she'd already told Giorgio Testa about Claudio's slip of tongue, and Claudio knew she and Giorgio were friends. The bitter cold Erika felt had faded to a numbing thrum inside her. Passersby darted ghostly around them in the vaporous mist under the low, confining porticoes of Via Po. Erika and Giorgio had thought they might achieve their work and then be protected by the international press before Claudio discovered their deed. Claudio, naturally no fool, and remembering Erika's collaboration with Giorgio the previous year, took only a fraction of a second to add: "It's that bastard who owns the *Cardinale*!" No denial on Erika's part could quell Claudio's fuming suspicion. They had parted ways right then and there, Claudio looking over his shoulder with eyes as icy as the air around them. Soon after, Erika and Giorgio shifted gears and rocketed out of Turin to work in hiding.

Erika had told only her landlady, Eugenia Sillano, about her dilemma and imminent flight. Now the train was pulling slowly into Bellinzona's station, brakes tapping just enough to make rising from her seat a jerky process. But she was eager to get off and call the signora.

She went to a pay phone in the station and, having carefully thought out her words, dialed the signora in Turin. It was three-thirty, most stores still closed for the afternoon pause, and as expected Signora Sillano was home.

"*Ciàu* Genia," Erika greeted her in Turinese, using the diminutive of the signora's first name.

Immediately the signora fell into the dialect, their agreed means of clandestine communication. Certainly, many in the city could speak and understand the dialect; not so many, however, would expect an American to chatter in it, and doing so might render Erika's voice more difficult to identify. *Playing cloak and daggers*: it made her feel a speck safer. Their communication, as always, was condensed to only a few sentences, in case the signora's phone had been tapped. Voghera was perfectly capable of it (as was DIGOS, of course); after all, he'd even shown Erika how to do it.

"*Cum al'è?*" Erika asked, and the signora replied she was fine.

"I've been inundated by relatives," Sillano continued in Turinese. "You'd think it was Christmas again."

"Anyone I know?"

"Maybe one. You remember Rinaldo? You two once met. You said he was dashing and looked like a movie star," the signora clarified.

"*Ah, sì, Rinaldo.*" Erika understood. The signora was mostly an introvert and receiving a rash of visitors didn't make a lot of sense. Only one man held any particular significance in their clandestine communications: the visiting relative with the film-star looks could only be Claudio Voghera.

"But everything's fine...?" Erika asked.

"*Sì, sì, sì!*"

Good—no fallout from Voghera's visit. Erika told the signora that things were status quo with her, and soon after they hung up.

She left the station, wondering how many others who knew her had been visited by Claudio. How was he getting people to engage? How was he presenting himself in order to even be let into their homes? Certainly, anything but an intelligence agent. As she walked to Dr. Betz's office a sudden wind gusted, leaving tree branches flailing and whirling Erika's hair to match her thoughts. She hunched her shoulders in her overcoat against assaults of January drafts skimming off January snow. She thought about wearing a scarf again. But the reminder of having almost been strangled by one last year kept the thought a wishful glimmer.

Hands in her pockets, her head turtled in her coat, she arrived at Betz's building. She pressed the buzzer next to his name and waited for the click of the opening door. Her ears stung with cold and her head was starting to pound. She couldn't help blaming the latter on this latest report about Claudio, though her nightly dreams and headaches had yet to subside.

Maybe it was time to tell Dr. Betz the entire truth about at least one of her dreams.

Chapter 8

Claudio Voghera found himself politely sipping coffee in yet another residence; this one, the Asti apartment of Erika's cousins the Marengos. However, instead of perching on the kind of simple kitchen chair offered by Signora Sillano, Voghera sat stiffly on an ornate, high-backed wooden chair in the formal dining room of Signor and Signora Marengo.

"It's been more than a month since we've heard from Erika," said the stately grey-haired Signora Marengo. "I've called Signora Sillano—Erika *doesn't* have a phone, you know—and she said Erika would be out of town for a while—*for a while*: what does that mean, and why didn't Erika tell us herself?"

Signora Marengo (the niece of Erika's grandfather) went on to express a frown more of irritation than concern, thought Voghera. Along with maybe a note of jealousy in her tone that Erika had told Sillano she was leaving without giving her blood relatives the courtesy of a simple call.

"And her landlady doesn't even know *where* she's gone," Signora Marengo emphasized. She adjusted the pearls resting just over the collar of her sky-blue cashmere sweater, a caressing gesture, interpreted by Voghera as self-dignifying. He could picture her thoughts: *why confide in someone you barely know, a country bumpkin to boot, rather than in us, the cousins you've known for years?*

Voghera glanced at the husband. While the signora signaled strait-laced self-possession, Signor Marengo sat smoking with his elbow on the dark-wood dining table, a lock of grey hair falling almost comically over his forehead and one suspender hanging rakishly off his shoulder. His large round blue eyes gave him a perpetually surprised look, Voghera thought, only now the owlish eyes turned sardonic. He shoved the table's crocheted centerpiece, with its vase of yellow day lilies, further away from him to make more room for his large glass ashtray.

"What's Erika—twenty-eight now? he growled. "Or maybe she needs to be fifty before she can come and go as she pleases."

Signora Marengo shot him an irritated glance and corrected him. "Erika's *twenty-six*, and if her parents have called in a detective, maybe there's something serious going on."

Voghera got the impression the two bickered all day long, with the smart-alec Marengo finding every opportunity to take his haughty wife down a peg. The old goat stubbed out his unfiltered cigarette, leaving the ashtray still wrinkling the crocheted centerpiece.

Voghera cleared his throat. "Yes, Erika's parents are concerned. Maybe you could tell me when you last saw her and what you talked about."

Marengo deferred to his wife with a jerk of his head that made the lock on his forehead swing like an upstart kid's.

"I can't remember what day it was," said Signora Marengo. "As I said it must be almost two months. We talked about the usual things—the long winter, that we expected her to come for Christmas lunch. But she said she was taking a trip over the holidays, going skiing with some friends. I expected her to at least call on Christmas Day, but she didn't. That's what got me concerned."

"And nettled you," her husband added.

Voghera peered at him. Time to take the wife's side. "And were *you* concerned, Signor Marengo, or *nettled*, when she didn't call?"

"Well," he muttered in a gravelly voice, "I'm concerned now. But that she was having too much fun to call on

Christmas didn't bother me."

"Mm," Voghera acknowledged. His questions were wasted on Marengo, a classic wise guy. He turned back with interest to the signora; this was the first time he'd heard the lie about "skiing." Erika hadn't even bothered to concoct it for her landlady—then again, he was sure the two were in some kind of league. "Where did she say she was going skiing?" he asked Signora Marengo.

The signora was thoughtful. "I don't think she was sure at the time. This was back in November...it wasn't near here, though." She glanced at her husband. "Do you remember what she said, Angelo?"

Angelo Marengo shrugged and shook his head. Voghera expected nothing less.

Then Marengo's large blue eyes jolted wider. He waved a triumphant hand. "Saint Moritz!"

"Are you sure, Angelo?" The signora looked highly doubtful.

"I'm *certain*. I remember thinking, *of all places in the Alps, they choose one of the most expensive resorts they can find.*"

They, Voghera repeated to himself. Erika didn't have "friends." As far as he knew she was a psychologically-screwed up, guilt-ridden loner. *Almost as if she craved danger*, he added cynically to himself.

He thanked the Marengos, assured them Erika was probably fine, and that he would be in touch with any news. He left his card.

The sun made a cameo appearance as Voghera drove his black Opel Ascona from Asti back to Turin. Although he'd learned little of substance from the couple Erika used to live with, the burst of brightness now shredding the clouds gave him a boost of confidence about his hunch—thanks to Marengo, the old smart-ass, the notion that Erika was in Switzerland was more alive than ever in Voghera. The Matterhorn, Saint Moritz:

Erika must have some secret desire to go to the frozen, politically-neutral country. He doubted she was holed up in either Saint Moritz or Zermatt—both extraordinarily expensive in winter—but she could be elsewhere in the country. It was still only a hunch, but when that's all you have, the hunch becomes your baby.

No colleague in DIGOS was passing Voghera information since his snafu. He thought about Moretti, the agent he'd worked under and informed about his slip-up with Erika. That Moretti was the only colleague even speaking to Voghera attested not only to their casual friendship, but to Moretti's appreciation of Voghera's work the previous winter doing a job that had got him shot. But not even Moretti would share information culled by DIGOS. Once he'd found out about Voghera's blunder, Moretti had given Voghera a grace period of almost a month to sort things out—Erika and Giorgio Testa *might not* be up to anything that would compromise the agency. But when the two disappeared from Turin, Moretti's only choice had been to sound the alarm. Yes, Moretti had finally agreed, Testa could be writing a "Matilde Fassino story" with Erika translating it.

DIGOS had mobilized, suspending Voghera and sending out agents to stop Testa and Erika. In terms of "stop," Moretti had refused to be specific, yet Voghera knew quite well that in DIGOS' sphere the word could be *all-encompassing*. Had they not, after all, "stopped" Matilde Fassino? Well, let DIGOS do what they wanted with Testa. *Voghera* would deal with stopping Erika.

Moretti and DIGOS had dubbed the case "Bonnie and Clyde," and who wouldn't covet being first to apprehend the two, given that sobriquet? Including, and perhaps most of all, Voghera, who not only wanted back into the pack, but who continued to register the relentless blow of Erika's betrayal.

As he drove into Turin, he felt a fresh stab-in-the back, his chest constricting with the eternal shock of it. He breathed in deeply and forced his thoughts back to the joy of his bolstered hunch.

And what if his hunch didn't play out…?

He shook his head as he steered down Corso Giulio Cesare. Only one way to find out.

Voghera unlocked his apartment door to the ringing of the telephone and was startled to hear Moretti himself on the line. Voghera hadn't heard from his colleague in over two weeks, so either Moretti had tapped into his thoughts or he was calling to relay another dressing-down from DIGOS.

Instead, he felt momentary relief when Moretti asked him how it was going, a *lets-go-out-for-a-drink-sometime* tone to his voice.

"Too much time on my hands," Voghera answered, misgiving creeping back into him.

"Getting bored, eh?" Moretti was in his late thirties, just that much older and more experienced to demand professional deference, which Voghera had always given him. Moretti was one of the best under-cover operators he'd known, but his excellence at dissimulation also made Voghera a little wary at the moment.

When Voghera didn't answer, Moretti turned up the geniality. "No need to worry, no one's checking up on you. But naturally we've been checking up on Bonnie and Clyde. So far we're still concentrating on Clyde, the mastermind."

Thanks for the info, thought Voghera, though it was hardly anything new. Other than make a couple of visits to the *Cardinale* newspaper office, he hadn't put any effort into Testa.

"But we're asking round about Erika now," Moretti said. "And guess what we've discovered…?"

Voghera barely realized he was holding his breath. "Go ahead," he said.

"Seems we're not the first to sniff around Erika's disappearance. Her landlady says a private detective came by to see her, someone employed by Erika's American family."

Voghera breathed out a silent sigh.

"Seems not only the 'police'—*our* cover, naturally—is concerned, but some guy called David Rosasco. 'Above average height, dark hair and blue eyes—a *beard* to boot...'" When Voghera remained silent, Moretti quipped, "Since when have you been growing a beard?"

Voghera revealed nothing and Moretti had nothing more to share. No clue even as to where in France Giorgio Testa might be hiding out, or where DIGOS planned to move on after questioning Signora Sillano. He refused to talk about the case and said only this about *David Rosasco*: "Our colleagues haven't heard anything from me that I think he's you, but they have their suspicions.

"Listen," he said, when Voghera wouldn't budge from his silence, "I'd just like to know if you got anything out of Eugenia Sillano. Our agent says her mouth's as tight as a crab's ass."

Voghera grunted.

"What was that?" Moretti said.

"Nothing. As you say, it's your case, not mine...So, you think you'll be interviewing more of Erika's acquaintances?"

"Hmm...David Rosasco's probably got there first, don't you think?" Silence once more. "Well, maybe we'll do Rosasco one better."

We'll see.

"Anyway, you and I'll have to have a drink sometime, Claudio..."

Voghera could almost see Moretti wink. "Sure," he answered, as if nothing had changed. "I'll get back to you."

But something had changed: it was time to get organized for an expedition to Switzerland.

Chapter 9

Giorgio Testa stood at the counter in Menton, France's station, asking about train schedules for Bern, Switzerland. He was planning to visit his friend Régine Farigoule, an ally in getting his sensational scoop out. He'd sent her the last of his story, which she'd passed on to Erika, and now he needed to meet with her to discuss how they would get the finished translation spirited to Ian Westcott in London. After all, she was the one who knew *The Guardian's* journalist. Giorgio would also ask after Erika. While Régine had seen her fairly recently, he hadn't set eyes on his American friend since they'd made their individual getaways from Turin, close to two months ago. Most of all, though, Giorgio longed to see Régine and spend time with her. They'd met only sporadically in their careers, having spent their longest time together during that first conference in Geneva. A long-distance friendship had bloomed, Régine expressing true kindness and concern when she'd learned of the fire in the *Cardinale* office last year. They'd kept in closer touch after that and now she was welcoming his visit. Maybe with more time shared, they would become even closer...

Giorgio sighed warmly at the prospect, then turned his thoughts back to his journey. He could always drive, but the Alps were crisscrossed with narrow, serpentine roads with scarce guardrails, and he didn't feel up to risking a daylong trek along hairpin turns, with lunatic drivers, such as the one the other day, popping up like jack-in-the-boxes. The physical discomfort he'd felt from almost hurtling off that cliff above Monte Carlo had yet to leave him. Now and then he could still feel his heart thump at rest, an uncomfortable sensation akin to having an alien presence inside him. He was tending towards the train for another reason: so he wouldn't have to cross the border in his car, which invited extreme scrutiny, especially by Swiss border guards, including, but not limited to, an examination of a vehicle's condition (the used Peugeot Giorgio had bought in Cluse verged on decrepit), a good look at your face, and then the rest of you if you were obliged to exit your car. Trains, on the other hand, carried so many people that guards, who hopped aboard at border stops, made quick sweeps through the carriages, half the time not even asking you to open your passport.

A ticket agent explained the Menton to Bern route: 353 kilometers, with two changes, both in Italy—a ten-hour train trip, a long day. He thought of driving again; he could shave off about three hours in respect to the train, but he would still have to travel through Italy; the only way to avoid that country by car was to head north towards Grenoble, then veer east into Switzerland, which would tack another hour or two onto the trip, and with just as much mountain to negotiate. How would he feel at the end of a day like that? Just envisioning it made him quit vacillating and buy a roundtrip ticket for the next day; departure: 6:15 a.m.

The next morning, blackness engulfed Giorgio's train as it sped east along the Mediterranean coast. In daylight he would have enjoyed watching line after line of thick-trunked palm trees sliding past his carriage window, their bushy fronds painting a limpid blue sky. In Italy he would have seen some growing in pods of four, their lush fronds almost grazing the ground. A native of Turin, he still found this Mediterranean beauty dazzling.

About fifteen minutes later the train coasted to a halt at the border in Ventimiglia, and Giorgio inhaled tensely. Dressed in a dark three-piece business suit, his modest dark bag visible above him through the metal bars of the luggage rack, he was the only person in his compartment. Until another traveler entered: a bearded young man in frayed jeans and a windbreaker, who swung an enormous backpack onto the rack and then sat down with a motorcycle magazine on his lap—an all-day traveler like him, only foreign, judged Giorgio. Then, before the conductor's whistle sounded, a middle-aged woman joined them, another early bird. She'd dragged a large suitcase aboard and was squinting up at the luggage rack. When she started looking round the compartment, Giorgio hoisted himself off his vinyl seat. "I'll do that for you," he said, and relieved her of the suitcase. He pointed at the luggage rack across from him and the woman nodded, thanked him, then looked back and forth at the seats facing one another. Giorgio sat back down next to the window. The young man across from him failed to glance up from his magazine, yet he was skinny and Giorgio figured the woman would sit on his side. Instead, she cast Giorgio a brief smile and took a place on his side, next to the door. One seat separated them, which put Giorgio at ease. He couldn't count how many times people avoided sitting next to him on buses and trams, as if his bulk might spill over onto to them. He smiled back politely, then looked out the window. He couldn't see any Italian railway police on the platform but knew they were boarding the train somewhere.

When he heard the door to the compartment next door slide open, then the words, "*Signori: documenti, per favore,*" he knew they'd arrived.

It wasn't long before the uniformed officer entered their own open door. "*Documenti,*" he repeated.

He scanned the three passengers, the woman and Giorgio already holding out their passports. The young man with the beard patted all his pockets, then, with a lost look, rose, stood on his seat and started rummaging through his backpack. That proved awkward, so he dragged the bag off the rack onto his seat, and began rummaging anew. The equally young policeman, clean-shaven and crisply-packaged in his uniform, gave a faint shake of his head. "*Signore,*" he repeated.

"Here it is, here it is!" the young man blurted breathlessly in American English.

With a tart look, the officer took it and began examining it page by page. At the end he studied the stamps of individual countries, while the young traveler stood with a red face and a worried frown. At last the officer slapped it shut and handed it back. "Please to not put your feet on the seat," was his only comment, expressly in English.

He turned to the opposite side of the compartment. The woman held a French passport, which he nodded at. He looked Giorgio over—from his close-cropped hair to his polished black shoes—and then also nodded at his Italian passport. Then he left the compartment, sliding the door shut with a strong jerk of his arm.

Giorgio exhaled relief, then sent a virtual smile to the absent-minded American across from him. The kid was now looking from his pockets to his backpack, as if considering for the first time where to seriously stow his passport. Finally he let out a frustrated sigh and zipped it into the pocket of his windbreaker.

Once over the border, the train continued along the coast in the dark, with Giorgio picturing each town displaying its perennial jewels of bougainvillea, oleander, geraniums, and the like. Giorgio's own Menton inn kept geraniums all winter in its window boxes, one reason he was fond of the place. Before long though, the train would snake northwards, and these Mediterranean jewels would be left behind. Not, however, until leaving Genoa, the city they were now pulling into. Time to change trains.

Giorgio looked at his watch: over two hours had passed since the start of his journey and he hadn't even opened the novel in the bag he was now pulling down from the luggage rack. The kid stayed put, evidently continuing his travels down the eastern arc of the Italian Riviera. The woman who shared his side of the compartment rose and Giorgio lifted her suitcase down. It was on the heavy side, so he offered to also carry it to her new platform. It was the least he could do since he had almost an hour's wait for his train to Milan.

After thanking him profusely, she revealed she too was taking the train to Milan. Her Italian betrayed not a blemish of foreign accent. Giorgio said nothing, of course, about her French passport, but it did strike him as odd. But not *terribly* odd, he revised, irritated at the state of hypervigilance he'd been forced to adopt. Many Italians lived in Menton. It didn't mean they were DIGOS agents, although the agency did employ its share of women.

Together they located their common platform, then decided to kill time having coffee. It was the French, or Italian woman's (Giorgio couldn't be certain which she was) invitation. "Thank you again," she said as Giorgio set down their bags next to their café table.

Giorgio gave a dismissive wave. "My pleasure."

The woman was pleasant enough—mid-fortyish, but youthful looking in her auburn coiffure, the ends of her hair turned up above her shoulders in 1960s style.

"My first coffee of the morning," she said, lifting her cappuccino to her lips and sighing pleasantly at Giorgio whose espresso was his second this morning. They were the only two seated in the café, most early-morning travelers snatching their pick-me-ups at the counter, where the noise of the coffee machine and the clicks of cups on saucers played familiar background music.

"I live in Menton, by the way," the woman volunteered. Her eyes, watching Giorgio over the rim of her cup, seemed to telegraph, *and you?*

Giorgio nodded at her. "I'm a traveling businessman—every hotel's my home." A clichéd response, though one that served Giorgio while he puzzled over the woman's assertion of living in Menton. "And yet you boarded the train in Ventimiglia...?" he asked casually.

"Oh no," she chuckled, flipping up her hair from under her collar. "I got on in Menton but needed to change compartments. Too many smokers in the other one. My husband hates when I return home reeking of cigarette smoke." She shrugged. "He's French."

Giorgio had no idea what the woman meant by her second remark. Probably nothing, but at least it could explain why she carried a French passport.

"You've been living in Menton long?" he asked.

"Since my marriage. Twenty years now." She paused, observing him. "But you're *Italian-Italian*..."

He thought for a moment. It was a curious expression. "Well, if you like, but I live in Paris," he lied. As it happened he was well acquainted with the city.

"Oh, how interesting!"

"Not really. I prefer it down here in the south where I do a lot of work—nicer weather."

The woman nodded appreciatively.

He would have liked to ask why she was going to Milan, but thought it wiser not to get more than a toe wet in this particular stream of conversation. "Well," he said, checking his watch, "I think I'll head over to the platform." He started to stand.

"Right," she responded, following suit. "If the train's already in, it'll be nice to get settled in a compartment."

Giorgio's gaze swiveled towards her then to the luggage on the floor.

"Sorry, I didn't mean we should share the same compartment." Flushing slightly, she maneuvered towards her suitcase.

"I've got it," he said, lifting it, then fetching his own. Busy with the two bags, he avoided her gaze. Then he told himself it would be silly to purposely distance himself from her on the two-hour-plus leg to Milan. He could steer their talk away from Menton or not even speak much at all, if he thought it judicious. He had his novel to start, after all.

"And I'd enjoy the company," he said, straightening with a barely audible grunt.

They exchanged modest smiles and made their way to the platform.

In hardly no time the train was climbing the Maritime Alps, soon to enter the land of snow and barren trees.

This time Giorgio and his travel mate sat alone in their compartment, settled across from one another, each next to the window. Giorgio had insisted Silvana (they'd finally exchanged names) sit facing the train's *senso di marcia*, her gaze in synch with the train's forward movement, while his traveled in reverse. Some people got motion sickness when looking in reverse. And again, it was the least he could do.

He took out his book, *Catch 22* (the Italian translation), and read while Silvana dozed on and off until they entered the Po River Valley. It was daylight now and nature's tableau had turned smoky-white with mist. They'd gone, thought Giorgio, from Monet's painting of Bordighera on the Riviera to his impressions of a Norman winter. Rain slashed the window as they glided to a stop in the town of Voghera. Giorgio hadn't noticed the Voghera stop on his itinerary and bristled at the sight of that name on the station's wall. He pictured Claudio Voghera slinking about Turin like an elongated shadow. His eyes drifted back to his watch: only nine-thirty. The day was stretching longer and longer. He drummed his stout fingers on the table under the window. *Let's get moving from here.*

"Where are we?" asked Silvana, shaking herself awake.

"Only Voghera," Giorgio huffed.

Her hand covered her mouth as she stretched and let out a high-pitched yawn. He was reminded of a sleek, self-satisfied cat—he found the pose both annoying and attractive.

"At least we're half way to Milan," she said.

"You take this route often?" Giorgio asked, conscious of a tinge of skepticism in his voice.

"When I visit my brother. Didn't I mention he lives in Milan?"

He shook his head. No, she hadn't. He'd been careful not

to ask about her business in Milan. His gaze returned to the window, beyond which rain and vapor now precluded seeing much of anything at all. He got up and pulled it down, letting the cold air sting his nostrils; it smelled of damp dirt on stone. The rain made it dark as dusk outside and he could see no one on the platform—*like a ghost stop*. When he heard Silvana draw a shivery breath he closed the window. No sooner had he done so than he felt the train jerk under his feet. *At last!*

"How about a game of briscola," Silvana proposed, as he sat back down. "Unless you'd rather keep reading."

Giorgio said he liked the game, pushing his paperback aside while she pulled a deck of cards from her purse and set them on the window table between them. He wondered whether she always carried cards when traveling alone—she probably enjoyed solitaire. At any rate, she was good at briscola and had won most of their games when the voice over the loudspeaker announced their arrival in Milan's Central Station. While Silvana gathered up her cards, he stood and lifted both their bags down. They gathered coats, which they'd each retrieved from their bags for the brutal change in weather, and filed out of the compartment.

Down on the platform, Giorgio said, "I guess you'll be going on to your brother's..."

Her nod seemed non-committal. Giorgio's gaze lingered over her. Her hair was trapped under her collar again and she flipped it back out. He found that gesture attractive as well. He was on the verge of saying, *If you'd like to have a bite to eat with me while I wait for my connection...*

But he stopped himself in time, instead saying, "I'll carry your suitcase to the exit. Are you taking a taxi?"

She was. "It's been nice company," she said as they walked up the platform. "I hope you have a smooth rest of your trip." She narrowed her eyes. "To *Innsbruck*, did you say?"

Yes, that was what he'd told her—Innsbruck, Austria.

They'd almost reached the station's concourse when gruff male shouts irrupted. Soldiers with machine guns were converging on the station, chasing passengers back down the platforms from where they'd come.

Indietro! Indietro! one soldier yelled at Giorgio and Silvana, ordering them back, one hand waving at them impatiently, the other resting on the machine gun draped across his torso.

Giorgio and Silvana locked shocked gazes, then let themselves be herded with the others towards the end of their train and into a carriage.

Chapter 10

Giorgio and his travel companion ducked into a train compartment and returned to seats by the window. Others passed them in the corridor, expressing anxious, fearful, and angry utterings—a stream of speculation: the Red Brigades, or one of the other communist terrorist bands? The Black Order, or another one of the fascist terrorist gangs?

Giorgio and Silvana merely looked at each other and shook their heads. *Che diavolo succede?*

What the hell's happening, indeed.

"Your brother will be worried if he's listening to the news," Giorgio said.

"And my husband too when this breaks in France." She sighed and put her elbows on the window table, her head between her hands. "And you?" she asked, looking across at Giorgio. "Will someone be waiting in Innsbruck for you?"

"No, fortunately." He didn't want to answer any more questions about his travels, so he stood and pulled down the window. Leaning out he saw two soldiers patrolling up and down the platform, heard shouts, the noise of boots scrambling on concrete farther away. As the soldiers approached he heard the word "bomb" crackle from one of their radios. They looked up at him, so he jerked his head back in, shut the window and sat back down. *Cazzo!*

"Might be unwise leaning out the window," Silvana observed. "But could you see anything?"

Giorgio glanced towards their open door. Tense chatter still chimed from people standing in the corridor. He got up and shut the door. Seated again, he said quietly, "I heard the word 'bomb' on one of the soldier's radios."

Silvana's eyes widened, then closed. She drew a deep breath and puffed it out. When she opened her eyes, she said, "So they won't let us escape the station. Two minutes earlier and I would've been out the door."

Giorgio shook his head in sympathy. "I guess their logic is that if there *is* a bomb, it'll be planted in the hub of the station, not on a particular train—not one that's arriving, anyway." *Hopefully*, he thought.

"*Jesus*. So we're safer in here..."

Giorgio gave a weak shrug.

"You remember what happened in 1969 in this station?" Silvana said.

"God, yes. Fascists, that time. Fortunately those bombs didn't go off."

Silvana nodded, sighed, then briefly closed her eyes again. "Can you believe we've been living with this nightmare for *ten years*?"

"Doesn't seem possible," Giorgio agreed. And yet he'd been writing about such events for most of his journalistic career: about the kidnapping and assassination of Aldo Moro by the Red Brigades last spring and the Brigades' killing of journalist Carlo Casalegno in Turin last year, by shooting him four times in the face. His own newspaper office was fire-bombed by fascist Black Order gang members. He'd written about everything but the Matilde Fassino kidnapping, which his signing of the state secrets act had forbidden him to do. He'd chafed at that prohibition for a year, until DIGOS had gone one step too far. Their obvious assassination of Matilde Fassino had in effect freed him from his constraints, in his view at least. Too bad DIGOS would see it differently.

He got up and pulled down the window once more. "Still soldiers on the platform," he reported to Silvana, "but they're too far away for me to hear anything." He pushed the window back up, then ventured out of the compartment to have a look in the corridor.

Same cramped crowd, spouting useless speculation.

When he came back in, Silvana asked if he could shut the door again. "They're setting my nerves on edge and I don't want them coming in here," she said.

Giorgio was pulling the door closed when the voices suddenly hushed, a different sort of racket replacing them.

"*Signori, ritornate negli scompartimenti,*" ordered a harsh male voice.

When Giorgio looked back into the corridor, a young soldier was shooing passengers towards the compartments with one arm, the other clamped to his machine gun. A chorus of worried complaints struck back up as people scurried to obey.

Cazzo, Giorgio swore to himself again. His and Silvana's compartment was the first in the carriage of that particular segment of the train, and the young soldier was now entering their space followed by a middle-aged railway police officer.

"*Documenti, per favore*," came the familiar request, firm though perfunctorily polite.

Giorgio stared at the police officer, doing his best to suppress an irritated and uneasy frown.

"We must see all travel documents," the officer said. The soldier behind the policeman moved a pace forwards, and it took all of one second for Giorgio to produce his passport from inside his jacket pocket. Silvana's French document was already in her outstretched hand.

The officer chose Silvana's passport first. "You were born in Milan," he stated dryly, flipping through the pages. "Naturalized French," he spoke over her 'yes.' "Let me see your ticket, please."

She extracted the rectangular, stiff-papered ticket from her purse and handed it over.

"Your destination is Milan," the officer stated. "What is the reason for your visit?"

"To see my brother and his family," she said mildly with a pleasant smile.

Giorgio couldn't help noting her calm after the exasperation she'd expressed just minutes before.

The officer returned her passport and ticket, then held his open hand out to Giorgio.

"Are you still living in Turin?" he asked, looking up from the page in the passport with photo and personal data.

Giorgio hesitated, sharply sensing Silvana's presence across from him. "Well, yes, basically. But I do business in France—Paris, Menton. You could say I live in Paris as well." He glanced at Silvana who was observing him with an aloof stare. "Sometimes," he continued with a nervous chuckle, "even my mother says she doesn't know which country I live in when people ask."

The officer looked him up and down. "Your ticket, please."

Cazzo. He removed it from his jacket pocket and, feeling suddenly over-heated, placed it in the officer's hand.

"Seems you don't just commute between France and Italy," the officer said, looking from the ticket to Giorgio and back."

"I should only be away for a few days," Giorgio said, his neck beginning to chafe and perspire beneath his stiffly buttoned shirt and the constraining knot of his tie.

"All of them in Bern?"

His collar was cutting into his neck; it was all he could do to resist loosening his tie. "Yes," he murmured, avoiding Silvana's eyes. *Please don't mention Innsbruck,* he pleaded silently to her. *Don't even give a curious look.*

"Then back to Turin?" the officer asked. "Or will you be returning to Paris?"

Giorgio's thoughts flickered like a frantic lightbulb trying to keep itself alight. "To Turin," he answered, completely clueless as to whether he'd made a wise choice.

The officer nodded, almost reluctantly it seemed, and placed both passport and ticket back into Giorgio's sweaty but grateful hand. "Your patience is appreciated," he said stiffly to both passengers before pivoting then adding over his shoulder,

"The train will be on its way as soon as possible." The soldier followed him out the door.

Giorgio stole a glance at Silvana. She wasn't looking at him, rather gazing through the doorway to the corridor. The police officer and his military escort had moved on to the next compartment. Giorgio didn't know what to be most grateful for: that the officer hadn't further questioned him about his "business," though he had a cover for that; that the train station hadn't blown up—at least not yet; or that Silvana hadn't proven him a liar.

He watched her on the sly until she finally took her eyes off the corridor and cast him a wry smile.

"About Innsbruck," he began. "I…" He started to rise. "Let me just close the door…"

"You don't have to on my account," she said coolly. "But if it would put *you* at ease…"

"No, no," he felt forced to say.

"You know?" she said, "you don't look like the type that needs to conceal his movements. Or maybe it's me—you didn't want me *following* you to Bern…" The emphasis she put on *following*, the indignant swing she gave her hair, made him tense all the more. If he could only loosen this *cazzo* of a tie and shirt, but now wasn't the moment to look distressed.

"No," he mumbled, shaking his head. "*Nothing* like that. It's this particular business…" Again he faltered.

"Never mind," she uttered, shrugging him off. "I don't need to hear about your *business*." She was gazing at him suspiciously now, and he wondered if she suspected him of some kind of mafia activity—distasteful, but on the other hand maybe useful at this moment.

"Anyway, sorry," he murmured, and got up to have another look at the corridor. The police officer and soldier were stalking back in his direction, so he ducked in and sat down next to the door. They passed the compartment, and then all Giorgio could hear was the heavy tread of boots and leather shoes. The train's door to the outside rumbled open, and a few seconds later slammed closed with the thud of a tomb being sealed.

Chapter 11

Erika sat watching the snow produce a thick frosting on the trees outside Dr. Betz's window. It had started with a powdered-sugar sprinkle, but now flakes the size of plates floated down uninterrupted, and the sky, instead of its usual late-afternoon grey, was assuming a pinkish-golden glow. The last time she'd witnessed such a sight was a year ago in Turin, when one of her wretched recurring dreams had woken her. She'd risen to have a look out the window and been dazzled by "daylight" in the middle of the night—a heavy carpet of snow on the rooftops and a golden-pink radiance, bright enough to go out and build a snowman by. The same sort of scene was forming in Bellinzona right now. Only last year she'd been an awestruck youth from San Diego beholding a stunning miracle of nature. Now, with all this snow, she knew she would have a slow wet slog to make when she left Dr. Betz's to go home.

"Does the snow make you anxious?" asked Dr. Betz. "I can understand if it does."

"Well, maybe a little. It just makes it a bit hard to get up the hill to my house in Cobbio."

"Mm," Betz murmured, watching her eyes flick back and forth from the room to the window. "Maybe we should talk about anxiety."

Erika frowned, but didn't know what to say.

"Are the dreams still disturbing you?" he prompted.

"I still have them but not every night. I mean I don't always remember them every night. But when I wake up in the morning, I feel lousy. Getting out of bed is like fighting something that's attacked me in my sleep."

"How does that feel?" Betz's voice was soft and mild. Like

73

Signora Sillano's—another reason she liked him.

"It's like I've been in a war all night long."

"A battle with your brother, the stabbing..."

The battle wasn't always with her brother, sometimes Claudio figured prominently. But still it was a war. "Whether I remember the dream or not, I still have to recover when I wake up—I'm exhausted, like I haven't slept at all, my head throbs, and I don't feel even nearly myself until I've had some coffee."

"Can you be more specific about the feeling the dream evokes?"

Erika remembered him asking this before—always concerned with the *feeling*. She thought about it again. The sensation could be heart-palpitating, leaving her breathless when she woke up. "Even if I can't remember the actual dream, I know I've had it. I can feel it in my chest, like I've got a caldron in there brewing disturbing things."

This morning, upon waking, she'd had the same sensation, only she recalled dreaming of Claudio. Somehow she had fallen into the moat of a medieval castle—not Bellinzona's castle, which had no moat, but the one in central Turin. Clods of dirt were falling down on her in shovelfuls, blinding her eyes. It was like a dark rain that still allowed glimpses of Claudio glowering down at her grave from the moat's edge. When she woke she was glad to be alive, but not completely glad. Some seconds later relief was replaced by a sense of punishment. But why should she feel punished for escaping Turin to help Giorgio publish his exposé? On the contrary, DIGOS deserved to be exposed and punished.

"When I was here last time," she said to the doctor, "you told me that all my dreams come from a part of me."

"It's true." The doctor leaned in more intently. His smile was brief but invited trust, also like Signora Sillano's. The comfort and confidence engraved in the signora's aged grooved face she also found in Doctor Betz's craggy handsomeless features. She had yet to see him in a suit and tie. Only white shirts under pullover sweaters, which also looked warm and comforting. This evening's was a forest green; she could imagine its softness.

"Everything we dream," he went on, "each segment of a dream, rises and coagulates from our deeper selves. Our dreams are organic, trying to make sense of our experiences."

Erika nodded thoughtfully. She decided to share last night's dream and began by describing the scene: the castle, the dark sky, the moat she'd fallen or been pushed into; only she didn't mention Claudio.

"I was being buried alive," she said. "Dirt shoveled down on me." Naturally he asked her what it felt like.

"Paralyzing fear. I couldn't manage to keep above the dirt. Clawing in slow-motion, you know?"

The doctor nodded.

"And the dirt was blinding me."

"So you couldn't see who was burying you?"

Erika shook her head, eyes averted from the doctor's gaze. "But I felt in some way like I was being punished. Then I woke up."

The doctor was sitting back now. One leg crossed L-shaped over his knee, he scribbled impassively in the file on his lap. He reviewed his notes for a moment before looking up and asking, "Do you think this dream might be related to the one in which you stab your brother?"

Erika thought about it. Frowning slightly, she glanced out the window. The silent snow was burying the city in brightness. "Maybe..." she said.

"Both have to do with death, with killing, if you will..."

The suggestion made Erika shudder, for suddenly she pictured her brother at the top of that moat instead of Claudio. So she *was* being punished. She swallowed heavily. Sensing the doctor's persistent stare she finally turned away from the window. His expression held the usual patient curiosity, only now his folder was closed and his eyes looked into hers with more kindness and concern. He nodded for her to respond. So she slowly said, "It could've been my brother at the top of the moat."

"You remember him, then…"

"Not really, but his face just came to me now." The doctor remained non-committal. It was *her* dream and therefore *she* had to make sense of it. "That's why I feel like I'm being punished," she offered. "Because I stab him in another dream…"

"Could be," said Betz, "but I'm wondering what he's done in your life that your dreams give him such power. Because even if he dies in them, he still comes back…You would agree that he has great power, at least in terms of your subconscious…?"

Erika nodded uncertainly, tried to break the dream down. Being buried alive by Claudio was evident. He was there trying to silence her for DIGOS and himself, and to *punish* her for betraying him. But equally undeniable was her own internal feeling of being punished, a feeling she *owned,* deserved even; this pain went deeper than the moat, burrowing inside her like an endless well. For there was no way she could reverse what had happened to her brother, Keith. That one act that had reshaped her life in such a mangled way that even ending up here in this mountain refuge could be traced back in part to it.

"Shall we try to analyze this power?" The doctor's voice was ever calm and patient, but Erika knew her attempts to stall had come to an end.

Her eyes darted to the window again. The snow granted no truce, its saucer-size flakes continuing to fall like surreal bombs. Her time was coming. She felt nauseated, waiting for the silent explosion inside her. If she could just keep watching the flakes fall one by one…

"Shall I shut the curtains?" Dr. Betz was standing up, indicating the window.

"I…I don't know." The scene outside was a mesmerizing diversion.

"How about if we shut the sheers and just part of the drape?"

That sounded okay, and Erika watched Betz close things to just a small patch of muted light.

"So," he resumed once seated. "Let's hear about your brother."

Funny what it feels like to have revealed a most-guarded secret, thought Erika as she stepped out into the street. Relief on one hand, mounting agitation on the other. "Calm yourself," she muttered under her breath. It was still snowing and so bright she felt practically blinded. Maybe this was due to her hypersensitive state, the rawness she still registered from her confession. For she had told Dr. Betz that her brother really was dead. "And I killed him."

She'd expected the doctor to pale, or at least cough or clear his throat, or something. Yet he'd remained stoically composed. It could have been a mask, for all she knew. But just voicing this confession had made Erika's stomach plummet like a runaway elevator. She must have looked the part too, for Betz had leaned in and asked if she was all right. She'd said she was, then hurried to add that her brother's death had been a terrible accident. After that she'd entered the semi-trance of recounting the event, the disassociation of voice and feelings that was her only means of communicating the dreadful incident.

She'd told Betz about her brother's ad nauseam mocking of her fencing skills. Keith valued hunting with their father, a *male* sport in which Erika was not invited to participate. "But it wasn't completely his fault. Our father fostered that in him." She'd voiced this to her own surprise, for it was the first time she'd truly realized this particular truth.

Then one day Erika invited her brother to give the sport a try. She lent him her new fencing gear while she used her old stuff, including her well-used Spanish foil. All the same he got frustrated, unable to score even one point on Erika. And then the unthinkable happened. In a maneuver in which she'd launched herself forwards, Erika's foil pierced Keith's neck, just under his mask. "He didn't have it pulled down far enough," she said to Betz. "It's happened before in fencing, but who could've imagined it would happen to us?" Her voice was small and distant, her gaze clinging to the patch of light in the gap in the drapes.

"But don't foils have little rubber bulbs on their end?" Betz had strayed from the matter at hand, and Erika jumped at the diversion.

"Yes, they do." She whipped back around to face him. "But they're plastic. Épées have them too. And with a saber, the blade's tip is welded over. So you shouldn't be able to penetrate jackets or skin—"

"Yes, yes, Betz interrupted, *but*..." His brows were arched in anticipation and Erika's brief perkiness shrank away.

"But," she said, her tone turning to leaden, "when the blade hit his neck..." She looked down at her shoes..."it broke."

"So the broken tip of the blade..." Betz said slowly.

She glanced up at him, her eyes imploring.

"Go on," he nudged. "You're almost there."

She heaved a shaky sigh. "It hit his carotid." She covered her face with her hands, her breath coming fast and short.

Dr. Betz bent towards her. "*Breathe now*, the way I showed you before—in deeply, out slowly through your mouth. That's right, keep it up."

Once Erika had calmed and her breath had returned to normal, she looked straight ahead and uttered in a voice filled with eternal disbelief, "He bled out."

She didn't think Dr. Betz would have anything to say apart from *It's all right; it wasn't your fault; you didn't mean to do it; it was an accident,* and to instruct her to repeat those things every time the accident revisited her.

Instead, he surprised her by talking about the nature of emotions, and anxiety in particular. When anxiety over the accident took hold of her, she was to first absorb the blow, then tell herself, *This sensation won't last; difficult emotions can't last—the organism, which is the body and mind, can't support them. They will pass.*

"But it is a blow, like getting punched in the gut and the air taken out of me. I have to use all my mental powers to push it away in the day, but when it comes back at night…"

"You musn't push it away," said Betz gently. "Tell yourself the feeling won't last and then embrace it."

Erika stared at him in disbelief.

"Yes, acknowledge the feeling and validate it. The harder you push it away, the more aggressively it will come back. *Breathe,* like you've just done for me. And then observe the sensation—ask why it might be visiting you in that particular moment; ask if this time the feeling is any different from before. In that way you can detach from it."

Erika nodded slowly, though she wasn't sure how this could help.

"And finally," Betz concluded, "nurture yourself. Make yourself a cup of tea. Do whatever it takes to pamper yourself. I know this a lot to absorb in such a short time, but I'd like you to practice it. The dreams might fade, but even if they don't, remember that dreams are only your subconscious trying to make sense of your experience—they are not the whole of you. You are not your dreams; you are not a person who repeatedly kills her brother."

They would follow up next time.

The appointment had gone over-time. And yet no one was waiting in the outer office when Erika left. In fact, she never crossed paths with anyone either arriving or leaving Dr. Betz's establishment. Not even a secretary occupied the desk in the reception room. Betz always scheduled their appointments himself. Perhaps Erika was always the last patient of the day. Maybe Betz kept only part-time hours. Or he worked in a hospital as well. All she knew at this moment was she felt as wrung-out as a floor mop. If ever she deserved pampering it was right now as she battled to get her umbrella up against a frosty wind, newly whipped up and turning the golden-pink glow of late afternoon into an obscuring white blizzard. When she got home she would make herself a stiff drink from the liquor trolley kept in the house, courtesy of owner Romano Rosselli.

As a gust of prickly crystals hit her face, wind blowing back her umbrella, she thought of Claudio with *his* well-stocked and well-used drinks trolley. She hadn't told Dr. Betz about the substitution she'd made regarding her dream of being buried in the moat. How could she talk about Claudio, without giving away the most immediate and dangerous secret she now held?

She did decide, however, to apply the doctor's advice to her anxiety about Claudio. *Embrace the fear, for it won't last.* And, she added, *Claudio will not win!*

Chapter 12

After a half-hour wait on the tracks, with Giorgio and Silvana closed in their compartment in mutually-agreed silence, the conductor finally announced the train would leave Milan's Central station for the nearby smaller Rogoredo station.

There Silvana got off to be picked up by her brother. Giorgio had to wait in the Rogoredo station another hour until finally the train was cleared to return to Milan Central, where he changed trains for Switzerland. The bomb scare, he would learn later, had been a hoax, with no one yet laying claim to it. After his ordeal in Italy, the border crossing in Switzerland was practically a stroll along the beach. Still, he didn't arrive in Bern until that evening and now sat with Régine in the living room of her flat.

"You know you can always change your mind and sleep here on the sofa," Régine said, patting the space between them.

"No, "Giorgio repeated, "I really appreciate the offer but I shouldn't spend too much time in your flat. It's a risk to you with everything that's going on."

It was a true sacrifice not to accept Régine's generosity, but he'd already booked a hotel. In more tranquil circumstances he would have canceled the reservation; he'd so looked forward to spending time with her. Yet he couldn't ignore what had happened this day. The traveler Silvana (who knew who she might really be?) was aware he was in Bern, could have easily found out what time his train arrived and relayed the information to someone here in the city. She would have given his description. His taxi could have been followed in the dark from the station...he probably shouldn't even be in Régine's flat at all—he should have called her and said they would meet the next day. He took a breath: *he had to tamp down his paranoia.*

She had fixed dinner for him and now they were sitting on the sofa, finishing a bottle of wine. He'd finally been able to strip off his tie and undo the top button of his shirt. He wanted to move closer to her on the sofa but once more feared his bulk might prove too aggressive. She was so small compared to him, compared to a woman like Erika, even. He should try reaching for her hand first, but now wasn't the appropriate time, since there was business to discuss.

They had alluded to it over dinner though they'd both agreed not to let it spoil their meal, and certainly not Giorgio's well-deserved interlude of relaxation, as Régine had affectionately expressed. Yes, she was kind and pretty and smart. The clichéd triad annoyed his writer's sensibilities, but he couldn't think how else to put it at the moment. He wanted to tell her how much he appreciated her. Caress her cheek. Her complexion had a pinkish glow, but in a womanly way considering she and Giorgio were about the same age. He wanted to stroke her dark hair...gaze deeply into those piercingly intelligent eyes...

"I talked to Ian yesterday," Régine said, abruptly quashing his fantasies.

He gazed in the direction of the clock on the sideboard: ten minutes to eleven. "And his patience is still holding, I hope?"

"Yes, but he'd like to see the finished product soon, since he still hasn't revealed anything to his editor at *The Guardian.*"

Giorgio nodded. "I'll be sure to nudge Erika along." With another glance at the clock, he said with regret, "But right now I'd better call a cab. We can go over business tomorrow."

"So you think you'll have to move from Menton," said Régine, as they rose from the sofa.

"After today, I don't have a choice. Menton's small—can't risk running into *Silvana* in the supermarket. Pity, I was really enjoying it down there."

"Especially compared to here." Régine motioned to the window. "I wonder if it's still snowing?"

Giorgio grunted. "At least it might give me some cover."

Yes, it was still snowing, and if that provided cover to Giorgio, it might well do the same for anyone who could be following him. With a last glance up and down Régine's empty street he ducked into his taxi.

Back in his hotel room he crawled into bed under the eiderdown, once again mulling over his bad luck. He should have driven to Bern the long way. Should have acknowledged the fickle danger of crossing through Italy. He would've had a car and he and Régine could have taken a lovely drive around the lakes. *He could have stayed in her flat.*

He should have repeated to Régine how much he'd enjoyed the evening—the food, the wine. And most of all *her company.* This latter he hadn't said. If he'd mentioned it, maybe she would have replied: *Another time you'll have to come and stay over here with me.* But when would that next time be? He needed to get back to Menton straight away and evacuate the inn. He'd planned to move soon again anyway but *calmly*, taking time to study where. That was another reason for this visit to Bern—to find out if it was feasible to live here, near Régine and closer to Erika. He felt responsible for both women who were risking so much to help him. Without Régine he wouldn't have found Ian Wescott of *The Guardian.* And without an English translation there would be no getting into *The Guardian.*

Now Bern was out of the question. Or was it? Who said Silvana was a spy? All he knew for certain was that she took offense too easily. But could that also be a cover, along with her tale of moving to his compartment because her husband hated the smell of cigarette smoke on her. *Christ*, he just didn't know and therefore couldn't take any chances, especially spending too much time here in Bern. Tomorrow Régine and he would meet to discuss how to get his translated manuscript safely to London. Then, he would tear up his return train ticket and rent a car to drive back to Menton and vacate the inn.

Ugh, he sighed, waking up a couple of hours later. He turned on his light and got out of bed to guzzle some water and loosen his tight dry throat (a bit too much wine this evening). He glanced out the window and verified a continuing cascade of white. *Cazzo*, in order to skirt Italy on the way back to Menton, he would have to drive ten hours, a good part of them through the mountains. *Correction*: if it were still snowing it could take *fifteen* hours. Refilling his glass in the bathroom, he noted how clean and crystal-crisp Swiss tap water tasted— fresh from the mountains without even a hint of chlorine: what balm to his hot dry throat. Yes, it would have been nice to live here!

He plunked down his glass and returned to his bed, giving a shiver at the thought of the road home. He snuggled back under the eiderdown.

Early the following morning Giorgio and Régine met in a café at the train station. He had just made reservations there to rent a car.

"Don't do the drive all in one day," Régine advised. "It may have stopped snowing for now but it's supposed to pick up again later."

It was six-thirty: with this break in the weather, he'd hoped to get lucky and drive straight through, arriving in Menton by seven or eight in the evening.

"And you'll have to drive a good stretch in the dark," Régine added.

Right: at least four hours if you counted both early morning and late afternoon. Giorgio knew this but enjoyed Régine's concern for him. "Any idea where I should stop for the night?" he asked.

"I'd say Annecy or Albertville," Régine replied after a moment's thought. "Depends on how tired you are."

Giorgio nodded. "Thanks—I'm sure I'll get at least as far as Albertville. Now, shall we talk about the manuscript's route to London?"

They agreed not to send the exposé by mail. Erika was typing with a carbon copy, but Giorgio still didn't want to risk even one copy going missing. He and Régine talked of potential couriers. Régine had someone she could vouch for, Giorgio had trusted colleagues too, but somehow he couldn't face releasing the manuscript from this intimate circle of three.

"I understand," said Régine. "Frankly, I'd feel devastated if something were to go wrong with someone I recommended."

"And *I'd* want to kill the guy I sent who screwed up." He shook his head and sighed roughly. "Whatever I decide I'll first have to clear out of Menton."

"Too bad you have to go back."

"True, but everything's there. And if I hurry, even if that woman on the train turns out to be a spy, DIGOS won't have had time to locate me. I told her I live in Paris. But I need to get started. I'd like to move somewhere here in Switzerland. Bern would be nice, but I don't think it would be wise after yesterday."

Régine agreed, and he wasn't sure if he'd been too forward in mentioning his preference for the city. "I'd like to be closer to Erika," he emphasized. "She's got no one in that speck of a mountain village, doesn't even have a phone."

"I've thought that myself. She's awfully brave," Régine added with a wistful look. "You've told me about the unsavory characters she's taken on in the past."

"Defying caution at times." He had the sense Erika was somehow trying to compensate for what had happened to her brother. Régine knew nothing of that and Giorgio didn't plan on telling her. It was Erika's private story to tell. "I guess it's 'youth,' he summed up.

"*Youth*," repeated Régine with a huff. "They're the ones who fight our wars, take the risks we want to avoid."

"Well that fits Erika."

The two gazed at each other for a moment, something meaningful passing between them.

"Anyway," said Giorgio glancing away, "we're due to get in touch when I get back to Menton. We're making an exception for her to phone my hotel..." He stopped. *Shit*—in five days, when he'd hoped she would have finished the translation. But he couldn't hang around Menton for another *five days*. He needed to be well out of there in no more than *two*.

When he told Régine, she said, "Do you have a backup plan in case something goes wrong?"

Giorgio tilted his head, an apologetic gesture. "*You*, as usual. You'll be the one she calls if she can't get me."

Régine nodded thoughtfully.

"Not an imposition, I hope?" Giorgio said.

"No, of course not." She smiled warmly. "Good—so Erika will be calling me when your hotel informs her you've checked out."

"Right. You'll have to tell her what happened yesterday and that I'm looking for a new hideout." He paused a moment, then added, "And if you wouldn't mind asking her how close she is to finishing the translation. And then..."

"I'll tell her we need to get it on its way to London *soon*." Régine looked pensive, staring out the café's entrance. The sound of trains whistling their departure, their combination of electric whizz and rumble as they glided away, invited more time for thought.

Giorgio was also in the midst of pondering. "Erika has the manuscript," he finally stated. "She'll be the last to be in possession of it until we hand it over to a courier..."

"When we decide *which* courier to trust."

"Which we agree won't be easy..."

"And time's running out."

Giorgio drew a breath: "I think Erika would be willing to take part."

"In transporting it to London...?"

Giorgio nodded. "I'm sure she'd take on the challenge."

Régine looked hard at him. "So you'd take advantage of her adventurous, *incautious* nature?"

"She wouldn't be incautious with the manuscript. But yes, I'm thinking along those lines." And hadn't Régine had the same thought ten minutes ago when they'd locked meaningful gazes? If she'd thought the same thing, would she admit it?

"You can't put her out there alone." Régine looked surprisingly indignant—defensive, motherly.

"But I wasn't suggesting she do it *alone*," Giorgio protested. "She and I would do it *together*."

"Then you'd both be at risk," Régine concluded, shaking her head.

So Régine cared as much about him as she did Erika. Nice to know. Giorgio dismissed his childishness and looked out the window into the darkness. "Let's think about it while I'm gone to Menton. I'll call you before I leave there. Maybe you could also think of a sensible place here in Switzerland where I can lie low..."

Régine agreed, laying a hand on his across the table.

"Well," he said, reluctant to release her touch, "I'd better hit the road and gain some time before the next dump of snow." From his jacket pocket he took out an envelope. Speaking of Erika, I've got this cash that needs wiring to her at the post office in Bellinzona. You don't mind doing it again?"

Régine took the envelope and tucked it into her purse. "Of course not. And if you ever get into a position where you can't supply money to her, I can always draw on my own funds."

Giorgio smiled and took back his hand. "I hope it won't come to that, but thanks."

"Not at all. Anyway," she said," nodding towards the window, "you'd better get going."

Outside, white crystals were beginning to pierce the blackness.

Giorgio sighed to himself. Contrary to Régine's advice he'd actually thought again of driving straight through to

Menton.

Cazzo!

Chapter 13

The snow in central Turin measured up to the tops of cars' tires. Plows had cleared the streets, merchants had shoveled the sidewalks, while icy berms mushroomed all over town. Claudio Voghera, wearing lightweight, waterproof hunting boots, tromped over the snow between two parked cars in order to cross the street. The dark-green, mid-calf boots reminded him of having missed out on boar hunting season last fall. He was supposed to have gone with Moretti and two other colleagues in November, but by then Moretti was already keeping him at arm's length over the Erika debacle. Voghera had considered hunting alone but didn't have a dog to help track the animal. And then there was that slight detail called danger—especially when encountering a male boar that could weigh 180 kilos, with razor-sharp tusks 20 centimeters long. One shot poorly placed and *addio*! He wasn't particularly afraid, but he wasn't stupid either; plus, his vow still stood: before going to any "happy hunting ground," as the American Redskins put it, he would track and apprehend Erika.

Voghera was still amazed at the girl's enthusiasm regarding his boar hunting. She'd wanted to join him and his group. Said she'd always longed to hunt and that tracking a boar had to be the most exhilarating of hunting experiences. He'd told her it wasn't like playing cowboys and Indians or Daniel Boone, a TV program dubbed in Italian that he'd watched as a kid. The *endeavor* (to Voghera, a more apt description than "sport") not only took sangfroid but also studious discipline and group tactics akin to battle. She'd insisted she could learn, that it wasn't for lack of discipline and focus that she'd earned fencing awards. "Fencing's been compared to playing chess," she'd said. And as far as courage was concerned, *hadn't she demonstrated her mettle last year?*

Voghera had to admit the girl was extraordinary—for a woman. But that's where things came to a halt. Moretti and the guys would have scoffed him out of the woods if he'd suggested inviting a twenty-six-year-old upstart female into their rough, frank-talking male crew. He hadn't repeated exactly as much to Erika but did allude to the exclusiveness of the longstanding group. "You're just as bad as my father," she'd retorted with disdain, meaning the father from whom she'd been estranged even before her brother's death.

Overall, Voghera didn't view himself as close-minded. (It wasn't in his nature and certainly wasn't good for his work.) He'd admired Erika's pluck from the start. It turned him on, even. But she'd gone too far in teaming up with Testa. Testa was in it for the fame and the dough—no doubt there. But Erika—why couldn't she get it through her goddamn childish head that Matilde Fassino, *the now deceased war criminal*, didn't matter?

Jesus, he had to stop wishing Erika was a tad more docile, like his ex-wife Nella. And even Nella had left him, taking their eight-year-old daughter. He hadn't seen his daughter for more than a year and the situation always left a taste of bile in his gullet that needed extinguishing.

He entered a café under the porticoes of Via Pietro Mica and went straight to the bar, wasting little thought on whether he ought to be drinking right now. After all, *un bianchino*—just a glass of white wine—didn't hurt anyone in the morning. And he was drinking less since Erika's defection—*somewhat*. He ordered the wine and put off the coffee chaser for when he would meet Moretti, in about fifteen minutes. Voghera had decided to take up his colleague's offer to "have that drink," though Voghera had specified meeting before noon. The later in the afternoon, the more tempting to start on Negronis, and he needed all his wits about him when sparring with a cunning bastard like Moretti.

Moretti was waiting for him in a café only a block away. Arriving first, he'd been able to choose their table and which side of it to sit at. He'd done that on purpose, Voghera surmised in the second or two it took to enter and spot his work friend. Of course Moretti's back was against the wall and his smile a charming gleam. His could be a disarming smile when coupled with the rest of his exotic looks—wavy dark hair, olive skin, and that startling contrast of sharp green eyes and flinty cheekbones. Erika had likened him to a prince from the Caucasus, but to Voghera, Flavio Moretti was merely a spook from Rome, who like most Romans could spin charm and a good story, one reason he excelled when undercover.

Moretti rose to shake Voghera's hand, wagging an "I knew it" finger at Voghera's short-cropped beard. He smiled, shook his head, but made no comment, and by the time the two were seated, the waitress had arrived.

"A dark beer," Moretti ordered.

"Coffee for me."

"Only coffee?" Moretti's brows rose in subtle though discernible disappointment.

Voghera nodded in affirmation to the waitress, and once she'd pivoted away, said, "I've got a dentist appointment afterwards. Don't want to smell like booze." He couldn't tell whether Moretti believed him, but already his friend was chuckling.

"Afraid you were turning into a teetotaler," he said. "Not good for our kind of work." Another gleaming smile.

Voghera nodded. Plenty of people didn't trust nondrinkers, especially men in the company of other men.

"But you're hanging in there…" The up-pitch in Moretti's tone suggested he was no wiser than he'd been after their phone conversation.

Naturally, thought Voghera, that couldn't be true. By now Moretti and DIGOS would have discovered Voghera's visit to

Erika's cousins and to her school.

"Hanging in there," he confirmed with a shrug, as the waitress arrived and set beer and coffee in front of them. He plucked a packet of sugar from the holder on the table and began the ritual of tearing it open and stirring the contents into his demitasse. Setting the small spoon whirling more than necessary, he gazed about the part of the room he could see, which wasn't much since Moretti had nabbed the seat against the wall. Voghera hadn't passed many patrons on the way in, still he hated having his back to the room.

"Any news you'd like to share?" Moretti asked after downing a draught of beer.

"News?"

"Well, maybe something illuminating about Erika..." He took another sip, a studious one this time. "You know how things can suddenly come to us intuitively, or a detail somehow emerges from the subconscious on its own..." *Right?* said Moretti's encouraging smile.

"I *wish*," Voghera replied with a grunt. His gaze caught on an abstract print framed on the wall in front of him. Ignoring Moretti, he tried to decipher the image which seemed to sport a naked woman riding a horse. Breasts were visible, but the animal she straddled could as easily pass for a centaur. As he squinted at it, the song "Runaway" suddenly interrupted his concentration. His eyes opened fully. *Who put that old relic on the jukebox?* Voghera had studied English, had heard the tune before, and could make out the gist of the song, which now sounded personally insulting. *Shut the fuck up*, he complained to himself.

"Something wrong?" asked Moretti.

"No," Voghera snapped back, a bit too quickly. "But maybe, for a change, *you'd* like to share something about *Bonnie and Clyde*?"

Moretti sighed and displayed his palms. "You know I can't say much with you suspended. But, as I mentioned before, we've been mainly trying to track down Testa. *And*, we think he's in France, and maybe not far from the border."

"Are you *sure*?" Voghera said, leaning in keenly. "How did you find out?"

"Can't go into that, but we think he's constantly on the move."

Voghera sat slowly back. So maybe Erika was close to Testa, in *French* Switzerland, for example. He pinched his chin, knew that Erika had studied a little French. But if Testa was on the move, so might she be.

"What are you thinking?" Moretti's head leaned shrewdly atilt.

"That maybe Erika isn't far from Testa," Voghera answered, giving nothing away; both Moretti and the others tasked with Bonnie and Clyde had surely suspected the same. "She could be in France as well."

Moretti gave an indulgent smile, whose twitch of condescension didn't escape Voghera. "That *has* crossed our minds."

"But if they're both on the move..."

"They won't be running together. Too risky."

True, Voghera told himself, tamping down his enthusiasm about Testa's being in France. The two would not be running together. "So do you have any intelligence on where Testa might move next?"

"Not yet."

And not in the same place as Erika. That was a given. So, he was back to his Switzerland hypothesis, with maybe a penchant for the French-speaking cantons.

"But so far it seems he's stayed in France," Moretti added.

Voghera blew out a breath and pushed away his empty cup and its saucer.

"Frustrated?" Moretti asked.

"No more than you, I imagine." Voghera gazed back at the horse-and-woman print, spotting a sliver of dark pubic hair on the woman.

"Hmph," Moretti muttered. "Not planning to take any

trips abroad?"

"Abroad? No."

"Not even a casual drive across the border into France?"

Voghera chuckled dryly. "A needle in a haystack."

Moretti nodded. "Maybe. But you know that if you ignore orders and go gung-ho on your own quest, you could get fired for good. And even worse."

Voghera narrowed his eyes, and Moretti quickly added, "*I* understand your motives completely. But the bosses may not. Let's leave it at that." He looked Voghera up and down with almost fondness. "Anyway, my friend, with that beard and cropped hair you'd be shit at disguise."

Voghera couldn't help smiling at that. During their last job together, Moretti had transformed himself into a radical hippy-looking terrorist type.

"So *stay put*," Moretti drove home.

Voghera's smile hardened. "Am I under house arrest? I'd planned an extensive hunting trip—you know, to kind of make up for last fall?"

One corner of Moretti's mouth twisted down. "Sorry about that, but the other guys..."

"It doesn't matter. I've always wanted to try boar hunting solitary style. More challenging and certainly a distraction from things."

"Don't be an ass." Moretti shook his head as if Voghera was the most hopeless of fools. More the fool now than when he'd blabbed to Erika.

"Well," Voghera replied, "the winter season's open. And I know of a dog I can borrow."

"*Fanculo*," Moretti scoffed.

Fuck you too, Voghera quipped to himself. He smiled yet said nothing, leaving Moretti with no retort for once and nothing to do but briskly finish his beer.

Moretti checked his watch, as did Voghera, in mutual understanding that the encounter had run its course.

"Let's stay in contact, eh?" Moretti said, when the two

men rose to leave the café.

With a less than honest smile, Voghera agreed. "When it's possible."

Moretti's lips parted, his head angled to one side, but he seemed to decide not to challenge Voghera's ambiguity. He waved a hand and the two parted ways.

Out on the street, the sinking grey sky menacing more snow, Voghera kicked a berm on the corner, sending snow toppling back onto the sidewalk. He hadn't given away anything to Moretti and yet he was sure his so-called friend was now tasked with keeping an eye on him.

He swung around the corner and entered another café. "Brandy, *a double*," he barked, then turned from the bar to scan the street outside the steamy window. He was almost disappointed not to see Moretti peering in bug-eyed like an anxious nanny.

Chapter 14

The previous day's slog home had left Erika cold, wet and awash in rumination. Today the snow was ever falling and Erika was still thinking about Dr. Betz, his advice and insight floating around in her mind like the arhythmic flakes outside the window.

Taking everything in at the end of their session had been hard and confusing, and she looked forward to fleshing things out during their next appointment. That would be in four days, since Betz had suggested they meet more often. In the meantime she repeated in her mind what she remembered as Betz's key points. When thoughts about her brother's death crept into her mind and brought her down, she must *not* push away the pain and anxiety but accept and embrace the feelings: validate them. She blew out her cheeks—*how unnatural that seemed.* Then, Betz had said she should nurture herself. *Pamper* herself, to use another of his words—*considerably easier.* Oh yes, he'd also said to observe the feelings with an investigative mind. So, *three* things to remember.

Alone here in the house, however, there were limits to pampering herself. A hot cup of tea next to the hot stove, or a whiskey, a book to read or the radio to listen to while she sat on her hard kitchen chair—she did those things already. Then, and most importantly, there was her work, stimulating rather than pampering, nurturing maybe in the sense she felt she was getting ever better at translating, but also anxiety-provoking. She had to get the translation finished and spirited away before Claudio or DIGOS came swooping down on her. Hypervigilance played its part, which indicated fear. And now suddenly, she realized she was putting Betz's investigative component to use. *Fear of the hounds pursuing her*: she'd already thought of it after leaving Dr. Betz's office. She could embrace that too, because somehow this intimacy with fear made her feel stronger.

Plus, what was the worst to fear? Claudio or DIGOS finding her and capturing the manuscript? Doing her in, even, so she couldn't talk? She knew they could eliminate her and Giorgio, but then they would have to do the same to Régine. After all, how could they be sure there weren't others who knew, or even that more manuscripts weren't out there?

She was standing, watching it snow outside, when she finally said *okay, time to do something therapeutic*. She strode over to the closet where she kept the épée she'd bought in Bellinzona. Then she found a file in a stash of tools in the kitchen. Sitting at the table, she began a new project. She removed the round plastic knob from the sword blade's tip, then started rasping the dull metal point—rasping and shaping; it would take some work but in the end she would have another lethal weapon to supplement her knife collection. She might never use the épée but the mere action of filing it, of forming it into a real weapon, gave her an extra sense of purpose—of agency.

When she got tired of filing she went back to her translation, worked another couple of hours, then rose stiffly to look out the window again. The weightless flakes were topping off an already formidable snowbank. She turned on the radio and found some palatable music, though she couldn't keep her eyes off the interminable rain of white. And at this moment she was gripped by perhaps the most grueling sensation of her solitary life: simple lonesomeness. Of course she knew it for what it was, knew its cloying nature, but now, with nothing but blinding white in front of her, she felt its heavy hollowness all the more. She needed to get out of the house, if only for a coffee at Cobbio's one and only café, yet she felt rooted in place by the oscillating, almost hypnotizing flakes. Finally she heaved herself from her inertia and went to put on her boots and coat.

The café was small and rustic—wood floors, ceiling beams, wood bar, wooden table and chairs—exactly what you'd expect to find in the Alps. And though Erika had already frequented the place, the couple who owned it always struck her as true mountain folk. Especially the husband, who wore a tiny gold, looped earring in one of his lobes—the sign of a Swiss mountain man.

Erika was the only patron in the café and took her coffee at the counter so she could chat. She asked the couple about the snow.

"Sometimes it'll come down for days," said the wife. She glanced out the window and added, "And this looks like one of those times."

"If you need provisions in Bellinzona," said the husband, "you'd better stock up soon. I've seen transportation come to a complete halt because of the snow." He nodded, half in concern, half in apology for the unpredictable, untamable wilds in which Erika now found herself.

"But things don't stop for long, do they?"

He shook his head. "There's no telling."

Before Erika could respond, the door opened and a couple Erika had seen before hurried in, slamming the door against the icy air. They greeted the café owners, but before settling at a table they stopped and looked at Erika.

"We've met," said the woman. "You're the American!"

Erika smiled and nodded. This was the Irish couple she'd encountered at Cobbio's small grocery store some weeks ago. The couple who owned a renovated stone house in Cobbio and who'd said they'd like to invite her for dinner.

In no time Erika was seated at their table and chattering in English. In a way it was like being beamed back to the States for a visit, but without the unbearable emotional baggage that had made her leave in the first place. She, who'd got used to speaking, thinking, even dreaming in Italian, found this conversation in her native language surreally relaxing and, she realized, she was parched for conversation.

The couple, Maeve and Brendan Hartigan, lived in Dublin most of the year, but enjoyed winters in the Alps.

"In Ireland, winter consists mostly of rain and fog," Brendan explained.

"And bone-chilling humidity," added Maeve.

"It's pretty cold here too," said Erika. *Especially when you come from Southern California.*

"Yes," Brendan agreed, "but it's a drier cold—much more bearable. And there's skiing and hiking. We'll be taking an extended ski trip soon."

"What Brendan's saying is it's a delightful seasonal retreat for a couple of pensioners. We've been coming here for three years now."

Maeve didn't look old enough to be retired; neither would Brendan, thought Erika, if he didn't have grey hair. Obviously, they were both very physically fit and this attracted her as well. She knew she shouldn't indulge in too much idle chatter, yet she couldn't resist the charming couple. Plus they were Irish, after all, and hardly likely to be spies. So when Maeve asked her to dinner that evening she readily accepted.

Leaving the café, a surge of joy zinged through her just thinking of spending an evening in someone else's home. Yet as she approached Casa Rosselli, the cheer turned soggy, disintegrating under the relentless snow and the familiar dread of being found out. Maybe she should make an excuse to cancel the dinner. Then she thought of Dr. Betz and what he'd said the other day. "You need to get out and meet people." Yes, that would help her morale, could even help with the dreams. On the other hand, he didn't understand the danger involved in raising her profile around the village. She needed to finish the translation, hand it off, and move on. Quite what the latter meant, she didn't know. She and Giorgio hadn't much discussed that phase of their journey. They would both need to work; the money earned from selling their exposé to

The Guardian wouldn't last forever. He'd told her that once the story was published, they might ease their way back to Turin. Again, it wouldn't be in DIGOS' interest to rub them out after the fact, not with Italy's democratic allies in the know.

And yet, Erika found it hard to imagine returning to teach English at Turin's Manhattan school. How could she just show up one day asking to teach again after an absence of almost two months? Granted she'd obtained emergency leave from the director, but she hadn't kept in touch with him, which on the surface seemed fairly disgraceful. But hell, right now it was risky enough merely checking in with Signora Sillano. All she could do was wait until this enterprise was finished and then visit the school's director, Doctor Longo, and apologize.

But she couldn't dwell on these things now. She'd chosen this path and would see it through. She felt restless, looked forward to going to the Hartigans' for dinner tonight. She would have to talk about some personal things, perhaps having family in Italy, then coming up here to Cobbio to...to what? She'd told Dr. Betz she was writing a novel. With all the fodder for psychological analysis she'd thrown his way, he hadn't asked her to expound on that. She wished she'd told him she was just *writing*, which wouldn't have been a lie at all. As for the Hartigans, since they'd barely met her, she would say she was here for a change of scene. From city life in...in...Asti? No, that would be like needing to escape city life in Bellinzona, since Asti wasn't much bigger. She would have to reveal that her home base was Turin. Too bad. Yet the Hartigans seemed worldly, and she didn't trust her knowledge of other big cities like Milan or Genoa, and certainly no place south of those. She didn't want to lie too much to the Hartigans. That was her problem in this gritty business. She didn't enjoy lying to people she liked.

As it turned out she didn't have to. The Hartigans were more interested in her life in southern California, which she depicted selectively, emphasizing the attractions of sunny San

Diego. And why would she leave that paradise? To take a GAP year, of sorts, to perfect her Italian.

"And now you find yourself caught between jagged white walls with no horizon to feast your eyes on as the sun sinks into the sea." Brendan Hartigan gave a beatific smile to punctuate his bard-like musing. Some of it was no doubt inspired by the wine he was drinking. His raven-haired wife Maeve, on the other hand, seemed to delight more in the food she'd prepared and Erika had praised.

"So what activities do you have planned for Cobbio?" asked Brendan, swirling a glass of red wine from a new bottle. He tasted it, gave a half nod, then refilled Erika's glass, along with Maeve's, who stopped him at two fingers, and then his own.

"Well, I've been getting settled in," said Erika. "Getting the house in order..."

"Must take a lot of work and planning," said Maeve, "with no washer or central heating. Things we take for granted in a remodeled house."

Erika gave another look around the Hartigans' dining-living area. Scandinavian-style furniture, statuettes and various souvenirs that seemed collected from different parts of the world. A fire crackled and hissed in the hearth.

"But when you're not doing household stuff," Brendan skipped on, "what do you like to do? Do you ski?"

"No, not really—haven't had much of a chance. But I like to hike..."

"Then you'll love it here. Have you hiked up to the monastery above Cobbio?"

Erika shook her head.

"Well, you'll have to wait till some of the snow melts." Brendan looked out the window into the black night, then got up and turned on an outside light. "Bugger," he said, which summed up the status quo.

"It's a marvelous hike," Maeve said, returning to the subject of the monastery. "And the nuns are lovely people.

Here they call it the *monastero*, but it's actually a nunnery."

"Is it a long climb?" Erika asked.

"Well, I'd call it a moderate hike in summer. Much more arduous this time of year, even dangerous, since the path will be snowed over. Wait till the snow melts, as Brendan says. But the hike will be well worth it when you reach the level of the monastery—the view is splendid."

Erika agreed she'd have to try it.

The evening continued with more jokes exchanged, Brendan's putting more wood on the fire, and Erika, though she knew it was late, didn't want to leave.

At around eleven, Brendan brought out a bottle of Irish whiskey. "This is special stuff," he said. The bottle was labeled Redbreast. "You'll need an extra shot of warmth before heading out in this cold."

Erika had already drunk enough to feel she could strike out in short sleeves. Still, she indulged in a shot of Redbreast with Brendan.

Then she set off, Maeve having promised another invitation to dinner and Brendan inviting her to hike with them sometime. As Erika waved and thanked them again, Maeve called out, "Remember, you can always use our washer!"

Her umbrella unfurled, Erika stumbled and swayed all the way home, no more than a five-minute walk. The umbrella should have kept her fairly dry, but it had done its own share of wobbling and when she staggered in through the door, it, her clothes and hair were sodden and dripping. She shed her coat and boots and dried the puddle on the stone floor. A hot shower would feel marvelous, but the thought of a cold dark walk to the end of the balcony in her bathrobe put the kibosh on that. It didn't matter anyway, and she felt good. Dr. Betz was right: all she needed was an interlude of jovial company to lighten her mind. She dried her hair with a towel, filled her two glass bottles with hot water, and took them to bed. She didn't even realize her feet were cold until she nestled them near the bottom of the bed and felt soothing, radiant heat. She barely managed to click off her nightlight before conking out.

The next morning she woke, free of unsettling dreams. The sky was also free of falling flakes, though it remained a sullen greyish-white. She'd planned to work all day on the translation, then remembered the warning of the café owner with the single pierced ear: stock up on provisions.

With this lull in the weather, she'd better go to Bellinzona to buy items unavailable here in Cobbio, such as typewriter ribbon, carbon paper, and liquid eraser.

By the time she boarded the train it was snowing again—*cazzo!* All the way to Bellinzona and back those great saucer-like flakes continued their silent bombardment. By the time Erika got indoors she was soaked again, this time from trying to juggle her bags and umbrella.

But she was glad to have made the trek, for the next morning she woke to the same maddening, monotonous scene. At least she was getting close to finishing the translation.

The day after, she received a visit from one of the Rosselli relatives in the village. Adriana, a niece of Casa Rosselli's owner, showed up at Erika's front door, shaking out her umbrella and stamping her boots before Erika ushered her inside.

She asked Erika if she had sufficient provisions. "Because the trains aren't running—too much snow."

"So it can actually happen—we're cut off?"

"Cars with chains might be able to travel, but if you depend on the trains," Adriana shook her head, "you're out of luck. And no one knows when they'll start back up."

Erika gritted her teeth. *Snowbound!*

Chapter 15

Not only had Giorgio failed to make it from Bern to Menton in one day, he hadn't even been able get as far south as Albertville. He'd had to stop farther north in Annecy, about forty kilometers inside France and still high in the mountains. Between Bern and Annecy he'd put on tire chains, but the journey had proved a white-knuckle affair all the same. A raging blizzard which broke out near Annecy had finally forced him to admit defeat. According to the hotel receptionist, he'd been lucky to find this narrow single room with a twin bed, and in a hotel with a fabled view of Annecy's ancient prison, perched on an isle in one of the many canals in the city. Thanking him, Giorgio had looked out at the blinding blizzard and thought, *what view*?

Cramped in his twin bed (he usually managed to obtain a larger bed when travelling) he endured a stuttering sleep, waking off and on in worry about getting back to Menton the following day. Towards morning he woke again, but this time with a similar sensation to when he was almost forced off the corniche above Monaco—that feeling that his heart was hiccupping. What had gone wrong with his nerves when it came to tough driving? He dressed before dawn and headed downstairs, noting that although the blizzard had ceased, snow was still falling. He would catch a quick breakfast and strike out early. But the breakfast room hadn't opened yet, so he crossed back to the reception, only to learn that the roads south were closed.

"For how long, do you think?" he asked.

The young man on duty shook his head studiously. "Hard to say. But of course I will keep you informed."

Giorgio thanked him and went back up to his room. He couldn't stay here indefinitely, he affirmed to himself as he paced the room, collecting his things. He sat down on the bed and stared at his bag. Then he fetched his coat and gloves and returned to the reception.

"Sorry to bother you again," he said to the clerk. "You did say the trains were running?"

"Oui, monsieur."

"Then do you know if it's possible to turn in a rental car here?"

"Here?" The young man looked unsure.

"I mean here in Annecy. I have a Europcar rental."

"*Ah, oui, bien sûr!* Europcar is located at the train station."

"Perfect! Could you point me in that direction?"

Giorgio retrieved his bag from his room, checked out of the hotel and drove to the station, where he found there was a train leaving for Menton in two hours. The route was hardly direct, looping west to Lyon, then south to Marseille, and finally northeast to Menton—an over nine-hour journey. "Or," said the ticket agent, "you could shorten the trip considerably by traveling through Italy."

"*Non, non, non, non,*" Giorgio cut the agent off before he could elaborate. On the bright side, he would reach his base by early evening, and letting the train do the driving would allow him to relax enough to think about where to relocate.

He returned the car, paid the extra for leaving it in Annecy, and bought his train ticket. Then, sighing heavily, he bought a coffee and a couple of croissants in the station restaurant and sat down to wait.

It was still dark when Giorgio left Annecy and dark again when he got to his family-run inn in Menton. The first thing he asked the wife manning the reception was if anyone had come calling for him.

Madame Goux frowned and shook her head. "You were

expecting someone?"

"No, madame, but unfortunately I'll have to leave your excellent establishment in a day and a half."

On the train he'd decided to move to Geneva. Who knew how long he would stay there, but the move should at least bump him off DIGOS' radar for a while, if indeed one of their agents might be on to him. The move would place him closer to Régine and Erika, their three cities forming a rough geographical triangle within Switzerland—Bern at the peak, Geneva at the left corner and Bellinzona at the right point. He liked the metaphor, the fact that he and the two women were joined wholeheartedly in this pursuit. In Marseille, during his layover to change trains, he'd found a travel agency near the station and asked about lodging in Geneva. He'd learned that in parts of Switzerland even trains were blocked by snow.

"Where might those areas be?" he'd asked.

"Not in Geneva," the female agent had assured him. "The lake has a mitigating effect on the cold. But we're hearing of pockets in the hinterland which are effectively snowbound. And we don't know when that will change." She glanced out the window towards Marseille's palm trees. "You'd never know it here," she'd said with a satisfied smile.

She'd booked him a hotel room (with a large bed) for two days hence in central Geneva. That would do for now.

Two days later he was behind the wheel again with all his belongings. Traveling the long way from Menton to Geneva (again, skirting Italian territory) should take about eight hours, he figured, depending on the roads. Snow continued to be forecast for the more northerly Alps, and if necessary he would spend the night somewhere. At least he would be well away from Menton and could relax his pace. He'd called Régine before leaving, relaying his Geneva hotel information and gently reminding her that Erika would be bound to call her in the next couple of days when she couldn't reach him in Menton. And again, could she ask Erika how close she was to finishing the translation?

The drive went smoothly until he neared Grenoble. Light snow showers, starting a half hour before, had now turned thick as down feathers. Cars in front of and behind him now slowed to a caterpillar's crawl. At this rate it could take four more hours to get to Geneva and he would have to pull over and put on chains again. He was tired. Tired from a week of frenzied travel and wary of another spell of hiccupping in his chest.

He took one of the Grenoble exits, entered the city, and after thirty minutes of inching from one hotel to another, finally found a vacancy.

After calling the hotel in Geneva to report his delay, he stretched out on the double bed he was fortunate enough to acquire and closed his eyes. He thought of Régine, he thought of Erika. He thought of his scoop. With all this dashing around he couldn't help feeling he should be getting closer to his goal—more work equaling more results. Silly, of course, when all his current effort now consisted of evading capture. His thoughts couldn't let go of the traveler Silvana. Did she really live in Menton, or had she lied, just as he had about his living in Paris?

With nothing to do but wait for the dinner hour, he went down to the front desk and asked where the nearest phonebooth might be. He preferred not to call Menton from the hotel.

"There's a Postes-Télégraphes-Téléphones office nearby," the woman said. "It'll be much warmer and drier than using a phonebooth."

He decided to walk to the PTT, rather than try to find a parking place on the street in the snow. He hadn't been out ten minutes before regretting having left his boots in the car. Yet didn't the clerk say the PTT was close? *Things are always farther away than people say*, he complained to himself as he slogged through the snow in his sneakers.

After another ten minutes, thinking he might now be lost, he found the PTT and sloshed inside, out of breath, with his heart pounding. He was assigned a booth, his call was put through, and soon he heard a voice he already missed—that of Madame Goux, owner of the inn he only left this morning. He sat down on the small bench to enjoy a bit of warm conversation.

"Ah, Monsieur Giorgio!" She sounded happy to hear from him, though they had talked only a few hours ago. "Could you already have reached Paris?"

"No, madame, I've decided to stop in"—he gave it half a second's thought—"in Lyon; just taking my time."

"Good decision. You looked awfully tired after your last trip."

"Just the nature of business travel," Giorgio said, appreciating Madame Goux's concern. "But I just wanted to make sure I left everything satisfactory after clearing out the room."

"Yes, you did—but you left a credit card behind."

Giorgio was taken aback. He'd only really called to see if he'd had any visitors since he left, not wanting to keep posing that question to Madame.

"Your credit card was lying under the bed," Madame clarified.

Giorgio sat forward, tightening his grip on the receiver. He hadn't wanted to carry both credit cards in his wallet, so about a month ago he'd locked his Diners Club card, which he rarely used, in the bottom of one of his suitcases. He could only figure that during his hurried packing and rearranging clothes it had fallen out. Then he must have kicked it absently under the bed.

Rounding out his thoughts, Madame Goux said, "It was under the bedspread, next to the leg of the bed. Would you like me to do something with it?"

For a significant moment Giorgio was tongue-tied.

"Monsieur Giorgio? Are you there?"

"Yes, yes," Giorgio answered. "I won't be able to return to pick the card up. At any rate, I have another credit card."

"Then shall I keep it just in case you return sometime? Or I could send it to you...?"

"No, no, madame." He ran his fingers through his hair. He should tell her to destroy it.

But before he could make that request, she said, *"Pardonnez-moi un instant, il y a quelqu'un à la reception."*

Someone had come to the reception. He waited. He would ask Madame if she could please cut up the Diners Club card when she was finished. He waited a little longer. *A guest with a question, or someone checking in?*

Then Madame was back. *"Monsieur Giorgio, vous avez un visiteur."*

What? He had a *visitor*!

He could hear a muffled masculine voice, to which Madame said, "Are you sure you don't wish to speak with him?" Her voice sounded more distant, as if she were holding the phone out.

Then a lower, more muffled response, as if Madame's interlocuter had taken a step back. In the telephone booth Giorgio was on his feet, holding his breath, trying to make out what the man was saying, but discerning nothing.

"Well, suit yourself," said Madame, the phone still held away from her cheek. "I still don't understand—"

She didn't finish her sentence. After a couple of seconds Giorgio could hear the whooshing of traffic in the road. Then nothing, as the door must have closed.

"Madame?" he said.

"Yes, yes, I'm here. I don't know why this fellow didn't want to talk to you after asking if you were staying here."

Giorgio sat back down on the bench, massaging his head in frustration. He said as patiently and casually as possible, "Did he ask anything else?"

"Yes, he wanted to know where you were going next. I told him back to Paris. He asked if you thought you could make it to Paris today. I said you were calling from Lyon, but somehow he didn't look convinced of that. You're not in some kind of trouble, are you?"

"No, madame, everything's fine. I don't know who he could be." Giorgio would have liked to ask for a description of his visitor, but thought better of further raising Madame's concerns. And a description wouldn't help unless the man turned out to look like Claudio Voghera. Giorgio knew no one else who worked for DIGOS. And if this man did happen to be Voghera, what difference would it make?

He tried to put Madame at ease by adding, "In business there's always competition, and resentment…"

Then he fell silent, at a loss for what else to say, when Madame piped up: "*Mon Dieu*, your credit card is gone!"

"What?"

"It was sitting right here on the counter. I'd removed it from my desk when you called. That man must've taken it!"

Giorgio let out a groan, clutching his head again.

"If this has something to do with business rivalry," she said, "you'd do well to rethink the trade, Monsieur Giorgio." He could picture her shaking her head.

"No doubt you're right," he sighed.

They wished each other well and rang off.

After paying for his call, Giorgio stepped out onto the porch of the PTT. He would have liked to take a taxi back to the hotel, but all he could see were private cars creeping and sliding along snow-caked streets in the encroaching twilight. Then he noticed a bluish glow to the air; the fallen snow had taken on a blue-white hue as well. In reality it had stopped snowing altogether.

He felt revived. He pulled his gloves on and his coat collar up and trouped back to the hotel in his wet sneakers. His mind was a thought-storm. His Diners Club card was no doubt in the hands of his pursuers—but he hadn't used the card in quite a while. DIGOS knew he had called Menton—they might somehow finagle their way to accessing the call record in Menton and discover he'd phoned from Grenoble. The many calls he'd made on the run now sparked in his head—but

DIGOS would be hard-pressed to obtain all targeted phone records in France.

He blew out a vaporous breath. He would finish his drive to Geneva tonight, this window of still and silent weather offered just for his escape.

Chapter 16

In Cobbio, snow was still falling, and Erika wondered if the whole of Alpine society had closed in on itself and shut down, or if only she found herself snowbound, waiting to be buried alive as in her dream about Claudio. Yesterday Romano Rosselli's niece, Adriana, had trudged over in the snow to tell her the trains had ground to a halt, and today she heard on the radio that train travel was still frozen. Even worse, perhaps, was that she had an appointment with Dr. Betz tomorrow. The thought of missing it whipped up the kind of anxiety he had counseled her to embrace and observe, a practice that was hard, to say the least, and one she still didn't fully understand. She should at least call him and tell him she might not be able to make the appointment.

She donned her weather-battle gear—including gloves and scarf this time—and struck out to the café to use the payphone. She also needed to phone Giorgio, but that call she would need to make from Bellinzona.

She'd never called the doctor before and found his phone ringing endlessly. *Why didn't he employ a receptionist?* Finally she hung up, acknowledging that his practice might be closed due to the weather.

She hiked back home and got back to her translation. After working two and a half hours straight, and feeling a fettering pain shoot through her shoulders, she stood up, stretched, dropped to do a few pushups, then went to retrieve her épée. Pulling on the thick workman's gloves she'd also found in the house, she resumed filing the épée's tip and sides into...well, not razor-sharpness, but at least edges that approached the roughness of glass shards. The harsh rasping sound that filled the kitchen could torture the ears of a bystander watching her. To Erika's ears it signaled satisfying progress.

She alternated activities, sharpening, typing, sharpening, typing, pivoting like an automaton, until twilight shadows began to slide down the mountain outside. At four o'clock, with the kitchen light already on, she wondered if Dr. Betz had been with a patient when she'd called earlier. His lack of a receptionist was really frustrating. How was it that a psychologist, a professional, couldn't manage to hire someone? It didn't make sense—Betz was good at his job, had helped Erika so far, as he must have helped plenty of people. Then of course she had never *seen* another patient in the waiting room. Her puzzlement was turning to hot impatience.

She rose and started pacing about the kitchen. *Shit*, she finally said, stopping. She'd better try to call again. So once more, she piled on boots and coat, gloves and scarf, turned off the stove, pulled the curtains shut, grabbed her umbrella and headed back out. If necessary she would wait in the café trying his number until six o'clock.

The couple who owned the café lifted their heads in surprise as she walked back in with a wave, stomping her boots on the floor mat and shaking snow off her umbrella. She plopped the umbrella into the common holder and crossed to the bar to order a cup of tea.

"Tea's best when it's this cold and nasty," the wife agreed as she turned to prepare Erika's *tè rosso*.

"I actually need to use the phone again, but it may take a while to get through."

"Take your time," said the husband, who was leafing through some receipts, his efforts setting his tiny gold earring toggling in the air. "We're not going anywhere until dinner time—and neither is the weather," he added shaking his head.

"You were right about the train stoppage. And the forecast says snow for at least another two days."

"Don't worry," said the wife, turning back with Erika's cup of tea. "I've never heard of the trains being grounded for days at a time." Erika wondered what "days at a time meant."

She sipped her tea, then left it on the counter while she went to make her call. The wife remotely reset the minute counter and Erika lifted the receiver of the telephone housed in a tall, semi-private nook.

She almost jumped when Dr. Betz answered on the first ring.

"Dr. Betz!" she stammered, identifying herself. "I thought your office might be closed because of the snow."

"No, no," the doctor said. "Though it *is* fairly challenging outside." He chuckled lightly, then turned serious. "Are you all right, Erika?"

Erika shifted her weight, edging closer to the phone. Though she was the only patron in the café, the owners stood practically within earshot. "I'm okay...well sort of...I have my appointment tomorrow, but as of today the trains still aren't running."

"And you're stuck in the village. How are you feeling?"

Filled with cabin-fever, she wanted to say. *Verging on claustrophobic.* "I'm okay," she repeated instead. "I'd hate to miss my appointment, though.

"Do you have a moment to talk right now?"

Erika looked back at the couple behind the bar. They were going about their business, the wife arranging cups and glasses, the husband having retreated to a back office. No one seemed to be listening. She pictured the phone's minute-counter. *Well*, she thought, since she hadn't paid for even one session with Betz so far, she could call this phone conference a payment of some kind. His voice was already instilling a blessed calm in her.

"Let me pull a chair over."

Dr. Betz's prescription for imposed isolation consisted of a strange and elaborate regime: ten minutes of focused breathing, while sitting with her eyes closed. Gradually she should work up to twenty minutes. Betz suggested breathing to the image and rhythm of ocean waves. At some point in the day, particularly when she felt anxious or agitated, she must do a walking exercise. Not simply *going for a walk,* but taking slow, leisurely steps and focusing on the movement and sensation of her feet with every step. "Do this for twenty minutes," he'd said, either outdoors or indoors. Obviously, Erika would have to perform this exercise *inside*. It sounded bizarre, meandering throughout the house as if in a trance.

And yet it didn't turn out to be some zombie-like rambling. The following day, snow still wafting down, Erika embarked on her so-called therapeutic walk. Step after contemplative step, she rounded the kitchen table, drifted into the unused living room then back to the kitchen. At first she couldn't help viewing the somber, deliberate movement as a kind of prison march. Then she remembered Betz's description of the exercise as a concentrated stroll, the way one steps in the sand on a beach. She wondered at Betz's choice of images. Stepping slowly and carefully through ocean sand; breathing in, like water sucked out to sea, and breathing out as the wave returns to crash on the beach: *very Southern California. Bravo, Betz!*

The stroll took her back into the living room, after which she moved towards the stairs. Consciously, she climbed, registering the difference in pressure and texture in the raising and setting of each foot on the stone steps. She roamed the upper floor, eyes aimed mostly at her feet, then climbed to the floor above it, which had two empty rooms. In the early century it must have accommodated a spillover of the Rosselli family of ten. Strangely, the awareness of her feet in space and time was causing a kind of calm inquisitiveness in her mind. Descending the stairs, she noticed the weight on her bones, whereas in climbing she'd felt the work of her thigh and calf muscles. She took a turn around the balcony outside, protected from the snow by the sheltering overhang, noticing the cold which in this instance didn't seem to bother her much. She rolled her sweater sleeves back and examined the goosebumps cropping up on her arms—*yes, their appearance seemed reasonable, normal.* She wondered what it would be like performing this exercise in the snow.

Back in the house she made another round of the bedrooms then returned to the ground floor. She looked at her watch—she'd only walked for ten minutes, but even so could sense a kind of flattening of her thoughts. She sat down, stretched her legs and folded her arms. For a long moment she felt at ease, placid and peaceful in the radiating warmth of the stove. Then curiosity about Betz crept back. Did all of his patients perform this exercise? *What patients?* she answered herself. She would like to cross paths with at least *one*. And why wasn't he charging her for her therapy? He'd said he would think about payment after evaluating possible effects of the therapy. She'd never heard of anything like that before either. All very nebulous, though this walking practice had turned out to be strangely satisfying. They'd made an appointment for four days hence, though she wouldn't mind seeing him before that; imagined him at this exact moment with her in Casa Rosselli—the two of them nestled near the stove, drinking hot mulled wine, their shoulders touching, chatting about casual things...

She shook her shoulders, pulling some sense back into herself. Betz was her *doctor*, though a peculiar one—and once more, a bout of circular enquiry came unleashed—*why no secretary, why no bill for treatment—a bizarre treatment at that—why no other patients*—only to be silenced by a knock on the front door.

Before springing to her feet Erika questioned who it could be. Only Adriana had come here to visit and that was just two days ago. Like last time, Erika gathered up her papers, whisked the work in progress out of the typewriter and shoved the stack into a drawer.

She opened the door. *"Adriana?"*

Romano Rosselli's niece had indeed returned, bearing not only news of a timely resumption of train travel (tomorrow, in fact) but an invitation to a party—or rather an unorthodox invitation, for Adriana and two of her cousins proposed the venue to be no other than Casa Rosselli. Erika's bewilderment led to an uneasy smile.

"This is a very old house," Adriana explained, when they were seated at the kitchen table, "and it's got a special oven outside. Have you seen it in that storage closet attached to the house?"

"Yeah, I wondered what it was used for."

"For roasting chestnuts, and it could make for a great winter party!"

Erika's heart made an involuntary leap of excitement. "*A party*," she said, smiling. Although when she saw Adriana's gaze flit over the typewriter, then around the room, past the drawer hiding her translation, her internal radar began beeping. She liked Adriana. Under normal circumstances she'd invite her friendship. But circumstances were far from normal. She shouldn't be getting cozy with anyone. She gazed out the window at the specter of white that seemed to magnify her caged and solitary existence day by day. She looked back at Adriana. She was a Rosselli, and Romano Rosselli had been Erika's grandparents' friend. Erika's grandparents had even met Adriana on one of their trips here. Then Dr. Betz's voice piped up: *You must engage with people, especially those your own age.* He had repeated this advice on the phone just yesterday. Adriana was only a little older than Erika. Surely she would qualify in Betz's estimation.

The tug-of-war didn't last long, the rope ceding pleasantly to Betz's advice on mental health.

And, Erika added to herself, she was nearing the end of her translation. Maybe it was time for a tiny celebration. "Who all do you think would be coming?"

Chapter 17

Claudio Voghera maintained a well-practiced vigilance regarding being tailed. Not that he expected to catch Moretti himself skulking in the shadows; even Moretti's disguises wouldn't fool Voghera. But Moretti had access to other agents for this kind of work, in all likelihood with DIGOS' blessing. Or, he could ring up a retired agent (someone unknown to Voghera) who might like to pad his monthly pension with a bit of surveillance work.

Voghera scratched at his chin, unused to his itchy close-cropped beard. He also wasn't used to being sidelined, shunted like a train from the main line into a siding. Shunted by his organization, shunted by his wife, shunted by Erika. Well, if anyone thought he would remain sidelined for long, they'd better think again. Or better yet, not pay attention at all as he slipped onto his own rogue rail.

He'd been studying which track to take. According to Moretti, DIGOS was searching for Giorgio Testa in France. But was that really true, since Moretti was possibly overseeing surveillance of Voghera himself? Moretti, in his capacity of semi-friend, seemed to be warning Voghera not to rile DIGOS by embarking on his own hunt. But in that case, why divulge anything at all?

Granted, DIGOS might well be operating unofficially in France, but that didn't mean they would find Testa there, nor did it mean Erika was situated near Testa.

He looked out the window of a café across the street from *Il Cardinale*. Though his focus wasn't on Testa per se, you never knew what the return addresses of the journalist's mail might reveal. Plus, the custodian had to be somewhat in cahoots with Testa, and shaking him down verbally gave Voghera some satisfaction. The guy never pushed back against the harassment, didn't threaten to call the police, which only reinforced Voghera's conclusion that the custodian and Testa maintained contact.

Voghera had just let off steam with another of these visits and now sat across the street with a hot Rum Punch in front of him He deserved the brandy-and-rum charged grog, given the unrelenting cold (it had snowed again yesterday) and the equally cold and lonely thoughts he couldn't help entertaining. His ponderings over where to find Erika never ended, only to circle back to his original hunch. Switzerland: it was close, and they spoke Italian in the south. Yes, *Italian*—wouldn't Erika feel more at home there than in a German or French-speaking canton or country? *She wanted to visit the Matterhorn,* said the owner of the Déjà Vu. *She'd planned a ski vacation in Saint Moritz,* claimed her old cousin in Asti. Glamorous, romantic, but bullshit! Especially since Erika didn't even know how to ski. If she'd fled to Switzerland, she would go to ground in a low-profile, low-cost little corner off the beaten track where she could at least communicate with Testa. Somewhere in Canton Ticino, most likely. *He hoped.*

He picked up the cinnamon stick resting diagonally in his glass cup and poked at bits of nail-shaped clove floating on the surface of the grog. Delicately he dunked a floating slice of orange then let it spring back up for air. Cinnamon, cloves, a slice of orange, how festive they looked. Hot Rum Punch, such a cheery drink to sip with friends in winter—the holiday season, which had just ended last Saturday, January sixth, with the Epiphany. Voghera had enjoyed little of it. He'd spent Christmas Day with his mother, forcing a dutiful smile while rumblings about Erika roiled his gut. Amidst all the food and drink, he'd even nursed a droplet of hope that Erika might still return. On New Year's Eve he'd got drunk at home alone, then endured a harrowing hangover on New Year's Day, one that had hammered him back to the nauseating likelihood that she would *not* return. No manifestation of Erika, *no epiphany*.

With the cinnamon stick he methodically stirred the hot grog, its innocent orange glow and spicy aroma somehow making him feel, or seem, less an alcoholic. He then took a spoon and plucked out all of its ornaments, tested the grog's temperature with his tongue and, satisfied the liquid was tepid enough, removed the cinnamon stick and guzzled the entire cupful.

At home he took out his map of Swiss and northern Italian highways, checking the route to the Swiss canton of Ticino. With another clear-weather window like today's he could reach Lugano, just over the border, in about three hours. That was encouraging. Then he would have to comb Lugano—not so encouraging. The city was the biggest in Canton Ticino and very high-profile. Locarno and Bellinzona stretched further afield, more towns than cities. The whole of Canton Ticino numbered less than half a million people, yet where among the map's specks of towns and villages might Erika be hiding?

If she was there at all. The idea was so flimsy, Voghera suddenly felt his insides deflate. He pushed back from the kitchen table and blew out a long sigh. Eyes closed, he used all his mental willpower to re-inflate his hunch. He must do something—*had* to.

He fought as his nerves clamored for another drink, then he shook his head. *No—time to get serious!*

He would leave tomorrow.

The next day the weather held cold and clear, and Voghera felt a refreshed determination as he motored out of Turin. Given he was suspended from DIGOS, he planned to spend a couple of days in Lugano to suss out which way the wind blew. An advantage to working by hunch was freedom to go wherever that wind flowed. He embodied that feeling now as he sped along the motorway behind the wheel of his Opal, pop hits piping from the radio, the car's heater streaming warm air.

He'd packed a few changes of clothes (including a suit and formal overcoat) and zipped a photo of Erika inside his black parka. His brown-handled hunting knife lay secured in its leather scabbard in the back of the glovebox. It was the only weapon he would risk taking across the border.

It took him a little less than three hours—continued clear weather, cleanish roads—to get to the Swiss border town of Chiasso. From there remained only twenty-seven kilometers to Lugano and that, he figured, he could cover in about twenty minutes. He'd be in Lugano in perfect time for lunch—another heartening thought.

Except in Chiasso, the Swiss border guard seemed in the mood to detain someone.

Voghera couldn't understand why he had to be the one; all his documents were in order, his passport, driver's license, car registration. He'd informed the guard of his "vacation" destination, and still the officer set out circling his car at a leisurely pace.

Coming to rest next to the right front tire, he declared: "It's bald."

"Where?" Voghera asked, striding up next to him.

The guard tapped the tire with the tip of his boot. "There."

Voghera bent down and frowned. "*That?* It's just a little worn at the edge."

"Nevertheless, it's illegal," the guard maintained matter-of-factly.

"But I've got chains in the trunk. I'll put them on if there's any hint of snow."

"That's not the point. We have regulations here."

The guard was a middle-aged man, looked like he'd been on the job for half a lifetime, so what did he need to prove? Voghera held back an impatient sigh, offering instead a pained smile. "Would you prefer I drove back to Milan and buy all new tires? I can't just buy one."

His attention fixed upon the tire's slightly-worn tread, the guard had avoided eye contact. Finally he glanced briefly at

Voghera, then rounded the car again, rechecking the other tires. He stopped at the back of the car. "Let's see your chains, then."

Quickly Voghera approached the trunk and opened it.

The guard squinted at the snake's nest of chains inside. "Take them out, please."

Voghera obeyed, laboriously untangling three sets of chains. Why hadn't he done this before he left? Hands filthy, he extracted one set and held them up in front of the officer.

The guard shook his head. "Are you sure these are the ones that fit?"

Voghera assured him they were, explaining he'd had to buy the other two sets on the spur of the moment.

The guard shook his head again, this time with a sour smile, and Voghera could imagine him grumbling to himself about scatterbrained, disorganized Italians. *Casinisti*: muddlers.

But at last he gave in. "You can put them back."

Voghera tossed the chains into the trunk and slammed the lid. He took out a handkerchief and wiped as much dirt off his hands as possible while the guard started back towards the front of the car. Once more he stopped next to the imperfect tire. He gazed inside the car, and Voghera threw his head back in exasperation. "The inside's not messy," he said, then hoped he wouldn't have to prove the assertion in detail. He felt like a schoolboy at the mercy of a custodian's petty power trip. *What's next, checking if my underwear's clean? Idiot!* He bit his tongue. He didn't think it illegal to carry a hunting knife in the car, but with this asshole...

The guard carried on towards the front of the car and then, without looking at Voghera, muttered, "You're free to proceed."

Voghera found a hotel in downtown, Italianate Lugano, checked in, then went to buy Swiss francs and have a late lunch. After a welcoming winter meal of polenta and rabbit he thought he'd better stretch his legs with a walk around the city center. In reality, worry about his mission was starting to mount again. Hitting the border, he'd felt an almost maniacal enthusiasm for his hunt. Now, his meal finished, he could no longer put off deciding how to proceed in these uncharted waters. What to do now: go through telephone books looking for *Rivoli, Erika*? Ridiculous to think that her name would be listed in a Swiss phonebook.

He kept walking and came across a stationery store where he bought a map of the city. About fifteen minutes later he'd arrived at the Parco Ciani on the edge of Lake Lugano. Even at this time of year, the park, with its vast lawns and winter-slender trees, offered a pleasant distraction. But Voghera couldn't afford to linger, and when a bracing breeze off the lake burned his face, he turned back towards the city center.

Ploughing ahead under arched porticoes, he soon approached a cinema. People were spilling out onto the sidewalk and mulling about in front of the marquee. He was snaking through the crowd when a collective cry arose. A series of flashes erupted next to him—photographers, reporters…? He tried to move on but was jostled, while voices again surged all around him. Finally he stayed put, weaving his gaze through rearing bodies to find out just what was going on.

It didn't take long. The cinema doors once more flew open, and liveried personnel pushed the crowd back until a space formed into which stepped a woman—blonde, bundled in fur and sporting large sunglasses. But not quite "bundled;" her fur coat swung wide open, displaying a mini-dress and knee-high boots. Another gust of cheering, with flashes exploding everywhere. "Mina!" the crowd started chanting. Voghera's jaw slackened as he stared more intently. Yes, it was her—Mina! One of Italy's most popular singers who had been living in Lugano for over ten years. He couldn't take his eyes off her: her brilliant smile, her long legs—she was as tall as Erika!

His observation lasted all of a minute, for Mina and her

male escort were swiftly whisked towards a waiting limousine. The crowd tried to follow, and next thing Voghera knew, a flash burst in front of his eyes. He shook his head to clear his vision. Not only his vision, but his head: a guy with a handheld video camera had turned up next to him and was filming the whole episode. A microphone was shoved under his nose. *"Cosa prova, Lei, in questo momento?"*

What was he feeling at this moment? He swore and forced his way out of the fray—hopefully his mug wouldn't turn up on the local news tonight. He strode back to the hotel, pondering what to do next. Lugano was *not* proving to be a good base. He would spend the night then move on tomorrow. He could play out his hunch from anywhere that had hotels.

The idea of moving on reinforced his feeling about working from intuition. Even without a lead he could change tack, if only based on a negative omen. And he could always double back to Lugano if the trail dictated so. That was valid operating procedure.

Back in his hotel room he displayed his map of Ticino on the bed. The two other principal cities of the canton—Bellinzona and Locarno—lay close. Either would do as a base. He frowned keenly at both on the map. No difference between them. He decided go by the alphabet: B before L.

Tomorrow morning he would leave for Bellinzona.

Chapter 18

A strong wind skimmed off Lake Geneva, forcing pedestrians into a hunch as they hurried along city streets amidst below-freezing chill factors. But at least it wasn't snowing.

Giorgio Testa was thankful for that. He'd arrived late the night before only to collect his key, climb to his room and collapse into a heavy, dreamless sleep. When booking the room from Marseille he'd made sure the hotel contained parking facilities. "It also has a restaurant," the charming young travel agent had said, "and I think a view of Lake Geneva, the largest lake in Switzerland." Though he could see no such sight from his window, he'd learned from the breakfast staff that the lake lay only about six short blocks away. As for the restaurant, it was a boon indeed. So far, he'd only had to go out to cancel his Diners Club card, directed to the proper bank by the desk clerk. Now he could hunker down in the hotel. His hairbreadth miss of the spook in Menton still caused his skin to prickle. He pictured the spy returning to Madame Goux's establishment to try to worm out guest Giorgio Testa's car license number. He couldn't shake the panoply of scenarios besetting him, rational and irrational.

Time to get busy. He took out his notebook, sat at the small desk in his room and started drafting. He'd left his portable typewriter in his car trunk, but could do without it for now. This piece would not be long, only an announcement of sorts explaining his disappearance from Turin, his now-certain flight from DIGOS (something previously just a probability), and his possible arrest, or even liquidation, by the Italian security services. He'd decided to get some kind of message out after the incident in the Milan train station, and now with DIGOS snuffling up his trail it was vital he get started. The announcement would accompany his Italian copy of the Matilde Fassino exposé (stored in his suitcase) and like the manuscript, would be destined for a Swiss bank safety deposit box. He would call on Régine for help with securing said box, so that if anything happened to him, she could release both the message and the exposé to the press.

He spent the afternoon scribbling and revising, went downstairs to the restaurant for a late lunch, and when darkness fell, ventured out to call Régine from a phone booth. Along with asking for help with bank logistics, he needed to inform her of his new location and ask if Erika had made contact. Just the prospect of telling Régine he was now in Geneva warmed him. *Finally we're in the same country.*

With wind rattling the phone booth's glass and hissing through its crevices, he learned that Erika had indeed called and been concerned by the Milan incident.

"And now that they're definitely on your heels," said Régine, "you must take special care."

He thanked her for the concern and she repeated the line *We're in this together.*

And might we be together for an even longer haul? he would have liked to ask, but not from a freezing phone booth over a hundred kilometers away.

Régine had wired Erika the money—"Thankfully she's almost finished with the translation!"—and now agreed to open a safety deposit box in her name for Giorgio's Italian manuscript. He didn't mention the accompanying message he was working on, preferring to avoid stirring up emotions; hopefully, the message would never be needed.

"So we'll meet to procure the safety deposit box," Régine summed up.

"Probably best to use a bank here in Geneva. DIGOS might know I've been to Bern."

"Geneva's not far. Let me check my schedule." She left the

phone for a moment, and despite the wind and the penetrating cold, Giorgio felt another gush of warmth.

"Giorgio? Looks like I can come the day after tomorrow. How long are you booked in your hotel?"

"I've already extended my reservation by two weeks."

"Could you see if the hotel has another vacant room?"

"Will do. I'll call you back tomorrow evening to confirm."

Actually, he had already checked and found there was no shortage of rooms in the hotel. Smiling, Giorgio hung up.

The following day he worked straight through, going downstairs only for meals and to bring up his typewriter. Balled-up pages filled the waste paper basket, and still the message he now finished (complete with details of being tracked through France) was far from elegant, but blunt and, he hoped, potentially alarming. Every "genre" of writing required an appropriate tone.

He paper-clipped it and placed it in the manilla envelope on top of the Matilde Fassino manuscript. Régine would have to sign and keep the key to the safety deposit box.

Régine's train arrived in Geneva just before noon the next day. She took a cab to the hotel and after checking in and receiving her room key, accompanied Giorgio to the restaurant for lunch.

"I hope the hotel restaurant suits you," he said. "I've only been out at night, and just to call you."

Régine laughed lightly. "Yes, you must stay underground!"

"Well, we have to go to the bank this afternoon, but I'm only too glad to chance it."

"As I said when you called back last night, this bank is so small and low-profile, no one on the street will even notice us entering the door."

It turned out to be true. Régine, a French-Swiss national, knew Geneva well, and the bank she'd chosen occupied a narrow slice of side street not far from the hotel. "There's a bank on every corner of every street in Switzerland," she said, and Giorgio grinned his acknowledgment. The wind had died down and so they decided to walk.

Inside the building, dressed in dark suits and overcoats, they took the elevator to the third floor, where a short, bespectacled man received them with a serene smile. Régine filled out papers for the safety deposit box, while Giorgio sat beside her. The banker asked for no details regarding Giorgio (introduced by Régine as "my associate, Monsieur Marca") only casting him the occasional placid smile. He looked more like a watchmaker than a banker, Giorgio thought. The little man then escorted Régine and Giorgio into an elevator leading to the basement, where all three entered a vault. The banker opened Régine's box, confided the key to her, then withdrew from the vault.

Giorgio and Régine gazed at the walls of gilt-trimmed boxes and then at each other. Giorgio nodded, and Régine opened her briefcase, removing the beige manilla envelope containing Giorgio's story and message to the press. She placed it in the felt-lined box, then looked back at Giorgio. "Shall I lock it in now?"

"Go ahead." Giorgio watched his scoop slide solemnly into the wall. For some reason, the thought of a body rolling into a morgue freezer crossed his mind.

Régine turned the key, then held it aloft between them. "I'll keep it safe," she said.

"I know you will." Giorgio extended a hand and closed it around Régine's. For all intents and purposes the gesture symbolized the soldering of trust and ongoing friendship; for Giorgio, however, Régine's warm, delicate fist in his represented a gentle step forward, if only for one long second.

Giorgio mentioned the beatific little banker as they headed back to the hotel through narrow lanes filled with clock and watch shops. "Nice that he didn't ask about me."

"In Swiss banks they don't ask questions." She flashed Giorgio a wry grin. "The lake's just down the street—shall we take a short walk?"

The wind had ceased and the low winter sun was winking between smears of cloud.

"...I guess a short one," Giorgio conceded.

They strolled along the quai du Mont-Blanc where they sat on a bench to admire Lake Geneva's famous Jet d'Eau. From there the lake began to open up wide and vast.

The Jet of Water shot up into the air like a skyscraper. "Or a huge ship's sail," Giorgio observed.

"Or a gigantic harp," said Régine. "See the individual streaks of water in the air, like strings? You should see it when there's a rainbow. Lucky the cold hasn't shut it down."

Soon the sun sank lower than the Jet's peak. A slight breeze rippled off the lake, and Régine gave a shiver. "I suppose we should head back."

Giorgio wanted to drape an arm around her and enfold her into his warmth, so they could enjoy the rest of the sunset. But yes, they needed to return to the hotel and hole up.

They each went to their rooms, then met again downstairs an hour and a half later for an early dinner. At six p.m., they were the only diners in the hotel restaurant, a long rectangular room with tables and banquettes, matching tablecloths and napkins. The mood-lighting served as a sensual reminder that it was dark as ink outside and time to relax.

"I wish I didn't have to leave so early tomorrow morning," Régine said with a sigh.

If only she knew the extent to which Giorgio agreed. "You *definitely* have to return to Bern tomorrow?" he asked.

"I've got a meeting with one of the news producers at eleven."

So this evening was it. Scenarios to the contrary swirled in his head: and if it started snowing between Geneva and Bern to the northeast, and the roads closed? What if Régine happened to twist her ankle stepping out of the hotel elevator and couldn't travel until seen by a doctor?

Naturally he didn't wish any misfortune on her and admonished himself for thinking like a cad. Better to start a conversation that could last late into the evening, accompanied by cordials and a nightcap.

"I've been thinking more about your story," said Régine. They were sharing a pot of cheese fondue and she had paused, holding her long fork in the air.

"Oh?" Since Giorgio didn't have a topic at his fingertips, he supposed this would do.

"Have you always wanted to do investigative journalism?"

Giorgio gave it some thought. He didn't want to prattle on about his year-long dream of producing a giant scoop. More modestly he said, "Not when I first studied journalism. But the times we're living in now, I guess I couldn't *not* be interested in something big like the Matilde Fassino affair."

"But you had to wait…"

"Almost a year, since I'd signed the State Secrets Act. Then when Erika told me about Fassino's assassination—"

"You saw a green light."

"Because *that* particular crime took place *after* I'd signed the Act."

Régine nodded wistfully. "Even though I'm a television journalist, I share the passion for a scoop that'll turn everyone's head, the scandal involved, the chance to make people *think*, if they're capable."

Giorgio saw that passion in Régine's gleaming dark eyes, in the red of her cheeks, in her animated gestures. As she dipped another piece of bread into the hot cheese, he refilled their glasses with Savoyard white wine.

"By *think*," she went on, "in the case of your story, it would be how one decides whether Matilde Fassino deserved her demise for what she did in the war."

"That's the discussion I'm aiming to spur. Spin off articles and so forth."

Régine acknowledged that once the story was published,

DIGOS would have a hard time justifying their pursuit of Giorgio and Erika. "The story will eventually make every newspaper in Europe."

Giorgio gave a brief smile. He didn't want to count his chickens. "Who knows how they'll comment on it?"

"The Left will play up her war crime. The right might claim human rights abuse—for the first time ever, mind you—because she's one of their own. Both sides could declare gross state overreach, each side according to its agenda." Régine gave a generous smile. "The centrist government could collapse."

Giorgio thought she looked absolutely gorgeous in this moment. His pride spiked, he said, "I wonder how it'll be seen in terms of ethics, with her stroke and then her murder and its cover-up."

"If she'd been prosecuted thirty years ago, she might have hanged for turning a vulnerable Jew in to the authorities for deportation to Auschwitz. Many readers will consider it delayed justice."

"Vigilante justice, which goes to the issue of government overreach..."

"I agree it's complex," said Régine, mopping up cheese at the bottom of the fondue pot. "You say you don't offer a solution in your story—and rightly so—but do you feel anything gut-wise, yourself?"

Speaking of his gut, Giorgio was happy to see Régine scraping the bottom of the pot with her bread. He would have liked to do so himself, but always avoided finishing the last of any food from a common platter or pot.

"You'd think I'd have decided by now," he said when she'd finished. "On the one hand there's the Jewish victim, Sara Lattes, hiding from the fascists throughout the war, finally finding freedom when peace came, only to die of tuberculosis. Then I go back to Fassino and her age and health risks, and the legal question. But now that DIGOS is after *me*..."

Régine nodded. "And after Erika too because of what she

knows."

"Right." Was he actually thinking so much about himself that he needed reminding about Erika? "Anyway," he stated, raising his hands, then letting them thud back on the table, "I've quit deliberating. Let the readers judge. And what about you?"

Régine shook her head. "I'm not going to shed tears over Matilde Fassino, but I'll be interested to learn the lengths to which others might defend her."

An ambiguous response, but from a journalist's point of view, entirely understandable. *Ambiguity*: in Fassino's case, a right tangle regarding the letter and the spirit of the law. But this wasn't what Giorgio wanted to spend the rest of the evening talking about.

Fortunately, the waiter arrived to clear their plates and hand them the dessert menu. Régine chose a slice of Charlotte aux Noisettes and Giorgio ordered apple sorbet topped with Calvados. "Under different circumstances," he said, "we could go for another walk after dinner."

"You mean the cold, and DIGOS, of course."

Giorgio threw up his hands again. "Exactly."

They finished their desserts, then ordered coffee. Giorgio didn't usually drink coffee in the evening but would do most anything to keep the evening rolling indefinitely. He didn't want to talk about Erika, though. So far, Régine hadn't mentioned his proposal to send Erika to London with a copy of the translated manuscript. He sensed this could stir up an argument.

"I can't remember if you said you completed all your education here in Geneva?" he tactically asked.

"Everything but university. I went to Zurich for that. We Swiss must be multi-lingual achievers, you know." Her smile included such a charming roll of her eyes, Giorgio wanted to reach over, take her by the cheeks and kiss her right there and then. He loved that French was her native language (and of course she spoke German and English too) but that her Italian was perfectly passable as well. He delighted in how they sometimes mixed the two languages, their special mélange—informal and, dare he say, fairly intimate?

They talked about their university days. "I almost went into performing arts," Giorgio said.

"*Really*—and what would you have specialized in?"

"Comedy seemed likely at the time. I had a friend who was a little shorter than me, skinny, with light hair and—how would you say—childlike blue eyes? We used to do Laurel and Hardy impersonations for the students, even in cafés. Got a bunch of laughs. 'Course, you can guess who played who."

Régine's expression seemed slightly sympathetic. He probably shouldn't have mentioned his Laurel and Hardy days (which lasted even beyond university). As if he was capitalizing on his weight instead of trying to lose it. "I had a mustache in those days," he added with a shrug.

"Well," Régine said, smiling, "I'm sure you and your friend had a good act."

"Mm," Giorgio concurred, looking moodily past her. Where could they go from here? Might as well offer a digestif. "How about a *génépi*, or something?" he asked. "Being from this area, you're probably familiar with it."

Indeed, she knew of the herby Alpine liqueur. "But I think I'll pass—let's not empty your wallet. The whole day's been a splurge."

Giorgio could feel his brow furrow. *Naturally* he was paying for things here in Geneva. She'd taken time out of an undoubtedly busy week to buy a train ticket to join him and open a safety deposit box for him. It would be utterly rude of him *not* to offer generous meals and drinks. Besides...

He leaned in as far as his bulk allowed. "Régine," he said. "As you say, we're partners in this endeavor. You've done me a great service in sponsoring the safety deposit box. You've had to rush over here, and tomorrow you have to hurry back early." He reached for her hand, which had been fidgeting with her demitasse on its saucer, and felt it become still. "I not only owe you a debt, I care very much for you." Silently he exhaled from a pair of full-to-exploding lungs. His heart beat a tattoo.

For a moment she gazed at their joined hands. "You're right," she said. "There's no one I'd rather work with than you." Slowly Giorgio withdrew his hand and waited for her to continue. "I care very much about you too," she said, looking up with affectionate eyes. "And what we've got going in this partnership, well, it's of such value and importance that I can't think of anything beyond it right now. You're my trusted friend and partner. Let's not jiggle the scales."

Not jiggle them now, or never? Giorgio understood her point, considering the nature of this enterprise, the diceyness, the danger, et cetera. And they weren't alone in their collaboration. Erika was out there too. In fact, he'd half expected Régine to mention her again. But what did Régine really feel about *him*? Had he effectively communicated his own feelings, his desire? He wasn't sure. In addition to meals, he had also planned to cover the cost of Régine's room. Now he was relieved he hadn't yet got to it. If she worried over the cost of a nice dinner, how would she have reacted to his paying her hotel bill?

The waiter reappeared. "*Madame, Monsieur: vous désirez encore quelque chose?*"

Giorgio and Régine looked at each other. When Régine remained silent, Giorgio resigned himself to asking for the check. "*No merci, l'addition, s'il vous plaît.*"

"*Tout de suite.*"

Once the waiter left, Giorgio managed to say, "I hope we'll remain friends and partners to the end." Then he thought, why did I say *the end?* Luckily Régine responded with a hearty, "*Mais bien sûr!*"

He settled the check with cash, and they left the dining room. They wouldn't see each other again before Régine left the next morning, but they vowed to meet again soon. Then time came for kisses on the cheeks—one side then the other; then one more. *Status quo confirmed.*

Chapter 19

The mess in Casa Rosselli seemed worse this morning than when Erika had gone to bed. The long kitchen table was strewn with chestnut shells, littered with empty bottles, crumpled paper napkins and miniature pastry wrappers. Plates and cutlery were smeared and encrusted with food. Glasses sat either empty or with abandoned splashes and slicks of red wine. The room smelt of burnt food and stale cigarette smoke.

The sight was both overwhelming and slightly nauseating to Erika, whose head must've weighed fifty pounds by the way she'd dizzily descended the stairs and swayed into the kitchen. Now standing before the mess, she not only balked at cleaning it up, she felt hopelessly merged with it. What time did everyone leave last night? Adriana and her sister, plus the sister's boyfriend had been there. And the two cousins—what were their names, the ones who filed to and fro from the outside oven into the house, bearing plates piled with steaming roasted chestnuts? Vittorio and Valdo? It hadn't seemed cold in the house despite the door propped open much of the time, laughter and shouting volleying throughout the house and the outdoors.

Erika cringed, squeezing her eyes shut. She should have tried to keep the noise down, but how could she have done, without seeming resentful of hosting the party? At least no one lived right next to her, and even if someone in the neighborhood had heard the ruckus, it wasn't as though she was unknown in the village. Not even an authentic hermit could live here invisibly. The whole Rosselli clan had been aware of her presence well before the party. *So*, nothing should have changed in the last twenty-four hours...she hoped.

Emitting a lengthy sigh she trudged back upstairs and along the balcony walkway to take a shower. The slapping tonic did her good. Steadier on her feet, she returned downstairs and commenced attacking the mess.

She paused where the boyfriend of Adriana's sister had sat. Erika had never met him before but something about him seemed familiar. Yet with much of the conversation whizzing back and forth in dialect (increasingly, as the drinks flowed), the more she'd had to struggle to keep up. Everyone was nice enough to translate into Italian when she didn't understand something, but at times laziness had got the best of her and she'd missed chunks of conversation.

Erika cleared the table and wiped down its oilcloth, emptied ashtrays and swept the floor. She looked at the stack of dinner and dessert plates next to the sink, the two sets of glasses bunched next to them, along with the grimy ashtrays. How could she have agreed so readily to host a party? And why hadn't she let Adriana help clean up afterwards rather than send her home? *Face it*—drunk as Erika was last night, she couldn't deal with anything beyond collapsing into bed. *Well, she wouldn't risk getting drunk again any time soon.*

She blew out a breath and rolled up her sleeves to tackle the dishwashing. It was noon and she had an appointment with Dr. Betz at four. If she hurried she could finish the dishes and still work a little on the manuscript. Even if she'd rather take two more aspirin and dive back under her duvet.

This time when Erika walked down the hall of the doctor's building, she passed his office to check the unmarked door next to it. Could this be a private exit from his inner office? Maybe people slipped out this way so as not to be recognized in a psychologist's office. She pushed down on the handle— locked. Or it could just be a utility closet. Erika had never seen an extra door in Betz's inner sanctum.

As usual, no one else graced the waiting room. She walked

up to what would normally be the secretary's station and took a good look around: at the desk, the phone, an ink blotter, a pencil holder spiked with a couple of pens and a pencil; no notepad, nothing personal such as framed photos, just an ordered, dust-free surface. Behind the desk stood a row of army-green file cabinets, three rows, equaling nine drawers, the only object on top, an old globe attached to a stand. She was about to sit in one of the waiting-room chairs, when Betz appeared and invited her down the inner corridor to his office.

"So, how have you been holding up since our phone conversation?" he asked, once they were seated, he in his swivel chair and Erika where she always sat, in the corner of the leather sofa by the window. He smiled mildly and Erika immediately felt a shimmer of warmth. Today he was wearing a dusky blue cabled sweater with, for the first time, no collared shirt underneath. His striking bare neck looked solid and strong, and his craggy features somehow complemented the complex weave of his sweater. She had to remind herself he'd asked her a question.

"Well," she said, "it's not snowing for now, so I was glad I could take the train." For the first time today she was aware of a note of optimism in her voice, compared to her earlier sighs and complaints over the state of the house, coupled with increasing worry about repercussions of the party.

"Mm, yes," said Dr. Betz. "I've been thinking about that— glad it's worked out."

Had he been thinking about *her* in particular these four days, or just about the effect of the weather on all his patients?

"And how are you feeling now?" *The question that always kicked off their sessions.*

Usually she would respond within the context of her harrying dreams and the physical exhaustion they caused, but today the question made her pause. She'd always felt a lightness of spirit when coming to an appointment with Betz— she looked forward to it, she liked him, and he was the only person she visited on a regular basis. This afternoon, a residue of the morning's hangover still trailed after her, but also, she had to admit, did doubts about the doctor and his prescriptions. Then again, the strange walking and breathing practices had helped during those trying days of smothering white, and she told him so.

"Have you tried the walking practice outside?"

"Not yet..."

"Try it. You might feel an even greater sense of spaciousness and tranquility."

Erika was already reveling in her freedom. As soon as it had stopped snowing and the trains started running, she'd rushed to Bellinzona. It was like coming back from the dead—visiting shops, including the city's little mall, where she'd spent some of the money Régine had wired her on a black, formfitting ski parka with a hood, so she wouldn't have to carry her umbrella when it snowed. She'd stopped for coffee at one of the high-end cafés, even flirted with visiting the castle again, but it was closed due to the snow build-up. Which was probably just as well; no need to run into Marzio, the guardian, on top of everyone else she was meeting lately.

"Good that you're getting out," Betz said. "Just going for aimless walks is nourishing when you live alone and don't know many people."

"I've actually met some people my age..."

"Wonderful!" Betz uncrossed the leg he always held at a right angle on his knee to support his notebook. "Socialize as much as possible," he said, leaning in.

Erika gave an obligatory nod while thinking just the opposite. Betz's praise was fine, but she did need to curb her social activities, even cut them out altogether. She must finish her translation. Between trips to Bellinzona, helping Adriana prepare for the party and cleaning up while nursing her headache, she'd lost precious work time. And over the phone Régine had told her of Giorgio's brush with danger in the Milan train station. She had no time to waste.

Betz sat back and finally got around to asking Erika about

her dreams.

"More or less the same," she said. "I haven't been remembering them lately, but I still wake up frazzled, with the feeling that something awful's just happened to me. But I don't have the headaches as often as before." (Except for today's, which *didn't* merit mentioning).

"I'm pleased about the lessening of the headaches, but the other symptoms..." For a moment Betz sat tapping the top of his fountain pen on his notebook, gazing pensively at Erika. His eyes never left hers and she felt their dark intensity penetrating deep inside her, searching for things kept well hidden. Erika drew a silent, quivering breath. Both aroused and uncomfortable, she wanted to shift her buttocks but found herself paralyzed.

Then the tapping stopped and Betz himself shifted in his chair. Looking at his notes, he said, "By the way, what kind of novel are you writing?"

The physical tension was slashed, only to be replaced with a new discomfort. Erika didn't respond straight away. On her first visit she told Betz she was working on a novel, but not what kind of novel. Did he now want to know the plot? She moved her gaze to his cabled sweater, taking in the tight weave that made her think of vertical arrowheads linked together, stretching up and up...She started to tell the story of a young woman who wants to climb a mountain in the Alps.

"An aspiration of yours?" Betz asked.

"In a way..."

"A way to surmount the tragedy in your past?"

"...Maybe..." She was bluffing her way through and hoped he would change subjects.

"Writing is healthy," he said, nodding. "And it can be particularly therapeutic in the form of autobiography."

He paused, and Erika hoped he had finished. "You might try it," he added. "But for now it looks as though we still need to work on those demons in our own way. How would you feel about being hypnotized?"

The golden light from the table lamp flickered a couple of times. Betz excused himself and leaned over to fiddle with it. It was fully dark outside and the unscrewing of the bulb threw the room into fractured shadows cast from streetlight. When he screwed the bulb back in, light once more filled the room and Erika winced—not at the dazzle, but as a delayed response to Betz's question. *Hypnotism: no, not at all.* She knew shrinks did this and didn't doubt its efficacy, but God knew what kind of beans you could spill when in a state like that. *And what was he really after?*

Betz must have guessed her fear and said, "No need to feel pressured. It's only one option, and people do have control of themselves when they're under."

Maybe. But there was no way she would allow herself to be put to the test. Still, she asked, "Do you hypnotize many of your patients?"

"Well, at the moment I don't have many patients. But I've used the practice successfully."

Not many patients. Erika wondered if the few he had were *non-paying*, like herself. Are we *guinea pigs*? She could feel her mouth tighten.

"Let's just let it be for now," Betz said, bestowing one of his benevolent smiles. "However, I do have another suggestion."

Erika tilted her head.

"Have you ever heard of Samatha meditation?"

Trying to relax, she said, "I've definitely heard of meditation. People have been doing it in California for years."

"Have you tried it?"

With meditation so wide-spread in her home state Erika hesitated to say *no*. She'd just never been interested, especially the way everybody and his mother in flamboyant, hippy attire proclaimed how *marvelous* it was. "I've never heard of *Samatha* meditation," she decided to say.

Betz smiled softly again. "It's a basic form of practice that calms and steadies the mind and strengthens concentration abilities."

Erika wondered why she would need to learn to concentrate better, but Betz was ahead of her. "There's a theory that in developing strong concentration skills, a person can learn to even control his dreams—or *hers*, in your case. Go to bed telling yourself 'I'm not going to have disturbing dreams tonight', and eventually, with plenty of practice, you could become able to change the course of your dreams if they don't suit you."

Control your dreams? Erika had a hard time believing this, though she didn't say so.

"Since you're a writer I thought this might especially appeal to you," Betz said. Erika gazed over his shoulder, trying to figure out what this was all about. She suddenly felt saturated, overwhelmed, and more doubtful than ever.

"Might this type of meditation appeal to you, Erika?"

Erika had already realized she was practicing a type of short meditation with the breathing exercises Betz had assigned her, so she asked, "Where would I do it, here?" She heard the skepticism in her tone.

"Not today, we don't have time. But I've made recordings where I guide the meditation practice. Do you have a tape player?"

Erika didn't.

"No problem. I have one right here you can borrow." Betz swiveled in his chair, rising to go to his desk. Out of a drawer he pulled a small compact black machine wound with its electrical cord. He set it on the desk, then from another drawer collected a cassette tape. Rummaging around, he found a plastic bag and placed both inside. Then he stood before Erika, bag proffered. "Here you are! Try to listen to the tape once a day."

She was almost taken aback. She couldn't remember his ever smiling broadly like this. His eyes were intelligent darts, his angular features made less rough by the smile. She averted her gaze, moving it over his strong bare neck, down his solid physique and the sharp alluring weave of his sweater, over his legs planted firmly apart in charcoal flannel trousers.

She inhaled another silent, stuttering breath. Then she met his eyes again. She stood up and took the bag.

"Shall we schedule another appointment for another four days hence?"

"...All right." Erika wondered if he'd caught the slight hesitation in her voice.

"Good," he said, crossing back to his desk and his appointment book. They scheduled the next visit and then he turned to shake her hand as he always did when they took their leave.

She felt his grip as firmer than usual, felt more friction between their hands, but his smile had retracted to its habitual avuncular mildness.

She left the office through the still, sterile waiting room. *I don't have many patients,* he'd said. And why was that? What kind of psychology practice was he running?

Why didn't she just ask him? Because she didn't want to confront him, didn't feel ready for that kind of thing. But she *could* take her own style of action, unorthodox as it might be. She took her time leaving the building, observing, reflecting, then made her way out along the sidewalk to a hardware store. She would need a tool or two.

At five o'clock it was pitch black, but storefront lights still blinked and beckoned.

Chapter 20

The six-p.m. train sped Erika through the night on her way back to Cobbio. After her session with Dr. Betz, she'd stopped at a hardware store and bought a small flashlight and a mini flat-head screwdriver. Still, she hadn't finished her shopping and decided to search out a different sort of store. The helpful clerk had steered her in the direction of a yarn store, and there she'd bought the rest of what she needed.

The shopping bags, plus the one with the tape recorder, now slouched on the train seat next to her, while she, as usual, sat next to the window. At intervals she glanced inside the bags, pensive, then bunched them back up. A shiver shot through her as her plan materialized. It should work, theoretically.

She was looking inside one of the bags again when someone entered her compartment.

"Is that seat free, or would you prefer to keep your shopping on it?"

Looking up, her eyes met the young guardian of downtown Bellinzona's castle—Marzio. She'd been thinking about him not two hours ago.

"*Disturbo?*" he pressed.

No, he wasn't bothering her, really...

"Have a seat," she said, shifting the bags to the left, between her and the window.

"*Erika*, right?" He unzipped his coat and stretched his legs.

Erika nodded. "And you're Marzio."

"We both have good memories." He smiled proudly.

"Been shopping in Bellinzona?"

He looked slightly different from how she'd remembered him on that twilit evening a few weeks ago. They'd spent about an hour in each other's company, first in the castle grounds then on the train back to Cobbio. Tonight he wasn't wearing his guard's uniform, and perhaps his hair was a tad longer; still there was something disconcerting in his features. "I've been doing *plenty* of shopping, since the trains have been running again. And you—still without a car?"

"Not *still*, but *again*." His lip curled as he shook his head "At least I'm not working at the moment."

"The castle's closed?"

"Until enough snow melts."

It was then that Erika recognized what made him look different this time. He reminded her of one of the partiers the night before—the boyfriend of Adriana's sister. Erika tried to scrutinize him on the sly. Could the two be related? Marzio looked a bit younger. They both had light-brown hair and similar noses, but Marzio's eyes were blue, while the other's were dark. It was hard to study him sufficiently from the side...

"That's a nice old house you live in, by the way."

"You've seen my house?" She tried not to sound alarmed.

"*Casa Rosselli*. Cobbio's small, I've seen it many times. Also, my brother was there for a party last night." He grinned. "I heard it was a good time."

Brothers. Erika sat dumbstruck. Yet why should she be surprised, given Cobbio's miniscule population? "Oh..." she managed to say. "If I'd known..."

"Don't worry, I haven't told my brother about you and me meeting at the castle."

What? She'd been about to say, *If I'd known, I would've invited you too.*

"I mean about sharing that joint," Marzio clarified. "My brother's kind of strait-laced. Likes to drink but thinks pot smokers are losers."

"Well, then I appreciate you not mentioning it."

Marzio shrugged. "Cobbio's conservative. You don't want to be smoking grass there...just a warning."

Erika didn't need any warnings. After last night, and now with Marzio's new connection to her, she was kicking herself all the more. Still unsure how to proceed, she glanced at the window and saw her jaundiced silhouette staring back. She wanted to punch it.

"But if you'd like to go out," Marzio continued, "you and I could go to Locarno or Lugano...we could be fairly anonymous there." He grinned again, and Erika felt her stomach sink. Under normal circumstances he could probably show her a good time. But *Jesus*, enough was enough—she'd pushed her luck too far.

"Erm..." she murmured. Should she say *I'm just too busy right now?* But he knew where she lived and might later show up unexpectedly. "It's just that..."

"Ah, you're seeing someone else..."

Perfect! Erika thought, though she heard the slight disappointment in Marzio's voice. With a decent dose of contriteness in her tone, she told him, "It's someone in Bellinzona." *And she wasn't even lying.*

Arriving in Cobbio, they parted ways with Marzio inviting Erika to visit the castle again when it reopened. Erika nodded and smiled obligingly. She walked up the hill to her house with a renewed sense of purpose. She would buckle down all day tomorrow with the translation. Then, tomorrow night, she would pay a visit to the man she was "seeing" in Bellinzona.

Well, she wouldn't exactly be *seeing* Dr. Betz...

The next evening, in preparation, Erika transferred her switchblade from her long grey overcoat to the outside pocket of her new black parka. Her roundtrip train ticket was already tucked in her jeans. She took one of the knitting needles she'd bought in Bellinzona and slipped it into the left inner breast pocket of the parka. Along with it she added the small flat-head screwdriver. Into the right pocket she placed the little flashlight. It was nine p.m. and her train to Bellinzona left at nine-thirty. She zipped up her parka, closed up the house, and started down the hill through the path between berms of snow.

Few people were on the train, the majority of late commuters traveling out of Bellinzona. Erika couldn't help patting the pockets she'd put to use. She thought she had everything she needed. She *hoped* she had everything. She could have brought her Instamatic camera; maybe she should have brought gloves—to avoid fingerprints, and all. Yet her fingerprints would already be on surfaces of Betz's office, since she was a patient. Plus nowhere in Switzerland, or Italy, were her fingerprints even on file.

The key now was getting through the entryway door of Betz's building. She didn't want to be caught tinkering with the lock right there on the public sidewalk. On her various visits she'd noticed that Betz's building also contained apartments. She would wait across the street in a dark doorway for someone to either go out or come in.

After half an hour of leaning against the door of a shadowed florist's shop she started stamping her feet. The parka she'd bought in Bellinzona, despite its label's claim of being *warm, lightweight, and breathable*, didn't cover her legs. She needed her long woolen coat for that, though it didn't have multiple pockets or a hood, like the one now shrouding Erika's head and part of her face. How much longer could she stand here in subfreezing temperatures?

And then she saw a man walking down the sidewalk towards her target. As he stopped and pulled his keys out, Erika crossed the street to join him. Under the streetlamp she projected a gleaming contrast of blond hair against a black fur-trimmed hood. She stopped next to the man, a vigorous-looking middle-aged sort, and smiled. "*Buona sera,*" she said, reaching into her pocket and jangling her own keys.

He smiled back and held up his hand. "I've got it." And with that Erika let him unlock the door and hold it open for her.

"I haven't seen you before," he said, letting the door thud shut, then following Erika to the elevator.

"I'm just visiting." She cast another smile at him, hoping he wouldn't ask, *visiting who*? But the Swiss weren't nosy. Though they did like to keep an orderly eye on things, they didn't ask strangers impertinent questions.

"*Bene,*" he said as they waited for the elevator.

Yes, *nice*. And it turned out to be even nicer when they entered and he pushed the button for the *third* floor, for she had no back-up plan if they had both exited on Betz's fourth floor.

"*Buona permanenza,*" he wished her as he left the elevator.

"*Grazie!*" She did hope to *enjoy her stay*, or at least make it *successful*.

The corridor light was on when Erika exited on the fourth floor. It might go off automatically, so she located a switch near Betz's door. She listened keenly for noise inside the office but heard only the static hum of the corridor light. She unzipped her parka. She was already starting to sweat and felt grateful not to have her heavy grey overcoat hanging on her like a duvet.

She took a breath, scanned the hall, then tried the door handle. Naturally it didn't budge—*no such beginner's luck*. Claudio had taught her how to pick a lock with his own equipment, had let her practice on his own door, but that had been the extent of her experience. She pulled out the screwdriver and inserted it in the keyhole. She turned it in the direction of a revolving key, but couldn't feel the lock's pressure point. She blew out a breath and pulled out the screwdriver. She tried again. This time the flat-head caught the lock and she pressed down, holding the tension. With her right hand she took out the 2.0 mm knitting needle and started the picking process, wiggling it in and raising it up and down above the screwdriver. She could hear one click, then another, but the screwdriver wouldn't yet act like a key. She drew another deep breath and looked around. Then the hallway light went out.

"Shit," she whispered. She pulled both tools out and stepped aside to feel along the wall. Wasn't the light switch closer to the door? *Damn it!* She removed her flashlight, shone it along the wall and punched the light back on. "Shit," she said again, stuffing the flashlight back into her parka, then stripping the jacket off and dropping it on the floor. She reinserted the screwdriver, caught the lock and held it down. Up and down she maneuvered her needle again. She was still sweating in her turtleneck and breathing heavily when at last she got all the pins up. Her screwdriver began to rotate, the lock clicked free, and Erika snatched up her jacket and entered the room.

Quietly she closed the door and extracted her flashlight again, its beam bobbing about the dark waiting room. Leaving her jacket with its lock-picking paraphernalia on a chair, she moved carefully towards the receptionist's desk and shot her beam of light over it. No difference from the day before yesterday. Behind it stood the same filing cabinets. She rounded the desk and checked its drawers—a stapler here, paperclips there, a couple of pens, another tape player. She thought of the one Betz had loaned her along with the meditation recording, which she hadn't yet listened to. Nothing wrong with his advice, fundamentally. But why did he only have a few patients? Did he also tell the others to meditate? Tell them they could control their dreadful dreams that way? Did he hypnotize them all?

Erika shrugged off the fixation and continued on to the filing cabinets. They all had small keyholes, and she inhaled heavily in preparation to pick their locks. But first she tried the drawers and was met by a hollow clang as each opened and slid smoothly on its runners. She began delving in. A pair of brass, owl-figured bookends in one. A small gong and striker in another, along with a couple of bracelets, one knotted, the other beaded. Incense and a few candles in a third. Another contained a bowl and short baton, reminiscent of a pestle and mortar, only made of metal. Also, a couple of Asian-looking masks. In one more, a sculpted tree whose leaves consisted of gemstones, probably fake ones, Erika surmised, as she shone her light closely on them. Three more drawers were empty, but the final one held a statue of a seated Buddha, his eyes closed in serene smile. *What a weird collection.* She found no files and came out of the receptionist area disappointed. She shot her flashlight around the waiting room again, poking its stream of light into every corner, then lowered the beam and proceeded towards the door to Betz's inner office. Naturally she tried the handle, but found it blocked. Why had Betz locked this door, with the outer door secured? He kept a different set of filing cabinets in his personal office, and they would have to contain his patient files. She sighed and rolled her shoulders. Then she flicked her fingers and went back to her jacket to fetch the screwdriver and knitting needle.

This time she was able to unlock the door in one go, with no need for light. She slid the tools into her back pocket, pulled her flashlight back out and slowly pushed the door open. Her beam moved across Betz's chair and desk, his bookshelves, the two vertical rows of filing cabinets. Would they be locked? She took a step inside. It was warmer in here, smelled stuffy. She crossed carefully to the desk and found the notebook Betz used during his sessions, plus his appointment book. She licked her lips in anticipation of getting her hands on them, finding just what kind of patients he treated; what he wrote about them— *what he wrote about her.*

She reached for the notebook, then leaped as if it were on fire. Something had moved behind her.

"Who are you? What are you doing here?" came a tense but controlled voice.

Erika spun around, pointing her flashlight at the voice, one she recognized. Her beam shone directly on Dr. Betz's white face and tousled hair. His eyes squinted back at the light and he raised a hand to block it. In those two seconds Erika also saw he was wearing a white undershirt and that a blanket covered half of him: *my God, he was sleeping here.*

Erika didn't wait for a third second to pass. She pivoted and streaked out of the office back into the waiting room. She was almost out the door to the corridor when she remembered her jacket. Dashing back in, she saw Betz's inner office light flash on. She grabbed the jacket off its chair and jogged out of the office towards the elevator. Its light indicated it had moved floors, so she yanked open the door to the stairs and trotted down them as fast as her meager light allowed. She pictured Betz calling the elevator and beating her to the ground floor, but her only choice was to continue racing down. On the next landing she punched on the stairwell light and threw her jacket and flashlight down the center of the stairwell. Then she began skipping every other stair, swinging round the landings, one hand gripping the banister, the other balancing against the wall.

The light was still on when she reached the ground floor. She gathered her jacket, swung it on and stowed the flashlight into her pocket. For a moment she stood breathless by the door to the foyer. Then she pushed the door open, prepared to meet an outraged Dr. Betz.

No such face appeared. She rushed out of the building, jogging down the street to the first crossroads. Turning the corner she glanced behind and finally slowed to a brisk stride. By the time she reached the train station she registered nothing but a thumping heart and a sweat-drenched body. She peeled off her jacket and went to check the timetable on the wall. There was a train leaving for Cobbio in half an hour.

She hated the idea of waiting. No telling who might show up in the station. Betz could have easily called the police, which was probably why he hadn't raced after her down to the foyer. She paced the brightly-lit station, looking for a secluded nook to wait in, and finally settled on the women's restroom, where she closed herself into a cubicle. Police weren't likely to check the ladies', since most burglars and home intruders were men. In the thick, still darkness of his inner office, Betz had said, "Who are you?" And when Erika turned around, she'd speared him with a blinding light. Not a very kind thing to do, but one that had likely made her unrecognizable.

With a sigh she sat down on the toilet seat and reached into her pocket for the offending flashlight. Though cracked it still worked when she tested it. Yet the minor satisfaction didn't last long. Slowly she reached back in her pocket—*no knife!* She checked her left pocket, knowing perfectly well she never kept the switchblade there. And indeed, all she felt were her keys. Frantically and irrationally she pawed through the entire jacket. *Christ!* The knife must have fallen out when she'd lunged back into Betz's dark outer office to grab her jacket before hightailing it down the hall. Why hadn't she zipped the pocket closed? Because ever since those life-threatening episodes in Turin last year, she'd wanted to keep quick access to the weapon.

Now the switchblade was irretrievably lost, just waiting to be found by Betz. *Shit, shit, shit!* After squeezing her eyes shut and rubbing her temples, she finally leaned back against the toilet tank and exhaled loudly. She checked her watch—fifteen minutes before her train left. She concentrated on her breathing—Betz style: first taking long, exaggerated breaths, then gradually lighter ones, while watching the flicking second hand on her watch. Ultimately she didn't hear her breathing at all. Ten more minutes had passed. Time to head for the platform.

Chapter 21

Voghera had settled for a two-star hotel near Bellinzona's train station. The first thing he asked after signing in was, "Do you get many Americans here?"

"No," the desk clerk had answered. "Once in a while in summer. But we're not like Lugano and Locarno, with their touristy lakes. Here we have our magnificent medieval castles. As soon as the snow melts a bit you should visit them, that is if you plan on staying awhile."

"As a matter of fact, I do."

Now, two days later, he'd canvassed Bellinzona, casually asking the same question about Americans in all the hotels and in various restaurants and cafés, only to receive more or less the same response. "Foreigners go to the lakes in summer and to ski spots in winter, mostly to Canton Grisons—Saint Moritz, and places like that."

As for waiters, Voghera wondered if they would recognize Erika's accent during their limited interactions with the American? Unlike the hotel personnel, they wouldn't ask to see a passport for simple transactions. She would sound foreign, but they might not be able to identify from where.

It was time to show her picture about, a more delicate procedure, and hope for the best. He had yet to visit any banks or the post office in Bellinzona during his inquiries. If Erika was here, she must frequent one or the other establishment to facilitate money operations—exchange lire for francs or receive money—from France, maybe, if Moretti could be believed about Giorgio Testa hiding there.

He had just finished a late lunch of risotto milanese. Time

152

for the main post office to open again. Before lunch he'd bought a post card showcasing Bellinzona's three castles, and had now finished writing a greeting to his eight-year-old daughter, Lina.

Dressed in wool slacks, a pullover sweater, tie and overcoat, he headed down the street to the main post office, entered, and stood second in one of the lines. Luckily it didn't take long to reach the window manned by a uniformed postal agent.

"*Buon giorno*," he said, and laid the postcard on counter.

"*Genova, Italia,*" the agent stated rhetorically.

"*Sì,*" Voghera confirmed. Little did the postman know that the only thing valid written on the card was Voghera's sincere greetings to his daughter:

"Beautiful winter scenery, sweetheart. Wish you were here with me.

Big hugs, Papà."

Apart from that, the card contained a phony surname—Lina *Minetto*—and a phony address in Italy. If only he could send a legitimate card to Lina; but Moretti was acquainted with Voghera's wife, and if he was snooping around he might somehow come across the card and its Bellinzona postmark. So, Voghera would have to make do with virtual wishes, which when put into words at least warmed him.

He paid for the postage, the postman stamped the card, then dropped it into a tray.

Voghera glanced behind him—three people in line—then turned back to the postman. "One other thing," he said. "I'm in Bellinzona to look into a missing-persons case." He extracted a business card, this particular one presenting him as *Loris Minetto, Investigatore Privato, Genova, Italia.*

The postman frowned at it, but before he could say anything, Voghera placed a photo on the counter. "Erika Rivoli. She's American, and I've been employed by her parents in the U.S. to locate her."

The postman gave the photo a decent glance then slid it back to Voghera. "Sorry, but I've never seen her. I can't speak for the others here, but I know we're not authorized to take time out for this kind of business. You can always make an appointment with our supervisor, though."

Voghera had expected just this kind of reception, yet he'd had amazing luck in the past in situations like this and always deemed the approach worth a try.

He thanked the postman and bid him *arrivederci*. He would not be going to the man's supervisor. The chance that *he*, screened off in a lofty office somewhere in the building, might have seen and remembered Erika was less likely than his noticing a huge house spider crossing his path.

Voghera moved on to try his ruse in a bank, exchanging a bit of currency but receiving the same unsurprising invitation to speak with a supervisor about missing persons. He visited various shops, showing Erika's photo to clerks, this time with a different story. Agitatedly, he claimed: "My girlfriend and I are here on vacation, but we've got separated. You didn't happen to see her?"

He knew the risks: unlike the tightly regulated and regimented bank and postal employees, any given store clerk, recognizing the photo proffered by Voghera, could eventually alert Erika. Still, he had to step up the search.

And the operation wasn't going well. In two stores the clerks, both women, handed back Erika's photo, their brows arched dubiously.

"And where did you say you're from?" asked one.

He *hadn't* said, but nonetheless offered: "Genoa."

She shook her head. "Sorry, I wish you luck." Voghera was certain she didn't wish him any such thing; probably the opposite, figuring he was out to coerce his "girlfriend" to return to him. As he left that particular shop, one filled with an array of aromatic cheeses, he chuckled darkly. *Yes, to coerce her.*

As dusk was now purpling the Alpine valley, Voghera decided to return to his hotel. But first, one more stab. He tried another café on the main drag, this time referring to Erika as his sister. "I can't believe we got separated," he complained, ordering a well-deserved caffè grappa. "We're just spending the night before heading east to ski..."

The barman handed Erika's photo back, shaking his head sympathetically. And now yet another café to which Voghera wouldn't be able to return. This evening, at the restaurant where he planned to dine, he would go back to simply asking, "Have you seen many Americans around?" Otherwise he would run out of places to eat and drink.

Back in his room, he turned up the heat, stripped down to his undershirt and boxers, and stretched out on the bed in what he himself could only describe as a brooding mood. There was no way he could question every merchant in the city of Bellinzona without eliciting gossip. So tomorrow he would drive to Locarno, the nearest city to Bellinzona, and recommence the process there. At least he'd have a change of scene. A nice drive, a lake to look at.

Writing to little Lina had first filled him with an almost adrenaline-filled joy. Now, thinking about her, a familiar aching helplessness returned to afflict him. His wife had moved away just over a year ago to Italy's northeastern, German-speaking South Tyrol, where she remained cloistered with Lina even at holidays. He could understand her mounting frustration with his work, which he would only describe as "special police services." Also his drinking. But not the isolating of their daughter. He had always been a decent father, and the only reason he'd avoided taking his wife to court to contest her exclusive custody of Lina was the risk of exposing his real job.

His wife was utterly irrational at times. He recalled their last explosive row—over the director Roman Polanski, of all things. She'd gone on a rant about the film director's escape from the U.S, fleeing charges related to unlawful sex with a minor. *A thirteen-year-old girl*, she'd repeated over and over again. Naturally, Voghera found that aspect of Polanski's personal life distasteful, but he'd loved the film *Chinatown*, so far his all-time favorite—the detective-noir plot, the actors, the 1930s California setting. He'd pointed out the film's critical acclaim and the awards it had won, and that a person could disapprove of a director's personal life but still appreciate his work. Only to have his wife pounce back with, "Don't you remember that John Huston's character sexually abuses his daughter?"

"Yes, but Polanski's portraying him as a villain!"

"Well, Polanski's still a pedophile, and *you* think it's just fine to help make him even richer!" Voghera had ignored the term *pedophile* (perhaps Polanski was more of a *Lolita* man) and had shaken his head.

"Typical of you to not take a stance," she'd hurled. "Nothing's ever black or white with you!"

"*Chinatown* is just a *movie. You're* the one who's nuts about movies," Voghera objected. He couldn't resist reminding her that she'd insisted on naming their daughter Melina, after the Greek actress Melina Mercouri. He'd grudgingly agreed to what he'd considered a silly idea but insisted on calling the little girl Lina.

"Well," his wife shot back, "at least Melina Mercouri is a dignified figure. She fought for democracy in her country and is now minister of culture!"

"Who cares? I'm talking about art. Would you rage like this against a fantastic painter because of his personal affairs? Or a great musician?"

"Yes, if he's a pervert like Polanski!"

Voghera had thrown his hands up. "Jesus, Bruna, you like that druggie centerfold singer Patty Pravo, who doesn't even have a decent voice! There's no having a rational conversation with you."

"*Really?* And what if the young girl Polanski molested had been *our* daughter? You'd still be standing in kilometric lines to get into his movies!"

Voghera had looked at her as if she were crazy. "But she's *not* our daughter, is she?"

He'd labeled her *obscurantist*, and that had done it. She'd moved out soon afterwards, right before Christmas of 1977.

Replaying the scene in his mind merely tanked Voghera's mood further. *Of course he'd kill Roman Polanski if the man ever laid a hand on Lina.* But how likely a scenario was that? He would have liked to reason with his wife that the movie world was its own milieu, like that of all the arts, full of contradictions and paradoxes which couldn't always be resolved. But he hadn't done. He knew she would link the statement to his own murky work.

And now Erika had turned *obscurantist* as well.

Early the next morning Voghera motored off to Locarno, flanked by greying snow berms on either side of the road—how quickly auto exhaust morphed their pristineness, like life's transmutations in general.

Locarno lay a tad closer to Bellinzona (a twenty-five-minute drive) than did Lugano, and after his initial visit to Lugano and his raucous encounter with reporters and fans of the singer Mina, he figured the city could wait.

Yet he wouldn't easily forget feasting his eyes on Mina in person. Her blazing smile, her long, gogo-booted legs, the talent and vitality pouring from her—the sexual current coursing beneath his belt at the mere thought of her.

If his wife had been there, she would have compared him to a salivating teenager. But he could defend his adoration of Mina. She was arguably the best Italian singer out there, with a sizzling voice range that left other voices shaking in her wake. And if Voghera's humble opinion of her artistry weren't enough, the venerable Louis Armstrong had dubbed Mina "the greatest white singer in the world."

And sexy as hell too! Again he pictured her emerging like a goddess from the cinema in Lugano. *And she was as tall as*

Erika, he repeated to himself.

In Locarno, Voghera employed similar ruses to those he had used in Bellinzona. At the hotels: *Any Americans here at the lake this time of year?* Poking his head into restaurants, cafés and shops while presenting his PI card: *Have you seen this missing person?* Or, alternatively: *I can't find my sister!* He even bought another postcard, this one spotlighting Locarno's palm-tree studded lake, and addressed it to a fake friend in Florence. In the post office he received the same shake of the head and referral to a supervisor. If in stopping for lunch he hadn't consumed the best ossobuco he'd ever tasted, he would have written the jaunt off as a total bust.

And then there remained the myriad villages that peppered the area around Italian Switzerland's three main cities. For the next two days Voghera combed the villages and hamlets between Locarno and Bellinzona: Gudo, Cugnasco, Gordola, Minusio; then back through Cadenazzo, Camorino, and Pianezza. One day he spent a good part of the afternoon in Ascona, a town five thousand strong, which shared a lakefront location near Locarno. But still nothing.

There were additional villages south of Locarno to investigate and villages north and south of Bellinzona. But how would Erika have arranged to hole-up in any of these two-horse, ice-encased places? Once more he spread out his map: south of Bellinzona black dots represented Giubiasco, Rivera, Toricella, Manno. North of Bellinzona: Arbedo-Castione, Gnosca, Cobbio, Preonzo. Or he could return to Lugano...

He tapped the map with insistent fingers, willing some kind of inspiration...

Chapter 22

Three days straight of sunshine in Geneva. The lake's emblematic Jet d'Eau sparkled with rainbow-like prisms of light. Giorgio sat on a bench watching it: today it resembled a great sloping flag, maybe an ethereal version of the Italian flag, with its shooting smears of red and green. Or an Italian flag on the wane, its fabric shredding, its colors blurred and fading.

He still felt tired from his flight through three countries in as many days, even though a week had now passed since the fiasco with Silvana in the Milan train station, the event that had triggered the race. Part of his fatigue could surely be put down to lethargy—little to do but languish here until Erika finished the translation. A lassitude that was hard to contest— oh, how those L-words fit his mood right now! And then there was the accompanying sense of despondency—*letdown*, to keep the alliteration rolling. He couldn't blame Régine for this aspect of his mood since he'd been the one to set his sights high. It was understandable that she wanted to keep things status quo, considering the stakes of their mutual enterprise. Yet somehow he'd felt there was more to her assertion—a slight stiffness on her part when they'd said good night before she left to return to Bern. Little to do with words, but rather a greater distance she'd put between them, even as they'd exchanged normal, amicable kisses on the cheeks. Maybe she was slightly fearful. If so, was she afraid of intimacy, or was he just projecting his own homegrown fear of not being pleasing to the opposite sex? Their relations would remain a muddle, in any case, until their mission was accomplished. In the meantime, he wondered how long he would go on experiencing what he could only describe as a strong case of both physical and emotional indigestion.

His gaze still pinned to the giant shooting fountain, he thought of when he and Régine sat together on this very bench. Then, he hadn't wanted to venture far or for long from the hotel, with DIGOS digging around the area. Yet maintaining strict, enduring vigilance grew harder by the hour now—the suffocating confinement of his hotel room, the near-same meals day after day in a restaurant that provided at best a paltry change of scene. He wondered if Erika was holding up any better in her mountain refuge. Their communication now ran exclusively through Régine, who'd said to him, "The girl has the resources of youth—I feel energized just speaking to her."

Well, Giorgio was ten years older than Erika and hardly in youthful shape, though not just because of his age. He needed to lose weight. *Eat less and exercise more*—yeah, he knew the ball-breaking refrain. Living the life of a recluse in Geneva was not helping. He'd just finished reading his novel *Catch 22*, and couldn't help relating to the hapless Yossarian. He barked a mocking laugh and jerked himself up off the bench. If he was going to stay outside any longer, exposed to God knew which pissant predator, he would at least get some decent walking in.

He backtracked along the lake walk to a bridge and crossed over the lake's narrow inlet of water. The Parc des Bastions was just on the other side, and for exercise Giorgio intended to walk the circuit of it. He slowed only briefly to observe the chess players. He'd seen giant chess played before in Bern, but this park hosted multiple "boards," checkered imprints in the concrete. He strolled by men in their winter coats, watching them lift chess pieces as tall as their knees and thighs and haul them about the board. Some of the younger men clip-clopped around in clogs which made the scene truly smack of Switzerland. He would have liked to take a turn on a board himself but limited himself to watching the end of just one game, when the loser, acknowledging checkmate, knocked his hip-high white king down onto its square.

Giorgio moved on across the grass and passed next to Reformation Wall, which honored John Calvin and Europe's principal Calvinist reformers—four gaunt figures sculpted in white stone, dour in their expressions and long patriarchal beards, confident of their foremost status among God's Elect. All held bibles, though one figure, his shoulders slightly edging beyond the others—probably Calvin—held his like a fig leaf in front of his pleated pastoral robes. Giorgio gave a wry chuckle, then realizing he wasn't getting any exercise quickened his pace, striding briskly back towards the bridge.

Crossing to the other side of the lake again, he made his way through the watch and clock quarter he'd already visited with Régine. He'd like to buy both her and Erika something nice for all their trouble on his account. Although watches and jewelry seemed rather personal, he would keep the idea in mind.

It was hard to keep Régine out of his thoughts, period, especially since they hadn't spoken since she'd left Geneva. He could call her this evening, their having established that he would phone regularly from a payphone; there was the status of Erika's translation to check on, with Erika reporting her progress to Régine and checking for updates from Giorgio's side. Yes, absolutely, he would call Régine after dinner.

The anticipation pumped him full of drive, and he struck out in energetic strides, taking a long roundabout way back to the hotel. *Exercise—that was the remedy!*

He arrived panting and sweating despite the brittle, skin-burning cold. Nevertheless, he would have to continue this walking regimen every day if he wanted to lose weight. In almost two months of exile, the only labor he'd put forth was racing from one city to the next, and even those exploits, though heart-pounding, could be technically defined as sedentary. As he passed the restaurant to the elevators, he vowed to order only a salad for dinner.

In his room he stretched out on his wide bed and plucked

up the new novel he'd bought the day before, Camus' *The Stranger*. The French was smooth and unadorned, and he liked to practice reading the language. He shifted about to get comfortable but still felt like he'd just been competing in a Formula 1 footrace. And now instead of a hiccupping in his chest, it felt like a fish was flopping inside him. He rolled over and left the bed to pour himself two fingers of the cognac he kept on the dresser. Slowly, the fish began to settle down. *Ah, better.*

That evening he kept to his vow and ordered a large *salade mixte* for dinner: lettuce, kernels of corn, and strips of red bell pepper. He did allow himself the accompaniment of three small slices of French baguette and a quarter carafe of red wine, but still he felt hunger's claws as he left the hotel restaurant. At least he was on his way to call Régine.

It was nine o'clock; she was home as he'd hoped, and answered on the second ring.

"Calling from a phone booth?" she said after they'd exchanged greetings.

"As always." Did he detect an awkwardness in her tone? A defensive residue lingering from his timid attempt at an advance during their last dinner together? He resisted jumping to conclusions.

"Good," said Régine. "But you're going to freeze to death if we talk long, so let me tell you straight away that Erika called yesterday—she's finished the translation!"

No mistaking this tone. "That's fabulous!" he joined in.

"Now, we all three need to meet somewhere and firm up plans. I'd thought of Montreux maybe, then it occurred to me we could meet closer to where Erika's staying. Locarno, perhaps. Would you mind traveling to Canton Ticino?"

"Not at all. Sounds perfect. So she'll bring the English manuscript and its copy, and of course my Italian copy."

"That's right."

"And then we'll talk about the logistics of getting the two

English copies to London."

"Yes…"

"We'll ask her if she'd mind taking one copy, while I take the other one." He heard what sounded like an intake of air over the line. "But naturally," he quickly added, "we'll assure her that it's fine if she doesn't feel comfortable with that idea, and we'll find another way." It sounded vague at this point. *Flou*, as they said in French—blurry, flimsy. But it would get sorted out, even if only he traveled to London.

"Yes," agreed Régine again, more solidly this time.

"Well then, you and Erika can work out the timing of our meeting. I can be in Locarno on any day that works for you two."

"Good. I'll look into where we can meet."

They agreed that Giorgio would call back three evenings hence, then rang off. Outside the phonebooth Giorgio welcomed the bulleting cold air which had the temporary effect of puncturing and leveling his spiking moods: elation over the completion of the translation—before long it would land in the hands of Ian Wescott of *The Guardian*—and the ongoing sense of foreboding about his chances with Régine. As for the former, at least he knew where things stood.

Locarno. Back in his room he located the Italian Swiss city on his map. Régine was right to take Erika's isolated situation into consideration. Meeting in Locarno would be easier for her. From Cobbio she could take the train to Bellinzona, and from there it looked like a direct shot to Locarno—it wouldn't take her long. He and Régine would no doubt have to change trains somewhere. Not that he was complaining; tomorrow he would walk over to the train station and find out the best route. Considering DIGOS could have unearthed his license plate number, he would not be taking his car.

The next day Giorgio stood scanning the glass-encased wall of trains scheduled to and from Geneva. He would have to spend almost the entire day journeying to Locarno. The arc of the route's rail trajectory stretched to Zurich in the far north, then south again to Locarno which lay roughly at the same latitude as Geneva; with all the train changes involved, to call the route "roundabout" seemed a gross understatement; a fool's way to go, considering there was an alternate route: an approximately three-hour journey, heading due east. Only one caveat: the rails crossed through a northern chunk of Italian territory which, according to his map, jutted like a bull's horn between French and Italian Switzerland. Granted, there would be only one stop, a change of trains in the Italian town of Domodossola, where normally the transfer would amount to a pleasant stroll. But when was the last time things had gone *normally* for Giorgio Testa? *Domodossola*: the Italian border checkpoint, meaning that before his train could chug on out to cross back across the border, a uniformed guard would climb on board, spouting: "Ladies and gentleman, passports, please!" Just recalling the Milan train station and Silvana, who could have been a Mata Hari pointing DIGOS onto his trail, made him clutch his head.

Cazzo, this would take some deliberating.

Chapter 23

Hooray! She had finished the translation and would meet Régine and Giorgio in Locarno, the day after tomorrow. But between now and then, she had an appointment with Betz—*tomorrow*, Erika grumbled.

The thought made her cringe: getting caught in his office, blinding him with her flashlight, then losing her switchblade—what a mess! She thought of calling Betz and canceling her session...telling him she would get back to him eventually to reschedule. But even that idea made her shift uncomfortably in her kitchen chair. Right now she didn't want to talk to him at all. She flicked her fingers and scooted her chair away from the kitchen stove, whose heat suddenly seemed cloying and oppressive. And if she did call Betz, what might he think of her canceling right after his office had been broken into?

She shook off the thought and got up to gaze out the window. Dusk had made great strides in darkening the sky since she'd looked out only a few minutes ago. How different things were in every way now: the completion of the translation, the meeting in Locarno about its delivery to London—two couriers would be employed, each with their own copy. Learning of Giorgio's close-call with DIGOS in France, Erika thought it best he not be one of the couriers. Naturally, Giorgio might insist otherwise, but there still remained a second courier to choose.

She'd become attached to her translation. It was the most important creation she had ever actualized—a work that reflected the words and style of Giorgio's original composition, with her own craft involved in translating idioms, reworking word order, taking liberties she thought best served the greater message of exposing DIGOS' crime. Giorgio might feel an umbilical cord connecting him to his Italian original, but *Auschwitz Collaborator Murdered* was Erika's child. She wanted to spirit one of the copies to London herself. In fact, she would only take one copy to the meeting in Locarno and inform Régine and Giorgio that she would be the courier of the other. As far as she knew, DIGOS and Claudio Voghera knew nothing of her whereabouts. If she didn't have to wait for Régine to explain arrangements with Ian Wescott of *The Guardian*, she'd be tempted to take the train north tomorrow—ditching Betz while she was at it. But she still had to get one copy to Giorgio and Régine.

She couldn't stop her thoughts from circling back to Betz. She had discovered nothing important in his office, only bric-a-brac related to meditation, or metaphysics, or who knew what? She certainly didn't. Then again, she hadn't had the chance to crack open the notebook in his inner office or check the file cabinets there. And why was he sleeping on the sofa? Working late? The whole weird scene made her want to grasp her head in her hands to try to squeeze some sense out of the situation. She'd infiltrated his office to learn more about his strange practice, to read his notes about her and discover who else he might be analyzing for free. She'd dared to pick a lock and still felt a rush of exhilaration when thinking about the act and the fact that no one had apprehended her. Hypervigilance regarding her greater situation also affected her drive to get to the bottom of anything she deemed suspicious—she knew that. On the other hand, she'd also let down her guard and allowed a party in her house. She would like to blame Betz for that, for prodding her into social activity and making her feel good about reporting her social success, though he could hardly be aware of the risk she'd taken.

She walked over to the kitchen credenza, on which sat the tape player and meditation cassette Betz had lent her, both still wrapped in their plastic bag. She didn't want to listen to Betz's voice. Just the thought inflicted hot embarrassment—at the arousal he'd caused in her, at falling short of her goal in his office, at his pushing more meditation and even hypnotism. She couldn't help bridling against some type of control he might be exerting over her. The breathing and walking practices had served their purpose during those long snowbound days; but that was then. As for his claims about the power to control dreams—well, that just sounded fantastical, even smacked of charlatanry.

Then again, she could she be overreacting. She sat back down next to the stove. When might hypervigilance hijack sensible suspicion and skepticism? Apart from the Betz break-in, Erika could think of an instance that had occurred the very evening she'd left the doctor's office to shop for burglary tools. It was dark, she was still reeling from her session with Betz, and she'd seen a man who looked vaguely like Claudio Voghera exit a café and turn into an adjacent side street. She'd blinked and squinted, quickened her pace to a trot, then reaching the corner, peered round and stared; there was no one in the narrow black strip of a street, nothing but shops whose neon lights seemed to wink at her alarm. She'd waited a good fifteen minutes at the entrance to the street, finally seeing sundry people leaving the shops, but no Claudio look-a-like. So she returned to the café from which he'd exited, only to learn from the barman that the man with shaggy dark hair, mustache and black parka, was a regular. "Been coming here for ten years."

Had it been daytime, would she have mistaken the man for Claudio? And who said Claudio might not try to disguise himself? A couple of days before that, she thought she'd spied his black Opal Ascona cruising down the street near Bellinzona's post office. She'd spotted its right rear side, grubby with winter weather, but traffic had impeded her view of the driver and the car's license plate. Her suspicion had only mounted with the observation that *only a foreigner would drive around Switzerland with a dirty car*. But could that instead have been *paranoia?* Frankly, with her manuscript completed and clamoring to be smuggled to London, and stalkers after Giorgio, she wasn't sure she could tell.

With that, she retrieved her épée from the broom closet and got to work on it. The blade was sharpening up nicely; the last time she'd pressed her thumb against its tip, more than a trickle of blood had spouted forth. Whetting, rasping, honing each side of the blade so that it could slash as well as skewer—was this intimate project paranoia-driven? She didn't think so, not when the act itself generated great calm and concentration in her, something strangely akin to those breathing exercises. No, it was not paranoia. Stalkers *were* out there and one of them could be after her, especially Claudio who had multiple motivations to find her, not least because in his mind she had betrayed him.

With her switchblade lost, she now possessed just two weapons—her stiletto and this épée, whose Spanish grip felt so comfortable, natural, and secure in her hand, as if it were an extension of her body. A burst of energy shot through her each time she gripped it. Hardly a practical weapon, not one you could waltz about town with—for that the stiletto she'd bought last year in Turin would have to suffice. It opened slowly compared to the switchblade; she had to pull the stiletto's blade manually into a locked position, unless she extracted the blade just enough to then flick it straight with a whip of the wrist. She would now have to start practicing that again.

Yet would she actually be capable of stabbing someone? Not just in the arm or leg, but in the torso in order to definitively stop that person from harming her? The question had visited her before, and her only response was to recall the incident last year when she'd had to defend herself against a fascist terrorist. Her attacker had wielded a pistol but Erika had managed to maneuver her switchblade against the assailant's neck, pressing its blade ever so lightly as to draw a droplet of blood, all in hopes of forcing her attacker to back down. With the appearance of witnesses it had worked, and yet that incident remained closest to testing her ability to kill willfully. Each time she thought of it, she concluded that if need be she would have to plunge knife into neck. So why did she continue to question herself? As she held her épée at full extension, she imagined it might be easier to kill from a distance.

Time to tamp down her thoughts. She'd pulled on her gloves, ready to resume filing her blade, when the doorbell rang. Automatically she scanned the kitchen for traces of her translating endeavor, but naturally the file folders were stowed in a drawer in the credenza. So, who could be at the door? Adriana again?

No: looking out the window, she saw Maeve Hartigan examining the house, arms hugging herself in her heavy woolen coat.

Erika snatched the épée from the floor and returned it and her gloves to the closet, before heading for the door.

"You don't have a phone, so I took the liberty of dropping in," the Irish woman said as Erika welcomed her inside.

"I've got no central heating either," Erika reminded her, "so I hope you don't mind us sitting in the kitchen next to the stove."

"You poor thing," Maeve sympathized, as Erika ushered her through and hung up her coat. "But I'm glad to see you've made a cozy setting for yourself. I have to admit I've been curious about your living conditions ever since you came for dinner."

"They're not so bad," Erika said, as she and Maeve settled in front of the stove. "By now I'm used to the house, it's completely furnished—it's home." And the sentiment felt close to authentic. Despite the snow and cold, regardless of her bouts of loneliness, this *was* her place, she was in charge, and Maeve was here, offering distraction from her tangled thoughts. "How about a cup of tea?"

"Is the pope Catholic?

Erika grinned.

"I think that's one of your American expressions," Maeve added. "But did you know, the Irish drink more tea per capita than any country in the world?" Maeve Hartigan hadn't stopped by merely for a cup of tea and a peek at Erika's digs. "Isn't it wonderful to have a reprieve from the snow!"

Erika agreed wholeheartedly.

"In fact, Brendan and I are finally able to plan our ski and hiking journey. To Canton Grisons. Have you been there?"

Erika hadn't. "But it sounds great. Every place I've seen so far in Switzerland is stunning."

"Well," Maeve said, "we know you haven't been able to get around much, and we thought you might like to join us on our trip. We know you don't ski, but you said you like to hike, and that's most of what I'll be doing—Brendan's the ski maniac. We're booking a reservation for five days in a resort, and we thought we could just as easily reserve two rooms as one—our treat."

Erika's face must have reflected astonishment, for Maeve said, "I know it's short notice, but Brendan and I have managed to snatch this opportunity, and we are very fond of you. Our reservation starts three days from now."

Three days from now. Yes, it could have been a marvelous opportunity, if it weren't for the timing. Three days from now she hoped to be on her way to London!

She reflected an instant, then said, "Nothing sounds more fun, and thanks a million for the invitation, Maeve. But it just so happens I'll be going away myself in a couple of days. A getaway abroad with friends."

Maeve congratulated her. "I'm sure you'll have a grand time. We'll try to invite you another time. A *raincheck*— another of your American sayings."

Erika agreed wholeheartedly.

They sipped tea and talked more of Switzerland's ubiquitous outdoor offerings. "And don't forget to take that hike up to Cobbio's monastery," Maeve said. "In the midst of all those nuns, the view is truly *heavenly*!"

Chapter 24

Over the last couple of days, the sky had gradually recast itself from a high arching blue to an ever-lowering white dome. Dry weather and roads had aided Claudio Voghera in day trips, where he crisscrossed Ticino from its lower, palm-studded lake elevations to its eagle's-nest villages higher in the mountains. He had just returned to Bellinzona from making a sweep of Ticino's largest city, Lugano, following his usual protocol and netting the same negative results: no Erika. Not even another Mina sighting. Having fairly covered (how could you sweep a city one hundred percent?) the cities of Ticino he would now have to turn his magnifying glass on the rest of the villages he'd listed—and they were many, spilling over the region like so many paper dots emptied from a hole punch.

Sitting at the desk of his Bellinzona hotel room, he gazed out the window at the cream-heavy sky. He should've managed to get his car washed while it was sunny; its grime was really getting to him. But now, according to weather reports, the forces of snow were once more gathering. No surprise with the rising humidity and dropping temperatures. Snow would make sifting through mountain villages on winding one-lane roads more challenging. Still, the villages offered hope. Erika could not make herself anonymous in a village. At any café, or shop, he need only toss out: "See many Americans around?" And if Erika had indeed burrowed somewhere in a village, the response would likely be: "Well, strangely, we have seen *one!*"

That's how he must view this needle-in-a haystack situation; no choice but to persevere in what had now become the principal purpose of his existence. An obsession, maybe, although a cool, keen one, sharpened further each time he thought of Erika playing Bonnie to Giorgio Testa's Clyde.

Going on four o'clock: he turned on his lamp. He would wait another hour, then set out for the café (one in which he hadn't used any of his missing-person ruses) for a Negroni before dinner. So far today, he'd only consumed a couple of glasses of wine with lunch—no shots in the cafés he'd canvassed in Lugano. He'd also succeeded in ignoring the flask of whiskey he kept in his car's glovebox. He inclined his head back to his map.

Five o'clock: completely black outside. Time for his reward. His shoes cracked the afternoon slush which had now stubbornly refrozen. The Swiss were expert at keeping streets and sidewalks clean enough to eat from, but meltwater could appear from anywhere and then freeze before maintenance crews managed to pounce on it with their brooms. The snow had made a partial retreat during these last sunny days, but even so, the law of winter in these parts could not be bent. Before the next barrage of blinding white, he would have to speed up his hunt. Already he could feel a change in the cold; slithering damp was now thickening into a solid, constricting, embrace. He buttoned his overcoat up to his Adam's apple and fractured another frozen puddle of water as he crossed the street.

Voghera appreciated the mood of this café: candlelit tables, wood paneling, low lounge music, and the presence of a woman he'd observed three times now in as many days. When he'd first spotted her from behind, as she entered in a heavy grey overcoat, his glass had frozen in front of his lips, his eyes stretching in their sockets—*Erika*. Then, she'd removed her coat and taken a seat, and disappointment had deflated him—she was *not* Erika. This woman was older, though she shared Erika's leggy height and short fluffy blond hair. She was fairer too, her eyebrows a white-blond that matched her cool looks. Voghera watched her, fascinated and aroused, he had to admit, by her frosty air.

Tonight she sat at one of the wood tables near the bar, sipping her usual Martini & Rossi red vermouth. But this time only one table stood between them.

He drained the last of his Negroni, then called the waiter to order another, having splurged like this each evening since first noticing the woman. He'd always waited for her to leave first, and this time had removed the non-prescriptive, black-framed glasses he'd procured in Turin as a partial disguise. He started eying her overtly. She looked up from examining her address book and blew out a stream of smoke from her cigarette. The gaze she returned was ice-blue. He responded with the attractive smile he knew to be his by nature. She rested her cigarette in its ashtray without looking away. Voghera finally said, in all honesty, "*Scusi*, but you remind me of someone."

He knew the line to be lame, however keeping close to the truth worked best in any strategy. And so it seemed to play out here, for she laughed lightly, then said, "Hopefully it's someone you like."

A slight gap separated her front teeth, the kind he found attractive in an actress whose name he couldn't recall. He wanted to keep her talking, this chilly, shivery kind of woman Alfred Hitchcock chose for his movies, the icy type that ultimately cracked under the seductive power of a dark-haired man.

Let time leisurely unspool. "Yes," he answered. "You could say it's someone I've liked."

The woman smiled and nodded. Then she lowered her gaze as if contemplating the distance between their two tables. Voghera didn't waste another second. He backed his chair smoothly away from his table and picked up his glass. "May I join you?"

No words, again, just another placid smile and nod.

This time he went back to presenting himself as David from Milan, here on business (so convenient for men to be *anywhere* on business). She was Carmen from Lugano, and she intoned: "Here to take a break from my husband."

Even Voghera, who considered himself basically unflappable by nature and profession, tripped over this. He emitted a half-stifled chuckle and took a swig of Negroni. "I like your honesty," he finally said with a meaningful look. As he'd noted before, she wore no wedding band.

"My husband's back in Lugano, there's no kids, so I'm here to sample a bit of Bellinzona."

"Good choice." *Excellent choice*.

"And you...you've come to this café for the last three evenings..."

Voghera smiled to himself. He hadn't been the only one *observing*. He said, "I'm on the road, don't like having dinner too early, and I haven't found a better place for an aperitif—or to meet someone." He raised his glass and let it hang in the air, confident in his desire, his will. His senses managed to discard the cigarette smoke in the room and capture her subtle, rose-scented perfume. He inhaled it deeply, and after three steady heartbeats Carmen also lifted her glass. Voghera kept his tumbler suspended, calmly waiting, until after another second she closed the gap with a welcoming "clink."

He tipped his head at her near-empty glass. "Another Martini *rosso*?"

They chose his hotel, the one closest to the café.

"Whoops," said Carmen, as in the flurry to get their clothes off, Voghera's spectacles hit the parquet floor.

"Never mind, cheap reading glasses," he murmured hotly into her neck, before nudging them aside with his foot.

When they finished undressing, Voghera stripped the eiderdown off the bed and folded Carmen and himself onto the sheet covering the mattress. Her skin was moon-white and cool to the touch, and he began to caress warmth into it, massaging her breasts, her belly, his fingers producing friction between her legs. She gasped and wrapped a leg around him, then agile as a gymnast, flipped onto his torso, and began to rub her groin against his.

Heart thudding, he could have taken her right then, but first he would make her gasp again. He rolled her back over, kissed her hard, then let his lips slide lower and lower, to her breasts, down her belly, between her legs. Then he heard it again—that desirous intake of breath, that soft cry of satisfaction.

"Don't stop," she whispered loudly, her hips heaving.

Voghera peered up. "You don't get this often..."

"My husband's hopeless."

Pleased, Voghera resumed his deep kissing.

"Madonna sovietica!" she exclaimed, shuddering.

Voghera slowed to a stop. What was that? Madonna *sovietica*? He'd heard that oath uttered nowhere apart from one miniscule village near Turin. At that time the expletive had amused him greatly—*Soviet Virgin Mary,* a spin on the Cold War and Italy's current communist-fascist violence. But where had Carmen picked it up?

"What's wrong?" She sounded annoyed.

He didn't answer straight away. Slowly he inched up her body. "You know, you're very funny," he said. "I haven't heard *Madonna sovietica* for a long time."

"What?" Then with the merest hint of hesitation, "You haven't heard that here?"

"No," he said with a chuckle. He was concentrating on her accent. It sounded local, but the Ticino accent was practically identical to the one just over the border in Italy.

"The only place I've heard that is near Turin." His hand was grazing her pubic hair, which in the light seeping from the room's entryway looked as stark-white as her skin.

"Well, I don't remember where I first heard it," Carmen said, ruffling his hair as if hinting: *time to get back to sex.* "It might've been a time when I was in Italy..."

That could be true, Voghera thought as she started stroking him. But his mood had changed, his radar pulsing and bleeping, telegraphing the possibility that Carmen could be

Moretti's spy sent to keep an eye on him. If so, he told himself, she was doing just that—an eye and more. He let her stroke him to near climax, then he kissed her and said, "Shall we?"

They rolled again and as he entered her and began thrusting, her legs encircled him. He straightened his arms and thrust harder, staring down as if trying to extract more of her story. Harder and harder he ploughed until she said, "David, you're ramming me like a train!"

He spent himself, then rolled onto his back, taking deep breaths. "Sorry," he said, "but you're so attractive."

A faint, dry laugh from her. "Well, I guess that could be a compliment."

"It is."

For a long moment they lay quiet, he resting, feeling his breathing calm, gathering his thoughts.

Then she spoke, asking him how long he planned to stay in Bellinzona.

"Not sure. It depends on how the rest of my meetings go." He didn't ask the same of her. Although she might be a mere adventurous housewife, it didn't pay to hang around any stranger too long.

They returned to silence. Voghera visualized what he'd left out on the desk: his map of Ticino. Normally a common tourist item, in his case littered with check marks. He recalled folding it shut before leaving the room. His passport remained in his inner overcoat pocket, which hung over the desk's chair along with bits and pieces of his and Carmen's clothing. Their more intimate wear formed a puddle on the floor.

He heard a languorous yawn. "I'm going to use the bathroom." He was going to say *turn your light on*, but she had already sprung out of bed and was negotiating the room by the anemic light from the entryway.

Once he heard the bathroom door close he turned his bedside light on and got up. On the desk he'd also left a sheet of paper with detailed directions to a remote village. He turned it over so its flipside again presented brochure images of

Bellinzona's castles and countryside. Then he started to get dressed.

He was standing in trousers and open shirt when Carmen emerged naked from the bathroom. "Oh," she said, looking surprised. "You're already dressed."

"I'm hungry. Why don't you let me take you to dinner?"

Nonchalantly she walked past him towards her abandoned clothes. As Voghera waited for an answer he buttoned his shirt, tucked it in and pulled on his sweater. He waited until Carmen finished dressing and they had only their coats to don, before returning to the subject. "There's a decent restaurant not far from here, or maybe you know of someplace..."

Carmen took her time answering, slowly sliding her coat off the chair. While he was helping her on with it, she finally said, "I think I'll pass." Her gaze lingered on the desk. "But," she added, picking up the tourist brochure, "you should see the castles, if you haven't already, at least the one right downtown. The snow's melted enough that it's finally open again." She set the brochure back down. "And it's worth it."

With that, she made her way leisurely to the door. Opening it, she smiled over her shoulder and said, "Maybe we'll see each other around."

Chapter 25

Giorgio gazed out his hotel room window at a sky sagging with leaden clouds. He thought of the declaration he'd recently written and stored in the neighborhood bank along with his original Italian-language scoop. So close they lay to him and yet absolutely inaccessible because Régine kept the key to their safety deposit box. Régine: even though her romantic side was also inaccessible to him (for now anyway), at least her business side remained rock solid. Whatever might happen, she would make sure that his declaration and scoop landed on newspaper desks throughout Europe. Giorgio, Régine, and Erika were already one step closer to their ultimate goal of getting the English translation to London. Tomorrow he would leave for their three-way meeting in Locarno, where he would receive one of Erika's translations which he would spirit to London. He hoped Erika would agree to be courier to the second one; if not, that task would fall to a colleague of Régine's who, Giorgio couldn't help thinking, might possess less enthusiasm and grit for the job.

Giorgio had decided to take the short route to Locarno by traveling through Italy. Highly unlikely that something disastrous would happen in Domodossola, a small mountain town, its train station simply a minor border checkpoint and hardly the kind of attractive terrorist target represented by a metropolis like Milan. He expected he would only have to flash the cover of his passport to the Italian officer who came aboard (similar to the routine in Genoa not long ago) and soon the train would be chugging over the border, back into Switzerland. What had clinched his decision, however, was the tightening time factor. Choosing the all-day train route, as

Swiss-safe as it seemed, might have obliged him to spend the night in Locarno. And he had no time to lose; as soon as he returned to Geneva tomorrow afternoon, he would pack for London and leave with Erika's manuscript the next morning.

His thoughts returned to the bomb scare in Milan's central station. He would include that episode in his new writing project. Yesterday he'd stayed put in the hotel, making an outline for a story entitled: *Reporting in the Years of Lead,* with the subtitle: *Experiences of bullets and bombs, both Red and Black.* Titles to tinker with at this early stage, and even now he thought to add "Personal" to "Experiences," as his ex-partner and friend Franco revolved back to center stage in his mind. He would reveal the harassment inflicted on their moderate Socialist newspaper, *Il Cardinale,* by both communist and fascist thugs; the beating of Franco by a fascist punk, followed by the fire-bombings of the *Cardinale* premises in which Franco had lost his life. The tragedy took place just over a year ago and still made Giorgio clench his teeth against feelings of guilt and sorrow at not being able to rescue Franco from the blaze. Of one thing he was certain: his memoir would be dedicated to his dear friend.

Out the window the sky grew greyer, and though it was only three in the afternoon, headlight beams moved lavalike along the streets. Snow was forecast for two days hence, when he would next have to drive over the border into France, through the mountains to Annecy, where he planned to remove his license plates and ditch his car. He would then take a train to Paris, and from there the train to Calais or Boulogne, then the ferry to England and another train to London. The entire journey would take him an entire day, and although snow was promised throughout the week, at least he would be able to sit comfortably in a train compartment for the majority of the journey. Erika, being American, might wonder why he wouldn't purchase plane tickets. But apart from the exorbitant cost, DIGOS could more easily monitor airports than they could hundreds of train routes.

The thought of that last leg on the train, that final fulfilling push, made him long for the journey, complicated as it was— long for when he would stride into the humming offices of *The Guardian*, briefcase containing the manuscript in hand, and announce in English: "Giorgio Testa to see Ian Westcott: he's expecting me."

At close to midnight, Giorgio fell asleep caressing that thought, only to wake from a dream as disturbing as the image of the bustling *Guardian* offices was satisfying.

A blonde woman on the train had slipped into his compartment where he sat alone in the dreamscape dark, the space illuminated only by rushing flashes of light from beyond the window. Silvana, she seemed to be, his traveling companion on the train trek through Italy. Only the real Silvana had dark hair, a contradiction that didn't seem to matter in his dreaming mind. She was somehow Silvana and he called her by that name as she unbuttoned his shirt and whispered how much she wanted him. She straddled him, he became hard, but he started worrying about his briefcase which had magically transferred itself to the luggage rack on the other side of the compartment. He knew it was there but Silvana's head was in the way, and her kisses dogged him each time he tried to check on it. He fought to see it through a paralysis of desire that kept him rooted to his bench seat as Silvana rubbed against him. Then suddenly the oscillations stopped. Silvana slithered off the banquette, serpent-like, and out the compartment door. He immediately knew the briefcase was gone. He twisted and grasped for a light to turn on, tried to haul himself out of a seat that held him like a super magnet, and attempted to yell in frustration. But of course no voice broke through, and he could only register the dreadful strain in his throat and chest.

When finally Giorgio burst into consciousness, he gasped and punched the switch to the lamp above the headboard, his heart thumping like a drummer in a rock band. His whole torso seemed to shake as each heartbeat thudded against his ribcage. He feared he would need brandy to calm the riot in his chest, but once he relaxed back against the headboard, breathing with his eyes closed, the hard-rock drumming slowly subsided—a good sign. He looked at his clock: five a.m. Pitch black out, though not too early to get up, so he did, trying to drain from his mind every last dreg of that ghastly dream. He took a slow, warm shower, dressed, then left for the station with his briefcase where he had breakfast while waiting for the eight-fifteen train to Locarno.

That Swiss trains kept time as efficiently as Swiss watches was a cliché Giorgio greatly appreciated today, and settled in his compartment he observed his watch's second-hand. When it reached the eight-fifteen mark, the train jerked forward and he let out a satisfied sigh.

A little over three hours later, the train pulled into the Domodossola station. Giorgio, who had perched forward to look out the window, now breathed in and sat back, determined to look relaxed and nonchalant in his business suit. Two others sat in his compartment, a man on his side, also clad in a business suit, and a woman opposite them who now got up as the train slowed to a stop. Giorgio had said no more than "Bonjour" to either of them. The woman looked fit, smoothly pulling her suitcase down from the luggage rack and whisking it out to the train's exit area. Giorgio and the businessman kept their gazes to themselves and soon the sound of the heavy metal door heaving open reached them. "*Signori, passaporti*," soon followed, as the border agent entered their compartment.

Both men responded briskly to the request. The agent took both passports, checked the page with their photos, and handed them back.

And yet, despite the agent's quick scan of passports, the duration of the stop in Domodossola dragged on, with Giorgio monitoring his watch like a doctor measuring blood pressure and forcing himself to keep seated when curiosity and anxiety urged him to have a look out along the corridor. He did finally stand and was about to slide the window down to view the entire platform, when the floor beneath his feet began to sway. At last the train was heaving forward, though Giorgio remained standing at the window until the station became a miniscule dot in the distance.

Arriving late in Locarno (the Italians' fault, naturally), Giorgio plunked down into a taxi which sped him to his rendezvous, a café next to the lake. He could have walked there, the café turned out to be so close, but of course he still paid a high fare. Régine and Erika signaled him over with cups already in front of them, and when Giorgio's and Erika's eyes met, he just stopped and stared. What a fantastic sight after almost two months!

They embraced, and when they broke apart and sat, Régine joked, "We should order champagne!"

But champagne would have to wait until their mission's completion, and after some brief small talk they got down to business.

Giorgio eyed a messenger bag next to Erika and smiled at her. "I hope there's a copy of the manuscript in there..."

"There is," Régine answered, "and Erika's volunteered to travel with the other copy to London."

"I only wish I could leave right away," Erika said, "but I'll have to go back to Cobbio to turn my house keys over to the caretaker and pack up." In addition to returning the keys to Adriana, there was also Casa Rosselli's electricity bill to pay at the post office in Bellinzona; if she didn't tend to it, Adriana would find herself in possession of it as well as the keys. Too bad neither Giorgio nor Régine had tasked her to go to London before now. Anyway, she would leave the day after tomorrow. And her appointment with Betz? She would cancel it since her session wasn't until later tomorrow afternoon. Now that she was entrusted with one of the manuscripts she felt unusually emboldened.

Giorgio nodded approval. As it turned out, they would both leave for London on the same day.

Régine swept the café with her gaze, and Giorgio commented, "Same couple sitting by the window, same old guy with his nose in his newspaper, same mother tending that baby in the stroller. Good job choosing this table." (They were seated at the back of the café where only the barman had a decent vantage point to observe them.) Giorgio gave her a smile that he hoped she would return, but Régine's attention squatted squarely on Erika, who was now reaching for her satchel.

Giorgio placed his briefcase in his lap and Erika slipped her translation and her copy of Giorgio's Italian manuscript into it. The transfer completed, Régine gave instructions regarding contact with Ian Westcott in London, and immediately afterwards the group broke up, all three leaving for their respective trains. A plan had been established in the event something went haywire on the way to London, be it a tail picked up or a problem with the trains. In either case Giorgio or Erika would call Régine who would arrange another courier to pick up the English manuscript and ferry it to London.

Giorgio had to resist temptation to read Erika's translation right there on the train. But he knew he must wait until he returned to his hotel room in Geneva. The briefcase was locked and he sat with it on his lap as the train charged back towards Domodossola. While still in the Locarno station he'd briefly debated canceling his present ticket and buying one for the northern route through Switzerland, which had no border to cross. But once more, speed and efficiency got the better of him. He could pack up late this afternoon and even leave tomorrow morning if he bought his train ticket to London upon arriving in Geneva's station. Just thinking about it made his pulse thrum, his heart leap—his scoop was ready for *The Guardian*. They could do some minor editing, no problem, since he would be there to check any changes. He and Wescott would work together!

He couldn't help musing about it all along the leg to Domodossola. Until his heart began drumming again. This time a slow beat, like in a classical orchestra, not in a hard rock band—just his anticipation, his *excitement* to finally realize this dream-project. He tried to think of something else: basking on the beach at Menton—what could be more relaxing? But the drumming continued and he had no brandy with him to calm it. He loosened his tie and undid his top shirt button. *So incredibly eerie to feel his heart thumping in his chest while he was at rest.*

His train arrived in Domodossola right on time; now if only the Italians could get it back on its way just as timely! He undid another shirt button, closed his eyes as he waited for passport control.

The next thing he knew, an excruciating bolt of lightning hit him, pain radiating down his arm and throughout his torso. He pulled at his shirt and lurched forward. Then he saw only black.

Chapter 26

Claudio Voghera tossed aside thoughts of the icy-hot Carmen. Even if she were a plant of Moretti's, what could be gained? Access to locating Erika, maybe? If that were the case, Voghera, ever vigilant, would have spotted Carmen well before three nights ago, especially if she'd followed him from Italy. And what kind of spy could Carmen be, since she seemed to be as glad to be quit of him as he was of her? The only thing that reminded him of her this morning was the brochure on his hotel room desk, showcasing Bellinzona's castles. She was right, the snow had melted enough to perhaps make a quick visit to the one downtown before heading out to canvass more villages. So far he'd done no sightseeing. Why not take fifteen minutes out to see a medieval castle only a ten-minute walk away?

It turned out to be a five-minute walk, which made him feel even better about pinching time from his work. Up the cobbled main street, then around towards the Migros supermarket, and there it loomed—a medieval megalith, replete with crenelated ramparts that eclipsed the supermarket's modern metal, turtle-shaped roof.

Voghera marched up the castle's walkway, which rose with the slope of the mountain, the narrow cobbled path hugged by ragged-rough walls. The brochure dated the castle as 1300s, and he could easily imagine these ramparts patrolled by men with swords and glinting armor. The path took him up into a walled grassy enclosure, with snow still lingering in low mounds to one side; its greyish-black tint made it look like it had been shed from the ancient stone walls themselves. There, the ramparts rose high, linked by two towers pricked with arrow slits. Voghera was glad he'd come.

He'd probably come just in time. A frigid breeze slapped his face and he could sense that snow was weighting the white sky, set to break through just as forecast. He crossed the grassy expanse, easily picturing a parade of clattering soldiers crossing in the same way. A quick climb to the ramparts revealed sloping hills terraced with brown, winter-brittle vineyards; a sweeping gaze out showed the many houses that had sprung up over the centuries; and as he gazed up, he could make out the second and third castles clinging ever higher up the mountain. *Impressive*—but now he had to return to his car and get on with his search. The promised snow and its chain of perturbations would wait for no one.

He set back across the parade ground, or whatever this great swath of grassy terrain was historically called, and was about to engage the cobbled path downhill, when a man in a guardian's uniform came up the path to meet him.

"Ah, a visitor finally!" the man enthused.

Voghera met his eyes with mild surprise. He was a youth, really, a lanky twenty-something, his visored cap pulled low over scraggly hair. A nametag read *Marzio Villa*.

"Would you like to hear the history of this place?" Villa asked, squaring his shoulders in a brass-buttoned jacket that looked slightly too large for his lean frame. His nose was red with cold and Voghera felt his own numb face must look the same.

"Maybe another time," he said. "A bit too busy right now."

The youth looked disappointed, but then he rallied. "Well," he said looking around him, "this marvelous construction has been here six hundred years and I'm sure it will still be here if you decide to come back."

The kid sounded almost corny in his eagerness, and Voghera thought he could at least give him an encouraging response. "You must be glad to get back into full swing, with the castle being closed for a while—hope you get more tourists." He was about to say *grazie* and *arrivederci*, when he hesitated.

Tourists. Foreigners. The castle must have been open some of the time during the last two months. Voghera canted his head and massaged his chin with his knuckles "Actually, in my business I'm interested in the tourist trade here."

The young Marzio Villa stretched his frame taller and gave Voghera an attentive frown.

"Americans," Voghera pronounced. "Get any here in winter?"

"Not *usually...*" the kid drawled out. "Too much snow, especially this year."

His tone seemed uncertain, thought Voghera. *Not usually* didn't necessarily mean none at all.

"But you might get one or two exceptions to the rule?" Voghera pressed.

"Well, there has been *one* American visitor." The kid didn't exactly look pleased about that, nor did he seem completely unpleased. *Disconcerted,* maybe.

"Someone passing through?" Voghera asked.

"Not exactly." With this, Villa half sighed, and Voghera sensed he looked slightly forlorn. Then the kid gave a little cough and straightened his shoulders again. "But no, apart from her, no one."

Voghera felt the cold drain from his face and the heat of growing exhilaration rise to take its place. He glanced at his watch. "Actually," he said, "I might just have time to hear about this castle."

He let the young guardian usher him back onto the grass clearing, where patiently he heard a spiel about the ancient dukes of Milan and their goal of constructing a string of defensive fortresses to keep northern invaders out. "No nobility lived in them. Just soldiers."

Voghera nodded appreciatively, though he was barely registering the information. *The lone American,* a *she,* who had visited the castle this winter. *Erika*—it had to be...

Voghera let the young guardian discourse on the various phases of the castle's construction. How the city sprang up next to it, etcetera, etcetera, then as Villa tapered off, he said, "Makes me wonder how interested an American would be in this history, compared to us Europeans…"

The kid gave a faint smile. "Well, the one who came here was very interested."

"She must be a visiting historian, or something…" Voghera enjoyed the feel of his subtle probing as it ramped up, the sharpening and twisting of thoughts into seemingly anodyne questions.

"No," Villa said. "She lives here…temporarily, I think."

"Bellinzona?"

The kid shook his head. "Cobbio, a village north of here."

Voghera thought he detected a sourness in the slight contorting of the kid's mouth. Had his contact with this woman been a disappointment? If so, they might be the same age—another possible clue.

But he would leave things as they were. Asking for a name would ring decidedly suspicious. As he left the castle, sloping down the stony path, he silently thanked the guardian-guide for his youthful, innocent revelations. He also gave a nod of thanks to Carmen, who'd proved broad-minded in many delightful ways, including nudging him into expanding his tourist horizons.

Voghera went straight back to his hotel and took out his map. Cobbio couldn't be more than a fifteen-minute drive from here. He sat back in his chair and exhaled a deep breath. And if Erika *was* hiding out in the village? *Well, bravo, Claudio! You should be promoted rather than sidelined from DIGOS!* He puffed out his cheeks contemptuously, wondered if those "elite" intelligence services were making the kind of progress he was.

He snatched up his map and keys and hurried down to his car. But once he was in it and racing out of town, he found himself letting up on the accelerator. He could almost *feel* Erika in Cobbio, holed up in some rustic inn clattering away at her typewriter. Then he pictured her sitting by the inn's hearth, reading over her notes—the work she was doing for Giorgio Testa—warming herself at the fire, sipping some kind of grog, cozy in her illusory cocoon.

Did she feel *happy*, working this coup? *Safe from him?* He'd like to ask her.

First he had to locate her, he told himself, coming out of his trance. Nothing guaranteed Erika was the woman referenced by the guide Marzio Villa. With that he flattened the gas pedal, his muscles hardening into a solid block of determination. He focused on the next curve in the road.

The car climbed higher into the mountains. Snow could come sooner here than in Bellinzona, he observed. Much still remained from the last storm, stained lumps clinging to grassy hillsides. The road was impeccably asphalted, so the ascent seemed gradual. But the sky's white vault was descending, the higher slopes offering the first target for the next storm bomb.

As he passed the sign announcing COBBIO, he slowed to trawling speed and pulled into a service station. He got out and stretched his legs, stretched arms and shoulders. He rolled his neck and felt little clicks as constricted muscles grudgingly loosened.

The village consisted of multiple levels—this one along the highway, with service facilities and a train station, then the terraced houses scaling the mountain. It was colder here, and looked even colder higher up the mountain in this ice-shackled landscape How long had this *American woman* (he would limit himself to this label until he knew decisively who she was) been staying there?

Voghera entered the door of the AGIP gas station and asked to have his tank topped. As he followed the attendant outside, a swift debate revved up his thoughts. *If the American woman had a car, chances were she would have filled up here, since he could spot no other gas stations.* But Erika had no car, unless she'd somehow found the funds to buy one.

"Is this the only gas station in town?"

The man gave Voghera a perturbed frown as he shoved the hose nozzle into Voghera's tank opening. "Why, something wrong with *AGIP*?"

"No, no." Deep grooves etched the attendant's forehead and made wobbly parenthetic marks around his small dark eyes. "I always fill up with AGIP in Milan," Voghera told him pleasantly.

"Well it's the *exact* same gas here."

Touchy type. Voghera waited, gazing farther up the mountain, high above the houses, at a cropping of white structures with a bell tower. Then he heard the gas pump halt and glanced at the attendant who clicked the trigger another couple of times before slamming the hose back in its holder. Voghera thought to ask about the white structure up the mountain, but figured it best not to invite more sarcasm. The man was clearly not enjoying his day.

Voghera checked the total on the gas pump and pulled out his francs. "*Grazie,*" he said, handing the sum over.

The man grunted his own *grazie*, then added an "*arrivederci*" that lacked of the spirit of the expression.

Voghera took one last intake of breath then decided to skip this man altogether and take his questions about foreigners further up the village.

He steered his car around the paved roads—not many of them he realized; this was a walking-path village—and finally stopped near a woman exiting a grey stone house. He rolled down his window and asked if there was a café in the village.

Moving quickly, bundled up and muffled with a scarf, she slowed long enough to point up the mountain. "It's up there on the left. But you'd be better off parking and walking. There's little room for cars up there."

Voghera thanked her and waved as he moseyed his Opel Ascona towards a shoulder and crunched it onto snow.

After a ten-minute climb, with only grey stone houses and snow in sight, he was about to head back down to ask someone else for directions. Then he crossed paths with a man and woman conversing in English.

"I think we should leave an hour earlier tomorrow morning," said the redhaired man.

"Well, I *suppose* we can," his companion answered. "*Buon giorno,*" she said to Voghera as they passed each other.

Voghera did more than a double take. Speechless, he turned and followed them.

"Excuse me," he said, opting for English. "I'm visiting the village."

"Oh!" exclaimed Brendan and Maeve Hartigan in unison. "Well," said Brendan, "if we can help you with something..."

Chapter 27

Erika's train pulled into Cobbio from Locarno at just after four p.m., with snowflakes falling thick and fast. Behind mountains that jutted from the valley like rugged skyscrapers, the sun had already set, plunging the valley into sub-freezing temperatures. She was wearing her new hooded parka, which had been fine in the lake-mitigated temperatures of Locarno. Up here, though, she once more noticed the cold clawing through her trousers.

She tugged her parka's zipper up and mentally programmed her visit to Bellinzona the next day: the train station to buy her ticket; the post office to pay the electricity bill; and a quick phone call to Dr. Betz to cancel her appointment. Then she would return to Cobbio, pack and leave her house keys with Adriana, telling her friend she would be traveling for a while. Excitement flooded her—the day after tomorrow she would leave for London!— and turned her hike up to the house into a series of brisk hops. Over the last two months she had turned into a mountain goat like the locals.

Lighting the kitchen stove and shedding her outdoor wear, she pondered what she would take with her to London, apart from her cherished manuscript. She couldn't bring all her belongings, only a small bag with maybe three changes of clothes, extra underwear, and toiletries. She would wear her overcoat. Her manuscript in its plastic sheath would rest in her messenger bag, along with her passport, train ticket, wallet, and instructions for contacting Ian Wescott in London. Her stiletto, her only portable weapon, would stick close to hand in her right coat pocket.

Her thoughts sprang back to the lost switchblade and

having to call Betz tomorrow. She didn't want to be completely shed of him. He *had* helped her, after all, especially with the anxiety over her brother's death. Even his breathing and meditation practices, the walking one especially, had granted her a patchy sense of groundedness. She could probably benefit more with continued sessions, if she could only figure out his strange situation. Dark things still lurked uncomfortably in her subconscious, shards of forgotten dreams still stinging her when she woke in the morning like scabs being torn off. Betz had told her that during the phase between sleep and full consciousness, the mind was raw, tender and vulnerable due to barriers let down to allow sleep's restorative functions. The doctor did have sensible things to say, but for a while she needed to distance herself from him— from the break-in and from those awkward moments of desiring him.

She poured herself two fingers of brandy to take the chill off while the stove warmed the room and, more pertinently, to take the edge off the excitement and confusion swirling inside her—a mix of adrenaline, pumped by her impending mission, and astonishment about the strange laws of attraction. How could she desire both Stefan Betz and Claudio Voghera, as unalike as a dolphin and a shark? Well, not really, but sort of. In all honesty, indulging in the memory of Claudio's lovemaking still caused her thighs to contract in pleasurable tension; seeing Betz's taut chest and neck in his V-neck sweater had done the same. Claudio's smile was classically magnetic. Yet when Betz had turned his full smile upon her during their last session, she'd been bowled over by his inner boy's joy breaking out of a sober man's rugged face.

She didn't want to fall for Stefan Betz—inconvenient in all ways—so it was just as well she would be putting some space between them.

Erika finished her brandy and crossed to the broom closet, with both Betz and Claudio trailing in her thoughts. The truth about Claudio, she reaffirmed with a somber shiver, was that he might well be disposed to kill her. They had never even hinted to each other that they might be in love—the only person she was fairly certain he loved was his estranged little daughter. Erika had never even heard him say he loved his mother. He had voiced no qualms about DIGOS killing Matilde Fassino, and what were his last words to her on that sidewalk in Turin? *Team up with Giorgio Testa and be prepared to expect the worst.* In Claudio's world, the worst equaled death.

She opened the closet and lifted her épée out by its grip. Its sides and tip were sharp enough now for whatever might be asked of it. She pulled out the practice pillow and set it on a chair, where she dealt it a few more stabs and slashes. She'd bought the cheap foam pillow in Bellinzona and now it was properly shredded, but she would have to wait to dispose of it until garbage day. She placed it back in the closet.

The next morning in snowy Bellinzona, Erika ticked off her errands. She went to the train station and sighed at the length of the voyage to London: Cobbio to Bellinzona; Bellinzona to Basel; Basel to Paris; Paris to London, via trains and ferry boat. It would take her all day and then some. She bought a ticket for leaving Cobbio at six-fifteen a.m. the following morning. At the post office she paid her electricity bill, then stopped at a store to buy some small travel-toiletries. After strolling around a bit more to put off the inevitable, she finally ducked into a phone booth to call Betz. He didn't answer. Should she just let it go? No, she should try going to his office.

In front of his building she halted, her pulse quickening as she stared at his buzzer on its brass plaque. What if Betz had asked other tenants in the building whether they'd seen anyone suspicious, or even new to the building, and had then learned of a tall blonde night visitor? Did she really need to do this? Yes, she told herself once more, because Betz might just suspect one of his patients of having broken in to his office, and his suspicions could only be bolstered if one of said patients skipped their appointment and then couldn't be contacted. For an instant she closed her eyes: *and if he'd found the switchblade?*

Under the overhang, she collapsed her umbrella, took a cold bracing breath that burned her nostrils, and pressed the buzzer.

And pressed it again, counting the seconds on her watch. After thirty tiny ticks she dropped her arm in frustration. *Why wasn't he answering? Was he with a patient? Might she miraculously cross paths with one, since her own appointment was only an hour from now?* At this stage she really didn't care about his phantom patients. She needed to cancel her session and get home and pack, then arrange with Adriana where to leave the keys.

She stamped her cold feet on the stone sidewalk. *Jesus*, now that she had a good reason to cut and run, she couldn't permit herself the convenience! She looked up and down the street. Maybe she should go to a café, order some hot tea, then try calling him again. Yes, that made sense.

She let out a vapory sigh and strode quickly down the street towards a café she knew around the block. By the time he answered his phone it might be time for her appointment, but he shouldn't mind since she didn't pay for her sessions, anyway.

She had just approached the corner when she stopped in her tracks, for none other than Dr. Betz himself had come round from the other side. She registered his surprise as he must have hers.

"Erika," he said, looking perplexed now. "Were you just at my building?"

"Well..."

"You're early." The doctor looked at his watch, then back at Erika. "And you're covered with snow."

It was true; in her eagerness to retreat from Betz's building she'd neglected to re-open her umbrella. Absently, she dusted her hair.

"And you're wet. Why don't you come to my office now and dry off."

Erika continued to gaze at him. In his hooded wool jacket he didn't look like the Betz she was used to. He was squinting at her now and his features appeared magnified by the hood hugging his head. Watery snow was dripping onto her forehead and down her neck, so she fumbled to get her umbrella open, while mumbling, "I tried calling you, Doctor, to tell you I'm going on vacation for a while." The umbrella finally burst open and Erika smiled up at him in nervous triumph.

"Well, come up to the office and you can tell me all about it. No use standing here in the cold."

"Well," Erika tried again, "I might not have time..."

"You mean before your session?" He already had a hand on Erika's shoulder, ready to shepherd her back towards the warmth of his office.

"I mean I'm leaving tomorrow," she explained, following along.

"Oh?" Betz paused to glance at her. "A sudden plan?" He had removed his hand from her shoulder but now she thought he might take her in hand again. Instead, he went on walking, picking his steps in the accumulating snow and ice.

"Not *sudden*," Erika specified, catching up to him. *Sudden*: like suddenly and suspiciously skipping out on an appointment. "I'd planned it in advance, but—"

"Here we go," Betz interrupted again as they approached his building. He already had his keys out. "Come on up and you can tell me the rest."

Should she emphasize, right here and now, that she didn't have time for anything more—no further explanations, no session? No, she should at least tell him something that would account for her cancelling at the last minute. *And now it really was the last minute.*

With every step through the lobby and into the elevator her thoughts scrabbled like mice escaped from a laboratory.

But as the groaning elevator wheeled them up to Betz's floor, Erika's focus moved to Betz himself as he unbuttoned his coat and pushed back his hood. His hair was flattened in parts and spiking in others. That, along with his face, ruddy from the cold, made him look like the classic young, absent-minded professor. Her confidence rose, threads of an excuse for her abrupt behavior already weaving into a silky, credible plait.

Betz unlocked the door and they went through the empty waiting room to his office. "Take your coat off, it's nice and warm here," he told her, as he did himself.

"I really can't stay." She could feel more than the heat from the radiators warming her as she took in Betz's confused gaze. "Actually, I need to cancel our session. I should've called this morning, but anyway I wanted to tell you I've been invited on a ski and hiking trip, but that my friends decided to leave earlier than scheduled, tomorrow morning, in fact, and I need to get ready this afternoon..." Inwardly, she was thankful for the Hartigans' invitation that inspired her story.

Still, Betz was eyeing her quizzically, as though wondering what kind of friends inconvenienced others. Or maybe he was sizing her up as the possible intruder of two nights ago.

"Well, as I said, I could use the time to prepare..."

Betz hung his coat on the stand next to the door. He smoothed his hair then turned back to smile at Erika. "But you're here now..."

"Yes..." She thought of looking at her watch for emphasis but changed her mind lest she appear even ruder. "I didn't want to stand you up."

"You could sit down for a moment, perhaps let your hair dry..."

He was looking right at her hair now and she felt a flush of embarrassment.

"You could take your coat off, let that dry some, too." He smiled graciously. "Get warm before you go out again—it's up to you..."

She felt silly continuing to stand there. She must either

state firmly that she hadn't time, or agree to sit for five minutes. She decided on the latter, once more wishing to deflect any iota of suspicion.

Once her coat was hung up, Erika scanned the leather sofa before sitting. No unusual dents or blankets folded next to it that might give a clue that someone had slept there. Maybe it was just a one-off occasion, though she couldn't help recalling Betz's mad, deer-in-the-headlight moment when nailed by her flashlight beam—so unlike his composed presence now. She took her usual place on the sofa, next to the window.

Betz leaned back in his chair and crossed his arms. "So, tell me about your upcoming trip."

Faithfully, Erika channeled the Hartigans' invitation, including as much of their itinerary as she could remember. The rest she invented.

"Grisons—wonderful ski resorts in that canton," responded Betz. "You'll have to tell me the highlights when you get back. And the name of the resort, if you like it. I might want to try it myself."

Erika could not for the life of her recall the name of where the Hartigans planned to stay. She didn't want to pull any famous flashy names out of her hat, like St. Moritz, the way she had with her cousins Elsa and Angelo, back when she was leaving Italy. In hindsight, even they might have thought she was trying to impress them.

"I'll definitely do that," she said to Betz. Yes, when she had time, she would have to interrogate the Hartigans about their trip. She looked out the window. Snow still fell like perpetually sifted flour. "I guess I'd better get going." It was never easy lying to Betz. Despite the warmth and intimacy of the room she felt a cold stone of lonely detachment in her stomach. Today she felt no arousal looking at him in his shirt and tie under his forest-green sweater. And she was glad, because she couldn't afford to feel rattled and befuddled at the very moment she had so much clear thinking to do in these coming days.

The thought of traveling to London under blanketing

snow brought on a sudden weariness.

"Is everything else all right, Erika?"

The question pulled her gaze from the window. "I'm fine. Just the snow. I need to get back home and get ready for tomorrow..."

"Mm. I hope your friends have a good four-wheel drive vehicle."

Erika nodded absently.

"Nothing to fear out there..."

Was that a statement or a question? She couldn't quite make out Betz's tone...

"Anyway," he resumed, as if he hadn't expected a response, "we can schedule your next session for when you return."

"Well, about that," Erika said, rising, "I'd better wait to make arrangements when I get back."

Betz hesitated, looked at her a little too long for comfort before acquiescing. "Whatever's more convenient for you."

As she donned her overcoat and entered the outer room, Erika slowed. Following Betz into his office, she hadn't noticed that he'd placed his statuette of the Buddha (the one she'd found in his file cabinet drawer) on the counter of the reception nook. It sat in its lotus position with a beckoning half smile. She looked back at Betz, who was lingering in his doorway. "I'll let you see yourself out," he said, and slowly and quietly closed his door.

Usually, he walked her as far as the reception nook. For a moment she studied the waiting room. Apart from the Buddha appearing on the counter, things looked basically the same as they normally did. Leisurely she advanced towards the door to the hallway, her eyes in sweeping mode.

And then she spied it. On the floor just under an armchair by the door. An object that almost blended with the gunmetal-grey floor tiles. Only this grey object had little silver rivets. Erika looked back at Betz's door; it was still shut. Slowly she squatted, pretending to pull the bottom of her pantleg over the top of her boot. *Had she actually kicked it under the chair unwittingly during her break-in?* One more time she glanced back at Betz's closed door, then snatched her switchblade out from under the chair and plunged it into her coat pocket.

Then she slipped out of the office.

Chapter 28

This was the second time he'd been in the hospital in just over a year. The last time, he was admitted into the Turin hospital specializing in burn injuries; fortunately, his burns had not been serious. This time Giorgio had no idea how he'd got here: in a bed, hooked up to machines, with an oxygen apparatus in his nostrils. Even more worrying were the electrodes patched to his chest. His right hand had two IV needles stuck in it, with tubes running up to dual bags of clear liquid. What had happened to him? Something had gone wrong on the train. Domodossola was the last stop he remembered.

He tried to sit up but practically swooned with the effort. He knew he was fat, but now his body felt elephant-sized, his head a giant boulder. Pain pinned him down, and the entire ordeal sent him sinking, his head swimming against a force that led nowhere but back to sleep.

Later, he surfaced again. This time into a subdued, yellowish glow. Had the time of day changed? He didn't even try to sit up. His eyes hurt, his whole body ached, but his head felt slightly clearer. He was in a room with four beds, his the only one occupied. With his left hand he rummaged round and found a call button. Within a minute, a nurse pushed the door fully open and arrived at his bedside.

"You're awake, Signor Testa, that is a good thing." The middle-aged woman spoke Italian with the accent of the Alps region around Ticino and Domodossola. Anxiety overtook the pain in his body. *Was he still in Italy?*

The nurse confirmed it so. "You're in the hospital of

Domodossola. You've been semi-unconscious since yesterday afternoon. Do you remember what happened to you?"

He'd been on his way back to Geneva when a strangling pain besieged him from nowhere. "I was in my railroad carriage," he said, his voice cracking with dryness, his throat tight and sore. "Waiting for the train to move on from Domodossola."

The nurse bent over his bed tray and poured him some water. He was able to drink on his own, a good sign, but the nurse pulled the glass from his lips before he could drain it.

"Not too much at one time," she said crisply.

He tightened his left hand around the glass, not out of defiance but in another wave of anxiety which verged on panic. "My things," he uttered with more force now, trying to sit up again, only to crash back onto his raised pillows in a fit of fiery pain. He attempted another croaking plea, but the nurse silenced him.

"*You must relax*, Signor Testa. Your things are just fine. Your wallet and identity documents are fine, your suit is in the closet, your bag as well, along with a brief case."

Silently Giorgio sighed, then closed his eyes, relishing a moment of sheer palpable relief.

"*Signor Testa*." At the nurse's prompt, his eyes fluttered open again. "You've had a mild heart attack," she said, "so don't exert yourself in any way, including worrying about your things."

A heart attack? Giorgio's eyes blinked rapidly.

"A *mild* heart attack," the nurse repeated. "The doctor will be in this afternoon to explain things to you."

A *mild heart attack*. He was trying to get his mind around it: *not a massive one, thank God*...still, he'd been here how long?

He lifted his left arm, only to let it thud back on the bed. *The damn thing still hurt*, and his watch was gone.

"As I said, Signor Testa, you must relax. If you're looking for your watch, it's in the closet." She checked her own watch.

"At the moment it's just after three o'clock."

In the afternoon, Giorgio deduced from the light streaming in from the window. He let it all sink in. What could he remember during this last twenty-four hours, apart from that one waking moment?

The nurse studied him with fairly kind but clinical eyes. "You look confused, and that's understandable. We've been giving you pain medication and sedatives, so don't be too concerned about your state of mind."

But he was concerned, not so much with the sedative-induced fog he felt—that, thank goodness, had lessened since he last woke—but with his *things*, as the nurse put it. He narrowed his eyes at her nameplate. "Sister Ursula, would it be all right if I reviewed some items in my briefcase?"

"Not right now. We'll see later, after the doctor has been in. I will give you more pain medication if you need it. And you will need to eat something soon, now that you're awake." She looked him up and down, then indicated the bag of clear liquid feeding one of his IV. "You can't live off that forever."

"I'm sure I can't, but right now I'm not hungry." He added wryly to himself: *although to look at me, you'd probably think I'm always hungry.* "And for now, I'll hold off on more pain medication." He felt tired and trapped, and even a little sick. At this moment he probably wouldn't be able to manage his briefcase anyway, and he wouldn't be asking the sister to help him with it. Thank goodness it was locked, with the key in his wallet.

"I *can* get your watch for you," Sister Ursula offered. The woman seemed eager to do *something* for him.

"*Please*," Giorgio said. "I would appreciate it."

She opened the closet door. Giorgio craned his neck to get a look at his briefcase, but the sister was in the way. After closing the door, she returned to Giorgio's bedside with the watch and signaled for his left wrist. Giorgio almost stopped her. He would rather handle his watch himself, but decided to let the sister continue in order to keep on her good side.

"Well," she said, "I'll leave you for now, Signor Testa."

"Thank you. And when did you say the doctor would be in?"

"Soon." She gave a clipped nod, then left the room.

Three o' five, Giorgio's watch read, the second hand still in action. With a stab of pain and nausea he stretched his right hand, fumbling with numb fingers to remove the watch, wind it, then strap it back on. His right hand throbbed, but at least he felt he'd regained some small grain of control.

Yet things were far from normal—the fact that he wasn't hungry, when he hadn't eaten in over twenty-four hours, attested to it. *A heart attack*, he groaned with a shiver of fear. But a *mild* one, he reminded himself, though he had no idea what that actually meant. The fact that he lay propped up, rather than supine, had to be a sign he was nowhere near death. Without turning his head, he gazed slit-eyed at his closet. Did the door come equipped with a lock? He couldn't keep awake to find out, and when his eyelids dropped so did Giorgio, back into soft fuzzy sleep.

He hadn't plunged deeply, when the door creaked open.

"*Buona sera.*"

Giorgio's head jerked up as a white-coated woman swished into the room. "I don't think it's too early to say *buona sera...*"

The sun had dipped behind the dour, jagged mountains, so no, thought Giorgio, it wasn't too early. "*Buona sera,*" he returned in kind.

"Signor Testa, I'm Doctor Traversi, your attending physician."

A woman doctor: yes, delightfully different. And youngish—might be just out of her residency. "Pleased to meet you, doctor, and thank you." Gingerly Giorgio held out his left hand, which the doctor shook delicately but warmly.

"You've been told by now that you've had a heart attack," Doctor Traversi went on.

"A mild one, according to Sister Ursula."

"Yes, you've been lucky. But it doesn't mean you should be in any hurry to leave here, nor start doing any paperwork."

Sister Ursula must have passed on his eagerness to get at his briefcase. Giorgio smiled pleasantly. "Well, whenever I can at least do some light reading..." He pictured Erika's manuscript. Without being drugged he wouldn't rest until he could see those papers, black on white, shining through their plastic sleeve. He glanced at the wooden wardrobe door; he could see no keyhole, so presumably it couldn't be locked.

The doctor was now sweeping back her long dark hair in order to hook on her stethoscope.

"Let's have a listen to your heart and lungs."

She wrote something down in his chart, then straightened and nodded. "We've got you stabilized, but you'll need to spend some days here so we can monitor you." She seemed to have caught Giorgio's sagging expression, so added firmly, "Your blood tests and EKG show your heart has not suffered irreversible damage but, as you can see, we will be keeping the electrodes on your chest as part of the monitoring process."

Tentatively Giorgio raised an index finger. "EKG?"

"It was done while you were unconscious.

"So my heart isn't damaged, then..."

"It was deprived of oxygen, but fortunately you were brought here quickly from the station. Now you must *rest*. We don't know about the condition of your arteries—how much blockage there could be. Fortunately you're young and your heart withstood the event, but we'll have to transfer you to a bigger hospital to do more tests."

"Transfer me?"

"Yes. Domodossola is a small town. We're looking at Biella, or Turin."

Turin? Giorgio's heart struck up a beat that he could feel all too well. He closed his eyes and willed it to stop.

"Signor Testa, you mustn't get agitated. We transfer patients to other hospitals as a matter of course. Plus," she added, glancing at her clipboard, "from your passport and identity card, we've learned you're actually *from* Turin. You would be going back home."

Going home? She might well suggest sending him to a Soviet gulag. He tried to calm his breathing. Naturally they'd examined his passport and identity card when they'd removed his clothes. "You've put my documents in a safe place, I assume..."

"Of course." Doctor Traversi finally smiled again. "And we'd also like to contact your family for you. Assure them you're all right."

Giorgio practically groaned aloud. This was getting far too complicated, yet at the moment he didn't feel the strength to do much arguing. He gave a dismissive wave with his left hand. "No worries there. I've been traveling with my business. None of my family expect to hear from me for some weeks." He did, however, have one more question for the doctor. He waited while she wrapped up the visit, nodding obligingly as she stressed once more that he relinquish himself to serious rest. Then he asked, "About the sedatives and pain medication, could we perhaps cut them down? They're making me very woozy."

"I understand. But Signor Testa, the only way through your condition is utmost rest, which above all means good sleep. Sleep is curative. You're on a blood thinner right now, but as far as your other medications are concerned, we'll reassess them later."

Giorgio thanked her, all the while swearing to himself. He wanted to be his utmost alert self. There was much to ponder and a closet containing a briefcase to keep an eye on.

And yet, as Doctor Traversi took her leave, Giorgio could feel himself sinking back into the sea of sleep. He barely saw the doctor's high heels and nyloned legs slip out the door before his head fell back on his pillows and his awareness collapsed.

That night, after Sister Ursula had taken away his empty dinner plates, he was determined to stay alert—alert to shadows, to sounds, to anything. Where were they keeping his passport, identity card, and wallet, by the way? The hospital must take these items very seriously. He would ask Sister Ursula. he wanted them as near as his briefcase. With DIGOS on his trail he wanted to be able to leave here at a moment's notice. He lifted his left arm high enough to rub his face, then let it fall. God, how such a simple gesture fatigued him.

He tried to concentrate on the footsteps treading the tile floor outside his door. Clogs, they mostly sounded like, typical hospital footwear—clip-clop, clip-clop, like the hooves of slender horses. Sister Ursula had fiddled with his IV drips again. More dope, no doubt—not strictly a catch-22 situation but damn close enough. Which reminded him of the new novel he'd bought and where the nurses might have stowed it.

He turned back to focusing on his auditory faculties. Was that a different sort of footfall he could hear? A set of regular leather-soled shoes? Were they heavy or light-weight? Jesus, it was like trying pick out the sound of one specific instrument played in an orchestra. He would have to ask about visiting hours. How late were outsiders allowed to penetrate these halls?

So many questions, so much to worry about...and yes, Sister Ursula must have topped off his pain meds, or his sedative, or who the hell knew what, because he was starting to drift away again. His head felt like it weighed as much as a whale, and the whale was diving for the bottom of the sea.

Chapter 29

Cobbio: what a quaint little village, full of the friendliest sort of folk, thought Claudio Voghera. No wonder Erika had ensconced herself here. How she had found a three-story house to inhabit was still a mystery, but even that, he thought, might eventually come to light.

Thanks to his walk with the Hartigans, he had learned exactly where the "American" lived.

"From Lugano, are you?" Mrs. Hartigan had said.

"Doing a survey?" Mr. Hartigan had added.

"For my business," Voghera had confirmed in the English he'd learned through DIGOS's courses. "We're looking for ways to make Ticino's villages more accessible to foreigners world-wide." And that was all it had taken for Mrs. Hartigan to announce that an American was indeed living in the village.

"An American! I'd like to inquire how she happened onto Cobbio at this time of year."

"We'd introduce you, but we're getting ready to leave tomorrow on a skiing trip."

"Well, I suppose I can ask where she lives at the café..."

"No need. Erika lives near us. If you walk along with us, we'll go right by her house."

Voghera couldn't decide which Hartigan had been more helpful; the couple sort of blended together in one musical chord of eagerness and enthusiasm. They'd said that Erika, the American who'd lived previously in Turin, might not be home at the moment since she also had a trip planned.

That was yesterday, and he'd cased Erika's house (*Casa Rosselli* was stylistically scrolled upon its front wall) for the rest of that day and into the evening when lights should have winked on inside. Voghera had almost decided the Hartigans were probably right. He'd almost returned to his car, which he'd moved and parked behind the gas station, slipping the surly service attendant ten francs. But just as he'd turned to descend the mountain path, he'd heard the unmistakable thud of boots plodding upwards over the packed snow.

With new snow falling fast, he'd pulled his hood over his head and hidden behind a blockish stone fountain at the front of the house. Soon, a black parka similar to his own came into view, only with fur rimming its hood. The hips that swayed beneath the parka were also unlike his own, and Voghera shifted excitedly on his haunches until a face took form which made his heart beat jubilantly. *Erika, at last! He shivered with pleasure. Had he ever doubted this moment would arrive?*

A messenger bag hung crossways over her. And though Voghera's blood had cooled some, his temper simmered on. *She wouldn't escape him again, the traitor.*

Swiftly she let herself in and slammed the door. He heard the clatter of a key turning before he could even move. Eventually he slid out from behind the fountain and sprinted to the stone porch next to the front door, where he crouched under the upper-floor balcony.

For a while he'd sat hunched against the house, his narrow gaze sifting through snowflakes that salted the dusk. His lock-picking set was in his car, but he wouldn't go fetch it; better to wait for Erika to go out, when he would search the unfamiliar house and hide in it, waiting for her.

Lamplight illuminated the house's ground floor but the curtains were closed. Voghera could only imagine Erika moving warmly and fluidly around the house while he sat hugging his knees in the icy damp that seeped into his bones. He thought of her preparing dinner, perhaps near a fire. Erika by firelight, feasting on a hot meal. He had a fleeting urge to take her by force but his body was too cold to respond. When he realized he could no longer feel his backside he forced his stiff limbs into motion and headed back out into the snow. Behind the fountain he snatched up the tree branch he'd used to sweep clean his footprints from the snow and repeated the process.

Tomorrow morning, *early*, he would be back and thoroughly equipped.

And now tomorrow was here, the snow relentless. Just before dawn, Voghera had parked once more behind the gas station and made his way up to Casa Rosselli by the glow of his small flashlight. With the branch behind the fountain he swept the snow smooth of his prints, then stored the branch at the side of the house. He walked silently back along the front porch to once more sit under the balcony and wait. Compared to last evening it felt like the Arctic—*always coldest at dawn; it can only get warmer*. But when would Erika wake up? And would she stay home all day since it was still snowing?

At last, as dawn completely dissolved, Voghera heard a door open and shut on the upper floor. He straightened to a squat. Almost nine o'clock—Erika sleeping late as usual, damn her, while he froze his balls off! He craned his neck to look up at the balcony but could hear no footsteps. Seconds later another door opened and shut further down the balcony, followed by the muted sound of rushing water. Soon after, doors opened and shut, in reverse—Erika back in the house. Voghera scurried down the porch in a crouch to where he could wait and watch at the corner of the house. His angle didn't afford a full view of the balcony, though during the previous day's visit he had observed its covered walkway and what he'd thought was some kind of storage room at the balcony's left end. A makeshift bathroom?

A lamp brightened behind the downstairs curtains—nine-thirty by Voghera's watch. About thirty minutes later, the light went off and seconds after that another came on upstairs. Erika dressing...?

Another half hour passed, until at last he heard the

jiggling lock of the downstairs door. He ducked back around the corner, under falling snowflakes that were gathering speed and becoming dense as wet flour. He waited, listening to the door thud shut and a key crank in the lock, before peering around to see Erika cross the yard to engage the footpath down the mountain. This morning she was wearing her familiar grey overcoat and holding her maroon umbrella above her head. He stood guard another fifteen minutes, in case she returned for something, then headed for the front door.

Out of habit he gazed left and right, though the nearest neighboring house lay beyond sight of the entrance to Casa Rosselli. He extracted his lock-picking tools and before long was slipping into the house. In the entryway he rubbed his hands together. Was there no heat in this place?

In front of him loomed a steep stone staircase, to the left a living area which he entered and scanned for radiators. None—only a small parlor with old-fashioned uncomfortable-looking furniture, which looked like it hadn't been used in fifty years. He went back past the staircase and stepped into a kitchen. Immediately a waning warmth touched his skin. There were no radiators here either, merely a stove sitting at the end of the room which he approached and gave a swift pat with his hand. Erika must have extinguished it before leaving. *Jesus, was this all that heated this place?*

Evidently so, for clutter claimed the kitchen, evidence that the room was *the* living area: a transistor radio on the buffet next to a plastic bag containing a tape recorder, a book lying on top of it. On the table, a newspaper and a magazine. Plus— and Voghera chuckled darkly—the *pièce de résistance*: a *typewriter*. No papers in sight, though plenty of drawers to stash them in. He would check all of them for evidence of Erika's betrayal, but first he needed to examine the entire house. On his way out of the kitchen he noticed a scrap of paper behind the radio: *Betz, 3 p.m.*—Erika's scrawl that included today's date. *An appointment*, and yet she'd left the house for it fairly early. Maybe she'd planned to be out most of the day, which boded well for him!

Cold fanned up from the stone floors. First he took the staircase to the uppermost floor, finding two dusty bedrooms looking as abandoned as the parlor. He descended to the level which held the balcony and there beheld the bedroom where Erika slept. Her little red travel alarm clock on the nightstand practically waved to him. Voghera's gaze travelled over the bed, a double bed topped by a thick white duvet. He sat on it, picked up the closest pillow and inhaled, but the pillow was too cold to return Erika's scent. Feeling its frigid caress on his cheek, he shivered and put it down. How the hell did she sleep here? The duvet couldn't keep her warm enough.

Somehow Erika had to have turned tougher, and maybe even smarter, since he'd last seen her. This place was no hearth-warmed Swiss chalet, with solicitous staff tending fires and bringing you hot mulled wine and steaming fondue.

He rose to investigate the wardrobe. Winter clothes, the black parka, an empty purse, plus the leather messenger bag Erika had been carrying yesterday—also empty. The drawers contained the usual underwear, warm socks, sweaters, but nothing else. He closed the wardrobe doors, then went back to the bedside table. It also had a drawer, which he opened...and grinned at its contents. Erika's pearl-handled stiletto shone back at him. He picked it up, turned it over in his hand against the window's light, then pocketed it. His fingers reached further inside the drawer and raked forth a pen and a small notebook. He pocketed the notebook. Then he stretched out on Erika's bed and stared at the ceiling. From the block of ice that was his mind, thoughts chipped off sharp and gelid as the air in the room. Had Erika had affairs in this icebox? Had her lips been icicles, her traitorous cunt cold and dry as an ice age cave?

Voghera heaved himself up off the bed. He had work to do, an entire house to comb before Erika came home, although if she did return unexpectedly he could count on an element of surprise. The temperature had dropped since he'd been lying there and instinctively he put his hands in his jacket pockets. He pulled out the little notebook he'd found in Erika's night table and flipped through it...then slowly sat down to digest each page. Notes they were indeed, words marked down with corresponding page numbers next to them: *Auschwitz collaborator* had an arrow after it pointing to an alternative expression—Auschwitz *war criminal*. On another line: *Matilde Fassino more criminal than her husband?* And yet another line: *DIGOS equally criminal?* He read through until the writing stopped—little editing notes, no doubt, for a translation of Giorgio Testa's exposé. Erika *and* Testa's *coup*! Voghera felt vindicated, wanted to rip off each page and stuff it into Moretti's mouth for not initially believing him about Erika and Giorgio Testa's threat to DIGOS.

But where was Erika hiding the *entire* story?

He returned to the top floor, systematically checking every drawer and wardrobe (including on top and behind), carefully turning mattresses over and replacing them just as they were. He came downstairs and searched the rest of Erika's bedroom, to no avail. So far he had not even found a telephone in the house.

On the ground floor, he checked the credenza in the parlor, looked under the dusty furniture cushions, then entered the kitchen, picking through the buffet and every drawer and cupboard in the room, once more placing everything back in its exact place to avert suspicion when Erika came home. He went back to the plastic bag on the buffet and took out the tape recorder. A cassette tape was already loaded in it, so he plugged the machine's cord into an outlet and hit "play." After about thirty seconds of a male voice giving instructions about breathing, he hit "stop." What was Erika into, here? Voghera hit fast-forward, stopped the tape, and pressed "play" again. Now the voice talked about perceiving sounds—sounds in the body, sounds in the room, sounds from outdoors. Voghera fast-forwarded once more, only to meet silence; no speaker at all. Alternating between "fast-forward" and "stop," he inched his way towards the end of the tape and once more caught the speaker: "If you think you did a good job attending to the object of meditation, you should congratulate yourself; if you think you could have done better, you should encourage yourself—no need to criticize yourself." *What the hell?* Voghera shook his head and rewound the tape, then unplugged the machine and placed it back in its plastic bag.

He approached the broom closet, opened it and sighed sourly at two brooms, a dustpan and some dust cloths. He removed the brooms and dustpan and poked his head in deeper. What he pulled out made him take a great breath: "Erika," he exhaled, "you clever little bitch!"

The object which he withdrew was none other than a fencing sword, with a big hand guard and a pronged crosspiece above the grip. Voghera got a purchase on it, though he wasn't sure he was holding it right, and shifted his fingers on the prongs. The blade seemed short, and upon inspecting it more closely he saw evidence of some kind of scraping, miniscule jagged edges. He grazed the blade with a bare finger and arched his brows at the sting and the blot of blood, which he automatically brought to his lips to wipe away. "*Cazzo*," he swore. *What kind of crazy state of mind was she in?* He set the sword aside and looked around the kitchen once more. He'd inspected every room in the house, including the bathroom at the end of the upstairs balcony, and still found no story with *Auschwitz* in its title. But it had to be here somewhere. He remembered the door outside on the porch. Some kind of storage area, he assumed, as he left the house to investigate.

The handle inclined and the door creaked open. No lock, Voghera noted with disappointment, and therefore probably nothing to hide in there. And indeed all he discovered was an old stone oven filled with ashes and, leaning against a wall, some garden tools draped with ancient grey cobwebs, the likes of which also laced the ceiling and corners of a room whose rough stone walls breathed must and damp.

He returned to the kitchen to replace the fencing sword in its closet. But as he poked it into the back, his hand grazed something soft. Immediately he extracted every object, berating himself for being so astonished by the sword he'd forgotten to check the rest of the space. He yanked out the soft object, which turned out to be a pillow—a strangely mutilated pillow. Slashes and punctures marred it as if it had been attacked by some maniac. He fingered its insides; nothing hidden in it. He laid it on the table and picked up the fencing sword, inserting its tip into the pillow's punctured points. A perfect match—Erika was using the pillow for sword practice. Was she practicing for *him*?

It wouldn't be the first time they'd tangled with weapons, and Voghera would not easily forget that particular prior incident. How frustrating: when they first met, he and Erika had been opponents, then they'd become lovers, and now they were back to square one. He returned the pillow and sword to the broom closet. All the curtains on the ground floor were closed—good. He sat on a kitchen chair and took out Erika's stiletto and his own hunting knife he'd brought from Turin. He placed them side by side on the table, examining the advantages of each weapon. The stiletto's blade was sleek and sharp-pointed, a retractable blade to carry in a pocket but whose cutting edge was dead dull. Voghera's hunting knife, instead, was every bit as slashing sharp as Erika's sword, a brutal blade capable of ripping open a boar's belly.

And the switchblade Erika had taken from him in that duel last year? No trace of it in the house, which meant that she might be carrying it on her.

Voghera, the hunter, returned his knife to the brown leather sheath attached to his belt and slid the retracted stiletto blade back into his coat pocket. Now he had only to wait.

Chapter 30

Dusk was thickening by the time Erika left Amelia's to return to her own house. Since Erika was leaving the next day, Amelia had suggested she lock up Casa Rosselli and leave the keys on the window ledge behind one of the ground-floor shutters. It wasn't likely Amelia would need to go into the house while Erika was gone, but in case she did, she could then return the keys to the window sill, allowing Erika convenient entry when she got back. Tiny Cobbio was trusting and companionable in arrangements like this.

With her umbrella unfurled against the snow, she picked her way up the hill to Casa Rosselli, carrying bandolier style a black canvas hold-all she'd bought that afternoon in Bellinzona after leaving Betz's office. She would need to pack light, taking clothes for only about a week, and the hold-all would allow her to move through her journey hands-free.

She let herself in her front door, leaving her umbrella in its stand and locking the door again. She turned on the kitchen light and set her keys on the buffet next to the radio. Naturally the radio would stay behind tomorrow and also the book lying next to it, *Il fondo del sacco*, by Ticino native Plinio Martini. During the long train treks ahead of her she could buy and then dispose of magazines and newspapers. *Stay light and lithe*, she reminded herself. On her way out of the kitchen she plucked up the scrap of paper marked with her appointment time with Betz. *Whew*—she had got through that encounter and recovered her switchblade to boot! She threw the note away and headed upstairs to pack.

She turned on her small night-table lamp (her usual practice, rather than wasting money on electricity generated by the big bright ceiling light) and started filling the hold-all, choosing basic items from the wardrobe. She decided to bring her black parka, with its multiple pockets and hood, and leave behind her umbrella and the grey overcoat she was still wearing in the cold bedroom. She considered the messenger bag that sat on the wardrobe shelf. No point in dragging it along for the purpose of transporting one item. When she retrieved her translation from its hiding place, it would nestle safely in its plastic sheath at the bottom of the hold-all. Granted, only a zipper kept the hold-all closed—no lock—but the bag's lightness and maneuverability trumped the advantages of even a small suitcase, which could be stolen and still broken into, lock or no lock. A suitcase would have to be stored on overhead luggage racks, whereas this bag could sit in her lap if her train compartment became too crowded for it to rest next to her. Erika breathed luxuriously, felt satisfied, almost excited, about the arrangement.

She tossed the parka on the bed, then glanced at her alarm clock, a small collapsible item that she would drop into the hold-all after it rattled her awake tomorrow morning at five a.m. Then she opened her nightstand drawer. For a moment, disorientation clouded her mind as she stared at the empty space. She reached deeper into the drawer—things were always sliding to the back—and brought forth a pen, which she tossed on the table. Her fingers raked the rest of the hollow, her shocked mind refusing to acknowledge the empty space. She pulled the drawer completely out. Not only had her stiletto disappeared but the notebook she kept to jot down manuscript ideas before she fell asleep.

Slowly she slid the drawer back in place. Suddenly the room felt even colder, a different kind of cold that seemed to coil inside her like a constricting snake, paralyzing her heart and lungs.

An involuntary gasp restarted her breathing. She whipped around to face the bedroom's entrance, and there stood a bearded Claudio Voghera, holding her stiletto, blade deployed, in his left hand and her épée in his right. He lifted the weapons, his eyes filled with mock marvel. Erika's insides plummeted.

"Well," he said, his expression twisting into something between a grin and a grimace, "look what I've found!"

Erika said nothing. She could still barely breathe.

"And best of all," Claudio continued, taking two steps into the room, "I've found *you*!"

Erika's night lamp sent Claudio's shadows splaying across the wall. The épée's black shadow looked immense. He must have scoured Casa Rosselli, turning up whatever he could. *But not everything*. He did not have either of the manuscripts in his hand. They, Erika intimately knew, would not be easy to unearth.

And yet he had found her. She could have asked a thousand questions about how he'd managed that—and no doubt he would have delighted in regaling her with his cleverness—but what did it matter? At this juncture she could afford to concentrate on only one thing, and that was getting out of the house.

She was tempted to slip her right hand into her pocket for the reassuring coolness of her switchblade, but Claudio must have noticed a nervous twitch of her fingers, for he pointed the épée at her hand, making a flicking gesture with it. He stepped closer and Erika stilled her fingers.

"Why don't you speak?" he demanded. "Too shocked at finding me here? Or maybe you're scared of your own weapons?" He lifted the épée again and made a show of examining it. Shaking his head, he said, "What the hell were you going to do with this thing—run me through? I saw what you did to that pillow downstairs—are you *that* frightened of me?"

He made a scoffing sound, then lowered the épée's tip to the floor, placed his left boot on the blade and brought his leg down hard, snapping the blade in two. What was left looked like a blunted dagger with a ridiculously large hilt.

Erika stared as he kicked the severed end aside, a blade that she'd finally finished sharpening into a stabbing, slashing weapon, one that should have been in her hands right now— one with which she could have handily prevailed against a knife-wielding Claudio. She gazed at the dwarfed stub in his grip; it could still be dangerous, its jagged blade capable of shredding flesh. She knew this from experience, from tragic personal experience.

"Want it back?" he asked, extending the stunted butt.

"What do *you* want?" Erika demanded, hot angry blood coursing back to her face, her heart punching her ribs.

Claudio gave an amused grunt and tossed the sword stump on the floor behind him. He flipped the stiletto to his right hand and aimed it at Erika's neck. Then he poked his left hand into his pocket and pulled her notebook.

"*This*," he said, and tossed it on the bed. "This proves I was right that you were up to something with Giorgio Testa." When Erika didn't respond he took another step towards her and raised his voice to a barking staccato. "You betrayed everything I told you in confidence! Now where is the shit you've written?"

Erika's heart was thumping harder. She had to calm herself, stop the hot pounding in her ears in order to think, to act. Claudio stood at the edge of the bed. If she reached into her pocket, he would leap at her with the stiletto before she could free the switchblade and snap open its blade. Her breath came shallow, another constriction. She willed it to sync with her thoughts and channeled Betz: *Know that you're breathing. Feel the breath come up from the earth and spread through your entire body.* She imagined her breath leveling, suffusing her arms and legs, bathing and priming them with oxygen. And still she said nothing.

"*Speak*, for Christ's sake!" shouted Claudio.

"It's gone," she said.

"*What's* gone?"

"Everything I've written."

"*Disappeared?* Gone up in smoke?" Claudio gave his blade a menacing twist.

"It's not here."

"So Giorgio Testa's got it? You don't have a copy yourself? I don't believe it!" He glanced around the room, and Erika took a step back.

"You won't find anything here," she said matter-of-factly. Her breaths and heartbeats were evening out.

"Then you'll take me to where you've put it."

The back of Erika's thighs brushed the bedstand. *Nowhere to go.* Her fingers twitched again.

"Empty your pockets," Claudio ordered, eyeing her hand.

Erika cast him a quizzical look.

"I know you've got my switchblade, so take it out and roll it towards the door. *Slowly!*"

So this was it. If Claudio came any closer he could push her onto the bed and stab her there. If she leapt to the side, so would he, and then he would strike. The fire in his eyes told her so—a flame of hatred and indignation, a blaze of pride and barely-contained patience. Time was up.

She pivoted and yanked her lamp off its stand, plunging the room into darkness. As she tried to maneuver, she tripped on the loose cord and toppled to the ground.

Claudio landed on her feet. He grappled for her legs but she kicked him and swung the lamp in his direction. Its metal shade must have struck his knife for she heard a clang and felt a jolt in her wrist. If only she could discard the lamp and deploy the switchblade, but there was neither sufficient time nor space.

Erika struck blindly with her lamp, flinched as she registered something stab at her booted ankle. Her lamp connected with something tender, for Claudio groaned. She could only avail herself of touch, of sound, of smell, and at the moment the musty odor of Claudio's snow-damp jacket crept up her body. They scrabbled, his elbow slamming her thigh, her knee knocking against his chest. Then a rending sound, coupled with pressure on her right arm—his blade must've torn her coat sleeve, luckily a glancing blow. She swung the lamp again, hit something hard, solid but not heavy, then inched up against the night table. Claudio hung on, his hand grasping her knee. Through all the clatter she could now hear his breath coming loud and heavy. Then she felt a stab of pain in her left calf, a pain which swiftly subsided as she focused on getting to her knife. With both hands she flung the lamp hard in front of her and heard a thud and a groan. She reached into her pocket...but felt nothing. She kicked at Claudio, but he didn't move.

She wriggled out from under him, ready to kick like a kangaroo. Yet he still didn't move. Carefully she reached around the floor but found no knife. She pushed to her feet and climbed onto the bed and then off at the end. Gingerly she trod towards the door to the landing, halting at every step to listen for movement from Claudio.

She tripped on something that clattered, but managed to make it to the doorway. She punched the light on just as Claudio was struggling to his feet. Half dazzled, she spotted what she'd tripped over—the épée hilt with the stunted blade. She scooped it up as Claudio, still gripping the stiletto, wobbled after her. Her blow with the lamp must have struck him in the head.

She punched off the light and lunged out of the room, navigating the stone steps as best she could in the dark. It didn't take long for the bedroom light to come back on.

In the kitchen she felt for her keys on the buffet, snatched them and dashed to the front door. Three clanking turns of the key and the door was open. As she crossed the threshold she heard Claudio's boots hit the bottom of the stairs. She turned and saw him advancing towards her. He was no longer wobbling and now carried a different knife—a thick hunting weapon. If she ran, and he knew how to throw this knife, she would receive a blade in the back. She backed away from him. Then Claudio stepped out of the house and slammed the door behind him.

Moonlight on the snow produced a pinkish-yellow glow, the kind of phenomenon that usually entranced Erika but that now filled her with worry. She needed to hide. Continuing to reverse her steps, she finally felt the crunch of snow under her boots. She thrust her makeshift dagger in Claudio's direction and he halted on the stone porch to stare at it.

He shook his head at her sorry weapon. "You really want to take me on with *that*?"

Erika knew that her only chance with the weapon would be to strike him in the face or neck. Still, she held the stunted épée in classic *en garde* position, the only way she knew to fight.

"And you're bleeding," Claudio added, pointing his knife at her left leg.

Erika wouldn't lower her eyes to look. But now that she had the brief luxury to think about it, she could feel a dull ache in her calf. She squeezed the épée's grip and held Claudio's gaze.

"I didn't want to have to stab you." He flashed a perturbed frown as he advanced a step towards her. "Why can't you come to your senses and cooperate?"

Erika's thoughts were too busy to allow her to speak.

"Listen, we really should get that wound of yours bandaged," he continued half sympathetically. And then in a more menacing tone, "And I would *hate* to see you get stabbed with *this*." The massive hunting blade rose towards her face. "Now where's that fucking story!?"

Naturally Claudio was right about his knife's superiority to her stub of a blade. So she waited, willing herself to patience, expecting him to advance again.

Which he did, and in that instant she hurled her blade at his face and sprinted towards the path that led to the mountain.

Chapter 31

Erika's broken stub of sword flew end over end to strike Voghera in the forehead. Stunned, he clasped his forehead with his left hand. *Christ*, he could have lost an eye. Only an instinctive duck downwards had saved him from serious injury. Still, there he was bleeding profusely from the wide gash in his forehead. He shook off the pain, wiped off the blood, and started running after Erika. He had sheathed his hunting knife so as not to fall on it if he tripped—but it wouldn't remain at his belt for long, only until he caught up with that devious bitch.

He wiped his brow again, wincing and gritting his teeth. *Jesus*, did she truly think he'd meant to kill her? Grudgingly he acknowledged this could be true. But up until she'd flung the butt of her sword at him, he'd planned only to threaten her if he couldn't reason with her. He might have had to hurt her...a little, but he'd figured she would give in before that and turn over the exposé. Yet now, as he panted his way up the path towards *who knew where*, blood dripping into his eyebrows, his head feeling like it had been sawed open, all he could think of was getting his hands on Erika, story or no story.

The public path was coming to an end, no roads or houses in sight. A gust of wind and swirling snow smacked his face, forcing him to mop both blood and water out of his eyes. *Cazzo*, he swore, squeezing his eyes shut against the pain, where was Erika headed? He stopped for a moment; he couldn't see her, but after the gust of wind he heard boots tramping through the snow up ahead. He pushed off again and finally got a glimpse of a silhouette hiking up the mountain. Christ, she was headed into the wilderness, where trees thickened and so did the darkness. Were they going to climb this *cazzo* of a mountain?

Erika had left the village path. The closest house to hers was the Hartigans'. But when she'd come home late this afternoon, she'd noticed their house was dark. They might have already left on their ski trip. As she engaged the mountain she thought their absence fortuitous. She didn't want to endanger anyone else.

She had got a good start, adrenaline and plain old hiking practice at high altitude propelling her at mountain-goat speed. A wind had now whipped up, though, and its steel-sharp cold was freezing her hands and face and whistling through the gaps Claudio had shredded in her coat. And she could feel the cold now in her lacerated calf, an electric pain that shot up and down her leg. She grasped exposed stumps, bushes, sapling trunks, anything visible that could help her labor up the mountain in the deep snow.

And where would she end up? From the point where she'd turned off the public path, only one destination seemed plausible—the monastery on the side of the mountain, the very place the Hartigans had recommended for a hike. Even Adriana had suggested they make the trek up there together once the path was clear of snow. But now here she was, only alone, with no discernible path, stumping through the snow in search of refuge. From anywhere in Cobbio you could admire the shine of the monastery's white stuccoed structure against the mountain. Only now Erika couldn't see it at all. But it was above her, she knew that. She only needed to *climb, climb, climb.*

Incessantly Voghera wiped his face of blood. Blood and damp and cold had stiffened one glove and now he was using the other to mop his forehead. The cold supposedly slowed blood flow, but his was a head wound and he knew he should stop and press some kind of heavy cloth to it for a good length of time. Time, however, he didn't have. So he plodded on up the mountain, only one hand free to cling to rocks and jutting vegetation to keep his balance.

Amidst the thick, dark trees, he had lost sight of Erika's silhouette and his own heavy breathing and swishing steps meant he could hear no noise above him. How far up would she climb before having to turn back? Recalling his vantage point in the village, the mountain's crest looked miles away.

But there was a building on the mountainside. He'd spotted it from the gas station. Was that where Erika was headed? *Where there's a functioning structure* (and he had no idea what function that structure served) *there has to be a pathway to it.* Still, who could find it in all this snow?

For a moment he felt lightheaded. His wound could not be too deep, he told himself, and under the thin skin of the forehead lay thick bone. No arteries, only veins. Nothing vital to damage. Yet how long would he keep bleeding? He stopped long enough to regain equilibrium, scooped up a handful of snow and plastered it to his wound. He wanted to howl with the pain but held steady and slapped the gash with another handful. That seemed to sort out his head and he struck out again.

Erika tripped over a snow-obscured rock and slid about a meter down the mountain. Her calf was throbbing, her light-blue corduroys stained dark with blood, though when she felt the material it was mostly stiff. Maybe she wouldn't lose much more blood. Her wound might only be superficial, but in the cold and dark, and without removing her trousers, how could she tell?

Her toes now ached with cold as well, and for a moment while sitting in the snow she considered heading back down to the village. Claudio might not even realize her change of direction, if he'd made it this far. She could retrieve the manuscripts and dash to the train station—buy a ticket to Lucerne, or anywhere for that matter, stay the night in a hotel, and rebook her ticket to leave tomorrow as planned. She'd be able to obtain bandages and disinfectant for her wound, even buy clothes to replace the snow-sodden, shredded and filthy ones she now wore...

But as fast as those thoughts galloped across her mind, so did the thought that Claudio might hear her make her way down. She had no idea where he was in relation to her, she could even run right into him—*weaponless*. Certainly he was furious enough to pursue her up the mountain. The blow she'd dealt him had been brutal enough to land him in the hospital. But *shit*—she couldn't be sure of anything. All she knew was she mustn't lose her advantage in distance over him. She picked herself up and resumed her ascent, blocking the pain in her leg with stubborn, blinding effort.

Voghera's gash was seeping less blood, the cold or the snow he kept applying to the wound finally slowing things down—or so he hoped. Still, his whole head ached as if it were being jack-hammered. He grabbed another handful of snow and pressed it to his forehead, holding his breath against the pain of icy sandlike crystals scraping the wound. He forged on. If Erika was indeed heading towards the building he'd spied, maybe she would find it closed. He halted an instant to check his watch: almost seven o'clock; hopefully there would be no one to take her in. And then what?

No use thinking about it at this point. With no footprints in front of him, he wasn't even sure he was headed in the right direction. He couldn't use his flashlight, since one hand had to mop his forehead of blood and the other grip whatever jutted from the snow. He imagined both Erika and him zigzagging up this mountain, taking whichever path of least resistance, winding around trees and rocks like they were slogging through an obstacle course. Only this course was swallowed in darkness.

He stumbled through a belt of trees and almost ploughed into one, its low leafless limbs snagging his jacket. He stopped to regain balance, the muscles in his legs burning with exertion. He'd had no hiking exercise in practically a year, having been excluded from Moretti's hunting group. His lungs cried for air, making him bend at the waist and rest his hands on his knees. Cold as the air was, he felt soaked with sweat, and blood was fountaining anew from his forehead. He almost fell over. *Cazzo—this can't go on!* He wrenched off his jacket and laid it in the snow. Then he pulled off both his sweater and shirt, piling them on his jacket, and started working fast. He removed his undershirt, ripping it into strips with his hunting knife so he could bandage his head with them. The initial rush of frigid air against his bare chest was almost refreshing, though not seconds later his torso began to stiffen like a block of ice. He threw his partially-unbuttoned shirt back over his head, along with his sweater, zipped up his coat, and then wrapped his head with the makeshift bandage. He checked that his knife was snapped in its sheath, then heaved himself forward. He swayed with his first step, shivering in his damp clothes, then pushed on.

In the shadows of the trees Erika could see no lights above her. No illumination signaling the monastery might be near. Had she passed it somehow? Climbed completely around it? She wouldn't be surprised, she felt so tired. And yet if she was above the monastery she should surely be able to see some kind of light below her...*how high up the mountain had she climbed?*

And how much longer would her leg hold out? She'd already begun half dragging it, and she found that lifting it out of the snow to take a step was like climbing a ladder out of a swimming pool. Never mind the pain that felt like a burrowing corkscrew. Her feet, on the other hand, had started warming up. A small compensation; *or was it*? Coming from San Diego, Erika had no idea what kind of effects severe cold produced. Her hands were numb; if someone were to cut off a finger, she didn't think she would feel it.

227

And then she saw footprints in the snow. They weren't large, definitely smaller than hers, and not too deep. Had a woman walked here? Bolts of exhilaration shot through her as she followed the tracks upward. Her breath came in chuffs, but her leg didn't hurt now, nor did she feel the cold. She waded steadily up the mountain, finally spotting a glimmer of light. Her heartbeats were pummeling her dry throat when she at last reached a great wooden gate fixed with two lamplights on either end. Immediately she made fists of her numb hands and started pounding on it. *This had to be the monastery, but Christ, were the nuns still up?*

She stopped hammering and managed to peel back her coat sleeve to check her watch—not quite eight o'clock. She pounded again—*someone had to hear her*—then stopped when she noticed a niche in the gate that housed a bell. She yanked its rope repeatedly and clanging erupted through the snow-hushed woods. The more she rang the bell, the more she became aware that the din could be heard up and down the mountain. *Please someone open the gate!*

In pain and exhaustion Voghera collapsed against a tree. Once more he was woozy and his legs felt rubbery. He removed a blood-encrusted glove and with a bare finger dabbed the bandage on his forehead. A blot of liquid appeared on his fingertip but at least blood wasn't oozing through the bandage. He rested there, trying to catch his seething breath. His legs were so weak that he didn't know if he'd be able to push off again. *And this reeling in his head. No*, now it was a ringing— *bells banging about in his head.* As his breathing became less labored he was able to stand straight, but the clanging continued until he realized the noise wasn't in his head but was coming from somewhere else—up the mountain? *From the building perched somewhere up there?* Encouraged, he drew a deep breath and took up the slog again. He hiked while bent at the waist, focusing on each of his steps. *One foot, then the other—he would make it.*

At last he reached a path of sorts. With his flashlight he traced footsteps heading up and down this patch of mountain. There was a light in the distance. He staggered after it up to a clearing and a large gate. This must be the building he'd seen from the village. But what *kind* of building, and where was Erika? One of the sets of footprints must be hers. He aimed his light above the gate, up to the roof, where a Christian cross beamed back at him. So this was a monastery. He leaned his back against the gate, his head swimming. *The bells—someone had been ringing bells here.*

Erika, was she inside? He couldn't think any longer. Slowly his body slid down the gate and he found himself sitting slumped in the snow. His head drooped, his chin hit his chest, and all went black.

Chapter 32

Cool water spilled over Erika's feet. She knew it to be cool when placing her wrist under the flow, though to her fingers and feet the temperature felt close to burning. She sat on the rim of an old-fashioned, stand-alone bathtub. Was this the only bathroom in the monastery? Sister Clotilde hadn't said, but all the same Erika didn't want to monopolize the room. The sister—the resident medic, it seemed—had told her to bathe her feet and hands in cool water, for she might have a case of pre-frostbite, or frostnip. And the sister had been right. Erika cringed at the thought of even a drop of warm touching the skin of her hands or feet. And yet she would next have to take a full cold bath—once again, instructed by Sister Clotilde, who had disinfected and sewn what had turned out to be a shallow wound in her calf. "I once taught nursing sciences," she told Erika.

Submerged in the half-full tub, Erika winced and shivered, her wound tight and painful in the cool water, though her hands and feet felt only warmth. She washed quickly, gasping as she stuck her head under the faucet and washed her snow-drenched hair. Then she left the tub, feet and hands a livid red, and dressed in plain flannel pajamas and dressing gown provided by the sister. She towel-dried her hair, luckily it was short, drained the tub, and left the bathroom for her meeting with a certain Mother Ludovica, the nun in charge of the monastery. While in the water, Erika had started formulating a story.

Apart from frostnip, Erika must have been in a state of semi-shock when the monastery gate finally opened to her. The sister who'd opened the gate had asked her what happened, but after hearing a mumbled, incoherent response the nun had whisked her into the main building and turned her over to Sister Clotilde.

Now she was being escorted, limping, down a wood-paneled corridor by another nun-in-habit. This one looked young, younger than Erika, and kept far more silent than the commanding and capable sister-medic. The young nun knocked on a door, which had no label, and in an instant it inched open and another sister, middle-aged, ushered Erika in. The young nun left while the middle-aged sister sat on a wooden straight-backed chair in the corner of the room. Three people present, Erika counted, including herself and an older nun behind a desk.

The woman smiled faintly. "Erika," she said by way of greeting. "Do sit down." She gestured to a small leather armchair across from the desk, and Erika obeyed. "I'm Mother Ludovica. Are you feeling better after your bath and Sister Clotilde's ministrations?"

She looked stern, spectacles perched hawkishly on the bridge of her nose, a classic Mother Superior, thought Erika. She felt ridiculous dressed in pajamas and slippers but nodded and found her voice. "Yes, thank you for coming to my aid. Thanks to everyone." She studiously avoided the word *rescue* as her story continued to crystalize in her mind.

Mother Ludovica granted Erika another aloof smile, though this time Erika thought she noted a slight sense of indulgence in the woman.

The expression quickly faded away. "Well, now that you're in a much more collected condition, perhaps you could tell us what happened to you out in the woods?" The mother's eyes remained fixed on Erika's, and Erika had an urge to glance back at the nun seated in the corner. No sound had come from her, not even a rustling of her habit. Erika wondered if the sister might be taking notes. In the pause, Mother Superior intensified her stare, her brows rising in expectation.

"Mother Ludovica," Erika began, "I can only say that I was stupid. I went out for a hike in the snow and got lost." She cleared her throat in a manner she hoped sounded earnest. "You can probably tell by my accent that I'm not from here." This time she did look back and found the sister in the corner not writing but sitting still and stoic as a statue. Embarrassed, Erika quickly turned back to face Mother Ludovica, the corners of whose mouth had turned skeptically down.

"Yes, we realize you're a foreigner," she said, and then more gently, "but that does not concern us. All supplicants are embraced here, though we are obliged to learn of their circumstances."

Erika shifted in her chair. *Obliged?* Obliged to find out *how* much about her? "Yes," she said, "I understand. I went hiking and got lost in the storm, then I slipped down a slope and ripped my coat and," she shook her head, "my leg too. I knew I was near the monastery, so instead of going all the way back to the village, I managed to reach you."

Erika couldn't tell how convincing she'd sounded, for Mother Ludovica continued to study her. "You know," she said mildly, "that if you're in any kind of danger we can call the police."

"Oh no," Erika protested. "Nothing like that. I'm just one of those Americans that like challenging sport. Again, quite stupid in this case." She shook her head and lowered her eyes in feigned embarrassment, and hoped Mother Ludovica would leave it at that.

When she looked up, the mother superior still seemed to be contemplating. "Well," she finally said, "I'm very glad we could help. Of course, you can spend the night here, rest your leg, unless you'd like to call for someone to come get you. Though I'm afraid your clothes are in a poor state..."

Erika exhaled almost audibly. "I'd be grateful to accept your hospitality and stay the night—I live alone..." She paused, unsure of what to say next.

"No need to explain," the mother said. "We'll keep an eye

on your wound tonight, then tomorrow, after a good night's rest, you can decide what to do."

And that concluded Erika's interview with Mother Ludovica. The middle-aged sister in the corner left to recall the young nun, who accompanied Erika to an empty sleeping cell. "I've put clean towels on the writing desk," she told Erika from the threshold, her eyes cast slightly down. "And I believe you know where the bathroom is, but if you need any assistance, my room is the cell next to yours." She indicated the direction. "Knock anytime." She'd almost closed the door, then stuck her head back in the room. "Oh," she added, reddening, "I almost forgot. Mother Ludovica has instructed our cook to heat up some minestrone for you. I'll bring you a tray."

After the sister left, Erika reclined on the twin bed, putting her feet up and leaning back against the spartan wooden headboard. A wooden cross hung on the wall above her head. On her night table sat a glass and a pitcher of water, flanked by a hand towel. The floor was also wooden and creaky. A plain wooden wardrobe, about the size of a stunted telephone booth, leaned against the wall next to the door. That was life in this monastery.

And Erika was fine with it. All she longed for was to fill her stomach with the promised hot minestrone, drink more water (she had already been given some earlier) and go to sleep.

If things were only that simple. Where was Claudio? Had he followed her all the way up here, and would he try to break into the monastery? The latter she doubted, though she easily imagined him staking out the premises, waiting to see if she came out. Well, in that case he'd be stuck in the cold and snow, injured maybe worse than she was. Erika shook her head. Who could predict what Claudio might be capable of, since he'd managed to track her from Turin to Cobbio.

She tucked her pillow between her back and the headboard and had almost dozed off when there was a tapping at the door. The young sister entered with Erika's tray: a bowl of steaming minestrone, a plate of bread and cheese, an apple, and another pitcher of water. Erika thanked her and, after the girl left, devoured it all. Then she shut off her night light and snuggled under the simple white duvet.

She only slept for an hour and a half, her watch indicating as much when she woke and turned the light back on. She considered the small lamp, about the same size as the one she'd armed herself with to battle Claudio. And if he was now outside, about to die of either his injuries or exposure? She shook herself: that was his choice to make, not hers. *If* he had been dogged enough to follow her up the mountain. With his track record so far, she would have to assume so. Or, he'd gone back to Casa Rosselli to continue searching for her manuscript. She highly doubted he would find it, but when she returned to the house he could easily be lying in wait.

The manuscript, the scoop. How important was it, she dared ask herself, in light of the ordeal she had just endured? Safe now, with a full stomach and a warm bed, she could take some stock. What intrinsic importance did the fascist Matilde Fassino have, after all? She'd proved herself a villain during the war, a true war criminal, but even before her kidnapping by communist thugs last year, she'd been old and feeble and probably wouldn't have lived all that much longer, anyway. Then with her stroke she'd become almost a living corpse— Erika had seen her in that hospital bed with her own eyes. Had this not been punishment enough for her horrible deeds?

Erika wondered if even Giorgio might have similar thoughts. Everything seemed to be a grand concert of manipulation for one's own ends, everyone maneuvering to steer the players in their own direction. Including DIGOS and Claudio. DIGOS had orchestrated Matilde Fassino's assassination, just in case she got well enough to talk about their involvement in her kidnapping. *Assassination*: the word almost always conjured evil connotations, and the Free Press had always labored to expose those who conducted such operations.

Giorgio represented the Free Press. How could she even consider dropping everything and letting him down? *No, that wouldn't happen.* Plus, half of this project was hers—*her* accomplishment, waiting to be brought to fruition; which shifted her thoughts to Claudio again: if after all the travails of this night, her drive to reach her goal hadn't diminished, neither would have his to thwart her and punish her for betraying him. He would pursue her until the sun burned out.

Claudio wouldn't find the manuscript, secreted along with Giorgio's original Italian script, yet how was she going to get to the hiding place unnoticed? Giorgio must have already left for London. She would try to call Régine tomorrow and get an update. At least one manuscript would be on its way to Ian Wescott of *The Guardian* newspaper.

She contemplated how she would leave the monastery tomorrow—limping in her ragged and dirty clothes, looking for transportation. She glanced at her train ticket to London which lay crumpled on the nightstand next to her, having survived the evening's ordeal. Even if she had to leave in her tattered clothes she could trade the ticket in for a new one with a later departure time. Even if she couldn't get safely back to Casa Rosselli, she could take a taxi to the station and get the hell out of Cobbio, beyond Claudio's clutches.

But the house would be left abandoned and unlocked, with the lights on. What would Adriana think if she came by? *Shit!*

And the nuns here—would they ask her more questions tomorrow morning? *Where she lived, who she knew?*

Erika squirmed in her bed and groaned at the pain in her calf. Sister Clotilde had given her some kind of pain medication but it was wearing off. Her wound not only felt tight but it burned now. She was tempted to get up and ask to be brought to the sister-medic by the young sister next door. Then again she didn't want to appear overly dependent on the nuns. Already she had the sensation of being a semi prisoner: escorted everywhere, given orders, interrogated by the Chief in Command—*sleeping in a cell*. That was an exaggeration, naturally, but she couldn't help hating this confinement, even though it was of her own making.

Finally she turned off her light, fatigue crushing her again. She was certain of only one thing: tomorrow she would leave here, no matter what.

Chapter 33

It was still dark outside when Erika was wakened by a knock at her convent-cell door. She sat up, disoriented at first, then turned on her bedside lamp. She cleared her throat and called out, "Come in," checking her watch—it was only six a.m.

The young sister opened the door a crack and murmured, "*Buon giorno*. We're serving breakfast in half an hour."

"Oh." Erika rubbed her eyes and smoothed down her hair. "Thank you, I'll..." It occurred to her that she had no idea where breakfast was served.

"I'll come back to get you at six-thirty," the young woman said. And then, blushing, added, "I'm sorry I woke you."

Erika sat back against the headboard. Due to sheer exhaustion she had been able to sleep through the discomfort in her leg, but now a pulsating pain made her wonder how she was going to get around. She pulled the covers off and swiveled to the side of the bed. Gingerly she put her foot on the floor and applied pressure. The throbbing intensified, but she was able to stand and take a hobbling step. The wound was a puncture wound, not terribly deep, but Jesus, she wasn't sure she could make it to the dining area, wherever it was.

Then she heard another knock. "Come in."

It was Sister Clotilde, bustling in with a kit. "I knew you'd feel worse this morning," she said, after they'd exchanged greetings. "Sit down and let's have a look at the leg."

The sister changed the dressing on Erika's wound and pronounced that things looked good since very little fluid had leaked through the stitches. She gave Erika more pain medication to be taken with breakfast. "*Always* take these with food," she emphasized. "I can leave this packet with you, but when you run out you'll have to get more from the pharmacy in the village." She stood and put her hands on her hips. "My work seems to have held, but if blood starts to leak through the bandage after you leave here, you'll have to see a doctor." She gave Erika a dubious look, then packed up her things.

"*Grazie,*" Erika said, picking up the blister packet of pills.

"Get ready for breakfast now," Sister Clotilde ordered, "so you can take one of those before the wound gets more painful. I'll send young Sister Chiara back in with a cane for you to use." *Sister Chiara*: she'd been too bashful to introduce herself.

It wasn't five minutes later that the change of shift took place. The young nun came back with a cane hooked over her forearm and carrying a stack of Erika's clothes, which she set on the desk. Erika had filled a large bowl with water to splash her face clean and was just drying off. She thanked the sister for the cane and asked if there was a comb she could use.

"Oh..." The sister reddened once more. "I think there's one with your clothes. We put everything back after we washed and mended them."

Erika stared at the pile on the desk. When did these women do all this? "Well, thank you...you didn't need to..."

The young nun didn't wait for Erika to finish. She merely nodded and said, "I'll be back in ten minutes, after you dress." She lowered her eyes and backed out of the room.

With breakfast at six-thirty Erika figured they would be finished by seven, and it would still be dark out. She wasn't sure whether to leave the monastery then or wait for daylight. There were also the perceptions of the sisters to consider. Why would someone recovering from a trauma wish to skip out before daybreak? And how would she get off the mountain? Going down the way she came up would be folly, even without an injured leg.

She dressed quickly, her patched corduroys and coat making her look like a rail-hopping hobo. What Sister Chiara had said about her things was true, though, about the contents of all her trouser pockets. A few months ago there would have also been a pack of cigarettes in her coat pocket, but she'd quit smoking to save money since arriving in Switzerland. Just as well, since the sisters might have been displeased to find her Marlboros.

She looked around for a mirror and spotted none. Picturing the nuns coiffed and veiled, with only their stark, bare faces showing, she sighed in resignation.

More tapping at the door. Young Sister Chiara entered, took one look at Erika standing haplessly with comb in hand, and pointed to the wardrobe. "There's a mirror on the inside of the door," she murmured. She cleared her throat, turning away while Erika found the mirror and ran her comb swiftly through her tousled locks, then they left the room, the sister in the lead, with Erika limping behind, supported by her cane.

The dining room had a long, wooden communal table. Only two of its twelve chairs were occupied, and this time Erika was obliged to sit with both Sister Clotilde and Mother Ludovica. Young Sister Chiara, her duty accomplished, glided silently out of the room. Mother Ludovica, sitting at the head of the table, indicated an empty chair across from Sister Clotilde, where Erika sat, the three of them forming a triangle. An uncomfortable one, sensed Erika immediately.

After returning Mother Ludovica's *buon giorno*, she stared uneasily at her place setting and the breakfast next to it: bread, butter and marmalade, a plate of cheese, two small ceramic carafes, one containing hot coffee, the other warmed milk—all and only for her, it seemed.

"I hope you slept well," said Mother Ludovica. "The other sisters are at chapel right now. This portion is for you."

So, under the scrutiny of the two senior nuns Erika poured herself coffee and sipped it, feeling like a bug under a magnifying glass. She didn't want to eat alone in front of them, but Sister Clotilde urged her and Erika tore off a piece of bread and cut herself a hunk of cheese so she could take her pain pill.

"By the way," said Mother Ludovica, "the snow has stopped. Ploughs are already working on the road to the village."

"There's a paved road?" Erika asked eagerly.

The mother superior gave an ironic little laugh. "It runs between villages. How else would we get our supplies?"

Erika brushed off the humor. *There was a road out of here!*

"I take that back," Mother Ludovica said. "Years ago, before the road was built, supplies had to be delivered by pack mule. They traveled the same path, more or less, as you must have last night. A formidable enterprise in even the best of weather." Head slightly atilt, the same faint fissure of a smile as last evening's, she paused to watch Erika. Sister Clotilde was observing her as well, and Erika felt she must explain herself: where she'd come from, where she was headed next...

"Then I'm glad I'm staying in Cobbio now instead of back then," she said, deciding to speak as transparently as possible. "I've been staying in a house in the village—kind of a retreat to do some writing and hiking." She thought of Casa Rosselli standing vacant and unlocked, of the hidden manuscripts, of Claudio lurking about...

"I have to say again how stupid it was of me to go out last night," she went on, "especially since early this morning I was supposed to leave on a trip...I'll have to change my train ticket..."

She hoped that was enough information to satisfy the sisters, and maybe it did satisfy Sister Clotilde who said, "Well, you have the packet of pain pills, but if you really must take a train today, I suggest stopping at the pharmacy first for disinfectant and extra bandages."

Erika nodded obligingly, still wondering how she would limp down to the village. Even on a paved road it would be a long walk. And then she would have to try and retrieve her stuff from the house, then hobble down the hill to the train station—"

Mother Ludovica spared her the headache. "When it gets light, I'll have one of the sisters drive you down to the village." She paused again, her smile more pointed now. "So you live all alone in the village, no family or friends?"

Erika responded with an amiable shrug. "I came here for the solitude. In that, maybe I'm not all that different from you."

Mother Ludovica glanced at Sister Clotilde and the two exchanged inscrutable looks. Erika could have done without making that last remark, but now she had to focus on getting out of the monastery and then out of Cobbio. She thanked the two sisters for the meals and hospitality.

On her own for the first time in the monastery halls, she made her way back to her cell, noting the silence and absence of the other sisters who must be still at chapel. She wondered who would drive her to the village.

It turned out to be the shy, yet faithful, Sister Chiara. At sun-up, car keys in hand, she knocked on the frame of Erika's open door.

While waiting, Erika had pondered the ever-present danger of running into Claudio. He had followed her from the house, and if he had waited up here all night in the snow he could have frozen to death. So would he have found the paved road back down to the village? If he'd got himself back down, would he be waiting, hidden, at Casa Rosselli, no matter how hurt he was?

Now, seated next to the young sister in an old white van, Erika decided to ask a favor. "Do you think you could wait while I grab my bag out of the house, then drive me down to the train station?" Erika shot her a nervous look. "It won't take me long, and I'm not sure if I can walk down there with my leg like this…"

Although there was no place to park near Casa Rosselli, a vehicle could engage the cobbled public path for deliveries. That was how Erika received the fuel for her stove. The sister, her pale blue eyes fastened to the road, might have been considering such logistics and didn't answer right away. Finally she gave an abrupt nod. "*Sì.*" Erika wanted to hug her.

She would have to hurry down to the house—and with her wounded leg, hurrying might not be an option—change clothes, retrieve her bag and the manuscripts, and rush—once more not likely—back to the van.

"*Grazie!*" she said to Sister Chiara.

And where would Claudio be?

The road down to the village had been long and tortuous, and at one point Voghera had almost asked the driver who'd picked him up in the night to stop and let him out to vomit. Normally he didn't get carsick but the pain and wooziness in his head must have triggered the horrible sensation. The man, who'd been driving down from another village, had shown concern at Voghera's sodden condition and bandaged forehead and wanted to take him to the hospital in Bellinzona. Voghera had declined. "I just made a foolish mistake trying to hike in the snow. I'll be all right." And so the driver had taken him to his car parked at the gas station on Cobbio's main road. There Voghera had used the rest of the torn undershirt stuffed in his jacket pocket to change the bandage on his forehead, after first dousing his wound with alcohol from the first-aid kit in his trunk. The dousing nearly made him faint but at least Voghera had braced himself for it, first taking copious swigs from the bottle of whiskey in his glovebox; and in that respect the agony wasn't nearly as debilitating as when it had spiked in unexpected and dizzying waves while he'd scrambled up the mountain. He'd used the rubbing alcohol to clean his entire face and hands, checking the job in his rearview mirror. Then he'd crawled into the back seat and rolled up in a blanket that also came from the trunk. A few more swigs of whiskey and he'd been able to sink into a fitful sleep.

Now smears of pearl grey were lightening the sky. And no more snow, thank God. An automatic reflex to stretch his limbs made Voghera groan with pain. His body felt broken. Yet he knew it wasn't; it had only been taxed to unhabitual limits. His head ached, not as badly as last night, and his bandage had held. He got out to clean snow off his windows and windshield, leaving most of the car camouflaged in white, then got behind the wheel and turned on the ignition. He would drive as far up into the village as possible. As he pulled out of the gas station parking lot, the attendant drove in. His eyes narrowed at Voghera who waved as he drove away.

He reached the level of the village where he'd first driven upon arriving in Cobbio, the point where a woman had told him there was nowhere to park. There he eased off the cobbled path and brought his car to a stop on the snow under a tree; perhaps someone owned the property, though no house flanked the little clearing. He headed up the mountain on foot, his stomach cramping with hunger, urging him up to Casa Rosselli. He had no idea whether Erika would return there, only that she was in a bad way herself and would eventually have to go somewhere. In the meantime he would find food and check the house again.

Cautiously he approached the house, and judging no one was there he went in and ate biscotti from a tin on the table, brushing crumbs into his hand and disposing of them in the waste paper basket under the sink. He searched the house. Nothing seemed to have changed since Erika's flight, same lights on, keys left in the inside front door lock. She hadn't returned from the monastery.

He searched the house again for her writings, but instead found the switchblade he was certain had been in Erika's coat pocket the night before. There it was lying on the floor near the broken, unplugged lamp which he had to admit had worked effectively as a weapon itself. The knot on his head proved it. He pocketed this knife too. But dammit, where was that fucking exposé? Last night, before their fight, he'd seen Erika return with a hold-all with which she'd started packing. Had she planned to place the manuscript in it, then take off to meet Testa? Could DIGOS have caught up with him?

Voghera returned outdoors to recheck the storage closet at the end of the porch. This time he removed everything that stood against the dusty wall, sending rakes and shovels clattering to the stone floor. He checked for crevices between the wall and ground and any place old bricks could be loose. There were a couple which Voghera pried away, shining his flashlight into shadowy recesses and finding nothing but more dust and cobwebs.

He left the storage space, slamming the door. Outside he scanned the property. Could Erika have *buried* her story somewhere in the garden?

And then he heard the sound of an engine interrupted by the clunking of changing gears, typical of an old vehicle. He strode up Casa Rosselli's path to have a look, hiding behind a snow-shrouded hedgerow on a small ridge overlooking the house. An old white van was chugging up the public pathway. *What the hell? You can't park here...*

The van stopped, ignition shutting off, just before the turn-off to Casa Rosselli's private pathway. And lo and behold, none other than Erika climbed out. She'd gotten a ride here, and no wonder because she was limping along with a cane. He could see a patch on her trouser leg where he'd stabbed her. Whoever inhabited the monastery had helped. *Too bad...or maybe not.*

His breath quickened as she approached. He waited for the van to leave but it sat there, stubbornly blocking the public path. Who the hell was driving it?

Erika turned onto the path to the house; he wanted to get behind her and catch her, so he stayed put in a crouch, his gaze swiveling from her to where the van was parked and back. Erika was slowly approaching the house and the van's engine still hadn't started up again. *Cazzo*, the driver must be waiting for her!

She was nearing the front door. *Was she coming back to collect her hold-all—and maybe her story? Why else return when it could be dangerous?* He crept along the hedgerow where there was a gap he could squeeze through leading down to the front garden. There he squatted and watched Erika enter the house. He would wait for her, let her collect what might be the manuscript, then ambush her when she came back out.

Not ten minutes later, Casa Rosselli's front door swung open with a creak that broke the snowy silence. Out stepped Erika, wearing jeans and the black hooded parka, the black hold-all he'd seen the night before slung crossways over her shoulder. He had to pounce now while she was locking the door. He shimmied through the narrow gap in the hedgerow, causing the winter-brittle branches to crack and Erika to pivot and look up. She pulled the keys from the door just as he slid down the ridge.

Chapter 34

*C*laudio! He skidded to an awkward stop in front of Erika as she'd just locked her door. She now stood on the porch with the keys in her right hand, her cane in her left, and the hold-all hanging across her. *Claudio:* though he had a bandaged forehead and looked like he'd slept rough, had two working legs and two free hands. *No contest.* She looked up the path towards the road where Sister Chiara waited.

Claudio glanced over his shoulder in the same direction then back at her. Grimacing, he demanded, "Where are you going with that bag? And who's parked on the road up there?"

Erika just shook her head.

"Put the bag down and kick it over to me," he said. Without waiting for a response, he peeled back his unzipped jacket and extracted his hunting knife from the sheath on his belt.

Erika stiffened and looked up towards the road again.

"I know whoever's waiting for you can't see us down here, so stop trying to distract me!" Claudio took a step closer, his knife pointed at Erika's chest.

"...But if I don't go back up, they'll come down to see what's going on."

"*Who will?*"

Erika ignored that. "Or they'll go get the police." Actually, Erika didn't even know where police were located in the village and hoped Sister Chiara would stay put in the van.

"Drop the hold-all and kick it over here," Claudio repeated. "And don't try to throw anything this time!"

With all the snow overnight, the stunted sword Erika had hurled at Claudio lay nowhere in sight. She gazed at Claudio's forehead. So that's where her throw must have landed. His bandage looked scruffy but otherwise fairly clean. "I'm sorry you got injured," she said, echoing approximately Claudio's sentiment of the night before concerning the wound he'd inflicted on her. She recognized the ambiguity in both their apologies.

Claudio's eyes darted to her leg. "You're limping. Where did you get help, the monastery?"

Erika ignored that too. She pictured Sister Chiara in the van's driver's seat. How long would she wait there...?

"I want that bag!" Claudio's grip tightened on his knife.

"Whatever you think I've written isn't in it."

"I'll see for myself." He took another step forward.

Erika pocketed the keys and raised her cane.

"Drop it!" Claudio flashed his knife at her.

She lowered the cane. It wasn't much use in her left hand, anyway. She set the hold-all on the ground in front her.

"Kick it over," Claudio ordered again, and Erika nudged it forward with her right foot. "Where were you going with this?" he repeated. "To meet Giorgio Testa with your translating? *Ma che cazzo!*

"Nothing you're interested in is in the bag," Erika said patiently.

Voghera smirked then hooked one of the bag's straps with his foot, dragging it towards him. He told Erika to sit.

"Right here?"

"Do it!"

Erika lowered herself onto the cold stone porch, laying her cane in front of her, while

Voghera took a step back and squatted to unzip the hold-all. He rummaged through clothes and toiletries, then finally stood back up, grunting "*cazzo*." He kicked the bag back towards Erika.

"I told you there's nothing in there," she said, resisting the instinct to look at the stone fountain situated a few paces behind Claudio and covered with snow.

"Then you'll take me to where it is. Now get up."

Pain drilled through her calf as Erika attempted to rise. She suppressed a gasp and used both hands to lever herself with her cane. When she reached a standing position, both hands were resting on it.

"Now you'll—"

Voghera was interrupted by the sound of an engine igniting and revving up.

"They're leaving you," he boasted.

"No, they're telling me to hurry up, and they'll come down here if I don't!" Her left hand rested on her right, which now gripped the cane's handle.

"Who?" Voghera insisted.

The sound of a honking horn reached them. Both Erika and Voghera jerked to attention and Erika swung her cane, teetering off balance. Deflecting the blow with his knife, Claudio grabbed her by the jacket with his left hand and pulled her into the snow.

Down she fell, with Voghera landing on top of her. She reached for her cane but felt nothing but cold snow.

"Jesus Christ, Erika, haven't you had enough?" Claudio had her pinned, his knife at her throat.

His breath smelled of whiskey, the bandage on his forehead slipping down to his eyebrows. Blood was trickling from the flapping purple gash in his forehead. A drop landed on Erika's eyelid. She blinked and shook her head, then froze abruptly when she felt Claudio's ice-cold blade nick her neck.

Her eyes must have stretched wide, for he said, "Calm down—it's only a scratch. But it'll be worse if you fight me!" He raised his left hand, pushing his bandage back up, but it wouldn't stay put. Erika's right hand continued to probe the snow for her cane. Instead, it encountered a hard lump with uneven edges.

The engine noise from the road came to a spluttering halt, the air regaining its chilly silence. A drop of blood landed between Erika's eyes. She blinked again. Claudio pushed up his bandage, this time grunting with either the pain or effort. Erika's fingers felt her sword's hilt, curled around its grip, and swept its jagged blade up against Claudio's left temple.

Claudio froze, and for Erika time seemed to slow as well. He stared at her, his blood continuing to drip onto her face like raindrops. Then she realized he wasn't all there. His vacant eyes looked right through her, his knife slipping in his hand. Then time sped up and he was back, hand tightening on the knife's handle. Erika had already moved the épée's ragged tip to the corner of his left eye. "Stop! If you don't want to lose an eye!"

Another droplet of blood fell right into her own eye, welling it like a rosy tear. She fought to keep her eye open for fear that closing it might give Claudio the chance to strike. Instead his head started to sway like a drunk's, his knife loosening again. His dead weight sank on top of her and Erika had to retract her own weapon to keep from goring his eye.

"Get off me!" she yelled.

Voghera was shaking his head, trying to snap back.

"Erika?" A voice from somewhere up the footpath leading to Casa Rosselli. *"Erika?"* Louder this time.

"Get off!" Erika repeated through gritted teeth, afraid to give Claudio a shove lest his knife slip and slice her.

Claudio must have finally heard the voice too. He rolled off her, staggered to his feet, and stood grimacing down at her for a couple of seconds that seemed like more than minutes to Erika. Then he lurched and ran stumbling towards the ridge he'd slid down from, and scrambled back up it.

Just then young Sister Chiara turned the corner off the path and into the front garden. "What's happened!" she cried, running towards Erika.

"I'm all right." Erika had lifted herself to her hands and knees and was wiping blood from her face with snow while alternately burying the stump of sword. Sister Chiara helped her to her feet.

"I fell down," Erika mumbled vaguely.

"There's blood on the snow...?" The sister's face was almost translucent with cold.

"It's nothing, maybe my leg..."

Sister Chiara shook her head in bewilderment.

"Could you hand me my cane?" Erika asked to distract her.

Supported by her recovered cane on one side and Sister Chiara on the other, Erika retrieved her hold-all.

"Should you go in and dry off?" the sister asked.

Out of the question. Erika had to resume her flight, and fast. She did stop for an instant to stare at the fountain on the other side of the snow-blanketed lawn. She sighed and closed her eyes. Claudio was probably watching.

"No," she said to the sister. "I'm fine." They could return to the van and continue on down to the station. Only there was nowhere to turn the van around and Erika apologetically expressed as much. Sister Chiara shrugged off Erika's concern, shoved the gear shift into reverse, and backed as expertly down the mountain as a professional trucker.

At the train station Erika thanked the young sister, once more apologizing for the inconvenience she'd caused. Sister Chiara seemed reluctant to leave.

"I'll be fine," Erika assured her. "Especially since Sister Clotilde's let me keep the cane."

Sister Chiara still seemed uneasy, looking Erika up and down with what Erika could only figure was the wish to reconcile where the blood on Casa Rosselli's snowy lawn had come from. Then, as if sensing she was straying into impertinent territory, the sister blushed and wished Erika well. Erika gave a brief wave as the sister climbed back into the monastery van. Then she limped quickly into the station to the payphones.

"Hello?" answered Régine in Bern.

"It's Erika. I'm in the Cobbio train station," she admitted lamely. "I was attacked by a DIGOS agent."

"*What?* Are you hurt?"

"I'm okay, but..." Erika shut her eyes, then spit out what had happened with Claudio. "He didn't get the manuscript, but I don't have it either. I..."

"Forget it," Régine practically ordered. "Just come meet me. Giorgio's in the hospital with a heart attack. You'll have to take charge of his copy."

In his Domodossola hospital bed, Giorgio could hardly lie still. In the last two days, Doctor Traversi had let him get up and sit in a chair, but that was it. Granted, just the effort of the transition made him feel he was carrying an extra sixty kilos, yet he was itching to get moving and somehow demonstrate he need not be transferred to the better-equipped hospital in Biella. Every one of the three nights he'd been here he'd worried about falling asleep, secretly not swallowing his sleeping pill, or whatever the hell it was that they called a "relaxant." He needed to hear who came and went, both in and out of his room and up and down the hospital hall. So far it seemed nobody had opened the closet containing his clothes and briefcase. He'd made certain he could tell—purely by chance when one day a nurse left behind a roll of masking tape in his room. Sitting in his chair, he'd leaned over to the counter on which the tape sat, snatched it up, and hauled himself to his feet. He'd ripped off a thin strip and taped it to the bottom of the closet doors. Barely noticeable due to the wardrobe's off-white color, it allowed him a modicum of surveillance in an otherwise helpless and frustrating situation—if anyone opened the door while he was asleep, he would see the unstuck tape when he woke.

But today Régine was coming, and he couldn't decide what enthused him more, getting the manuscript moving or merely feasting his eyes on this woman he found so roundly attractive. He shifted in his bed again, and the mattress springs groaned in response.

And then he heard her voice in the corridor. In French-accented Italian she was pronouncing the words for *my husband*—"*mio marito*." By phone this morning they had agreed on the ruse, and Giorgio was taking vicarious joy in it.

"Giorgio!" she exclaimed, as she came through the door, a nurse on her heels. She approached his bed and gave him a clipped kiss on the lips, her hand lingering in a squeeze to his shoulder. Her lips felt dry yet thoroughly warm, and they were full lips, he mused.

As they reverted to French, the nurse backed out of the room and Giorgio was left to savor the short but intimate contact they'd just had.

"I was so worried," she said, when they found themselves alone. "First, about you and then...well, you know...Her gaze swept the room with a look of nervous anticipation.

"Not to worry. Both I and the manuscript are fine, just as I told you on the phone."

"But to finally get here and see you..."

She almost did sound like a wife. A rush of passion and affection surged through Giorgio. Wishing her hand could remain on his shoulder, he reluctantly invited her to sit, indicating the chair next to the wardrobe. "You've had a long journey," he said.

"Not long at all. Only two hours from Bern to Domodossola by train. And tell me about you. Have they said any more about moving you?"

Giorgio gave a vague wave of his hand. "*In the next few days*, they say—they probably won't tell me until the morning they load me into an ambulance." He sighed disgustedly. "So it'll be a relief to get this business moving again." He nodded towards the wardrobe. "My briefcase is in there. Take it—it's got everything we need."

Régine nodded and stood to open the wardrobe and lift out the black briefcase.

"It's still locked, isn't it?" Giorgio couldn't help asking, though he had checked on the briefcase when he'd put that subtle speck of tape on the bottom of the wardrobe's door. The door didn't even stick when Régine opened it.

"It's locked," she confirmed.

"Before you leave I'll get the nurse to fetch the key, they're keeping everything that was in my pockets in an office." He continued to admire the briefcase, telling himself once again that the mission was still on.

"And Erika's on her way to Bern," he said, feeling the need to repeat what he already knew to be so.

Régine nodded and looked at her watch. "I've planned my return to be home when she gets there."

"I'm not happy she has to finish this alone, especially after what happened in Cobbio and that scum Voghera still out there." The flush of anger made his heart quicken, and a pain shot through him. He drew a breath and let it out slowly.

Régine appeared to have noticed the contraction in his brow. "Don't get worked up," she said. "You look ashen as it is, and you've got to get well."

Giorgio nodded soberly, though he felt no more at ease.

And then Régine blurted something entirely unexpected: "I've decided to accompany Erika to London."

Giorgio's eyes widened. *When had she come to that decision?* He didn't know how to respond. *Now he would have to worry about both women.*

"With her crippled leg," Régine continued, "I can't let her go alone."

Giorgio considered arguing but could only perceive himself looking like a cad. Erika was *wounded for God's sake. She was barely better off than he was.* But Régine was so petite and vulnerable, especially compared to Erika who was tall and fit and had twice fought off Voghera. Then he felt ashamed for even comparing them, the two women who meant most to him right now. He cleared his throat...

"Hopefully you're not going to try and talk me out of it," Régine pressed on.

"No, but you'll have to go prepared." He couldn't think of what else to say. His eyes scanned Régine's business suit, nylons, and high-heels. "Wear trousers and boots," he said, and felt that was the weakest of advice. "And—"

"Yes, I'll be careful. We both will."

Once more Giorgio nodded soberly, all the while picturing everything that could go wrong.

Chapter 35

The going had been cold and shaky back to his car, his head still woozy, his legs stiff and sore from the prior night's climb, and Voghera once again felt he might pass out. Yet carefully descending the hill from Casa Rosselli, he had managed to keep pace with the white van as it slowly backed down carrying Erika. A nun had been driving it, and not a bad driver considering the snaky road down to the main highway. He had kept hidden behind trees and snow banks, managing to reach his car where he waited for the van to arrive at the bottom of the village. Once he'd heard it halt, he started his car and headed down after it, following it to Cobbio's train station, where it had deposited Erika and driven off.

Now, in the state he was in—his clothes filthy, his forehead bloody and aching—he hesitated following Erika into the station. Instead, he remained parked, where once more he downed some whiskey and cleaned up his face with rubbing alcohol. In the sunny daylight he even found a large plaster at the bottom of his first-aid kit and stuck it to his forehead. He started the car again for heat and leaned back against the driver's seat to rest, to think. Either Erika had a ticket and was inside the station to board a train, or she would be buying a ticket and boarding a train. In any case he couldn't tail her right now.

He jerked awake out of a dozing state and turned off the engine. No blood had leaked from the plaster, so he combed his hair, brushed off his clothes as best he could, and headed towards the station. From a vantage point just inside the door, he gazed around the entry area but couldn't spot Erika.

Cautiously he went to the board listing train times to Bellinzona. Wherever Erika might be headed, Bellinzona would be the first stop for any train leaving Cobbio for a larger destination.

And indeed one had left just ten minutes ago. He returned to his car and took to the road.

In Bellinzona, Voghera returned to his hotel to clean up, pack up, and check out. Stopping at a pharmacy he bought more large plasters and some pain killers and then drove to the station. He entered the place a new man: clean-shaven, wearing his suit and navy-blue overcoat, his homburg tilted low to hide his bandaged forehead.

His gaze raked the travelers coming and going in this larger train station, though it still didn't snag on Erika. He crossed to the destinations board. From Bellinzona you could get practically anywhere, though many places required a change of train. He made a list of cities reached directly from Bellinzona: Zurich, Lucerne, Basel, Milan. He could skip the last one—highly improbable that Erika would go back to Italy. Reaching Geneva required a change in either Olten or Zurich, and Bern a change in Lucerne. From any of these cities she could leave the country. Barring Italy, where could Erika ultimately be headed? To meet Giorgio Testa somewhere in France, where DIGOS had tracked the journalist? He jotted down the next departure time for each of the directly accessible cities and their platform numbers.

The first train departing, heading for Zurich, was scheduled to leave in five minutes. When Voghera reached the outdoor platform, he found a few people waiting, but none of them Erika. From there he could see the other platforms, but still no Erika. He checked his list. The next train was due to depart for Lucerne in twenty minutes, so he went back into the station house. He hesitated to check the waiting room. Erika would surely have taken a seat where she could see who entered. He would wait out of sight until passengers stood to board the train for Lucerne.

And his plan paid off. Peering out from the side of a newsstand, five minutes before the train for Lucerne was due to depart, he spied Erika making her way towards the platform. She was still using a cane but limping along quickly.

He followed her to the platform as the train pulled in and at a distance watched her climb its steps. She tossed her cane up into the train, then hauled herself aboard using the vertical side bars, her hold-all hanging in front of her. He was tempted to hop on after her. But that wouldn't do with his car here, plus he had no ticket and didn't wish to risk a potentially loud confrontation with the conductor. So he waited while the train's doors remained open, a straggler entering here and there. Waited for the conductor to blow his whistle and slam the doors shut. Waited while the train lurched away from the station. And when it had gained speed, and there was no way Erika could get off, he withdrew back into the station house.

So Erika was headed to Lucerne. But was Lucerne her final destination? Or Bern, maybe? He checked his watch. Erika's train should arrive in Lucerne in about an hour and forty-five minutes. Could he drive there in time to intercept her?

At the information desk he learned that traveling to Lucerne by train or car would take about the same amount of time. So if Erika's final destination was indeed Lucerne, he might be able to make it there before she left its station. But if she intended to change trains...?

He needed to sit down. He needed food and a pain killer.

Ten minutes later, he called Moretti from a pay phone.

"Where the hell are you?" barked the DIGOS agent.

"In Switzerland."

"*Switzerland*..." Moretti sounded pensive. "Have you found Erika?"

Voghera smiled to himself. No surprise, Moretti's suspecting what he was up to. "As a matter of fact I have. She just got on a train from Bellinzona to Lucerne, but she could change in Lucerne and travel to Bern, or elsewhere."

"*Bern.*" Moretti paused. "So you tracked her down. Congratulations, though don't hold your breath about getting back into the boss's good graces just yet."

Voghera ignored that last part. Right now he cared more about catching Erika than about the opinions of his bosses. "What about Giorgio Testa? Getting anywhere on that?"

More hesitation from Moretti. "*Testa*, well we're not sure..."

"Listen," Voghera shot back. "He's written an exposé about the agency, everything that's happened in the last year, and Erika's translated it into English. She's hidden it somewhere but I think she may be on her way to meet Testa. They're going to sell it, for Christ's sake, no doubt to an English or American paper."

"Well, you *have* been busy. But so have we." Then grudgingly: "So, I'll tell you: we received confirmation that Testa's been in Bern and Geneva. A hotel room in Geneva and a friend in Bern. But for the moment he's unaccounted for."

Bern again. "Who's Testa's friend in Bern?"

Moretti sighed. "I guess you're in as good a place as anyone to know. Her name's Régine Farigoule, also a journalist. I'm going to send our agent to Bern from Geneva."

"Which agent?"

"Bruni. But don't get in his way. I mean it."

Luciano Bruni. Voghera didn't much care for him—an oily type; not beneath slyly disobeying orders and working for his own benefit. "Maybe he should stay in Geneva in case Testa shows up..."

"And let you deal with Erika on your own? Seems you've already lost her...As a matter of fact, just stay where you are. *No*, come back to Turin."

Voghera started to protest, but Moretti cut him off. "I know you'll do what you want, but I'm giving you this order for the record: *come back.*"

The noon sun made a smiting comeback. On the train to meet Régine in Bern, Erika felt its might as if a giant spotlight were shining through her compartment window to highlight her and her losses. No English manuscript, no Italian original, nothing with her but the clothes on her back and the few in her hold-all; *and no weapons*. If it weren't for Giorgio's copy of her translation...well, they'd be screwed. With it she could at least get back on track to London.

She shook her head and pulled down the window shade. Giorgio in the hospital, Claudio still on the loose...

"Could you put that shade back up a bit?" came the voice of a passenger on the other side of the compartment.

Erika peered at the woman, almost as if she had appeared out of thin air. But of course the elderly woman had been sharing Erika's compartment since Erika's change of train in Lucerne. She pulled up the shade, then moved to a seat near the door next to the corridor, away from the sun's direct line of fire.

"I just feel the need for a bit of warm light after all this dreadful weather," the woman said, almost apologetically.

"Sure, no problem," Erika acknowledged and turned back to her grim musings.

Régine had told her about Giorgio's collapse on the train in Domodossola, Italy, and that he would be transferred to another hospital in Italy. "He's in stable condition but in no shape to travel to London," she'd said. "So I'm going to get his copy of the manuscript for you today." Erika thanked the stars Giorgio had been strong enough to survive. With his copy of her translation she could do the rest.

She pictured her own copy, along with Giorgio's Italian original, secreted behind a loose stone at the base of the fountain in Casa Rosselli's front garden. Erika had planned to retrieve it the night before, when it was completely dark, just before Claudio had burst in on her. Instead she'd had to flee to the nuns, and now the plastic-bound package might lie buried forever. With snow piled halfway up the fountain's walls, no one was likely to stumble across it until spring or summer, when Casa Rosselli's owner Romano might return from the States for a visit. And only then if he did any gardening around the loose stone.

But none of that mattered now. She had to move forward with the way things were. Erika remembered Dr. Betz talking in that vein after she'd confessed the tragedy of her brother's death. "You have to recognize things you can't change for what they are. Arguing with the unarguable only leads to a second level of suffering." *A second arrow*, he'd called it. Naturally he was right. Erika had launched quivers of guilt-tipped arrows at herself. "Channel your thoughts towards *remorse*, Betz had counseled, not *guilt*. You never meant to harm your brother. Remorse frees you to carry on in a more skillful way; guilt keeps you stuck in the pain of the past."

Well, now for the first time in days she'd been able to actually sit at length and think about her present predicament. And she was once more feeling guilty, this time about not having finished the translation sooner. If she hadn't insisted on *perfecting* it so diligently, worried how her greenhorn writing would be received in London by such a high-profile newspaper as *The Guardian*. Worried she might not do Giorgio's original version justice. And so Claudio had succeeded in finding her. But then Betz's rejoinder would be something like: "You were only doing your best at that given time, during those specific conditions. Instead of wallowing in more counterproductive guilt, view it as a learning experience. Work with what you've got now—get on with the task."

Oh, she would.

It was past seven o'clock when Erika's train pulled into Bern's station. She felt wrung out and wanted to take a taxi directly to Régine's apartment. But now wasn't the time to act impulsively. If somehow she'd been followed (Claudio's resources were not to be underestimated) then one taxi could easily follow another. So she would walk. Lame as she was, she could at least get to Bern's bear pit, alert for any tail, and from there take the bus she'd used before that stopped on Régine's street. She adjusted the hold-all hanging crossways on her right side, firmly gripped her cane with her left hand, and struck out into the night.

As Erika reached the building, she heard the main door click open before she could press the buzzer next to Régine's name. She entered the foyer and took the elevator to Régine's floor, and there again she didn't have to ring, since Régine was waiting on the threshold to usher her into the flat.

"You must have seen me limping up the street from the bus stop," Erika said, after they'd brushed cheeks.

"From my window."

Régine fussed over Erika's leg, insisted on seeing the wound, and after applying more disinfectant to it, taped on a new bandage. "You can't take these things lightly," was her pronouncement.

Over dinner they talked about Giorgio. "The doctors think he'll recover all right, but he'll have to do so in the hospital in Biella."

"At least you were able to get the manuscript," said Erika.

Régine nodded, then paused. "...And I'm going to go with you to London."

Erika stared at her. When she started to speak, Régine shook her head. "Don't say no. Your leg is in bad shape and you'll need help."

"I..."

"No argument. Now your leg will need a little rest, so I propose we leave tomorrow evening."

Erika shook her head. "But—"

"No buts."

Erika sighed. *Whose idea was this, Giorgio's?* She didn't know what to make of it and could only tense her jaw and wonder how to get around it.

Chapter 36

Voghera had kept the gas pedal almost floored during most of his drive to Bern, only to discover that Erika's train had beaten him there—if indeed she had taken the connecting train from Lucerne. If so, in Lucerne she must have lucked out with an immediate connection to Bern.

But he wasn't daunted. He had the name of Giorgio Testa's journalist friend, had copied her address from a Bern telephone book, had bought a Bern city map, and driven to her apartment building. There, he'd discovered Régine Farigoule's floor from the plaque on the front of the building displaying names with their corresponding floors and intercom buttons. Now he waited in his car across the street, his stakeout mode allowing him to shed some of the tension constricting his whole body during the long drive from Bellinzona.

His homburg sat on the passenger seat along with the sandwiches and bottled water he'd bought in the Bern station. He checked his watch: eight p.m. He was still wearing his suit and overcoat. He would have to wear them all night.

He'd gotten no restorative sleep in two days and after an hour of sitting still with a full belly he fought to keep awake. When the pain in his forehead returned like a brick hurled at him, he allowed himself only a loud, drawn-out groan, rejecting the deliverance of more pain killers or even whiskey, lest they should send him sinking lead-like into a bottomless slumber.

In short, he felt like shit but managed to keep collected by watching the light behind the two curtained windows he had determined were Régine's; that, and surveilling the street for signs of the DIGOS agent Bruni. Maybe Moretti would change his mind and keep Bruni in Geneva, especially since Giorgio Testa still had a hotel room there. Testa was the bigger fish, after all. Grimacing, Voghera chuckled at his own pun as pain lanced through his forehead again. He exhaled a tight breath, then returned his weary, burning eyes to the windows. The hell with Moretti—he would stick to Erika's trail like gum on her shoe despite what DIGOS decided or ordered.

A light went off behind one of the curtains. Had Régine extinguished it, or even Erika? She had to be in that flat. Where else would she have gone unless to Geneva to meet Testa? Only in that case she would have traveled from Bellinzona to Zurich or Olten, *not to Lucerne which led to Bern*. Again he thought of Bruni, with his slick-backed hair and even slicker personality. Voghera half wished he hadn't said anything to Moretti about train travel to Bern. But then he wouldn't have learned of Régine Farigoule. Why would Erika have come to Bern if not to meet Testa's friend? Unless Bern had merely been another transit station out of Switzerland. And yet, the last time Voghera saw Erika, she didn't even have a manuscript to take with her.

So, back to square one—to waiting.

He clicked his key in the ignition and turned on the car's radio, low. *Cazzo*, nothing but German music. He twisted the tuning knob until he happened onto a station in French. *Much better*. French was the first foreign language he'd studied; then English. French had come easier, though words in songs often rushed by him, like the ones in this melody now wafting from the radio. Something like, "Je n'étais pas aimé"...No, that couldn't be right. Yet the words had already flown by, and he had to rest his head back and brace himself for another wave of pain.

Then the second window went black and Voghera turned the music down even lower. Had Erika and Régine gone to bed? Would there be a guestroom? He couldn't help picturing them both undressing, though he had no idea what Régine looked like. Maybe dark haired and voluptuous to contrast with Erika's cool fairness. Voghera's groin pulsed to match his swelling imagination. He turned the music back up. His fantasies would keep the pain in his head at bay.

Dammit, he'd fallen asleep! Frozen and aching, unable to distinguish which hurt more, his head or the rest of his body, he rubbed his face and looked up at Régine Farigoule's windows. A light had come back on. He punched off the radio and pulled back his coat sleeve: eleven past five a.m., according to his watch. Who up there was stirring so early?

Voghera rolled his window down a crack. Then the light went off. Someone had either got up for a glass of water or a pee, or they were leaving. He sat up straighter, gripping his steering wheel.

He waited, his gaze glued to the front of Régine's building. For a minute or so his fingers tapped the wheel. He almost sat back when he heard the noise of a car's engine in the street on the side of Regine's building. A spray of headlights came his way and he ducked down in his seat. The spray flooded the intersection, froze for an instant, then swept to the right. Voghera deliberated: should he follow the car or stay put? But the coincidence was too compelling—the only light in the building going on and off in Farigoule's flat, and then a car leaving...Apartment buildings had back-ways in and out. Someone could have left from there.

Voghera's engine growled to life. He made a U-turn and followed the car, keeping his own headlights off until he engaged more traffic.

The distance he kept made it impossible to see who was driving the target vehicle, and once more Voghera questioned having abandoned his stakeout. He checked his rearview mirror: a car behind him, then another behind that easing out as if to pass, then pulling back into place. A tailing maneuver?

Voghera had no time to muse over whether he'd acquired a tail or not, for the target car ahead now turned into a parking spot near the train station. Voghera pulled into a spot across the street from the car and extinguished his lights. A moment later Erika exited the passenger side of the target vehicle: the height, the cane and limp— unmistakable in the street light. It seemed Erika was moving faster than she had last night. The driver, who must be Régine, had shut down her vehicle and stayed put. *What was going on?*

Then a knock on his rear window. Voghera whipped around. *Shit*, someone was approaching the front passenger seat window. Then, bent at the waist, none other than Bruni presented his mug.

Voghera rolled down the window and for half a second the two men stared at each other. Voghera shook his head. "So you left Régine Farigoule's building—*bravo!*"

"*Ciao* to you too," the DIGOS agent said sarcastically. "You left as well." Bruni was wrapped up in coat, gloves, and scarf, tepid streetlight shadowing his face, which made his sly, almost lewd smile more irritating when he said, "It seems you've finally found your Erika...too bad she's lame now."

Voghera ignored both the grin and the comment. "But you haven't found Giorgio Testa. You should still be watching the building."

"*You* should let me in the car before I freeze my balls off."

Voghera gave a begrudging sigh. He tossed his homburg onto one of the back seats and the wrappings from his meal onto the other, then leaned over to unlock the door.

Bruni slid inside. "How do you know Testa's not in that car?" he asked, indicating the target vehicle.

"Because he's so fat he'd take up the entire back seat."

Bruni squinted at the car. "Can't be sure..."

"So go check. He's *your* mark."

Bruni gave him a sidelong look. "What happened to your head?"

Voghera just shrugged his shoulders. Bruni continued to eye him askance, taking his time opening the door and getting out, but he then strode briskly across the street. He passed Régine Farigoule's vehicle, but instead of coming right back he walked straight into the station.

Voghera sucked in a breath. He wanted to go after him but resisted risking a confrontation in public. The car that had ferried Erika to the station was still waiting, which should mean Erika would return. *God damn that dick, Bruni!*

Then out he came from the station, avoiding Farigoule's car this time and crossing the street to approach Voghera's vehicle once more from behind.

He climbed in and sat silent, chewing his lip, prompting Voghera to bark, "*Well?*"

"No Testa in the car. But Erika's at a ticket line."

"No surprise, since she's in a train station."

"She doesn't know me, so no harm done looking."

Voghera had to swallow his impatience, keep it down with a clenched jaw. "So, are you going to sit here holding my hand or go back and stake out the apartment building?"

Bruni gave a blunt chuckle. Once more he leisurely opened the door. "I'm going to check the flat."

"What, break in?"

"Or just make a little noise to see if the fat man responds."

"He might not be there," Voghera said, suddenly alarmed at the idea of Bruni nosing around a space where Erika might return.

"Well if he's not, I'll have another chat with Moretti."

"He'll probably send you back to Geneva."

"*Shit,*" said Bruni, his tone bored and despising. He got out and slammed the door.

"*Cazzo,*" Voghera swore. In his mirror he watched Bruni stroll back towards wherever his car was parked. He hoped the idiot wasn't planning to enter Farigoule's flat. Voghera couldn't be sure whether Testa was there or not, but if Bruni broke in and perhaps got caught by Régine and Erika on their return? Just thinking of what Bruni might do in that scenario made Voghera writhe in his seat.

He looked back at the station. What was taking Erika so long in there?

Never change lines and think the one next to you will move faster. Still, it was something people continued to test, be it changing lanes while driving, waiting in the grocery store, or as she'd done five minutes ago, switching lines at the ticket office. *So many people here so early*, and now she was behind a couple who couldn't seem to make up their minds—about what, Erika didn't know since she could barely hear the conversation for the echoing hubbub around her and the announcements from the loudspeaker; plus, the couple's conversation was in German.

Erika and Régine had arrived at the station before dawn to buy their tickets for London under cover of darkness. Régine had proposed Erika wait in the car, but Erika had argued that she wouldn't be able use a clutch with her injured leg if they needed to take quick flight from Claudio, whose description Erika had given to Régine.

Claudio: she wouldn't put it past him to have tracked her to Régine's apartment. And Régine: did she have to insist on coming along to London? Naturally she had an interest in seeing the project through—it truly belonged to all three of them. But Erika couldn't help sensing the petite, ultra-feminine woman might slow her down in some way. *Funny, that*, considering Erika's own hobbling state.

Erika flicked her fingers, a tic that extended her digits to match her ultra-stretched nerves. *Would this couple in front of her ever finish?* As if to answer, they now started arguing with each other. If she ever got to the window, Erika was tempted to buy one sole ticket and take off now. But even though she had brought the manuscript with her, hidden beneath her new parka, she couldn't. The big schedule board with its revolving numbers and letters told her that a train for Basel, where she would connect to Paris, had just left.

Finally Erika saw the man of the couple pay the station agent and scoop up his tickets. She heard his "*danke schön*" and "*auf wiedersehen*," and then, at last, it was her turn.

For a moment she stood silent, gazing up at the schedule board. A train was set to leave for Geneva shortly. It would take longer to get to Geneva than to Basel, but she could still get to Paris from there...

The ticket agent said something in German and Erika stepped up to the window, still pondering. He spoke in French and she still didn't answer. He blew out a breath, but before he could try another tack she finally snapped to attention. Others were waiting behind her and she could hear their grousing and almost feel their breath on her neck. "Italian or English?" she asked the agent.

"*English*," he replied, hardly hiding his exasperation.

"Two one-way tickets to London, please" she said. "On this evening's train."

She left the station still half deliberating. How long would Régine have waited here in her car if Erika had ditched her and taken the next train to Geneva? What would Régine *and Giorgio* have said when they learned Erika had bought herself a ticket with Régine's money, then left Régine behind?

She opened the car door and maneuvered stiffly inside. *God damn leg.*

"All taken care of?" Régine asked anxiously.

Erika smiled weakly. "All taken care of."

They drove back to Régine's flat, with Régine doing most of the talking. "You bought first-class tickets, then?"

Yes, Erika had done so, though she would have preferred saving money by going second class. But Régine was paying for the entire trip, so why not enjoy the plush, more thickly-padded seats in first class?

"It'll be night, with fewer people in first class, so we'll be able to sleep some."

Truly, Erika couldn't imagine sleeping during such a critical, potentially-fraught journey. They would have to remain on guard; or at least Erika would do so.

"We'll have about four hours to get some rest before we

change trains in Paris. No sleeping after that, because it won't take us long to get from Paris to Calais. We *are* going to cross the Channel at Calais?"

"Yes, except it'll take about the same amount of time to get there as from Basel to Paris," Erika felt the need to correct. "But sure," she added. "By then we'll be getting closer to London."

"And the ferry. Have you ever taken it across the English Channel before, Erika?"

"Once, years ago with my grandparents."

"Well let's keep our fingers crossed for smooth sailing. Those waters can be rough, and if you're prone to seasickness..."

Seasickness was the least of Erika's worries.

"And then, the train from Folkestone to London. And then—we'll have made it!"

"Right." But Erika couldn't make herself match Régine's enthusiasm. This was her mission, and despite her handicapped leg she still couldn't help envisioning Régine as a potential second handicap. Miles from ever practicing a martial art such as fencing, worlds from wielding a knife to defend herself, Régine was the epitome of feminine daintiness in Erika's mind.

As they pulled into Régine's street, Erika stifled a sigh, and felt a shiver of foreboding.

Chapter 37

Claudio Voghera followed the car carrying Erika back to Régine Farigoule's apartment building. The car slowed in front of an iron gate at the side of the building, which started slowly opening. Operated by the driver's remote-control device, concluded Voghera. Indeed the car turned into the driveway of the yawning gate. Voghera coasted by, *merely another car passing in the night*, and found his same spot still vacant across the street from the front of the building. He shut off his engine and dashed out, jogging down to the gate. Slow-moving as it was, the gate clanged shut just as he arrived. Voghera extracted his flashlight to examine it. Apart from the segment of iron bars that swung open and shut, there stood a little pedestrian gateway for owners with a key. Voghera checked its lock and found it ripe for picking. He aimed his flashlight's beam through the iron bars, observing another paved driveway to the right leading downward towards a lower level—to below-ground garages, no doubt. His adrenaline had spiked since encountering the agent Bruni and following Erika to the train station, melting his pain and fatigue. He strode back to his car to collect his lock-picking tools, a running ticker tape of questions marching across his mind.

Where was Erika headed next? What had Bruni found out, and where was he now? Voghera had not once seen where the DIGOS agent had parked. If he'd come back to surveil the building, he would also be tracking Voghera's movements. *Would it be too much to hope that he'd driven off back to Geneva?*

Reaching his car, Voghera wrenched off his overcoat and tossed it next to his homburg in the back seat. He pulled the necessary lockpicking tools from his kit in the trunk and slipped them into his suit-jacket pocket.

Back at the gate, he resurveyed the entire barrier with his small flashlight. The bars were low, about his height, and the pedestrian gate had a horizontal bar running through it midway. He looked around and could see no one in the blackness broken only by a puddle of streetlight at the end of the block. He stowed his flashlight in his jacket, then grasped the vertical bars, and pressing the tip of his shoe on the horizontal bar, he vaulted over the gate. Much quicker and simpler, he said to himself as he landed on the other side, though his legs protested in pain.

His flashlight led him to a courtyard, where he stopped before entering the well-lit space of greenery alternated with concrete walking paths. Here, there had to be a backdoor exit from the building for those intending to use the pedestrian gate, but Voghera did not want to risk being seen searching for it in the illuminated courtyard. He went back to where the inner driveway led down to the garages. Gravity pulled at him as he descended into the depths, and he kept his fingers crossed that no one would decide to drive out of the complex. There was nowhere to hide and only room for one car at a time in this tunnel.

Burrowing further he at last arrived at a clearing roofed by a metal grille. There, he could make out a set of large metal doors with numbers on them—the individual garages. He passed a few of them, finally finding a light to punch on that illuminated the space—garages with keyholes, plus another passageway featuring more garages.

But where was a door leading into the building?

It felt frigid here, as cold as above ground. Dank too. He walked on, directing his beam in front of him until he came to a passageway, dark and narrow. He found a light and punched it on too, and... *lo and behold, there was a door at the end!* As he approached it, it rattled, and he had to back out of the passageway and take cover behind one of the concrete pillars supporting the underground complex.

A sole woman carrying a purse and briefcase came into the clearing and turned towards the set of garages furthest from Voghera. He drew a breath. Could the woman be Régine Farigoule, leaving again? The woman stopped in front of a garage about four doors down from the clearing. After setting her briefcase on the cement she unlocked the metal door and swung it open. Next, she released the latches on the second, connecting door, and swung that one open too. Then she picked up her briefcase, went in and started her car. Voghera slipped back into the passageway and listened to the woman back out, then stop to get out and close the garage. When the sound of her car approached he flattened himself against a wall as the headlights swept past and the car headed out of the underground complex. Not Régine's car.

He headed for the door from which the woman had emerged, and finding it locked, picked his way inside, where he punched on another light revealing yet another tunnel with an unlocked door at its end. Stepping over the threshold, for an instant he let go of the door which flew shut with a deafening thud that concussed his eardrums. With a start Voghera found himself inside a space housing an elevator whose numbers indicated that it ran to the building's top floor. Stairs led upwards as well, which he mounted cautiously to a lighted lobby.

He noted the elevator and the mailboxes mounted on a wall, each one encased in clear glass. A few contained fliers, including the one labeled FARIGOULE.

Now what to do: take the stairs or the elevator?

At six-thirty, dawn's arrival was still distant. If only the same could be said of the intruder in the flat now pointing a pistol at Erika and Régine. The man's mouth was a thinly-traced line whose lips disappeared altogether in his grim pursing of them. His thick eyebrows sat on sockets heavy as cave walls, the outer extremes obscuring the corners of his eyes. He looked strong as a tank.

Having broken in while Erika and Régine were at the station, he'd got a good start at ransacking the flat, and now, in Italian, demanded to know where Giorgio Testa was.

"Who are *you*? demanded Régine, in turn.

"Never mind," said the man. "Where's Testa!"

"We've got nothing to do with him," Régine answered.

"That's an obvious lie. We know you're connected—all three of you!"

"But his business is not ours," Régine emphasized.

Erika was always impressed at how readily Régine switched from her native French to the English they spoke when alone, to Italian. Yet like Giorgio she was a journalist, in her case a Swiss journalist, and her trade required knowledge of the major languages of her country, plus English. Régine's Italian sounded charming, with its lacey, lyrical French accent, even as she argued in what must be dread and angst with the intruder amidst the rubble of her living room.

"Oh really?" he mocked. "And the story he's written?" His pistol shifted to Erika. "The one *you've* translated into English for some newspaper?"

"Who says I've done that?"

"Cut the shit. Have you passed your translation to Testa?"

"I don't know anything about a translation, or a story." *Claudio*, she thought. He must have told this stranger about the existence of her translation, which meant the intruder, who would not identify himself, could only work for DIGOS. But when and where had they talked? Where was Claudio at this moment? With the manuscript still tucked in the waistband of her jeans and covered by her sweater and parka, she thought it best to speak as little as possible.

"Both of you know Giorgio Testa." The man's pistol swayed back and forth between Erika and Régine; whoever spoke received its aim.

Now it was Régine's turn to stare down the barrel as she said, "I met Giorgio at a conference but I don't really know him."

"When did you see him last?"

"I can't remember...a couple of years ago at another conference...?" she seemed to ask herself quizzically. Despite trying to maintain her cool, her face was flushed and her fingers fidgety. Erika wished she would unlace them and let her hands rest at her sides.

"*Bullshit.*" The intruder shook his head. His pistol swung towards Erika. "And you?"

Erika still held her cane, resting both hands on its handle as if to support herself. "Sometime back in Turin..." She tilted her head for effect. "I don't remember exactly when."

"*Bullshit* to both of you! You two only know each other through Testa. What are you doing here, *Erika*, and why were you buying tickets at the train station?"

Erika tried not to look surprised. So he had followed Régine and her to the station and got back here before they did. Why had he left them on their own when they could have fled on a train?

"Give me the tickets," the man demanded before Erika could answer. He extended his gun instead of his hand.

Erika had barely pulled the tickets free from her pocket before he snatched them from her. She squeezed her cane's handle.

"*London!*" he declared, stepping back to scrutinize them.

"We're taking a trip together," Régine said.

"I'll bet you are!" He stuffed the tickets in his overcoat pocket. "And taking the translation with you. So where is it?" The pistol's aim rotated back and forth again. Erika remained quiet.

Régine, however, seemed to need to keep him talking. "You've taken the flat apart. Surely you would have found what you're looking for if it were here..."

"You got back before I could search the bedroom."

Erika could almost feel Régine stiffen. In her mind Giorgio's briefcase lay locked in the back of her wardrobe.

Except the briefcase wasn't locked anymore and Erika held the key in her jeans pocket and the manuscript close to her body.

"Come on." The intruder pointed his pistol towards the hall. "Down to the bedroom."

As the three entered the room, Régine's fingers fidgeted non-stop.

"We must be getting close," the man observed with a sneer. "Now put your hands to use and start emptying that dresser. And *you, gimp*," he told Erika, "stay back against the wall."

Erika obliged, adjusting her grip on her cane as she watched Régine pull open a drawer.

"Throw the shit on the floor," ordered the intruder.

Régine did as she was told until the dresser was gutted, its contents littering the floor like flotsam from a sinking cruise ship.

"Now open the wardrobe and do the same," the intruder commanded.

Régine wrung her hands.

"Do it!"

Clothes and shoes joined the jetsam on the floor, until finally Régine stood rigid facing the black briefcase.

"Now what do we have here? Kick it over to me."

Régine, in her high heels, did her best to nudge the briefcase towards the intruder.

"Stand back," he said, and Erika watched Régine's eyes widen as the tabs clicked and the briefcase stretched open. She expected Régine to gasp at its empty contents, but Régine managed to restrain herself.

"Your work briefcase?" the man asked matter-of-factly. Régine nodded dumbly. "*Shit*," he sighed sharply. "All right, over to the bed and start stripping it."

Erika watched as the duvet landed on the floor, then the pillow cases, followed by their pillows.

The intruder directed Régine to smooth her hands over the bottom sheet. "That's right," he said in mock encouragement. "Now lift the mattress." Régine could only hoist a corner of it.

"I'll help," said Erika, and started limping towards the bed.

"No!" ordered the intruder. But it was too late. Erika tripped over a shoe and landed on top of the duvet.

"Christ!" the man shouted, as Régine lurched towards Erika in concern. He lunged towards both of them, and when he was within reach, Erika thrust out her cane and hooked his ankle.

He fell face-down onto Régine's shoes. On her knees Erika struck him hard twice on the back of the head with her cane, using both hands. His fingers loosened their grip on the pistol and Erika battered them with equal ferocity, then swept the pistol out of his reach with the cane's tip. He shook his head and attempted to rise, only to receive another blow to the head which flattened him once more.

Still on her knees Erika scrambled to grab the pistol. She reached into the intruder's coat pocket and pulled out the train tickets as well. When she noticed his left hand contract in a spasm she whacked that one too. Régine, who'd retreated to the side of the wardrobe, looked on aghast. Hoisting herself to her feet, Erika wondered if Régine might be in shock. In the lull of trying to assess the situation, keeping an eye on the inert intruder, she heard the floor creak in the living room.

Voghera had to pick his way through the mass of objects strewn on the living room floor—books, sofa cushions, a broken lamp, a glass ashtray, chipped but otherwise intact, various and sundry knick-knacks. *Evidently, Bruni had decided to make himself at home.* The parquet floor echoed under the soles of Voghera's leather shoes and he held his hunting knife poised in front of him for the reception he might receive when entering the hall, from where he'd heard a crashing sound and desperate grunts.

But all noise had subsided now, and when he stepped in

to the short hall he was greeted with Erika pointing a pistol at him. Voghera halted and stared. *Shock*—yes, he felt a little of that. *Surprise*—*no*. Bruni had clearly underestimated her, even in her crippled state.

"Drop the knife," she commanded, her eyes flicking from him to the bedroom and back.

Voghera barked a sharp laugh. "*Brava!* But who's in the bedroom that needs to be watched?" He took a step forward and Erika brandished the gun.

"I'll shoot," she warned.

"I don't think you're capable of it," Voghera said, though his steps stilled.

Erika shook her head slowly. "Your feet, your legs...I could start with them right now, but I'm not the best aim, and in this small space I might hit something higher..."

Voghera knew she was right; even if she couldn't bring herself to kill him straight away, she wouldn't have qualms about wounding him again. And then gunfire would ring throughout the building. *What the hell was going on with Bruni?*

As if to supply Voghera with the answer, Erika called into the bedroom without shifting her gaze: "Régine, is he still unconscious?"

"I think so," came a female voice in response.

"And you've called the police?"

"Doing it right now."

"Hurry," Erika said, and Voghera could now hear the jingling of a phone's rotating dial.

Cazzo, this was Bern, the capital of Switzerland. The cops would respond in no time. After a short silence he could now hear Régine relating her emergency: "Two armed intruders, one with a gun..."

Voghera tuned out the rest, wishing Bruni would wake the hell up and announce whether he'd found the manuscript in the flat, since clearly he hadn't found Testa there. Before the phone call to the police, Voghera had even hoped Bruni could recover consciousness and take Régine hostage. But now both men would have to cut and run.

He heard a series of male groans and mumblings coming from the bedroom. *Hallelujah*: *Come on, Bruni, pick your ass up and do something!*

Then Régine stepped out into the hall to Erika's side. The pretty, petite woman whose waxen face reflected her fear said, "He can't see. At least that's what he says."

"What?" Erika exclaimed.

"I think you hit him too many times at the base of the head. He can't even stand up."

"Well, let's not depend on that." Erika extended the pistol at Voghera. "Get back into the living room. And drop that knife!"

Voghera started backing up, with Erika limping along with her cane.

"I mean it!" she cried, when he refused to relinquish the hunting knife. She aimed at his legs. "I'll shoot you!"

"What will the cops think of that?"

"I'll tell them I got hold of the gun and had no choice."

"Even if I turn my back?" And Voghera did just that. He presented his back to Erika, then walked to the door. With a quick smirk over his shoulder, he opened it and left.

"*Shit*," he said as he hustled out of the building. When he thought of Bruni, he muttered, "*Fuck him.*"

Chapter 38

Erika and Régine stared at the intruder who had managed to get to his knees. He kept squeezing his eyes shut, then opening them and shaking his head.

Régine looked at her watch. "The police will be here soon."

Erika, her pistol pointed at the intruder, now had misgivings about the police coming. The intruder would be arrested and taken away; detectives would be called in, not only to question *him*, but also Régine and Erika. Their story about coming home to a burglar in the house would probably be believed on the surface, but what tricky thing might this DIGOS agent say in his own defense? Would the police let Erika leave for London?

The way Régine was gnawing her lower lip, she seemed to be mulling over the same scenario. A healthy color had returned to her face and she suddenly said, "We've got to get him out of here."

Erika drew in a breath and gave a knowing nod. "Right," she said, then asked the intruder, "Can you see now?"

"Well enough." The man shook his head again and finally stood.

Erika extended the pistol and told him not to move.

"I just want to get out of here, like *she* advised." He waved a hand at Régine, then stooped to brace both hands on his knees.

"Agreed," said Régine. "Leave now and I'll report that you got away."

"*Christ*," the intruder uttered, managing to stand erect again.

Erika and Régine moved aside so he could make his way

out into the living room, his hand grazing the wall for balance. He gripped the door jamb as he opened the door, then staggered out of the flat.

Régine had barely shut and locked the door when Erika announced, "I'm leaving too."

"*What?*"

"I've got the manuscript here, under my jacket," she said, patting her belly.

The look on Régine's face spelled confusion and then relief.

"I took it with me to the station," Erika explained. "Just to keep it safe."

"But I'll have to stay here until the police arrive."

"Right. And it would be better if they didn't find me here, otherwise I don't know when I'd be able to leave. I'll take this too," she said, zipping the pistol into her jacket pocket, "then get rid of it along the way somewhere. Tell the police he took off with it when you called them. You won't even need to mention me."

Régine looked at Erika with a mix of worry and admiration. "All right, I'll call a taxi for you, but you've got to take special care, especially with that leg of yours."

"I will, but I've got to go now. No time for a taxi." She gathered the contents of her hold-all that were strewn on the floor, tossing them back in willy-nilly.

"Wait," said Régine, retrieving her handbag. "Take this with you." She pulled out an envelope and handed it to Erika. "I had it prepared for our departure tonight—French francs and English pounds."

For a moment Erika felt awkward. Then she thanked Régine and accepted the envelope.

"It's for our common goal," Régine added. "Ian Wescott's address and phone number are in there too."

With her hold-all zipped and hanging across her bandolier-style, Erika stood by the door facing Régine. "You take care too. I'll call you from somewhere along the way."

They exchanged kisses on the cheeks. When Erika opened the door, Régine took her by the shoulders. *"Be careful,"* she said in a quavering voice. And then she hugged Erika and kissed her on the lips.

Released from Régine's embrace, Erika stood stiff as stucco, confusion and embarrassment coursing through her. Then the urgency of the moment reeled her back in, and giving a brief smile and nod, she left the flat.

As she limped away she could sense Régine's presence watching her. She didn't look back. The elevator was already at Régine's floor and Erika ducked inside.

Down in the lobby, the doors opened to reveal three uniformed policemen, one standing apart, talking on a radio. The two in front of the doors spoke to her in German.

"Italiano?" she asked.

The younger of the two offered a *buon giorno* and asked where she was going.

She told them she had an early train to Basel to catch.

"Do you live in the building?"

Shit! "No, I've just been visiting."

She was worried they'd ask who she'd been staying with, when two other German-speaking police with radios appeared from the stairwell to report something. One pointed towards the ceiling, probably to indicate Régine's floor. Other officers must have climbed the stairs to Régine's flat.

Erika hoped her demeanor conveyed calm and patience as she waited with her heart thumping in her chest. A couple of times the officers darted concerned glances at her and she wondered if she looked flushed.

The Italian-speaking policeman finally asked, "Are you driving to the station?"

"No, I'm taking the bus."

"Well, it's still dark out and we've got reports of intruders in the area. Better to take a taxi."

"Oh," said Erika, trying to look disconcerted and finding it most easy. "That means I'll have to go back up and call for one." *And the police will be in Régine's flat!* "It's just that with this limp, even taking the elevator wears me out. I'm out of breath right now."

More consultation in German. Erika noted a nod from the Italian-speaking officer.

"I'll drive you there," he said to her.

"Or you could just drop me off at the bus stop, it's only at the end of the block..." She wanted no leisurely drive that could lead to more questions.

"At the end of the block..." he repeated. "We've got officers stationed there..."

"Oh, then I should be perfectly fine walking."

"It won't be too hard on you...? He glanced at her cane.

"No, no, I'm used to walking."

Well then why did you say that merely taking the elevator tired you? she was afraid he'd ask.

But he didn't. Squawks from the radios were distracting him and the German-speaking officers were already re-engaging him in conversation.

"I'll be on my way then," Erika said. "*Buon giorno.*"

The men nodded to her, directing distracted *buon giornos* and *guten tags* at her as she limped out of the building, slowly at first, then gaining speed when reaching the sidewalk.

Outdoors, police watched her walk to the bus stop. If Claudio and the DIGOS agent were prowling about they dared not move against her. And both knew she was in possession of the pistol.

At the bus stop she encountered a man carrying a briefcase. "*Guten tag,*" he said, and Erika wished him the same in her accented way. He indicated the lingering police presence and said something else, to which Erika once more responded with: "*Italiano?*" The man shook his head, smiling and shrugging. They waited in silence.

Aboard the bus Erika surveyed the seats and chose one near the front where she could get off quickly. The man sat two rows behind her. She wondered about him...

But he didn't get off at the station, and once inside the building Erika swept her gaze throughout the echoing space, then joined the early-morning commuters at a ticket line. She would have to rebook for the earliest departure. She waited her turn wondering whether Voghera and the DIGOS agent had been able to reconnect somewhere after leaving Régine's building. The police in the lobby had warned of intruders but had not mentioned arresting any. And the DIGOS man had scrutinized Erika's tickets before she could get them back. He knew she would be going to London and could have told Voghera.

She flicked her fingers, anxious, indecisive. Maybe she should buy a ticket only as far as Paris and lie low there for a bit...

The schedule board above her displayed a train leaving for Geneva in seven minutes. Her original ticket had her going through Basel...the DIGOS agent would remember that too.

She decided to dash for the Geneva-bound train.

Weaving warily through the crowd as fast she could, she reached the platform sweating. She was preparing to haul herself aboard when a male voice called out behind her.

Instinctively she flipped her cane to her right hand and swung round ready to defend herself.

"Oh!" a complete stranger uttered, taking a swift step back from her. Erika lowered her cane, and the man went on to say something in German to which Erika shook her head, displaying the palm of her left hand.

"No German," she responded this time.

"English?" Erika gave a reluctant nod, and he went on to say, "I was only going to ask if you needed help boarding..."

"Thank you, but I'll just toss my bag up..."

"Here, let me climb aboard with it," he said in formal but friendly English. "Then I'll help you get on."

Erika hesitated, her eyes flickering up and down the platform. The conductor's whistle blew. The man, no more than about thirty, climbed the steps and held his hand out for Erika's bag.

She handed it to him, then let him half pull her aboard. The conductor appeared on the platform behind her and slammed the door shut.

As the train lurched, Erika steadied herself and thanked the young man; then, pointedly, she headed down the corridor opposite from where he was standing. In her haste to gain the platform in time she hadn't even checked which carriage to board. This one turned out to be a second-class class carriage, though it hardly mattered; she merely found the first empty compartment, swung her bag onto the luggage rack, and dropped heavily into a seat. For an instant her eyes closed, then popped back open. She got up again and checked the corridor—no sign of either of Claudio or the DIGOS man.

No sooner had she sat back down than the door to her compartment slid open and a young couple entered. They were speaking French and chattered on as the young man stowed their luggage on the rack. Some peace and quiet would have been nice, but maybe having company was for the best, the bubbly conversation helping to keep her alert and her aggressors away. As the train droned out of the station in the still-pitch-black morning, she felt a dull headache creep up on her and wanted to close her eyes again. *Vigilance*, she reminded herself and focused on the cheery volley of French.

Once more the compartment door slid open. "*Fahrkarten, billets, biglietti,*" the conductor announced in a voice that seemed hoarse from decades of duty on the Swiss railway.

Shit, she knew someone would come through asking to see tickets. Letting the French-speaking couple show theirs first, Erika rummaged in her pocket for her own, knowing it was not valid, with neither the time nor the destination correct.

"English?" Erika inquired demurely. Better that this husky, grizzled man judge her an ignorant foreigner from afar who had unwittingly messed up.

He nodded brusquely, his hat's visor clipping the air in a stiff salute. "Ticket, please."

Erika handed it to him. Behind his spectacles he squinted at it, then shook his head. "Miss, you're on the wrong train at the wrong time," he said in a censuring tone. The French-speaking couple looked on in curiosity.

"I'm sorry," Erika said. "I needed to catch this train to Geneva and I didn't have time to change my original ticket...could I do it here on this train?"

"That is *not* how things are customarily done." He peered skeptically at Erika as if she were some silly schoolgirl. "You'll lose what you paid for this ticket"—he waved it in the air—"that's meant to take you all the way to London tonight."

"I know," said Erika, trying to look contrite. She had known this from the moment she'd decided to abandon the ticket window in Bern's station. Purchasing a train ticket while aboard was frowned upon in Italy as well.

The conductor shook his head once more. "I can issue you a ticket to Geneva, but you'll pay the cost plus a fine."

Erika readily agreed.

Sighing gruffly, he opened the satchel hanging off his shoulder and pulled out a booklet whose pages were separated by carbon copies. Inwardly Erika also sighed when thinking she would have to stand in line in Geneva's station to buy another ticket for Paris. She had the cash with her, though she wouldn't waste it on first class.

As if tuning in on her thoughts, the conductor said, "I'm issuing you a first-class ticket since that's what you paid for initially. We'll call it a type of credit due. So you'll have to move down two carriages to the first class compartments."

"Thank you," Erika expressed earnestly, "but I don't mind staying here."

"Rules are rules. You originally paid for first class, so you'll move along down there." And with that, the scrupulous conductor left the compartment.

Erika glanced at the French-speaking couple. Grins spread across their faces. "*This is Switzerland: rules are rules!*" said the amused young man in staccato English.

Erika grinned back, though her smile didn't last long. She would have to limp her way through two carriages.

Making her way down the corridor, she suddenly thought of Régine. *Jesus, what was that kiss about?*

As if enough curves hadn't been thrown at her! Dear God, what next?

Chapter 39

Voghera and Bruni stood on the platform watching the train to Geneva snake loudly out of Bern's station, Voghera's thoughts forming for the umpteenth time: *Where the hell is Erika ultimately headed, and where is that goddamn tell-all story she and Testa concocted?*

It didn't take long for Bruni, who had caught up to Voghera at the station, to weigh in.

"She's on her way to London," he informed Voghera smugly. "That's what her tickets said."

"You got hold of tickets?"

"Two—I assume the other one was for Testa's friend, or for Testa himself."

"And Erika was scheduled to leave now?" *Then why did they go back to the flat?*

"The tickets were for *tonight*—so she must have boarded without anything valid."

"You don't still have the tickets?"

Bruni sighed and looked away.

"You lost them—*bravo!*" Voghera shook his head. "Well, unless Testa was meant to show up today, that counts him out."

"*Maybe*," said Bruni enigmatically. "Instead of going back to Geneva right away, I think I'll watch the flat for a while in case he shows up with the story."

"You think that's wise?"

"I checked with Moretti from a payphone; backup's being sent to Geneva."

"And you didn't find anything in the flat...?"

Bruni shook his head.

"You checked *everywhere*..." Voghera peered at Bruni doubtfully.

"*What do you think?*"

"I *know,* not *think,* that Erika did a number on you, and that's how she escaped. I wonder how she managed that?"

"I'm going back now," said Bruni, ignoring the question.

"Watch out for the cops. You don't look up to snuff." Voghera's tone wasn't sarcastic. Bruni seemed woozy, his gait unsteady, and he kept blinking hard.

"What's your next move?" he asked Voghera.

"I don't know yet."

"Drive to London? You should've jumped on the train after her!"

"Testa could also be on his way to London."

"With his car and stuff still in Geneva?"

"He could've left on a train in a rush, just like Erika."

For a moment the two men exchanged inquiring looks. Then they had nothing left to share, and Bruni had started blinking again. "You'll be able to make it back to the flat...?" asked Voghera.

Bruni gave a dismissive wave, leaving Voghera alone on the platform.

Everything seemed muddled to Voghera. Why had Testa abandoned his hotel room without taking his stuff? Was he on his way to Bern to meet Erika? Was he already traveling to London? He wouldn't be bringing the manuscript to Erika, if Erika's translation into English had been the final step. Unless there was more than one copy, in which case Testa could ferry his own to London from Geneva.

Another copy: very likely. One could even have been mailed to London. But Voghera refused to allow that possibility to dishearten him. He'd come too far, had gotten too close—to *Erika*. She had always been his primary mark—his personal prize. And Erika wouldn't be going to London without her English translation. *She had to be in possession of it.*

Voghera's car awaited him across from the station. *Drive all the way to London?* No, only to Geneva. And from Geneva Erika would take a train to Paris, then another train and a ferry across the Channel, the most practical route to England by train from these parts of Europe.

Voghera crossed the station to the information window and asked how long was the wait in Geneva for a connection to Paris. "If someone took the train that just left," he added.

A quick look at the schedules. "One hour and five minutes, monsieur," said the pretty blonde employee.

Once more Voghera was wearing his homburg and overcoat. He gave the blonde a parting smile while tipping his hat.

A one hour and five-minute wait in Geneva, Voghera repeated to himself as he left the station. He could easily drive there and intercept Erika at the station. And if she got in trouble with her invalid ticket...? She would wriggle her way clear. Didn't she always? Voghera acknowledged the thought with a weary sigh, then gave his hat brim a decisive tug lower as he crossed the street to his car.

The argument in the hospital in Domodossola hadn't lasted long. Giorgio was leaving, and they couldn't talk him out of it. *Responsibility* and *liability*: those loaded terms he understood quite well. He would take responsibility for his own health. Anything rather than return to Turin, to where the hospital had received final instructions to send him—*tomorrow*.

For the last couple of days he'd been allowed to walk around the hospital. Granted, he tired easily and felt slow, but that needn't stop him from getting on a train to Geneva. He'd already called the hotel to assure them of his return. He would see how he felt upon arriving. He might even be able to travel on to London to meet Erika and Régine—at least accompany them into *The Guardian's* offices, so that together they could deliver the sizzling manuscript to Ian Westcott. Then afterwards, they could pop three corks from three bottles of champagne. A bolt of both excitement and apprehension shot through him. They were so close to their goal!

He was dressed in his suit when Sister Ursula came into the room, clip-clopping in her white wooden clogs.

"I have your personal effects," she said, laying passport, identity card, wallet, and train ticket on Giorgio's tray. She looked at him askance, shaking her head slowly.

"Don't worry, Sister," he said, pocketing all of the items, and smiling at her, "I'll be seeing my own doctor soon in Geneva."

The nurse's lips parted for an instant, then came together again. Giorgio knew she was thinking about what Doctor Traversi had said. *Since he was reluctant to be transferred to another hospital, why not let this hospital transfer his records to his doctor in Geneva? And what about his GP in Turin, where his Italian identity card specified his residence? As an Italian citizen, his hospital stay in Domodossola would be covered by the National Health, but wouldn't Signor Testa's GP like to be apprised of things?* Since Giorgio had already evaded those questions, he limited himself to casting a brief, polite smile at Sister Ursula, then returned to readying himself for his departure.

When the taxi he'd summoned arrived at the hospital's entrance, he couldn't drop onto the back seat fast enough and slam the door. "To the train station!"

While waiting for his train he called Régine to tell her he'd left the hospital and to call him at his hotel in Geneva before she and Erika left this evening. But no one answered. Where could she be with the sun barely up? Taking care of things in Bern before leaving? Was Erika with her?

Frowning, he hung up and went to the station café to order an espresso. He wanted to explain to Régine the reason he'd checked himself out of the hospital and that he planned to join Erika and her in London. He drummed his fingers on the café counter. *Where were they?*

Bern to Geneva. No more than two hours. Voghera had been on the road heading south for over one hour but had not yet approached the majestically long Lake Geneva. Once there, he would cruise along its coast for almost another hour. He pictured Erika's train charging along somewhere nearby. If he hadn't had to stop to fuel-up and buy a map, then visit a pharmacy to purchase a most important item, he could have even beaten her to Geneva and watched her dismount from the train. And then cornered her and searched her for the manuscript.

Of course, that would be difficult to do in a crowd. Maybe he should tail her onto her train to Paris...leave his car in Geneva, paying for parking if need be. Better to catch her completely unawares—plus she might still have Bruni's gun. He ran a hand through his hair and inhaled deeply. By now the sun had crept into the eastern sky behind him, its rays splashing onto the road in front of him.

He gave the gas pedal a hard punch.

Erika's nerves wouldn't settle, despite the Swiss cultural magazine she'd found and was trying to read. The manuscript in its envelope pricked and chafed the skin under her sweater whenever she changed positions. She needed to transfer it into the hold-all, but didn't want to do so in front of the passenger sitting across from her reading his newspaper. She hadn't found an empty first-class compartment and a sign on the nearest WC had declared that water closet *out of order*. She didn't feel like hobbling all the way to another carriage with her hold-all to find a working WC, so she remained seated and uncomfortable, continuing to ponder what could have happened to Claudio and the DIGOS agent. She was pretty sure Claudio had escaped the police, but his colleague might not have.

She consulted her watch: more than an hour left until Geneva. When she reached the station she would call Régine, who eventually (once the police left her building) should have called Giorgio with the latest update and a warning that DIGOS was close on their trail. How had that agent found Régine in Bern, and was it he who'd tipped off Claudio as to Régine's residence? If DIGOS knew about Régine, they could also have zeroed in on Giorgio's hideout in Geneva. At least he was safe in the hospital...for now.

She crossed her legs and felt the manuscript scrape her again. She'd been carrying it this way for too long. The guy across from her still had his nose in his newspaper, so she stood and turned towards her seat and the luggage rack. She lifted her sweater and yanked out the manuscript, then reached for her parka on the seat and wrapped it up. That would do for now. As she sat back down she heard a bored sigh and the crackle of another page being turned.

Chapter 40

Giorgio debarked from the train in Geneva and walked slowly down the platform towards the station's hub. All he'd done so far this morning was sit—in a taxi, in the train—but he felt exhausted all the same. When he reached his hotel he would have to lie down and rest. He wanted to buy his ticket to London now so he could check out of the hotel tomorrow morning and leave, but he acknowledged he would have to give his body a bit of time to recuperate; he would see how he felt later in the afternoon.

With Régine and Erika scheduled to depart this evening, why had no one answered at Régine's when he'd telephoned a second time from the station in Domodossola? Once more he reminded himself that they'd probably gone out to do last-minute errands. *They:* he understood Régine might be busy, but Erika should stay put in the apartment until departure time so as not to risk being spotted by Voghera, who could very well still be on her trail. He would call again as soon as he got back to the hotel.

Yes, he was tired, it was noon, and he was also hungry. Maybe he should get a bite to eat right here in the station before having to negotiate the taxi stand.

He wove his way near the platforms through an anthill of passengers. Next to a platform with a Paris-bound train, he stopped to catch his breath. *Paris:* that would be his route as well. Practically all trains headed to London went through Paris.

As he started to move on, he did a double-take. Was that *Erika* boarding the train to Paris? He could only see the back of the woman, but her build and thick blond hair looked like

Erika's. His heart gave a lurch. For an instant, other travelers milling around the train blocked his view, then the blonde came back into view. She wore a black parka, like the one Giorgio had last seen Erika in when she'd met him in Locarno to deliver the English translation. He edged closer to the platform to get a better look. The woman was making an effort to get on the train as if she'd been injured—*again like Erika*. He could see no cane, but according to Régine Erika was using one. Then the woman reached the top of the train's steps and disappeared inside.

What the hell? He stared at the train. Passengers were still climbing aboard. He would have liked to maneuver through the crowd to the platform to peer up into the windows. But he was still breathing heavily so he waited, watching stragglers dash onto the train at the last minute. Then the conductor blew his whistle and the doors were shoved closed in a series of loud thuds that resounded up and down the platform. The sheer agitation of the moment made Giorgio's heart thud as well. His chest felt heavy, and he now stood almost panting as the train began to glide out of the station.

In the station's café he sat with an empty shot of brandy in front of him and a half-eaten croissant—catching his breath, waiting for the heaviness in his chest to subside, reflecting. If the woman had indeed been Erika, why had she changed plans to leave at this hour? And what about Régine? She should have been there helping Erika onto the train...

Maybe he should call Régine again before taking a taxi back to his hotel...

Then he slapped his croissant down onto its plate. Régine and Erika were *not* slated to leave Switzerland from Geneva, but from Basel—*Basel to Paris*. How could he have let his imagination get carried away like that? He hoisted himself to his feet to head out to the taxi stand. In ten minutes he'd be back in his hotel. Then he would call Régine.

Voghera had boarded the Geneva-to-Paris train one carriage down from Erika's. From his lowered window he'd watched the platform in case Erika should retreat from the train at the last minute. But naturally she hadn't. She'd bought her ticket in the station, then gone to sit on a bench on the platform. Voghera had followed suit, also purchasing a ticket to Paris, though instead of waiting on the platform, he'd stood surveilling her from the crowd.

He'd been able to arrange parking for his car and now sat calmly with his homburg pulled down low, gazing at the empty seat across the compartment, internalizing the rhythms of the rocking train, its metallic, repetitive *clug-clung, clug-clung,* a meditative constant. Earlier he had stealthily observed Erika settle into her own compartment in the next carriage. With her physical challenges she would not likely attempt moving to a different carriage such as his, a maneuver that required crossing through a noisy enclosed space where the articulated floor of the train was in constant movement. Yes, he could relax for a while. Not only could Erika not spot him here, she had no further opportunity to escape the train.

The only problem was the daylight and the fact that Erika was not alone in her compartment. Voghera required darkness. Darkness and an opportunity to isolate her. He must prowl in the heart of the night when passengers could not fight off sleep.

Giorgio's cab dropped him off in front of his hotel's entrance. He now needed desperately to rest. Necktie in his jacket pocket, top shirt button undone, he inhaled, then started to push through the hotel's revolving door. He didn't quite make it. Two men grasped his arms. He struggled, the pure force of his bulk throwing one of the men off aside.

The other extracted a pistol. "You're coming with us, Testa," he snarled. Giorgio turned towards the sidewalk. A glance or two was cast his way, but otherwise foot traffic continued its quotidian pace. No one seemed to notice the gun pressed against his back.

"You wouldn't shoot me here," he said, gasping.

"Wouldn't I? Feel the silencer?"

Giorgio could feel nothing but an instrument poking his ribs and his heart thumping as if someone were hammering his chest. In the pounding pain he ripped open two shirt buttons and heaved himself against the door. As it revolved he fell downwards into the narrow gap between panes of glass. He tried to pull himself to his feet but failed, instead lying crumpled, half conscious, trapped.

"He's blocked us out," exclaimed the man who'd been forcefully shrugged off by Giorgio. "How do we get to him?"

The other slipped his pistol into the belt under his jacket and gave a quick, sweeping glance around him. So far no one seemed to be paying attention.

"I don't think he's scrunched up in there on purpose, the other man said. "Look at him. His eyes are closed and his face is red."

"*Cazzo!*" the armed man swore. "What the hell's wrong with him?"

"A heart attack...? A stroke...?"

"*Shit*, his face is turning darker."

A woman from inside was now trying to exit the hotel. She turned and ran back to the reception.

"Come on," said the man with the pistol, "they'll call for an ambulance."

"But..." his partner objected.

"*Move*—Bruni's already searched the room, anyway."

It was after five in the afternoon, and already dark, when Erika's Paris-bound train pulled into the Gare de Lyon. Lights illuminating the Paris station, Erika climbed down from the train with the help of one of her compartment mates.

"I'm actually getting practiced at doing this," she added to the thanks she expressed to the young man.

"Well, I hope you completely recover soon," he said,

before they separated on the platform.

Voghera smiled to himself, having watched the exchange from the shadows of the crowd waiting to debark inside the door. He let a few more people get off, then cautiously descended himself, keeping the limping Erika in sight. He wondered whether she had bought a ticket through to London from the Geneva ticket office. He imagined so, but had not bought one himself. First, he would wait to see whether she headed straight to another platform.

Around the busy station he tracked her. She couldn't seem to decide where to go and threw frequent glances around her.

He tailed her to the station's exit, where she stepped out into the blackness and hobbled towards the taxi stand. But instead of entering the long queue she just stood and gazed out at the city, its lights winking back at her.

Voghera noted a shiver of her shoulders, a tremor of the hold-all draped across her. Yes, it was freezing cold here in Paris too.

Finally she turned and stumped her way back into the station.

Erika cursed her limp. Her plan had been to lie low in Paris for a few days—but why, really, especially in the shape she was in? On the train from Geneva, she'd already considered the prospect of such a stay-over less and less attractive. She had no idea where to find an economical hotel, and who knew what Claudio and his DIGOS colleague were up to at the moment? The only certainty was that Ian Westcott was waiting in London for her manuscript. Any further delay didn't make sense. If Claudio were following her right now, with his expertise at avoiding detection, he could easily tail her to a hotel, break into her room, and steal the manuscript. Staying on trains made more sense. Handing over the manuscript in London as swiftly as possible was paramount.

Erika made her way to the information desk, where she learned from the English-speaking agent that a train for

London was scheduled to leave from Paris's Gare du Nord train station in a little over two hours.

"Could I buy a ticket in this station?" she asked in English.

"It would be smoother from the Gare du Nord—just a taxi ride away, unless Mademoiselle wishes to take the métro or the bus." She observed Erika's cane. "Perhaps a taxi might be better?"

Erika agreed.

Voghera slipped into a taxi two down from Erika's. "Wherever that cab's going," he told the driver in French, pointing towards the vehicle carrying Erika, "follow it."

Both cabs wrestled with rush-hour traffic, muscling around the Bastille, creeping towards the Hôtel de Ville—then a *halt*. A swarm of cars respecting no marked lanes honked and revved their engines.

In broken English the taxi driver told Erika that there was a pedestrian demonstration going on at the Hôtel de Ville. In the dark, Erika couldn't make out much, only the headlights of cars chomping at the bit to break free of the gnarly tangle.

"Time?" she asked timidly.

The driver blew out his cheeks and shook his head. Erika didn't understand the comment he made in French, only its sarcastic tone. The only way to take it was philosophically.

About ten minutes later, Voghera's driver had slalomed through the knotty mess at the Hôtel de Ville, but he had lost the target taxi. "*Je suis désolé, monsieur*," he apologized.

Voghera asked him if he knew from which station trains for London departed.

"*De La Gare du Nord, bien sûr.*"

"*A la Gare du Nord, alors!*"

Voghera spilled out of the taxi and rushed into the Gare du Nord. This station teemed with humanity as well, with no sign of Erika. He made his way to the ticket offices, and there in one of the long lines she stood, looking around her at intervals.

He crossed over to the information window and learned he had time to make the next train to London. He need only join a ticket-purchasing line immediately.

He tacked himself onto Erika's line, standing several travelers behind her. His only worry was which way Erika's head would swivel once she'd bought her ticket and left the line. After about fifteen minutes he checked his watch: six-thirty; departure time: seven o' four.

At last Erika reached the window. Voghera watched her converse with the ticket agent; then finally a ticket appeared on the counter and Erika pulled money out of a trouser pocket. She pocketed her change but still stood at the counter. *Come on, Erika, get moving so I can buy my own ticket!* A minute or so passed in which Voghera could only imagine the agent explaining the procedure regarding the ferry at the Channel and the reboarding of a train at either Dover or Folkestone. Voghera blew out a breath and checked his watch again: six forty-five.

Finally Erika rearranged her hold-all and made to turn. Voghera dropped to the floor in pretense of tying his shoe. When he stood he observed her making her way towards what had to be her platform.

He exhaled a tense sigh. *Cazzo*, would he make it in time with three people in line ahead of him?

Chapter 41

With darkness's mantle fully enveloping the countryside, Erika could observe only distorted reflections in the window of her lighted train compartment.

She was tired and her leg ached with all the hustling to make the trains and climbing on and off them. It seemed the wound itself didn't hurt as much as the muscles overly-employed to sustain what she called her "power-limping." Rather than a sense of anxiousness and anticipation to get to London, at the moment she merely felt relief at being able to sit in her compartment for three hours, before having to alight and then board the ferry for a Channel crossing of approximately an hour and a half, depending on the seas. And after that, a train ride of an hour and a half to London. Adding in layovers, the whole journey would take close to eleven hours, with an expected arrival time in London at around six a.m. the following morning. She didn't dare dwell on it. *Just one leg at a time*, she told herself with a twisted smile at the double entendre.

Then she remembered she still had to check in with Régine before arriving in London. She should have called from Paris but as it was she'd barely made the train on time; maybe there would be time in Calais before boarding the ferry. The thought gave her pause. *That kiss.* Would Régine try to explain herself? Then again, there might be nothing to explain. Perhaps Régine had just got carried away with her well-wishes and worry about Erika. She had hugged Erika hard, after all, which was perfectly normal considering the dangers inherent in the whole operation.

Then again she couldn't deny the queasy, floating feeling in her gut. Régine liked her in a way she hadn't expected, but she would have to push that aside for now.

She rubbed her leg—nothing ambiguous about that discomfort—and thought about taking one of the pain pills Sister Clotilde had supplied her with. She'd downed one the night before at Régine's and enjoyed the sleep of an angel slumbering weightlessly on a cloud. But she didn't want to risk falling asleep now. All the same, she let her eyes close, her arm draped snuggly over the hold-all sitting on the seat next to her, her manuscript tucked tightly inside it. *Just a little rest...*

Her head jolted forward as the compartment door slid open and a woman with two little boys entered.

"Mummy," one began, but the woman gave an immediate British-accented order: "Sit down and be quiet for a while."

This woman also seemed weary. The two boys moved down towards the window across from Erika, and their mother, after hoisting bags onto the luggage rack, sat next to them and massaged her forehead. Erika judged the boy next to the window to be about eight years old, his brother maybe six. Soon they both started to fidget.

"When will it be *my* turn to sit by the window?" the littler one asked.

"Don't start!" Their mother pulled some children's books from a bag next to her feet. "Here—read quietly." Now she massaged her temples.

After watching the boys leaf through their books, pinching the pages with friction-filled fingers, Erika rested her head back once more and closed her eyes.

Then she heard in a small voice: "Are you tired too?"

Her eyes flipped open. "Just a bit," she answered the littler one. Their mother was dozing, her head jerking up each time her chin fell towards her chest.

Both boys had blond, moppish hair. "Is it nice sitting by the window?" the littler one asked.

"Leave her alone," his brother scolded. "We're meant to

be reading." Then to Erika: "Sorry, miss. I'll change places with him."

"No, it's fine," Erika said, smiling. Sitting alone on her side of the compartment, she had room to move closer to the door. "Would you like to sit here, next to the window?" she asked the little brother.

"Oh yes!" The boy clapped his hands together and shimmied off his seat.

Just then, his mother snapped awake. "What are you doing, Geoffrey?"

"I've offered to let him sit by the window," Erika said. "It's no trouble, really. I've already moved."

"Then thank you. We've been traveling all day."

Erika could sympathize. She was about to ask where they'd come from but decided not to when the mother pinched the bridge of her nose and closed her eyes again. Erika turned her attention to the little boy Geoffrey. He was on his knees tracing his yellowish reflection in the train window with his finger.

Erika watched, admiring the creative way in which the boy could silently amuse himself. When his brother said, "Don't mind him, he's daft," the mother sighed and said, "Roger, keep your comments to yourself."

Her hold-all to her left and her jacket to her right, Erika settled back again to watch Geoffrey trace other abstract reflections on the window.

Erika was not the only one to take a speeding trip in a tube-shaped vehicle.

Giorgio had come to semi-consciousness in an ambulance, paramedics asking him a battery of questions. *Did he know his name and where he was? Did he know what day it was and what had happened to him?* He'd answered all their questions, feeling fairly alert until a needle entered his vein and he faded out once more.

He woke in a hospital room—*again*—hooked up to all the

usual paraphernalia. This time he was informed that he would not be leaving soon, regardless of the fact that he was able to talk and move all his limbs. Had he suffered another heart attack? The doctor didn't know yet. Procedures had to be performed, and in the meantime Monsieur Testa was not to move without permission.

He felt like he'd been hit by a phantom truck that had left no bruises. Those bastards from DIGOS were responsible for causing him this setback. They'd found his hotel, maybe even ransacked his room. Tricked the desk clerk perhaps; he wouldn't put anything past them. But the sons of bitches would have found *nothing* there. No Matilde Fassino manuscript to rush back to Turin, only his typewriter and the bare beginnings of his autobiographical piece.

It was dark out, and he wondered if Régine and Erika had left for London. The medical staff, happy to know he had a "wife," allowed him to place a call.

"Holy shit!" he exclaimed when Régine informed him of the events of the last twenty-four hours.

"But where are *you*?" she asked. "I called the hospital and they told me you'd left."

"Well, I tried calling you too."

"You must have called while I was tied up with the police. It hasn't been easy dealing with them and I'll have more questions to answer...but where *are* you now?"

When he told her, assuring her he was all right, she said, "Giorgio, how could you leave against medical advice?"

"They were going to send me to a hospital in Turin. I couldn't risk going back there."

Régine could only reply, "Oh God!" Followed by, "Of course I'll come to you as soon as I can. I've haven't heard from Erika yet, but maybe she hasn't had time to call from a station."

"I'm sure she's moving north as fast as she can. She'll call." And he too hoped that would be soon. When Régine didn't comment, he broke what seemed an uncomfortable pause. "I hope the police won't bother you for too much longer."

"So do I."

Another pause. "And be careful when you get to Geneva. We can't know who's still skulking about."

Despite all this trouble, he welcomed Régine's promised visit. With all his beaten and battered heart!

Voghera considered himself a lucky man indeed. His ticket to London grasped in one hand, his bag in the other, he had jogged to the platform, overcoat flapping, and leaped onto the train for Calais. He hadn't taken one complete breath when the floor beneath his feet began to rock as the train jerked away from the station. Finding an empty compartment he'd folded onto a seat, fanning his face with his hat as he gazed at this watch: five past seven o'clock. With three hours at his disposal before arriving in Calais, he could surely locate Erika and neutralize her in order to seize the manuscript. Part two of his plan wouldn't be easy on a train full of travelers, yet he would dog her until he was successful.

About fifteen minutes later, a man entered the compartment hauling two big suitcases. Voghera watched him swing one after the other onto the luggage rack before sitting down on the opposite side of the compartment. He gave a perfunctory nod and smile, which Voghera returned—a sort of shorthand exchanged by anonymous men on a train who wished to pass the evening in solitude. Voghera waited another five minutes; sometimes it took boarders a long while to get settled in a compartment. Finicky types might search the entire train for an empty compartment to themselves and never find one. Voghera didn't want to run into Erika in the lighted corridor in case *she* was still looking.

When the five minutes were up, he rose to spy on the other compartments.

"Ow!" cried the little boy, Geoffrey.

Growing tired of tracing window reflections on Erika's

side of the compartment, he had stood on the seat, then dropped to his knees again—this time onto Erika's jacket.

He rubbed one knee with his hand. "What was that?" he asked Erika, who swiftly scooped up her jacket and bunched it into her lap.

"Geoffrey," his mother called. "Come away from the window and sit back down next to me."

"Ohhh," complained the boy.

"None of that! You'll give the nice lady her seat back." As Geoffrey returned to her, sulking, his mother apologized to Erika.

Erika smiled graciously, though she didn't argue with the woman's decision. Geoffrey's knee had landed on the pistol zipped in her jacket pocket. Up until now she'd had more pressing concerns than the pistol. But as she felt its weight on her thighs, the potential consequences of the weapon loomed larger and larger.

She eyed the mother of the two boys. The woman was British, so she might know how things would unfold once they arrived on English soil.

Casually, she asked, "Are you and the boys returning home?"

"Yes," the mother answered. "And after our visit in France I'm looking forward to it."

"But Granny's *going* to get better, right...?" the older boy Roger chimed in.

"Now that's enough about Granny," his mother chided, though she reached around Geoffrey's back and gave the older boy a soothing pat on the shoulder.

Erika waited a moment, then said, "I suppose there'll be some type of passport check when we get to England?"

"Oh yes. And customs control. It's not like going from country to country on the continent, where they usually just ask to see your passport."

Erika could sense herself tense inside, the pistol in her lap feeling warmer and heavier by the moment. "So they inspect your possessions?"

"Not everyone's. Sometimes people look suspicious, other times it might be a random check." The woman gave Erika a sympathetic smile. "Don't worry, the process is very professional, not humiliating at all."

Erika took all that in with a polite nod and a knotted stomach. *Professionalism: that's exactly what worried her.* What if her nerves betrayed her and they decided to search her? There was nowhere she could hide this gun. She hadn't liked taking it in the first place but had needed to get it out of Régine's flat. She couldn't imagine any use for it on the train, even if Claudio or DIGOS were following her. The uproar and chaos following a gun going off didn't bear contemplating. She'd never even handled a handgun before (barring that one time her father had allowed her to go target-shooting with him and her brother) and had barely figured out how to put this gun's safety on. Unlike a sword or a knife, the pistol had felt awkward in her hand while she was confronting Claudio in Régine's flat, despite her bravado. And now it was urgently time to get rid of it.

Chapter 42

The train was a long, articulated beast. Voghera didn't know how many carriages comprised the whole, but he would check one after the other until he located Erika's compartment, beginning with second-class cars. Perhaps Erika was flush enough to afford a first-class seat, but Voghera doubted it. It made sense to start with second class, to which end he first made a sweep of compartments in his own second-class carriage. Fortunately, compartment seats didn't face the corridor, so Erika would need to be constantly looking to the side in order to spot him through the upper-glass half of the door connecting her compartment to the corridor. Still, Voghera was careful. His hat pulled down low, he peered into compartments from the edge of their windows, proceeding quietly in that manner until he completed his search of his own carriage.

Next, he crossed through the jointed section of the train, an enclosed, cramped, loudly clattering space that exuded the smell of industrial grease. Here, it was dark, and metal segments of floor shifted so that you felt like you stood wobbling above the tracks—not dangerous, but not terribly pleasant either, especially for a cripple; yet it was the only way to get from one carriage to another. Erika might do well to avoid these dark, cold cells and stay put once she found a compartment.

Having executed his search of this second carriage, he was just emerging into the third, when he heard arguing coming from the nearest compartment. He leaned back against the wall, glimpsing his jaundiced reflection in the window across the corridor as he listened to the bickering: two small children, one a boy judging by the timbre of his British-accented voice.

"Quit kicking me!" the voice said.

"Stop it, both of you!" a woman's voice interjected. "Roger, come over here now and sit by me. Geoffrey, you can sit next to the window for now. And both of you keep quiet." After a pause, Voghera heard her speak in an entirely different tone, evidently to someone else in the compartment. "Sorry they're such a nuisance."

"It's no problem," came the voice of her interlocuter. "They're not bothering me."

Voghera froze and flattened himself further against the wall. *Erika*, in a compartment with a mother and two kids. He recognized her voice even in English. Yet he needed to be sure, so ever so cautiously he peered into the compartment. From this vantage point he could see the woman and her two children—two boys. He backed away before they could notice him. Erika had to be sitting across from them. Once more he ventured a peek and this time spied a cane resting against a seat across from mother and boys. He pivoted and headed straight back into the gloomy cell between carriages. *Erika, in the midst of a family.* Not the ideal situation for his plan, but not impossible either. With one carriage lying between them, he would move back and forth to keep an eye on her.

Erika truly didn't mind the boys. She had nothing to read, and they at least provided a distraction. A distraction from boredom *and* a fleeting distraction from the problem of how to ditch the gun. Already she had hobbled to the WC, thinking she might dispose of it there, but could find no place to hide the weapon in the small, smelly loo. The pistol had to be secreted in a place where no one in the train could stumble onto it. Which really left only one alternative: to chuck it *out* of the train from a window in the corridor. It might flail for a second in the train's air displacement, but it would then land on solid ground and in solid darkness. When to do it, though? It was now eighty-thirty p.m. With another hour and a half to go before arriving in Calais, people were still sporadically roaming the corridor. The conductor had come by, asking to see tickets; conductors also made rounds. She would wait another half hour, or so, for things to settle down.

Shit—suddenly it was going on nine-thirty, with the train due in Calais at ten after ten. Erika couldn't chance tossing the gun from a window in her own corridor, not with the boys still charged up and bouncing around. It seemed their traipsing back and forth to the WC made for a diversion their mother could tolerate. Plus, Erika had to be careful about opening a train's window in the dead of a winter's night, an action easily inviting suspicion in and of itself. If she were to proceed with the plan, it would be better to move to another carriage where no one had seen her before—surreptitiously extract the pistol from her jacket and, using her body as a semi-screen, drop it from the window.

Inhaling a bracing breath, she pushed herself up off her seat and grasped her cane. With her parka on and the manuscript once more tucked beneath her trouser waistband, she crossed to the open door. "It just needs a little exercise," she answered, when Geoffrey asked if her leg hurt awfully bad.

She knew she would have to tackle the enclosed, swaying passageway between carriages, and with her cane. No way around it. She pulled open the door, icy drafts and smells of metal and grease assailing her before she even stepped into the space. She stumbled on the moving metal plates beneath her feet, barely keeping her balance while reaching for the door connecting to the next carriage. She caught it and pulled herself through. As she staggered into this new corridor she told herself she wouldn't be attempting to reach any other carriages; this one had to do, for she would still have to make it back to her compartment the same damn way.

In respect to her own carriage, this one seemed no different: well-lighted, some compartment doors open, others closed, chatter rising from various quarters; yet no one, apart from herself, occupying the corridor. Considering the time—nine-thirty—people would soon be packing up to arrive in Calais. She had to work fast.

She chose a window and peeled off her jacket. Holding it in front of her as she faced the window, she gave a glance around, then unzipped the right-hand pocket. She pulled at the window, but couldn't slide it down with one hand. *For the love of God, was it stuck?*

She bellied up to the bottom half of the window and with her jacket wedged there, used both hands to wiggle the window down.

"What are you doing, there? Why are you opening the window?" said a man who must have seen her from his compartment.

"Um...a little fresh air?" Erika offered feebly as she turned to face him, hands gripping her jacket.

"At this *hour*, and with this *cold*? I'm sorry but my wife doesn't fancy catching pneumonia on her way home. Here, if you've got your whiff of *fresh air*, let me close that window. We're almost in Calais, you can get plenty of air on the ferry."

Erika gave in.

Back in her compartment she contemplated other scenarios. Try another window? *Where?* By the time she managed to make it to a different carriage she would probably find its corridor brimming with people longing to debark. Hmm...*debarking*: might she be able to toss the gun under the train once she got off? If not, maybe find somewhere to hide it in the Calais station?

Ditching a pistol was not like hiding a knife. A knife could fit in many a crevice. Her thoughts drifted to the knives she'd lost back in Cobbio. The switchblade appearing under the chair in Dr. Betz's waiting room. Had the doctor actually put it there, thinking Erika truly needed it for some kind of defense? She would like to just bluntly ask him now. Tell him of her plight. Reveal all—how comforting a thought at this point. What therapeutic advice might he have? Erika missed Stephen

Betz: his earnest urge to understand and help her, his meditation exercises, his soft but solid voice. And that patch of strong bare chest exposed by his V-necked sweater...the image brought heat to her cheeks.

Seriously, as soon as all this was over she would make an appointment to see him again. In the meantime she could try the breathing meditation right here. She need only straighten her posture and close her eyes...

"Can we trade places now?"

Erika's meditation came to a halt before she could exhale her first mindful breath.

"Oh, for goodness' sake!" the woman said to the older boy, Roger. "There's nothing to *see* out the window."

"I know, but I like resting my book on the little table while I read."

"You have to wait!" countered the younger Geoffrey.

As their mother ordered them for the umpteenth time to calm down, Erika considered changing compartments to conduct her meditation. Finding someplace solitary, if only for the mere twenty minutes left of the journey. She remembered seeing a vacant compartment in the carriage when she'd gone to the WC. But her leg throbbed, and when they arrived in Calais she would have to face what she now likened to a forced march.

Voghera had also returned to his compartment, where he sat reviewing what he'd witnessed when last going to check on Erika. He'd just started to emerge from that articulated space between carriages when he spotted Erika flattened against a corridor window. He'd ducked back, closing the door to a crack in order to spy out. Erika had been trying to pull the window down. What on earth for? he'd asked himself, alarmed. With her parka bunched up in front of her against the bottom of the window, she'd finally succeeded, when a man strode out of his compartment to object. Erika had limped away and Voghera had set himself to follow, hoping to trap her inside the opposite articulated space. But damn it! The man who'd complained about the open window had followed her in order to open the door and help her through the dark and shaky space before returning to his own compartment—no doubt considering himself a gentleman redeemed.

What the hell had Erika been up to?

Now, his head resting back against the headrest of his seat, Voghera knocked a few ideas around his mind like billiard balls. Before hobbling away from the window, Erika had put the parka back on. Why take it off in the first place? And why hobble to another carriage to open a window? Crazy!

Before moving away from the window, Erika had also zipped up the right-hand pocket of the parka—only that one— as if to keep something important from falling out; where she'd carried a knife in the past...

...Or maybe the pistol she'd menaced him with in the flat in Bern. Had she brought it with her, fearing another encounter with him? A grave risk, no matter how you looked at it. Before long they'd embark on the ferry and then face customs in Folkestone, England. Voghera had already constructed a story in case his bag was searched and his hunting knife discovered. *Being an avid boar hunter in Italy, he had heard of the superior knife craftsmanship in Britain* (the latter an invention, but flattery was always worth a shot) *and had merely brought his own knife along to make comparisons before buying a new one.* If the story didn't move the custom agents, and they confiscated the weapon from him anyhow, it wouldn't much matter.

But if Erika were to get caught with a gun? The consequences would be dire; no way to explain the packing of a pistol in a country where not even the police carried one. Guards would arrest her and that would be the end of the line. Erika and Testa's scoop would be stymied, even though there could be another manuscript out there somewhere. Probably with Testa—but let DIGOS deal with that eventuality, as he had his hands full with Erika, who, he now realized, might have tried tossing the gun out the train window before arriving in England.

Voghera sat forward, flexing his fists as they hung between his thighs. He checked his watch: almost arrival time for Calais. He would see how things played out there and then on the ferry, because after his failed attempt to trap Erika between carriages, and the little time now left, his only option was to persevere over the seas. He stood up and pulled his bag from the luggage rack. Time to make his way towards Erika's compartment and keep an even closer eye on her.

Chapter 43

While passengers filed off the train at the Calais Maritime station, Erika stood aside on the platform, a biting sea wind lashing her face. The ferry was huge, its boarding plank with hand rails located just beyond the station platform, with passengers shunted to it directly from the train. Baggage handlers were loading luggage aboard. Erika noted that her compartment mate relinquished her three suitcases to baggage handlers and seemed relieved of the responsibility; the boys were enough to keep a grip on. Erika, on the other hand, kept her own hold-all, her manuscript still tucked next to her body.

As she observed one traveler after another head up the plank, she wondered if after the last of the stragglers were aboard she might be able to drop the pistol into the narrow gap next to the train between the platform and the rails. But she would have to first extract it from her pocket on this well-lighted platform, with ever-present railroad and ferry personnel. A stray glance from one of them could nail her. She didn't even know who would be the last to get off the train—the conductor? The engineer? Which doors would they exit from? Her gaze swiveled back to the ferry: how many seats were there inside? Did they over-sell tickets the way the railroads did sometimes? She might have time to go into the station and try to ditch the gun there...

A uniformed man approached her. "*Il faut embarquer tout de suite, mademoiselle.*" Then in English: "You must board now, miss."

"All right," Erika said, waiting another second.

But the man added more forcefully in English, "We're

expecting a strong storm, so you must move along."

"The WC?" she asked.

"*Aboard the ferry,*" he answered with undisguised impatience. Then he must have noticed her cane, and added more gently, "Do you need assistance?"

"No, no, thank you anyway." Reluctantly she limped towards the plank, her hair tugged every which way by the wind.

The boat was vast: two levels, with a snack bar at boarding level and plenty of seats in long rows. Through portholes one could gaze out at the sea—and actually see it in daytime. Voghera sat towards the back, watching Erika four rows ahead. From her seat next to the aisle, she had got up to purchase a sandwich and a bottle of Orangina, but now, half an hour into the crossing, she hadn't budged again. They were scheduled to arrive in Folkestone within the next hour, but Voghera doubted they would arrive so soon. The sea was throwing a winter fit. Not that he could see its wild protests through the dark portholes, but he could certainly feel the boat's bucking and dipping. He too had bought something to eat and had finished a small pizza and drunk a coffee in his seat.

In strange contrast, Erika hadn't touched her food. She sat frozen, her head never moving. Voghera had confirmed this after venturing out into the aisle to get a closer look at her. He wondered if she might be seasick. She wouldn't be the first. One of the most hardened DIGOS agents he knew was famed for dodging assignments that required boating across anything larger than a small lake. Seasickness seemed ironic when applied to Erika as well. She was utterly unafraid of heights, something many a macho man couldn't boast of. He couldn't help recalling last year, when she'd ventured out at night onto the roof of her fourth-story attic flat. With aplomb, she'd thrown his jacket down onto the sidewalk to him after having forced him to withdraw from her apartment. Yes, he'd been foiled by her that time too. A list of such embarrassments started forming in his mind but was interrupted by an announcement over the loudspeaker. First in French, and then the English: "We regret to inform you that due to rough seas we will be making land in Folkestone approximately one-half hour later than scheduled."

Groans rose among the passengers like a flock of pigeons in Venice's St. Mark's square. If Erika was indeed seasick, she must be groaning as well. Voghera, instead, was grateful, though he offered a gratuitous complaint in solidarity with the woman sitting two seats down from him with her two boys. Voghera smiled to himself at this irony as well—finding himself joined in his row by the little family he'd spied on the train in Erika's compartment. She was a pretty woman despite the fatigue visible in her eyes. But of course he couldn't stay here now that they'd moved in. The boys were loud, and if Erika did finally manage to get up and move about—and she *must* for his sake—she might easily spot the family and stop to say hello. He waited while rain now began to spit at the porthole. Could the weather get any worse? Then he got up to change rows.

Erika sat with her eyes closed, fearing she would throw up at any moment. This had never happened to her in California. Then again, she'd only gone out on small boats near the coast or around the San Diego harbor, and the seas had never raged like this one. What the hell was happening to her? She couldn't even glance out of the corner of her eye without feeling her stomach lurch towards her esophagus. On the seat next to her sat a tray with a bottle of Orangina and a sandwich. She'd bought them upon embarking, had the tray delivered by staff, but soon realized that just the smell of the sandwich made her want to retch. When she heard the announcement about their late arrival in Folkestone she didn't know whether to moan or acknowledge a possible glint of opportunity. Maybe she would eventually get over this seasickness; then she could venture about the boat looking for a place to dispose of the gun. At this point, however, she couldn't even picture making a move to stand up. Just imagining it almost brought bile to her mouth.

She actually did moan, and an older woman sitting two seats down from her said in French-accented English, "You really are suffering, aren't you, my dear?"

Erika's first instinct was to turn towards the sound, an impulse she quickly regretted as her head spun and her stomach flipped. She let out another groan.

"Is this the first time you've been seasick?" the woman asked.

Erika managed a barely perceptible nod.

"Ah, well I see you haven't eaten your meal or drunk your Orangina."

At those words Erika raised a hand. *No talk of food.*

"Well, you know there is a solution to this."

Erika opened her eyes to slits.

"You should drink some tea."

Erika shut her eyes again.

"The kind of tea for seasickness."

"Oh?" A spark of hope ignited.

"Yes. Do let me procure some for you. It can't hurt to try it."

Erika drew a deep breath, then exhaled audibly. "Okay. Thank you." Within seconds she could feel the woman brush against her knees as she crossed to the aisle. Erika was trying to remember what she looked like from their initial nods of greeting.

When the woman returned, Erika could feel her bent over her. She forced herself to open her eyes and saw a woman younger than her voice suggested—forties at best, but with a motherly smile. She held two cups. "Here: hold on to these while I pass through."

Erika took the cups, making sure they didn't spill as the woman got resettled, then looked straight ahead again. "Thank you."

"You'll need to drink both cups." The woman held the

second cup so that Erika could start on the first. "It's mint tea—very good for nausea."

Despite her fear Erika swallowed a little liquid. She took another sip, then another. Little by little she was able to move her eyes about.

Voghera, now sitting three rows behind Erika, had observed the goings-on: the woman's arrival with two cups, her return to her seat, and now Erika's head gradually moving. Then, having once more stepped out into the aisle, he'd inched closer and glimpsed Erika sipping from one of the cups while the older woman held the other without drinking it. It seemed the woman might be nursing Erika out of her seasickness, for Erika could now move her upper body. Good. But when would she get up, if only to go to the WC?

Back in his seat, he looked at his watch: another hour to go. He removed his hat and placed it on the seat next to him. Having to wear it so much was irritating the wound on his forehead, even though he kept the wound cushioned with bandages. Feeling his impatience heat up, he picked up the hat and set it lightly back on his head, then rose to get another coffee.

Erika's stomach felt soothed by some sort of magic balm. She still felt lightheaded, but at least she could now turn and face the woman who'd helped and have a brief chat with her. She almost regretted the decision when twenty minutes later, they were still talking about the woman's daughter and son-in-law who lived in Essex. The woman shook her head. "She got married way too young." When Erika finally extricated herself, claiming a need for the WC, the woman voiced concern. "Will you be all right on your own?"

"Oh yes," said Erika brightly. "Thanks to you and the tea." Yes, thank God for the tea!

She wasn't going to the WC only to relieve herself. With only half an hour more to sail, *come hell or high water*—she grimaced at the pun—*she would rid herself of this gun!*

Receiving directions from the kind woman, Erika made her way towards the other side of the ferry and locked herself in the WC. She leaned against the door. She was okay, and fortunately this WC didn't stink; because just recalling the smell in the train's loo made her nausea rear up like a cobra. But where to hide the pistol? This WC was no bigger than the train's had been.

After relieving herself, she set back out. *Jesus*, she thought, after checking her watch. Only about forty-five minutes left to sail. Yes, there had been that announcement of a delay, but who could count on clock time with these roiling seas? They could arrive later, or even earlier than predicted.

She would have to check out the upper level of the ferry.

Voghera had drunk his coffee at the snack bar, glad to be on his feet, and was now returning to his row. First, though, he walked over to check on Erika.

...And found her seat empty. She'd finally got up, but *Jesus*, where the hell had she hobbled off to? He tilted his hat brim lower, patted his coat pocket, where his pharmacy purchase lay, and set off for the WC.

And found it empty as well.

He combed the entire lower deck. No sign of Erika here! Could she have limp-climbed to the upper deck? He'd seen her hold-all still sitting next to her seat, so it couldn't be a matter of her having changed places. Had she perhaps spotted him and gone to hide?

He reached the stairs, taking them two at a time.

Making a sweep of the ship's upper level, he found a similar seating configuration and a WC as well. He tried its handle but the door was locked, so he waited in front of it. If Erika appeared when it opened he would shove her right back in and lock both of them inside. By now he was certain she must be carrying the manuscript on her person, having hidden it there before her scuffle with Bruni in Régine Farigoule's flat.

Surely, she wouldn't leave it vulnerable in the hold-all while limping around the ship, knowing that he, Voghera, could easily be following her.

From inside the WC he heard the industrial sucking of a flushing toilet. He waited, flexing his fists, sweat forming under his hat. *He craved to see her up close again, longed to look her in the eye as she recognized she was trapped.* Then the door opened and he found himself face-to-face with one of the blond-haired English boys he'd been sitting near. The boy gave a grin and a cheery "hello!" and then scampered off, leaving Voghera grim-faced.

Now where to look?

The only areas he hadn't checked were the outside decks, where no one in their right mind would go during a storm like this. And yet...

He found an exit door and pushed it open.

The door almost slammed him back inside, so strong was the wind. He squashed his hat down and pushed through, his unbuttoned overcoat snapping every which way and rain whipping his face in rhythmic waves.

Erika couldn't have come out here...?

He half-walked, half-skidded over the rain-slick deck to the railing, where he squinted down at the sea, which heaved and lurched like a black monster. There was no moonlight, though light from inside the ship glowed outward through the window-glass.

He could not sight even a silhouette of Erika on this side of the ship, and so holding onto the railing he fairly skated around the bow to the other side.

And there she was, hood up, sliding along the railing herself.

Almost slipping to his knees he staggered back to a recessed part of the boat. Black rain lashing his vision, he questioned whether the silhouette he beheld really was Erika. Then lightning slashed the sky, spotlighting a cane lying about a meter from her feet. For a couple of seconds she halted as charged air hissed with electricity. Then she resumed edging along the rail, at last coming to a halt and staring down into the roaring, pitching sea. Voghera understood. On this part of the ferry, there were no windows or doors giving on to the outer deck.

And sure enough, after looking right and then left, she unzipped her jacket pocket and pulled out a pistol. Voghera couldn't make out its details, but the size and shape left little to the imagination. Erika's arm drew back, then pitched forward. And though Voghera couldn't actually see the gun fly he knew it was gone when Erika's empty hand returned to the rail.

Perfect. His hypothesis verified, he reached into his own pocket, pulling out a rag and the chloroform he'd acquired. He gave the rag a good dousing.

Erika exhaled a grateful sigh. She was completely drenched and felt slightly nauseous again, but it didn't matter. She had athletically hurled the pistol in an arc so that it would plummet far away from any eyes fixed upon the portals. Though not much could be distinguished through the dark windows, the act still left her feeling reinvigorated. Now she needed to get back inside.

She maneuvered back along the railing to retrieve her cane. But before she could reach for it, she glimpsed a charging black mass out of the corner of her eye. An arm snaked around her while a hand shoved a cloth to her face. A sharp, piercing odor assailed her nostrils, competing with that of the rain- and brine-suffused wind. She twisted and stretched against the grip on her, pulled and scratched at the hand at her mouth, while rain belted her face and eyes so she could barely see. Her feet scrambled to rise up and push off against the rail, but they simply slipped and slid off. Everything was soaked; even the cloth covering her nose and mouth was wet.

Suddenly her stomach lurched and vomit spewed onto the cloth. She fought not to aspirate it, but the cloth quickly retreated. Erika, now staggering, turned as another zigzag of lightening illuminated the sky and the face of Claudio Voghera.

She shook her head, wiped her mouth with a sleeve, and felt another surge of nausea. Voghera shoved her back against the railing. The soiled cloth dropped from his hand as he gripped her by the shoulders.

For a moment all sound receded around her. His face was now a somber silhouette in the lost illumination of the lightning. A hat sat soaked on his head, collapsed to one side by the flogging wind and rain. A patch of white was peeling from his forehead—the spot where she'd cut him. She wanted to hurt him again, disable him at least with a kick to the groin, but she knew she lacked the balance. Her unstable leg, the glistening deck—she couldn't risk buckling at his feet, or worse, falling over the railing.

His grip on her shoulders tightened, as if the spy in him had been infiltrating her thoughts. Still, he stayed silent. There was a lull in the wind and water dripped steadily from the brim of his hat.

Then the wind whipped back up and Erika broke their silence. "Can't you just give this up?" she shouted in exhausted desperation. "What do you want?"

He pulled her closer. "You, of course. I want *you*."

Erika wobbled, confused, her worsening nausea not helping the situation. "You mean..." She stopped herself in time. He couldn't know she had the manuscript.

Once more he seemed to be riding the surf of her mind. "Oh, I'd like your news story too," he said almost incidentally. "But catching you, where there's no place left to run..." His tone was grim again. "I had to do that."

He reached between them and began unzipping Erika's parka. She blocked his arm and they grappled.

"You want to get daring?" he yelled, and pushed her shoulders so she bent back over the railing. Her breath was suspended. She was afraid to move. Voghera ripped open her jacket and reached underneath her sweater to yank out the manuscript.

By now its manilla envelope was soggy. Erika's eyes went wide as he held it up towards the stormy sky in one hand, the other clenching Erika. For a moment his head swiveled from her to the envelope and back. He didn't seem to know what to do, and for a second or two the manuscript remained suspended between sea and ship; just enough time for Erika to deliver a blow with the heel of her hand to his forehead.

His head dropped, the hand that had held Erika springing to his wound. Erika reached for the envelope which escaped her and fell to the deck. As she dived after it, Claudio pounced, the manilla envelope shredding as they scrabbled for it. Abruptly Erika stopped, feeling her stomach rise to her throat. Without preamble, she threw up.

Vomit spilled onto the envelope. Erika shuddered and wiped her mouth. When she looked up, Claudio, now hatless, his bandage flapping over one eye, was gasping.

They both collapsed back against the railing.

Chapter 44

*M*ais, qu'est que vous foutez là?!* What the hell are you two doing out here?!"

Erika and Voghera looked up to see a man sheathed from head to toe in waterproof gear. Shivering with cold, sitting in briny water, neither of them had a response to offer. Exhausted, spent of words and actions, they simply stared blankly back.

"*Faut rentrer dedans tout de suite!*" he shouted at them in French, following in English with, "You must go back inside now!"

Sodden and shaky, Erika and Voghera finally got to their feet. The manuscript lay between them and Erika bent to snatch it up. Claudio didn't try to stop her, both of them watching it disintegrate further, pieces peeling off, its print bleeding in the rain. Erika gathered up what she could.

"Hurry up!" ordered the man. "We'll be in port soon."

Erika retrieved her cane and they both followed him.

"This door was supposed to be locked," he complained, as the three entered the boat's enclosed space. "No one is allowed outside during storms like this." Shaking his head, he shot both of them a *you-must-be-mad* look, then added, "I hope you have dry clothes with you. We can't have water all over the place."

They both nodded dumbly.

***

Sitting across from each other in their compartment on the train from Folkestone to London, Erika and Claudio took stock of each other. It was five-thirty in the morning and they'd both been on the move for twenty-four hours. From a kiosk on the ferry, Erika had bought some magazines in order to make use of their plastic bags. One now contained the shredded manuscript, the other the wet clothes she didn't want in her hold-all. It was Claudio who proposed they sit together. Their mutual exhaustion of both mind and body, the virtual disintegrated state of the manuscript, and the presence of another passenger in the compartment, had convinced Erika to accept. Plus, she wanted to know what had driven him this far.

"You didn't throw it in the sea," Erika said in Italian about the manuscript, patting it in its plastic bag next to her.

After what seemed a reflective pause, Claudio said, "No. I needed it as well."

"To show DIGOS..."

Voghera shrugged an acknowledgement.

"But you didn't fight me any further for it..."

Voghera shook his head wearily. "Fight for what? Dregs? Anyway, there's probably another copy out there, so why bother."

"*Why bother?* You've stalked me this far, knifed me, chased me through two horrible storms?" She glanced at the man sitting by the window, who gave no hint of comprehending Italian.

Voghera didn't answer. His eyes were bloodshot and rimmed red, hollowed below by purple half-circles.

Erika remained quiet as well. Then finally she said, "I betrayed you last November."

Voghera's eyes slowly met hers. "Like a thief in the night. You didn't care, but I was able to catch you in the end—that's what counts. Now your story is in ruins—that's compensation enough." His voice was hoarse with feeling. Then he added casually, "If there's another copy out there, DIGOS can chase it forever, for all I care."

Erika was amazed at the passion in his first declaration

and the matter-of-factness in the second. She shied away from the former—the realization that Claudio must care for her more than she ever did for him—and so addressed the latter. "You're not worried about the publication of a presumed copy?"

"DIGOS will deny knowledge of anything they're accused of. And the State could still prosecute Testa—and *you*—for breaking the terms of the State Secrets document you both signed last year."

"Even though the murder of Matilde Fassino happened *after* that?"

"*Murder*. That's *hearsay*, isn't it? Pure speculation." Voghera cracked a cynical smile.

"Well, her kidnapping isn't—there's plenty of proof of that."

"Mm. And in that case, *I* was following orders." He closed his eyes.

So, Claudio still offered no expression of remorse, no niggling conscience regarding Matilde Fassino, her stroke, and then her murder. The murder of a woman who'd tried to have a Jew sent to Auschwitz—which could amount to attempted murder in and of itself. So, who was ultimately more guilty, Matilde Fassino or DIGOS? She and Claudio had already gone round and round about that more than once, and so they fell silent, each absorbed in the clouds of thought that floated through their respective minds. Erika, when she reached London, would bring the "dregs" of the manuscript to Ian Westcott and explain what had happened. She would inform him of the copy hidden in Cobbio. She would finally call Régine, and the two of them could retrieve it. As long as Ian Westcott had patience, all was not lost. And yet Claudio, despite his nonchalance about copies of the manuscript, was still sitting here with her.

"If you're satisfied we're even," she asked him, "why didn't you turn back when we docked in Folkestone?"

He drew an audible breath and opened his eyes. "Too tired

to make that trip back without some rest. Plus, we needed to have this little talk on terra firma." His reddened eyes became keenly focused on her. "I've witnessed you scared and wounded, living on the edge of your nerves. I'd rather have the old Erika back now, fully, or almost fully restored."

Erika wasn't sure what to make of that. "Well, I'm still limping."

"And I've still got a gash on my head and a horrible headache."

"Mm," Erika murmured, "*still even.*"

Claudio gave a kind of *que sera sera* smile, then once again closed his eyes. On the ferry there had been a small first-aid station, where they'd both had their wounds disinfected and patched up once more. Erika observed Claudio's furrowed brow below his new bandage as he rested. The pain in her leg had also flared. Maybe now she could safely resort to one of Sister Clotilde's pain killers. At the moment Claudio didn't seem to be a threat. *At the moment. Yet how long did he plan to stay in London? Would he follow her all over the city?*

While Erika and Voghera rolled through the English countryside towards London, Giorgio kept checking his watch in his Geneva hospital room. They'd served him breakfast early in the morning and now he could only wait for Régine to arrive from Bern. Hopefully all was sorted with the police and she'd heard from Erika. It had been over twenty-four hours since DIGOS had raided her place and Erika had escaped. As for Régine, he only hoped there was no one from DIGOS still in Bern to tail her to him.

One thing was certain: this time he would not leave the hospital prematurely. The good news was that according to the doctors he hadn't had another heart attack. All the same, he'd suffered inordinate strain during his tussle with the two DIGOS agents. If he didn't resign himself to total rest now, a further attack could be fatal—the cardiologist's words. So he would lie here recuperating. Not that he was even *tempted* to go anywhere the way he felt—basically like an elephant had run him down. And anyway, here in the hospital he was probably as safe from DIGOS as one could imagine. He was just closing his eyes in relief when he heard a knock on the door, followed by the arrival of the nurse.

"You have a visitor, Monsieur Testa."

Giorgio brightened, did his best to sit up straighter, then stiffened like setting concrete; for in walked none other than that bastard from DIGOS, Flavio Moretti.

The prick's smile was subtle, though undisguisedly smug. Unbidden, he plunked himself down in Giorgio's bedside chair and calmly said, "*At last.*"

Giorgio tried not to show the panic he felt, and instead looked away. It was Moretti who last year, while undercover, coordinated the kidnapping of the octogenarian Matilde Fassino in order to entrap and arrest members of the Red Brigades. And Claudio Voghera had been Moretti's lieutenant. Had it been Moretti, or someone higher up, who had ordered Matilde Fassino's recent murder?

Never mind, Moretti was bad enough. Giorgio could remember his disguise from a year ago—bellbottom jeans, long thick hippy hair. Though his dark wavy hair was now cropped close as a banker's and he wore a suit to match, the gleam in his green eyes was still arresting.

At last, he'd said, but Giorgio gave no reply.

"You're right," Moretti continued. "Who cares about small talk, though you do look like you've been through a car demolition process. Heart attack?"

Still no answer.

"Mm. Can't say I'm surprised."

Giorgio folded his arms across his ample chest and stared straight ahead at the opposite wall.

"It wasn't hard to find you. Just needed to call the Geneva hospitals after you collapsed. But we haven't found your scoop yet—the one undoubtedly intended for a liberal British newspaper." Moretti shook his head, gave an ironic smile.

"Probably with Erika, your partner in crime."

"*What* crime?" Giorgio finally thundered, spreading his arms, his eyes darkening with outrage. "We're not kidnappers. We're not killers!"

"Ah, good—tongue's finally oiled up. The crime would be breaking the State Secrets Act? You do you recall that both you and Erika Rivoli signed that?"

"But you have *no* proof of any crime. By your own admission you've found no *scoop*, as you call it."

Moretti sighed. "No, not yet. But we'll see how one of my other agents gets along. Due to catch up with Erika any time now."

"*Voghera*," Giorgio spat, narrowing his eyes. He clammed up again. *Why hadn't Erika contacted Régine yet?*

"Doesn't matter," Moretti went on. "We'll be watching you, and as soon as any kind of story about us comes out, you'll feel the bite of the handcuffs."

Once more Giorgio looked away. For now Moretti couldn't touch him. Not only was there no evidence, but Giorgio was protected here in the hospital. If the Italians couldn't kidnap him, they would have to apply for extradition. And only with convincing evidence of a crime having been committed.

"Well," said Moretti, slapping his knees. "I'd better let you get back to convalescing."

Giorgio looked at him with utter scorn. *You mean, you hope I'll have another heart attack and die in here.*

"Can't tell you how much I've enjoyed this visit," said Moretti, rising to his feet. "Take care of yourself." He winked, then left the room.

As the door swung shut, Giorgio could feel himself deflate inside, in part from relief to be rid of Moretti. *For now.* But he also felt a great void at being found. He'd held out for so long. Still, he reminded himself, Moretti had *nothing* on him for the present, and if necessary he would remain here in Switzerland forever. *In Switzerland, with Régine.*

He consulted his watch again. *Please, come soon, my*

darling, with news of Erika. We have so much to share!

Chapter 45

Régine didn't arrive at the hospital until almost two o'clock. She kissed him on both cheeks and reiterated her shock at what had happened and her relief that his condition hadn't taken a turn for the worse. Then she said, "I didn't tell the personnel that I'm your wife this time. We can't keep up that masquerade here in Switzerland."

Giorgio gave an obligatory nod. Naturally they wouldn't maintain the deception indefinitely, and yet the word "masquerade" sounded harsh, as if they were miscreants rather than good friends and partners just looking out for each other.

Then they addressed Régine's situation. Tentatively she said, "The police detained me at their station all morning..."

"They had a lot of questions, then?"

"Yes..." Sitting next to Giorgio's bed, she examined her hands folded in her lap.

Her fingers began fidgeting, and Giorgio said, "What did they ask that kept you there for hours?"

Régine sighed and looked up at her friend. "They didn't believe my story about the break-in. They suspected I was holding something back, which of course I was. They said that by the looks of my rifled flat, the intruder had to be looking for something specific."

Giorgio wanted to reach over and take her hand, reassure her that he would remain her ally whatever had happened. But he restrained himself, instead giving his most compassionate look. "It's not your fault," he said warmly. "They're only doing their job."

"They pointed out that even the sheets were removed

from my bed." Her cheeks flared red. "That DIGOS agent made me take them off, he was so intent on finding the manuscript." She threw up her hands in helplessness.

"There was nothing you could do, my friend," Giorgio said. "The man had a gun. You were lucky to get out unhurt."

Régine gave a small nod, then continued to unburden herself. "The police detective kept pressing me to reveal more. At one point he even suggested that my flat looked like drug dealers had torn through it looking for some stolen stash—as if I was a dealer myself. I wanted to say, *Do I look like a drug dealer?* Of course I didn't. I know drug dealers come in all shapes and colors and that my defensiveness would have made him even more suspicious."

Giorgio shook his head, grooves of sympathy in his frown. "Régine, dear, if you told them the truth, it is perfectly fine."

"I had to." Régine paused, her shoulders slumping.

"Of course you did and it doesn't matter." *But what all did you tell them?* Giorgio wanted to ask, though he didn't wish to pressure her.

He didn't have to wait long for an answer. "I told them about your scoop and that there were people out there who didn't want it published. They wanted to know who, and I said the Italian secret services. At the mention of that name the detective shut down the interview. He didn't even ask me what the manuscript was about, though he did ask if it was still in my possession, which of course it's not."

Giorgio stared ahead, drumming his fingers on his thigh. When he looked back at Régine, their eyes met in mutual speculation. Giorgio was first to speak. "It's above a mere police detective's competence. He'll have to turn the case over to Swiss intelligence."

"Just what I've been thinking. All he said was that someone would get back to me and that I should not leave the country."

"Good thing you and I are in the *same* country," Giorgio said, beaming. He had hoped to express more in a similar vein, about how important it was that they were close to each other and could support each other, but Régine responded only with a distracted "True." So he let what else he might say drop. He recalled when she'd come to Geneva to help secure a safe-deposit box for his original Italian manuscript and the accompanying declaration of his pursuit by DIGOS. How he'd tried to express his feelings for her then, only for her to respond that in her present frame of mind she could only concentrate on business. Considering what she'd now said about masquerading as his wife, he was beginning to feel less sure that she would ever engage in anything beyond business and a "friendship" with him.

"I still haven't heard from Erika," she said, sighing heavily and rubbing her forehead. "I shouldn't have let her go on her own."

And in those sentiments Giorgio both heard and saw deep feelings—her worried brow, her almost haunted eyes, her anxious tone that stretched beyond anything motherly. Everything had always been about Erika, all the concern, the worry, even the joy and admiration. Régine loved her.

This time Giorgio didn't scold himself for not thinking enough about their friend and collaborator. Régine burned up enough worry for both of them.

At first a strange numbness filled him. Naturally he hoped Erika was safe and sound and expressed as much. Then he felt something shift inside him—a painful grinding of gears. And so he would try shifting his concentration to gathering and unifying all his hopes for his scoop—let it arrive in London safe and intact, onto the desk of Ian Westcott! It was all he could do to force this focus.

"I'd better get back to Bern in case she calls," Régine said, reeling him back to the moment. "But I wanted to first make sure you were all right."

"I'm fine," he said in a neutral tone.

"I'll be in touch," she said, and as she left the room, he closed his eyes.

When Voghera and Erika debarked at London's Victoria Station, they stood dumbly amid the noise and bustle. All Voghera's mind could handle was finding a hotel. He felt like he was sleepwalking, and Erika looked equally exhausted.

"Where did you plan to stay?" he asked her.

She responded with a suspicious gaze. "Why, can't you find your own hotel?"

"Sorry, but unlike *you* with your excellent plan, I didn't see a travel agent to book a hotel before I left."

"Well, I didn't either. And if I had, why would I tell you?"

"Oh, come on. I think we're beyond games now."

"*Games?* It wasn't *me* who attacked *you* three times. Were you trying to *kill* me?"

"No, no." Voghera protested, lifting his hands in surrender. "But all that's over now."

"So you say. Anyway, I don't have the name of a hotel because you and that DIGOS thug made me leave prematurely."

"If it means anything, I don't like the *thug* either." *Would that help smooth some of Erika's rough, sleep-deprived edges?*

"Humph," Erika scoffed. "Well, I guess I'll have to find a tourist booth and ask."

Voghera let Erika take the lead in English and she succeeded in finding a hotel near the station. When he'd asked her if she really objected to their staying in the same place, she'd merely shrugged. So they took two rooms in a modest hotel called the Saint George, and after they'd each had a nap and shower, they found a pub for a bite to eat.

"So, are you going to try to make something good of that ruined manuscript?" Voghera had pushed away his empty plate of shepherd's pie and was now finishing his pint of ale. He sat back watching her.

Erika had finished her dish before him and was gazing about the pub. "A lot of people seem to be just drinking beer for lunch."

Voghera didn't shift his gaze. "Interesting observation, but do you mind answering my question?"

Erika finally looked him in the eye. "Why? Do you plan on following me all over London to find out? If you do, you'll tail me to *The Guardian* newspaper office, where I'll be meeting someone."

"Of course." Voghera cocked his head. "But what'll he think of that unreadable mess? It's in shreds."

"Not much, probably. But I still owe him the courtesy of a visit."

Voghera sighed and finished his pint. For a long moment neither of them spoke. What was he to do now that he'd caught her and foiled her plan? "How about traveling back together?" he finally asked.

At first Erika looked incensed enough to shout at him. Then her features relaxed. "Claudio, you and I are alike. We like to take risks to achieve and win. One reason I enjoyed being with you for those months. We did have something...*electric*. But philosophically, ethically, our relationship didn't work. I draw lines where you refuse to."

"So you've become a moralist."

"No, I just realize certain limits. You obviously have the right to your own limits as long as they don't impinge on mine."

"But why help Testa try to ruin me?"

She held up the bag containing the dregs of the manuscript, which she couldn't seem to abandon. "You've won this time, so let's just leave it at that." She turned to watch a group of suited young people conversing excitedly as they drank their pints.

So she wouldn't budge; wouldn't bend flexibly with him anymore. "I miss our old times together," he said in a deliberately nostalgic tone, lest she sense his hurt.

Again, she didn't respond right away. "...We did have times I'll always remember, but I've moved on."

Moved on—how quaint, how convenient. "Will you go back to Switzerland?"

"At some point," she said guardedly. "I have things to square away with the house."

"I can't imagine you living there."

"Another thing you don't understand about me, I guess."

He pictured the cold stone floors, the icy bedroom, the kitchen stove supplying the only heat to the house...and remembered the tape recorder on the kitchen buffet. He leaned forward. "What was that tape I found in the recorder in your kitchen? Some mumbo-jumbo about breathing and meditation..."

For a moment Erika looked puzzled. Then she relaxed back in her chair. "Ah, that. I haven't listened to it yet but meditation's become my new pastime, my new pursuit. And I've found an excellent teacher. It was probably his voice you heard on the tape."

Voghera studied her expression, perceived some type of blitheness when she mentioned meditation and her teacher. What kind of change had she undergone since November? Not one he could readily understand. He wasn't sure he even wanted to. They might as well be inhabiting parallel universes. There was no use trying to force things any further. He would pack up and leave London—tell Moretti the manuscript had been lost at sea. Moretti might be less than satisfied, with no concrete proof that Voghera had been right all along, but what else was there to do? Erika had declared he had won; did she realize he had lost as well, in other ways?

.

Erika hadn't truly embodied the stoicism she'd projected to Claudio. After putting off the reporting of her reversal of fortune as long as possible, she finally phoned Régine. She had to swallow hard before she could even say hello.

"At last! Régine exclaimed, and carried on about how worried she'd been. "Giorgio and I both have been."

Upon learning of Giorgio's second attack, Erika's spirits

plummeted further.

"But he's all right," said Régine. "He'll be as happy as I am to know you're safe in London."

That at least was good news. Still, how to tell Régine about this second failure? Twice now she'd been thwarted and the manuscript was now useless. "I do plan to see Ian Westcott, but..."

"What's wrong? Did something happen?"

After hearing about Erika's ordeal on the ferry, Régine let out a long sigh.

"I'm sorry," was all that Erika could summon, and she knew it wasn't enough.

"No, don't be," Régine added quickly. "You've been practically through a war. We all have. The important thing is we're all three still standing. "I've had a setback as well."

Régine recounted her confession to the Swiss police and Erika shook her head in amazement. "What will that mean?"

"Giorgio and I don't know; maybe for now we might feel fairly safe...?"

Régine sounded hopeful, but who really knew what the shift to Swiss secret services investigating Italian secret services might portend. "At least there's still the manuscript hidden in Cobbio," Erika said to contribute something positive and certain.

"Exactly. And Giorgio's copy of his original is secure in a safety deposit box in Geneva. An account he's written about this whole odyssey is also there."

"So we're still in decent shape."

"I think so, though I don't want you taking the lead all alone again."

Erika bristled. Régine could not have survived against Claudio. He would have taken her down during their first encounter and forced her to reveal the manuscript's location. And Régine was *not* her mother. She was...*what* was she to Erika? What did she *want* to be?

"Anyway," Régine swiftly continued, "we can talk about it

when you return to Switzerland. You can stay at my place while we figure things out."

Erika refrained from either agreeing or arguing. The first step was to face Ian Westcott and explain the delay with the manuscript.

There again, Régine chimed in. "I'll call him right away and explain. He'll already know what happened when you arrive."

"I'll be sure to add *all* the gritty details."

Chapter 46

Ian Wescott, lead reporter of *The Guardian's* foreign affairs' section, looked like a red-haired Santa Claus. Jolly, until his keen eyes narrowed behind his spectacles and fixated Erika. "My bosses had counted on Testa's manuscript arriving by now," he said. Gently he added, "I'm sorry, Miss Rivoli, they're now talking about a story with a different angle."

Erika shifted in her chair on the opposite side of Westcott's desk. She'd told him of her copy in Cobbio and now repeated her plea. "Really, it won't take long to get the copy up here. Régine can retrieve it and deliver it herself tomorrow, or the day after. There shouldn't be any more danger."

"Yes, we spoke about it when she called, but I told her as well that my bosses were starting to lose enthusiasm for that story." Wescott stroked his rusty-red beard. "It's not that *I* don't still believe in it...but they do have a point about a different angle."

"A different *angle*?" Erika sat forward. Fatigue and frustration were turning her nerves into sparking wires. She had no idea what Wescott meant. She tried to breathe the Betz way.

"Actually, when Régine called yesterday, an idea came to me. And your recounting of everything you've gone through to get this story to us has made it even stronger and more vivid." Westcott picked up a pen and tapped his front teeth with it while Erika waited, absently scooting closer to the edge of her chair.

"Do you think you and Testa still have energy for writing?" He put down the pen and folded his hands on his desk.

Erika couldn't speak for Giorgio, though from what Régine had said about him he hadn't lost heart. "Yes," she said. "I do, at least."

"Well, if you and Testa feel up to it, and you like the sound of it, I'll run this idea past my superiors: *a personal account of your and Testa's trials and tribulations while traveling with a manuscript* that exposes DIGOS." He smiled at the idea. "The bosses have been talking about stories taking a more personal angle, something that could net more readers. Naturally, sensational pieces do this. Only your story would also include the key contents of your scoop—politics and intrigue wrapped up in the danger of your endeavor to bring it to light."

Slowly Erika sat back in her chair. *A different story. Starting from scratch. A whole new effort.* But a story about *her*, and Giorgio of course, and even Régine who'd also faced a gun. Three reporters battling to get the truth out. She recalled Régine's mention of Giorgio's having written something of the sort and placed it in a safety deposit box. So they might not have to start completely from zero...

"Does Régine know?" she asked.

"I've told her; she sounds open to it."

So Régine will have likely phoned Giorgio by now and informed him. "I'd like to do it," she said. "And I think Giorgio will be on board. We could work together from the start, with me translating."

"Good. Talk it over with him and we'll confirm it. Oh, and I *would* still like to read the manuscript that's incited all this drama, if you wouldn't mind sending it to me."

"I'd be happy to!"

After being taken to dinner and on a pub-crawl by Ian Wescott, after visiting the British Museum and the Houses of Parliament, Erika returned to Cobbio. By phone she had also secured an agreement to meet Régine and Giorgio in Geneva. By now Erika had discarded her cane and was almost able to resume her athletic gait around the village. She'd walked unaided to Adriana's, telling her friend about the tourist sights of London—*a short but enjoyable vacation*—and picked up provisions she needed for Casa Rosselli. From Cobbio's café she phoned and made an appointment to see Dr. Betz.

It seemed eons since she'd sat in the doctor's waiting room. Yet, naturally, nothing had changed in less than a week: the same grey-tiled floor, onto which her switchblade had once fallen and then conveniently, almost magically, reappeared. Betz's globe was still perched on the filing cabinet, a symbol of the doctor's worldly knowledge and experience. And the Buddha statue still sat on the receptionist-counter. The statue wore its closed-eyed, cloudless expression, and Erika found it welcoming.

Stefan Betz, when he opened his inner door, greeted her with an almost identically placid smile.

"I'm glad you could take me so soon," said Erika, once she was settled in her usual spot on the sofa next to the window.

"You had a nice ski vacation?" responded Betz.

Erika lowered her gaze to her hands. "It was fine."

"Any place you'd like to recommend?"

"Well...I actually went to London instead."

Betz's dark eyebrows rose.

"It's a long story." Should she really tell him the whole saga, with all its detailed twists and turns, along with the history with Claudio? She decided not to. Not today. It didn't matter anyway, now. If anything, she should tell him about her new project. But she hesitated, wondering if he might still suspect her of breaking into his office.

"Well, you're back in snowy Cobbio now," he said.

It wasn't literally snowing today, yet she understood the pleasantry. "Yes, I'm settled back into the house..." She wasn't sure what else to say, how to proceed. While away she'd imagined spilling her guts to him about her true purpose in Cobbio. Now she felt blocked. Her gaze wandered past his shoulder to his desk with its appointment book, to his files on the shelf above it. There weren't many files and none of their spines were labeled.

"Do you have many patients?" she abruptly asked.

Betz gave a quizzical smile. A slight pause ensued, and then he said, "Not many at the moment. I also do research."

"Oh." Erika felt uneasy, her *oh* seemed a silly response. "It's just that I never see anyone else here." *Not even a receptionist.* That sounded stupid too. Just because she hadn't crossed paths with another patient didn't mean no others existed. And maybe Betz simply couldn't afford a receptionist. She was starting to get nervous. She should stop her enquiries before Betz could put two and two together regarding the break-in.

"Erika, is there something worrying you?" he asked.

"No...I..."

"About my research," he said, "maybe this might be the right moment to let you know my plans."

His plans. What did they have to do with *her*? The leather sofa creaked as she straightened on it.

"You know I've taught you breathing and walking exercises. I've suggested mindful ways to engage with your past." He paused when Erika tilted her head. "*Mindfulness,*" he explained, is a philosophy based on being at one and at ease with the here and now. It uses many Buddhist techniques, including mindful breathing and meditation." Erika's posture sharpened even further. "By *it,*" he clarified, I mean both teachers and students. I'm actually doing research as I study to be a teacher of mindfulness."

Erika tried to digest all this but could only shake her head.

"I know I've just dropped a lot on you," Betz said with a sympathetic smile, "but going back to our work together, I hope some of these techniques and teachings about how to handle guilt and anxiety have helped."

Erika drew a breath, then acknowledged they had. That's why she'd returned...still, what did he mean by *plans*?

"I'm happy to know you've been helped. You and my select

other patients. Maybe I should have told you at the start that I was using mindfulness in my treatments, but to burden patients with such a complicated philosophy at the beginning, expecting them to understand this type of holistic approach to psychology in one fell swoop might have been counterproductive. And I myself was actually working with these methods in increments. From starting with simple applications of techniques and concepts, little by little things grew..."

After this complex information drop, as he put it, Betz himself seemed to be at a loss for words. Frowning, he scratched his head, and Erika, who had actually followed his explanation fairly well, spoke to relieve his discomfort. "Maybe all this is why you haven't been charging me for treatments."

"Yes," he affirmed, nodding and leaning forward. "You've helped me as much as it seems I've helped you."

"But you said you have plans..."

"True. I'm coming to the end in terms of my psychology practice. Financially, you see, I can't sustain continuing to work like this."

"But you could start charging patients." The image of Betz sleeping on this very sofa she was sitting on came to mind.

"No, that wouldn't be right. At this point I've given myself completely over to mindfulness studies and couldn't take payment for your generous collaboration." He put his notebook down and smiled again, this time with a kind of serene confidence. "I'll have to go abroad to continue my studies."

Erika was now feeling anxious. "Will you still be working as a psychologist?"

"Not after February. I'll be moving to England. That's where my mindfulness training will take place."

To England! Erika's stomach plunged as if she'd stepped into an abandoned mineshaft. *Abandoned*—that's how she felt.

"Erika, you might be feeling a bit lost right now..."

She managed to gather herself. "I didn't know you also spoke English."

"I'm not the best of speakers," Betz said, chuckling, "but we Swiss learn to adapt to languages pretty well. It's our history of survival."

Erika knew this to be true. "Maybe I'd like to continue with what you've taught me, learn as much about it as I can..."

"We *can* continue, and you can definitely learn more—there's no limit!"

"So we'll still have at least a month together..."

"Certainly. And perhaps you could come visit sometime in England—check out what's going on in the Mindfulness World."

Erika nodded in reflection. Maybe...

Still, when she left Betz's office, a heavy hollowness swelled within her; a hollowness that hurt. Betz always said that painful emotions couldn't last. The human organism couldn't support them, and change occurred in the mind-and-body moods just as readily as it did in nature. That the sun had broken through the clouds in this moment was obvious proof, though not of the nature Erika would have liked to experience right now. Hands plunged in her parka pockets, she headed to the station to catch the train back to Cobbio.

*England...*she mused.

Erika declined Régine's invitation to stay in her flat in Bern. She had her own space in Cobbio and things to do there. That Régine wanted to exert control over her movements still chafed. Régine didn't want Erika "going it alone" again. Well, this situation had now changed as well. She and Giorgio would be working on a new story, assuming Giorgio agreed. And to this effect, the three of them planned to meet in Geneva in Giorgio's hotel where he would be continuing his convalescence.

Three days after returning to Cobbio, Erika boarded the Bellinzona-to-Geneva train which, including a change in

Zurich, amounted to an almost five-hour journey. Once more, Régine had offered her flat for Erika to spend the night before returning to Cobbio. Erika had declined that invitation as well, instead booking a room in Giorgio's hotel. It wasn't easy to navigate Régine's ways. She had politely declined Régine's invitations, yet she still had the rest of Régine's money that she needed to return. And as Ian Westcott's primary contact, Régine would remain part of the project to get a new story out.

Erika couldn't, however, ignore Régine's intimate attitude towards her, and with DIGOS still dogging Giorgio, the waters remained unsettled, if not turbulent. As her train sped from Zurich to Geneva, she contended with a sucking feeling, like low barometric pressure pulling her down, dampening her mood. She longed for light to clear and calm the waters, to lift the pressure. But as Betz had pointed out, wishing accomplished nothing. Embrace the discomfort; do what you can to disentangle your feelings and allow them to move through like a passing storm.

From the Geneva station she took a taxi to Giorgio's hotel, where Régine met her in the lobby. Erika felt herself stiffen as they brushed cheeks. Then Régine stood back, taking Erika in with an appreciative gaze.

"You look no worse for wear. And you're not using your cane."

Erika displayed her empty palms. "My leg's much better."

"Would you like to get a coffee in the restaurant before we go up?" With a raised finger she indicated Giorgio's floor.

"I'm fine." Something came spontaneously to her. "You know, with everything going on, and maybe a new project to tackle, I'd like to just concentrate on business as thoroughly as possible." This was a feeble attempt to extricate herself, yet strangely, a light of understanding seemed to spark in Régine's eyes.

"I understand," she said. Then with an almost imperceptible sigh, "I absolutely do."

A king-sized bed filled a large part of Giorgio's room. Fully dressed, he was sitting atop the bedspread, propped against the headboard. Erika and he exchanged kisses on the cheeks, with Erika attentive to how much pressure she exerted while leaning on him.

"Don't be afraid," Giorgio said, chuckling. "It would seem I'm indestructible!"

He didn't exactly look that way, with great dark circles under his eyes. Erika even thought he'd lost weight. Nevertheless, she told him he looked good for someone whose heart had twice flattened him.

"And you, my dear," he responded, "look healthy and fit as ever."

At his invitation, she and Régine took the two seats at the table where his typewriter squatted.

"So, where should we begin?" offered Régine.

And from there things commenced to take shape. Giorgio, however, seemed coolish towards Régine. But who could be sure? Erika thought. Given Giorgio's health, the waxing and waning of moods could be normal—he'd been through his own kind of war. And, naturally, all three of them were having to start anew, a daunting enterprise, with perhaps DIGOS and even the Swiss intelligence services still to contend with.

"You've already made a start with your written declaration in the safety deposit box," Régine reminded Giorgio.

"I have," he said, "but *you'll* have to retrieve it, since you're the one who signed for the box."

"Of course I will."

Giorgio gave a vague nod which Erika couldn't interpret. Maybe his condition made him tired and impatient. "And you're certain Westcott's editors won't back out and leave us hanging this time?" Giorgio added.

"He assures me they won't. And I've already told you that *The Guardian* is paying us a compensation fee for the first story. But they'd like us to make good time with the second."

Easy for Régine to say, thought Erika, since she wouldn't

be doing any of the writing. And yet, with Betz leaving, Erika was itching to get something new started.

"Giorgio," she said, "you and I can work together; I mean really closely, so I can translate it practically as fast as you compose it." More than that, Erika herself would be composing the section covering the ordeals of her journey. That prospect, in and of itself, had now become weighty in her mind. Hadn't Betz said some time ago that she should write her autobiography, or something to that effect?

"Well," Giorgio pronounced with a resigned grunt, "I guess I can't lie around forever doing nothing." He shot a wink at Erika. "Might as well have a notebook sitting on my chest."

"So, we're all in?" asked Régine. "Giorgio?"

"...Yes."

"Erika?"

She almost said *all for one and one for all*, but limited herself to a mature "Here's to our ongoing partnership, and to the story behind the story!"

Acknowledgements

Many thanks to my critique partners, authors Paula Riley and the late Bill Kuechler, and to beta-readers Angela Sell and Cora Robey. Your sharp eyes have saved me over and over again!

Much appreciation, as well, to my mates on the ground in Switzerland, Amelia Boffelli and Albertina and Tiziano Villa, with whom I first became friends in the 1970s, when I lived in this icy wonderland called Ticino, and whom I still visit today. Alas, like everywhere else on this planet, Ticino's climate has changed, and winters in this Swiss canton now produce little snow. But at least friendship is constant!